THE SABRAEL CONFESSION

CONFESSION

The Heavenly War Chronicles

Stephen J Smith

ISBN: 1508974527
ISBN-13: 978-1508974529
Library of Congress Control Number: 2015904804
CreateSpace Independent Publishing Platform
North Charleston, South Carolina

For Kelly, the love of my life. Thank you for supporting me in following my dreams.

And for Ava, my little cutie. You inspire me every day. I can't wait for when you're old enough to read this.

ACKNOWLEDGEMENTS

I'd like to give a special thank you to a few people without whom this book never would have been published:

Kathryn Allen, my amazingly talented cover artist. Your inspiring design and encouragement gave me the final push to share this story with the world.

My incredible copy editor, Amalia Oulahan, whose keen eye sees all. Thanks for taking the journey with me.

All my friends and family who have anxiously awaited this book. Your support means the world to me.

To God and His angels. Without you, there is no book. In every way that statement can be understood.

And to my mom, who read every draft along the way, and who has been my biggest fan since the beginning. I love you!

THE SABRAEL
CONFESSION

PROLOGUE

Lightning electrified the night, searing a phantom silhouette onto the roiling darkness. Racing through the relentless downpour, a lone figure swept wisps of drenched hair from his eyes and glanced up at the raging sky. Another flash, then thunder which rocked the Vatican City streets. The man ran harder.

Despite the late hour and empty streets, he scanned every alcove, every dark recess. As angry lightning streaked the sky again, he recoiled from the darting shape he realized was only his shadow. Scrambling up the steps to his front door, he jammed a key into the rusted lock and rushed inside, slamming the door against the storm.

Hand still clutching the knob, he tried to listen over the hammering of his heart. Only muffled thunder rumbled in the otherwise perfect stillness. Relieved, he slipped off his rain-soaked poncho, revealing a thick book clutched tight to his chest beneath, its cover worn with age. He dropped it onto an almost equally worn desk beneath sagging, overloaded bookshelves. Smoothing the white collar at his neck, he switched on a lamp to inspect his prize.

Yellowed pages thin as the skin on the hands turning them were covered in ancient scrawl—Aramaic—the language spoken in the time of Christ. Hand-drawn diagrams and symbols filled each margin. Most were beyond the priest. What he could read confirmed what he'd suspected at the vaults; this was a book of instruction. Rites and rituals lost to antiquity, forgotten or even condemned by the church. The priest had risked all to slip the book past security from the restricted stacks without permission. He whispered the words as he scanned the precious text. Five pages, then his finger stopped. Tracing back, he read that last line again.

"It cannot be," he whispered in Italian.

Reaching to a column of books stacked beside the desk, he retrieved one nearly as old as the stolen volume. Opening to a dog-eared page, he analyzed the texts side-by-side.

"My God! It's still there!" Knocking over his chair in his rush back to the bookshelves, he yanked out another volume from his personal collection.

Night suddenly turned to day as lightning struck the street directly outside. The priest blinked away the momentary blindness. As his vision cleared, he sank to his knees.

Standing in the scorched street, staring at the house, a figure clad in black seemed oblivious to the storm. Long coat and hair matted in the downpour, his thin lips drew a suicide slit across his pallid face. Where his eyes should be, empty sockets were fixed on the house.

The priest dropped the book, hands trembling, and gasped, "Adramelec!"

Impossibly hearing the name over the storm, the figure scowled, flashing gritted teeth. A fiery green glow suddenly filled his empty sockets. With inhuman speed, he flew forward, bursting through the window and slamming into the kneeling priest.

The rain poured harder, the lightning and thunder escalating over the Holy See. Only the first of the priest's agonizing screams escaped through the shattered window.

The rest were drowned out by the fury of the storm.

INTRODUCTION

The wind has been howling for hours. The man on the television says a severe storm is headed for the county. The oak trees out front sway in the growing gale, each leaf holding onto its respective branch for dear life, desperate to remain connected to its kin. In the distance, black clouds creep nearer. Slowly. Almost imperceptible. The sky holds a certain fascination for me that way, so like a beautiful painting just out of reach. These moments have become my favorite; the brief period before a storm when the air has the heavy feel and scent of the coming rain, and if you listen carefully, you can just make out the distant rumble of far-off thunder. There's an energy riding the air in these moments, an energy one cannot describe, only feel.

Perhaps it's this energy that has finally driven me to pick up this pen.

It's been nearly three weeks since Michael left me, bewildered and in the possession of four blank notebooks. In the time since, they've remained exactly as he left them, a constant reminder of his bizarre request. I'm not really sure why now, after so many days of avoiding it, I finally decided to begin doing that which he asked me to do. Maybe it's the energy of the coming storm being channeled through me somehow, or maybe it's simply that once the storm begins, I'll be shut inside the house, and since it's three o'clock on a Sunday, I also know there won't be anything on worth watching. But maybe it's more than that.

I must admit, though I didn't touch Michael's gifts, the notion of his request has been churning in my mind since the second he left. At first, I wanted nothing to do with it. *How could Michael bring this to me*, I thought, *this assignment from on high?* Yet despite my anger, in spite of it even, the idea grew, and soon it seemed the world revolved around nothing else. Everywhere I go, something or someone whispers to me, plunges into my thoughts to add another fragment to the story I've been asked to tell. These same whispers have also been telling me the reasons *why* I should write what Michael asked, why it's so important. When I went to watch our local Little League team—the Firebirds—play, all throughout the game little hints and messages came floating to me. At the grocery store last Wednesday, as I watched a cashier named Louise swipe items across her scanner in a bored stupor, long-forgotten events started aligning into sequences. Those moments when I look around and realize how uninformed the world is about the truth, when I want to shake mankind awake to what's happening with so few truly aware—those moments have drawn me to this.

But what am I about to write? The sheer magnitude of what Michael proposed is indescribable. The size of this undertaking has kept me from sleep, from food, from even glancing at these notebooks without a sense of distress, even fear … yet all tinged with a strange eagerness and curiosity. In the past weeks, I've spent entire nights staring with bloodshot eyes at the ceiling fan, my mind racing after the whirling blades, weaving together the strands of my life without my consent. Even now, in the very act of writing, I find myself skirting the duty, and yet I know I can't escape it. It seems the decision was never really mine to make. It was made even before Michael appeared in my living room, wings spread grandly behind him, an aura of white light surrounding his entire being in that spectacle of an entrance he so loves to perform. He knew I wouldn't be able to resist in the end, that eventually I would sit here to record all those details and emotions I've so longed to let slip from my memory forever. He knew because he knows me; he knows I've always wanted this chance to reach out to so many and allow them to know what was never revealed before.

There's so much to tell, how can I possibly fit it all in? It seems impossible, and yet I must try. The mirror across the room reflects the image of a man in his early thirties with short blond hair and bright blue eyes. But that mirror will not expose what I truly am—or was, at least. To do what Michael has asked, I must ignore the mirror, turn a deaf ear to the thunder growing louder each minute, pretend I don't smell the lilac floating on the breeze. If I am to allow myself to conjure my past, I must wholly forget my present, the pain of which will drive me mad if viewed in the same light. I must force myself to do this, because if I don't, then all the world will ever have from me will be a few pages of meaningless chatter, and there's so much more I need to tell. For the sake of all those who wish to know more, who already suspect more, I will close the window now and light this candle before me as my guide home when the tale is through, for without it I fear I might never wish to return. I'm going to let myself escape into the past, to give to you my life's memoirs, long and painful as they might be.

My name is Sabrael, and I was once an angel of the Lord.

CHAPTER ONE

There was a time when Heaven was not yet split. Before the burning of golden skies. Before the clash of weapons and the cries of suffering. Before brother stood against brother and armies formed out of the ranks of friends to shed the blood of those we once loved.

I remember that time, because I was there.

It is a strange thing to think I witnessed not one, but two wars between kin. God willing, there will never be a third. The thought of another haunts my dreams, the pained screams of angels lingering in my ears even now. There is no other sound like it. Especially when the screams are your own.

But as I said, it was not always as it is now.

⇥⇤

Created long before the first stirring of life on Earth, I was among the first beings in existence. On white wings I flew among my brothers in Heaven, the host of God's holy angels, and together we lived solely for Him.

Heaven in that time was much different than it is now, but its magnificence was no less striking. Everywhere there was beauty to make one weep: sweeping fields of brilliant flowers, unending forests, cities the likes of which I have never seen since. Streams coursed through buildings to plummet over waterfalls into the nothingness outside the walls. Richly colored banners flew from every building; flowers grew from every surface; vast canyons housed entire mountains. The only way to understand is to see it. It was nature, architecture, art and imagination seamlessly fused. Or rather, that's what we designed it to be.

In the earliest days, the kingdom comprised seven interconnected halls. Each had its own distinctive look, its own colors and, eventually, architectural style. Colossal archways stood at each crossroads between them. They had no names or rank; one knew where he was simply by the hue of the banners. Charged with the duty of making our own paradise, the host was divided into seven groups and each angel given a specific role in the beautification of his assigned hall. In the hall designated by deep crimson and gold, my task was to produce all manner of flora, placing it wherever I saw fit. As my brothers raised great structures, diverted rivers and manipulated everything else, I followed, adding floral accents to the spreading beauty. With no need for roots or water in the spiritual plane, the immaterial, my flowers sprouted from any surface, even stone, forever arranged as I conceived them. At the rate we moved, I thought our work would be done quickly, but as fast as we finished, more work was created.

Despite the great effort spent decorating the halls, there were times when no angel was at work or play. Times when the entire host was called to the eighth hall, the region none of us had a hand in creating—the Hall of Song.

The Hall of Song was the only true hall in an earthly sense. Constructed of stone comparable in appearance to burnished obsidian, it was the hub that connected the seven halls, and the grandest of them all. Towering above every other structure in the kingdom, it was more impressive than anything we could have imagined ourselves. Colors glinted within the walls like fireflies; shimmering banners fluttered from the stone itself; intricate carvings decorated every recess. Pathways lined in flowers funneled from each of the seven halls through the great archways into a common area outside the Hall where a stairway led to double doors so massive, dozens of us could fly through at once.

Inside, the Hall of Song was no less brilliant. A long passageway of immeasurably tall columns emblazoned with the names of every angel opened into an enormous worship area where concentric rows of seats stretched from the floor to the ceiling, each a bit higher than the last. These were the seats of the angelic choir, the host of God's children. The first circle, composed of just four chairs, sat at the foot of our reason for meeting.

Misleadingly simple in appearance, the throne of the Almighty sat in the center of it all. It wasn't a chair, but instead a raised dais where God could stand surrounded by us all. When gathered there, we would sing praises for all His work in creating us and the kingdom. Our love and thanks projected in voices not of sound but emotion, and as we sang, His light filled not only the Hall but each of us as well.

The light. I had almost managed to forget it. My God, has it been so long?

Illuminating everything, the light of the Almighty could be felt everywhere. Every corner of the kingdom knew its warmth. It came from everywhere at once, piercing into the very essence of all it touched. If He laid a hand on a stone, that stone would glow with His love for a certain period even after He had moved on. There were no shadows because of this, nowhere without the presence of God's grace. I still yearned for that light centuries after I was without it.

But I get ahead of myself.

That was the way of it in the earliest days; our time divided among assignments and praise. It was an existence of pure happiness. Between gatherings, my brothers would congregate to play, converse, or compose new praises for when the call was next heard.

But I was not among them.

So full of God's love was I when we were still new and Heaven was young, I devoted all my time to showing the Almighty that love. I could not ignore my duties as my brothers did, for I felt it reflected a reluctance to perform my assigned task. While the others played games or sat around chatting, I hunted for the next place in need of decoration. If ever I took a rest, it was simply to visit other halls and admire the work there. Studying their fields or analyzing their forests, I was always learning tricks from my brothers' craft to enhance my own. Do not misunderstand me in thinking I was not captivated by it all, for I was. There were times when I felt breathless with the beauty before me. It was the perfect paradise, and I the tourist with an eternity to marvel at every nuance. But the desire to show the Almighty my appreciation always came before all else.

I might have remained that way forever, isolated from my kin, had it not been for him.

Tracing my hands along the trees on one of my excursions into Heaven's many forests, I stopped to admire how even the leaves on the branches around me were spread evenly, no leaf crowding or growing larger than its brothers. All was in perfect harmony, down to the smallest detail. On my knees with folded hands, I thanked the Almighty for bestowing upon us the ability to bring such wonder to the kingdom.

It was then I sensed I was being watched.

The feeling wasn't one of fear, for in that time fear did not exist. Merely the realization of eyes upon me. Cautious footsteps grew nearer, then stopped. I looked back down the path and met the gaze of glowing cobalt eyes.

Lucifer.

Crouched a short distance away, my brother peered at me from beneath golden curls with what I can best describe as delighted curiosity. His childlike features did not at all reflect his station. He was one of the four angels who held the honor of sitting closest to God in our gatherings. I couldn't believe he was there. Our eyes locked, neither of us speaking for a long moment. Then Lucifer laughed.

I couldn't help my smile at the absurdity of it. "You followed me all this way just to laugh at me?"

"So! The enigmatic Sabrael can talk! They didn't believe me, but I knew it."

"They?" I asked, shocked. "Whom do you mean?"

Lucifer's wings fluttered as he strode toward me. I was surprised to find that despite his youthful features, he stood only a measure shorter than me. He smirked and said, "Many even think you were made without a voice, for no one has ever heard you speak. Makes me something of a pioneer talking to you, does it not?"

It was probably true. When we sang in the Hall, my voice was just one of many, and outside, I kept to myself. "I didn't realize I was cause for such concern," I said.

As he moved, the folds of Lucifer's robe unfurled from his body, as all our robes do in the spiritual plane. A common misconception for millennia has been that our robes are just clothing, but in truth, it's more symbiotic. Standing still, an angel's body and robe appear as one contiguous form. In motion, however, the robe stretches out like a solar flare to follow in a sweeping trail. While the robe can be gathered, shifted and even cut, it can never be removed. It's part of our being.

Lucifer glowed as if he were the Almighty's light made tangible. The only contrast to the brightness of his skin and golden hair was his eyes. With no need for adjusting to light in the immaterial, we have no corneas or pupils. An angel's eyes simply glow one uniform color the whole way through. Lucifer's were a striking cobalt shade unlike any I'd ever seen. I could see why his was a seat so close to the Almighty's.

Lucifer went on, "The question then becomes: If you can talk, why have you remained silent for so long?"

"I suppose I just don't have anything interesting to say."

"I doubt that. Besides, at this point, you saying anything at all would draw a crowd."

"Then maybe I just have nothing to say to those who do nothing but stand around and talk away their time."

"Is it so wrong to converse with your brothers?" he asked.

"Just because we are outside the Hall of Song does not mean we should refrain from showing our love. I find it difficult to speak to those who do not seem to understand that."

Lucifer smiled. "I think I see. By studying creation and everything around you, you feel you show Him your appreciation and thanks. And by taking a break, they do not?"

"Exactly."

Lucifer patted the tree nearest him like a pet. "I've been watching you for some time, Sabrael. I hope you don't mind my saying, but I've been somewhat fascinated by you."

"Me? Why?"

"You claim to appreciate creation, yet somehow you manage to overlook your own brothers as though they themselves pale in comparison to what they have wrought."

"That's not what I meant…"

"No? Then come with me. Let me introduce you to the brothers you so easily ignore."

"I am honored you would offer, but I do not think I fit among them," I said.

"How do you know?" Lucifer contested. "You spend all your time with trees."

"I've listened," I replied. "They talk about their jobs but do not act on them. They talk about each other and how great they are.

They play games. I would rather spend my time showing my love for Him."

"Can you not see that those *are* the ways they show their love? They plan new ways to carry out their duties so they never become routine. They play to celebrate existence and happiness, and complimenting one another spreads His love among them. They do not hide their love like a secret as you do. We are meant to love Him, yes, but does this not include helping each other grow in that love? Do you truly believe He wants you to exist in silence when so many could benefit from your way of expressing adoration?"

Never before had I thought this way about our purpose. Never before had I heard the reason for the breaks between gatherings so clearly defined, the reason for letting us design the look of the halls. Lucifer's explanation of how our praise was connected to everything around us made so much sense. I felt immensely ignorant. I wanted to apologize for my naivety, but I didn't get the chance.

"Come," Lucifer beckoned as we heard the call like the blaring of trumpets. "The host is gathering."

The two of us flew together to the Hall of Song, talking the whole way. It was incredible. To think that I was personally speaking with Lucifer was unfathomable! Even more astonishing, he was just a normal angel, like me.

Flocks of our brothers flew in from every hall, wings spread and robes trailing. Their shocked stares as we passed reflected how I felt. I followed Lucifer through the great doors into the colonnade leading to the worship area.

"Promise me you will not slip back into solitude after this, Sabrael. At the very least, come talk to me. Find me in the hall of blue banners. You have a beautiful voice; do not be afraid to use it."

He headed for his seat at the foot of God's throne. Adorned with great wings on its high back, it was far more regal than my seat, which lacked any decoration at all. Taking my place high above, I watched the stream of angels pouring into the Hall. Row after row, the fluttering of wings came from every direction as they settled themselves. Pairs of glowing eyes met mine more than once as I listened to the echo of thousands of voices, innumerable conversations spreading from the floor to the ceiling high above. But all were silenced the moment He entered.

In a blaze of gentle light, the Almighty appeared and took His throne. The reaction was immediate. The entire host burst into song, our voices first absorbed, then amplified by the shining black walls to a volume impossible for human ears to stand. While we sang, the Almighty smiled and sent His love through the blinding, soothing light.

Hymns poured forth from my lips as they always had, but it was different this time, for as my voice rang out I didn't tune out the vast number of my brothers singing with me. With wings folded and white robes still against their bodies, the angels of the host were indeed magnificent. Each of my brothers reflected his love for the Almighty; each added his own distinct voice. It was a harmony of existence, a symphony of perfection. I couldn't believe I'd never recognized it before. How could I have been so closed off?

I looked far down to the first circle where Lucifer sat in his ornate chair, singing so strongly I thought I could make out his voice above the rest. As if sensing my gaze, he looked up and gave me a knowing smile. Only later would I realize what that look meant.

I had just unwittingly become Lucifer's personal pupil.

CHAPTER TWO

Lucifer, I soon learned, was quite the celebrity. Everywhere he went, his name was called out by those desperate for his attention. He floated from angel to angel like he knew everyone and, always at his side, I flew as his wide-eyed companion. While most of my brothers had long ago settled into groups with whom they mingled between gatherings, Lucifer was ever on the prowl, conversing just long enough to elicit an outburst of laughter before moving on. He knew everything about everyone—names, duties, even their stations under God—without ever having to ask. They loved him dearly for this, competed for his praise, and Lucifer, the gallivanting master of our Heavenly society, ate it up.

Right from the start, it was clear what a wonderful blessing I'd been given in the attention of such a respected figure in the Heavenly hierarchy. I was welcomed into any group I approached and sought after by those I did not. So many new friends greeted me that it was hard to keep track sometimes. It was shocking to think that only a short time before, I'd been entirely unknown. That is, save for my reputation as the bizarre mute.

The wonder that my brothers held for Lucifer in his presence was nothing compared to that when he was away, though. Some spoke of him as if he were a deity, raving about how they'd won a kind word from him or how important he was to the host. Eavesdropping on these conversations, I was unnerved. Something didn't seem right in their tone. When they started speaking of me in the same way, my apprehension quickly turned to concern. The old rumors had indeed changed. Instead of a mute, I was now Lucifer's "silent disciple." The way they said it, it was like some prestigious honor, or even a role to be envied. They seemed to revere me. Me! I couldn't believe it. It wasn't just one or two angels who spoke this way either—it was everyone. I heard it so often, I actually began to wonder if there was some truth to it. It may sound disingenuous to say that I didn't enjoy the attention, but it was honestly more disturbing than anything.

The rumors reached their worst during those times when Lucifer went missing. He would often disappear without a trace for long periods. One instant he would be conversing with some circle of angels, and the next he'd be gone. Whispers would spread. Where did he go? What was he doing? Why did he not tell anyone about it? My reaction the first time was to worry that he'd abandoned me. He returned, as he always would, but even to me he would never say where he'd been. This was like fuel on the fire of my brothers' speculative gossip. Rumors ran wild as the frequency of his disappearances increased, and we were all left wondering where he went to escape from everyone … and why.

The answer wouldn't come from Lucifer. Instead, it came from my brother Raphael.

I was first introduced to Raphael during one of Lucifer's many absences. Actually, "introduced" is the wrong word; I should say I was approached. Another of my brothers who sat in the circle closest to God, he was also well-known and respected, but was nearly Lucifer's opposite in demeanor. Reserved and respectful, Raphael spent his time observing the rest of us from a distance. Few noticed him; most never knew he was watching. I only did when he started following me around. His emerald eyes seemed always to be there, staring from across the crowds. He would appear when I roamed the forests, when I was at work in my own hall. He was everywhere I went, as though he always knew my next move. I tried to ignore him, tried to keep my eyes averted, though I felt each time I looked away, he crept nearer. I thought if I could keep from acknowledging him, he might lose interest and find someone else to haunt.

I was wrong.

"Sabrael?" The voice startled me as I considered the arrangement of a newly completed mural. I turned to find Raphael standing near me, his auburn hair flowing down over his shoulders. His complexion was flawless, like a polished statue. "You missed a spot."

"It's intentional," I replied, at once both nervous and glad to finally speak to my silent shadow. "Sometimes the negative space is just as important."

He regarded me for a long moment. "I can see why you're the one. May I sit?"

"The one?" I asked. "Do you always speak in riddles?"

Raphael seated himself, wings folding as he ran his hand over a daisy, careful not to damage it. His glowing eyes radiated calm. I was a bit taken by the perfection of his features, the absolute symmetry. He was almost as striking as even Lucifer.

"The angel who walks at Lucifer's side. I heard Lucifer had taken on something of an apprentice. I decided to find out who the lucky angel might be, and behold, you are the one."

"Tell me, Raphael, why do our brothers care so much about with whom Lucifer speaks?"

Raphael laughed, softening his statuesque face. "Surely you must know."

But I did not.

His smile faded, his face once again blank and perfect. "Because of who he is, his place in the host." He paused, searching my face for a glimmer of the knowledge he was about to impart. "He was the first of us, Sabrael, at one time the only being in existence next to God Himself. None of us knows how long creation was just the two of them before another was created. Lucifer has always been closest to God, and serves as His sole confidant in many matters. You must notice it when Lucifer is summoned away to speak privately with the Almighty. That's why everyone cares so much; to be close to Lucifer is to be closer to God."

Dread swelled inside me with each word, the scent of the flowers making me sick, which was a feat since I didn't even know what being sick was. Why had Lucifer not told me? Why would he hide such a thing from the one he brought so close? But Raphael wasn't finished.

"Never before has Lucifer allowed any to get as close to him as you are; never before has any been brave enough to try. You have become something of a legend. Doesn't help that you were silent for so long. Many think you were kept isolated for a reason. I have heard different theories of what that might be, but the most common is that you were chosen to be trained by Lucifer even then."

"Trained for what?" I managed to ask around the tightness in my throat. My worries were coming to fruition.

"To join Lucifer in his private discussions with God."

My breath caught with the shock of these words. Some of the flowers around us uprooted and floated up. Raphael smirked and plucked one from the air.

"That's the rumor anyway. I simply wondered if you might possess some unique talent to explain his interest. You realize that Michael and Gabriel are both just as curious. As the first created after Lucifer, how do you think they'd take it were you to be invited behind closed doors before us? You've been the subject of very interesting discussions as of late."

I could hardly find my voice. It's hard enough finding out such a secret about a close friend, something kept from you for so long, but when the secret is actually about you… Lucifer, the angel who charmed me from solitude, the child of light I followed in adoration, had hidden from me perhaps the most important aspect of himself for the entirety of the time I'd known him. Why would he seek me out, befriend me and then withhold all this? I didn't feel angered or betrayed; again, these emotions didn't yet exist. I was concerned. Perhaps there was something troubling going on. "Now that you have met me," I began again, "what 'unique talent' have you found? I'm sure you see there's nothing to give truth to the rumors."

Raphael's warm, emerald gaze was still fixed on me. "Time will tell."

He rose from the ground and I asked, "Will you at least speak to the others? Tell them to end all these rumors and speculation."

He looked down at me, smile spreading, and said, "Where's the fun in that?" Raphael spread his wings and soared back toward the Hall of Song, a gentle wind lifting my hair in his wake. I watched the glowing streak of his robe until it was gone.

I attempted to continue my work, but the more I pondered his words, the more curiosity took hold. Lucifer was the only angel in Heaven with whom God spoke when He would speak to no other, the only angel allowed to know things kept from the rest of us. This wasn't something of which to be ashamed. My mind raced, tender petals wilting between my fingers as my attention drifted from the mural. I wanted answers, needed them, and no amount of duty or work would bring them. I spread my wings and took flight to search for Lucifer.

I finally found him alone in his hall, wings curled around him like a shield on the bank of a rushing stream. My feet silently touched down and I folded my wings to my back to crouch beside my brother. "Lucifer, we need to talk," I began, but as my gaze found his eyes, I recoiled in terror.

Lucifer remained still. He peered at me through the corners of his eyes, and I saw in them something never before encountered in Heaven—despair. I nearly cried out as a teardrop fell from his chin to join the innumerable drops of the stream. While crying may be the first act of human life, no angel had ever cried before. We didn't even know it was possible. Awful thoughts that my brother had somehow injured himself filled my mind. Unsure of what to do, I hid my eyes from him. Lucifer saw this and covered his face, wiping away his tears even as new ones instantly rose in their place. "Leave me here!" Lucifer said. "I am afraid beyond what I ever imagined was possible. I do not want you to feel it as well."

I forced my shaking hands from my eyes. He knew this feeling, knew it by name. *Afraid.* "What is happening to you? What caused this?"

Lucifer turned his face toward me for the first time. It seemed this *afraid* had gathered entirely in his eyes. Why had it not spread throughout his whole body? Perhaps it would not look so startling. Tears ran down his face and dangled from his chin before falling to strike the surface of the stream, disappearing into its current. I hoped we wouldn't need to retrieve them.

"Sabrael," Lucifer sobbed, "It is our brothers. They draw this river from within me."

"This has happened before?" I asked, shocked. How did our brothers have the power to do this? More puzzling than that, I didn't know what I could do to help. What I was seeing had been impossible before that moment. How could I know what might be done to stop his crying when I didn't even know what crying was?

"All I have ever done, I have done in His honor," Lucifer said, his face hidden again behind his golden locks. "I have never done anything that did not praise God. I do not understand them! Can they not see I am no higher than them in any way?"

"Higher? What are you talking about?" I asked, hoping that letting him talk would help him to stop crying somehow.

A trembling sob escaped his lips. "The others believe because I was first, that I speak to Him in private, and because they feel my assigned tasks surpass theirs in importance and scale, that I am somehow above the rest of you. They believe that I am not as you are or as they are, but something between angel and God." I listened without answering, horrified by what he was saying yet wanting him to go on. "They look at me with reverence and speak to me with this … tone. Always as I perform my tasks or sing the praise of God, they try to please and mimic me in the hopes of gaining my favor. But they do not need it, and already have it!

"When we gather to sing, I feel their gazes upon me rather than on He who deserves such adoration. Worse, our brothers have even started singing hymns written to honor me! Can you fathom that? I hear them everywhere I go. I cannot escape them! The gatherings have become misery because of those horrid songs. I have been forced to disappear, to find places where I can hide from those who would call me something I am not."

"Why not simply tell them all this?" He was already shaking his head. "Surely they would stop if you show them you are just a servant of God as they are."

"I have already tried, on many occasions. They listen with deaf ears as they look with glazed eyes. It is useless to try to discuss this with them."

"Yet you discuss it with me," I said. It was more a statement than a question, but his expression became one of terror. He thought I meant it in thanks, like a devoted apostle. But that was not my intent. "Lucifer, do you know what the others are saying about me?"

The shock in his eyes returned to sadness. He clearly did. Even now, as I write this, I'm still in awe of the range of emotions Lucifer had to deal with in that time, every one strange and new to Heaven. Even his horrific tears must have held a kind of fearful fascination. I saw the maelstrom raging inside him, yet I was unable to empathize. I was focused on the question Raphael had planted in my mind, and I would not be swayed.

"Our brothers believe me to be your apprentice. They think you are training me to be like you, to enter the Almighty's confidence at your side. They believe you chose me from among them instead of befriending me. Is this true? Am I somehow different from the rest of the host?"

Lucifer's face cringed, new tears spilling over his cheeks. "Yes!"

My heart was racing so hard, my entire body quivered.

Lucifer wiped the heel of his hand across his face. "Can you not understand that yours is the best way to see creation? You see Heaven and all within as no one else does, for you see it all as the beautiful work of God. From the pillars in the Hall of Song to our very brothers, we're all pieces in one big demonstration of His love."

Lucifer stood and paced, his tears dropping in a wounded trail along the ground. He reached out to the nearest tree and as his hand touched the bark, he stopped as though remembering something.

"When I first introduced myself to you back in that forest, you were marveling at everything around you. Not at how any one tree might be better than another because it was bigger, or one patch of moss over another because it had a more complex pattern. Each thing within that forest was just as beautiful and important as everything else, and you showed that by giving everything equal amounts of your attention. What makes you special is that you see our brothers the same way. You look from angel to angel and see what makes each one unique. This is a wonderful ability, brother, for you see every angel as equal. Yours is an indiscriminant view of creation, and for this reason you are special among us."

"That's not true. You are a throne angel, Lucifer; you sit closer to God than any of the rest of us. I'm in awe of you, could never think of myself as your equal," I protested.

Lucifer crouched down beside me. "But you see us both as equals under God. In this horrible time when so many of our brothers turn their admiration toward me, I yearned for someone who would not see me as superior, who would not laud me for things I am simply meant to do. I was alone and needed a friend, not another admirer.

You are that friend. You who see all equally. You who love all for who they are rather than for the placement of their seat in the Hall. You who knows it is God who deserves our praise. I knew I could trust you, so yes, I did choose you. But it was an innocent decision. I beg you; forgive me for not telling you all this, Sabrael, but I feared even you might begin to see me for my rank rather than for whom you know me to be."

To say I felt remorse would be a terrible understatement. I could not hide my shame for coming to accuse him. My brother had been suffering in despair every moment I had known him, and I never even noticed. Only then did I gain a bit of understanding of how Lucifer felt, of how trapped he was in the scrutiny of the host. He must have been stronger than even I imagined, dealing with this for so long without ever mentioning it to anyone, without showing how deeply it affected him.

"I cannot tell you how sorry I am that our brothers have drawn you into this," Lucifer said, staring back into the stream. "I never wanted you to get caught up in how they see me. Perhaps it would be best if you stop speaking to me altogether."

"No!" I said, appalled that he would even suggest it. "I will not let you face this with no one on your side."

The angelic choir suddenly burst into song, silvery voices re-sounding throughout Heaven and filling it with the praise of God. Lucifer's eyes widened and he bolted to his feet, shouting over the countless voices, "We are not there! We are missing the gathering!"

"He will understand," I assured Lucifer, hoping this was true. "When He asks why we were not there, tell Him all of this and He will make it well again."

Lucifer wiped away the last remaining tears. "How can you be so sure?"

I smiled. "He's our creator. He could never be angry with us."

Lucifer stared at me for a moment, then nodded. "You're right. Of course you're right. I will not hide this torment any longer." I rose from the ground and Lucifer embraced me. "You are a good friend. Truly special, I mean that. I shall not forget this in my discussion with God."

He soared into the air to seek a private meeting with the Almighty. The image of his tears stuck in my mind. Just the thought of them stirred feelings of horror within me, but I was relieved my words had helped. Hopefully he would now be able to find peace.

⟫⟩ ⟨⟪

It was only a short time before the misdirected praise was silenced. Lucifer spoke with the Almighty and God commanded the false praise to stop. The Almighty reminded us that to view anyone as more important than the rest was to idolize that angel, and this was strictly forbidden. The first commandment given to Moses was, "You shall have no other gods," and this was a reflection of the command we were given in Heaven. My brothers who had been singing for Lucifer were ashamed. The praise of Lucifer dwindled to whispers, then disappeared. All the songs in Heaven were once again in honor of the Almighty alone.

Soon, Lucifer was his jovial self again and even rejoined our conversations between the gatherings. I was delighted to have Lucifer back, but to say he was the old Lucifer again is not entirely true. In certain ways, the experience had left an indelible mark. Sometimes when he spoke there was an awkward tension, as though he was giving a glimpse of something he was embarrassed about. It was also soon evident that Lucifer had become obsessed with the future of Heaven and the role of the host within it. He believed change was coming, that the status quo of our beautifying Heaven couldn't last forever and eventually something more must come of our existence. I listened, skeptical, thinking it nothing more than innocent speculation by a mind recently released of heavy burden.

I was too happy to see Lucifer liberated of his oppression to suspect anything else.

Only Michael recognized something was wrong.

Amidst the happiness of Heaven, Michael, who held a list of responsibilities second only to Lucifer's, walked as an apparition of despair through the halls of paradise. Michael, who regarded his duties with great honor and allowed himself little activity outside them, was the only one who saw something that even I, Lucifer's closest companion, did not detect.

I remember it well. While walking with Lucifer in the hall of greenish banners, I stopped to inspect the artistry of a field adorned with vibrant flowers. When I looked up, it was to the sight of Michael sitting alone some distance away, a black and white smudge in the vista of otherwise brilliant color. I asked Lucifer, "Have you spoken with Michael recently?"

"Why would I want to bring myself down? I am perfectly content being content, thank you," Lucifer joked. But he couldn't conceal the strangeness of his grin.

"Something is wrong. I have never seen him so ... reclusive. I wonder what happened to cause him to be like this."

Lucifer looked at Michael and his smile faded. There was a bit of annoyance behind his gaze, though at what I couldn't tell. He shrugged and said nothing.

"You know what happened," I said, realizing it even as I spoke the words. "Tell me. Perhaps we can help him. Maybe he has discovered fear, as you did." When his eyes returned to me, they burned with concern. Or was it anger? "Do you not want to help him?"

"What makes you think he wants or needs help, Sabrael?" he said. The response threw me. Something was definitely wrong. "We should return to the others. This hall bores me."

"What aren't you telling me? What's wrong with you?"

"His sadness is caused by me!" Lucifer shouted, his calm gone. "Does it change anything, knowing that?" He glared at me, the annoyance held so precariously in check now fully apparent.

"You? I … I don't understand," I said.

"No, I doubt you would. Wallowing in your innocence. How could you understand?" Lucifer pointed at Michael. "That's why I did not come to you, but went to him instead."

"For what?" It chilled me how timid my voice sounded compared to his.

Lucifer sighed. "I am changing. Things I cannot explain are happening to me, and while I do not fully understand them, I do know that I am now unlike any of you." I looked at him, trying to understand what he meant, but how could I? I was naïve, not innocent. All my experiences in Heaven couldn't help me understand what he meant. Lucifer, seeing my confusion, finally threw up his hands, then caught me with a fierce look.

For the first time in my existence, I was truly afraid of him.

"Do you know why we praise God?" he asked me, his face drawing near, eyes narrowed.

For a moment, I waited to see if such a ridiculous question was rhetorical. "He's our creator. He gave us life and a paradise in which to live it." My hands shook under the strain of Lucifer's icy glare. "We praise Him because He loves us."

"If that's so, why does He demand that we spend our lives singing *about* Him *to* Him? Why not just allow us to enjoy this paradise and each other's company?" I opened my mouth, unsure of what I was going to say, but this time he answered himself. "It's because God feels something no other has felt in all the time we have existed. This feeling drives Him to demand that we spend our precious time praising Him instead of living as we should be … for ourselves." Lucifer's eyes widened, giving his face a maniacal look. "But I know something he does not."

"Impossible!" Fear was coming into my voice as a tremble. "He knows all. To say He does not is unthinkable."

Lucifer smiled with amused ferocity. "How do we know that? How can we be sure that everything He says is true, or that He really created this vast paradise of which neither you nor I will ever know the bounds? Were you there to see Him create it? What proof do we have that He knows everything He claims to?"

My mind was racing yet my tongue was frozen. I said the first thing that came to mind. "We know because He has felt things none of us have, and knows things none of us know."

Lucifer laughed and patted me on the back, the ferocity momentarily dispelled by a sinister gaiety. "And there it is. The reason you remain loyal—because He 'feels things we do not' and 'knows things we do not.' Well let me tell you something…" He leaned close, so no one eavesdropping could hear. "I too feel things you do not, and know things you do not."

I didn't understand, but he knew I wouldn't and continued. "That's why I spoke with Michael, and that's the reason he sulks now. I told him of this feeling only God and I share; what I believe it means. But you know how Michael gets. He does not understand this new feeling, or why I received it, and when Michael does not understand something, it must be unholy. He begged me to go before God, confess what's going on, but I cannot do that yet. Not until I know more. All that little discussion did was make him worry."

"Should he worry? Should I?"

Lucifer smirked. "So eager to get it out of me? So desperate to learn what horrid ailment has infected my fragile mind?"

"I am only trying to understand," I said. The sweet hyacinth scent turned sour with my nervous tension.

Lucifer shook his head, disgusted. "When the others sang my praise, I was afraid. Each word from their lips grieved me; each note they sang brought tremors of fear. I asked God to end it. With their silence, I was free again. Happy, for a time. It's what I wanted. But lately … lately I have been missing it."

Lucifer traced a circle in the dust with his finger. His eyes turned from me, I was released of the fear he was causing. As though the malice of moments earlier had only been imagined.

"I do not yet understand it. It's unlike anything I've ever known, this feeling. The very mention of my name now brings a sense of importance, even power. I wonder why I never felt it before. It is wonderful, Sabrael. Nothing I know compares, save that moment when God's gaze falls upon you. I do not—cannot—understand why He doesn't allow all to feel it. I crave it constantly, even find myself humming the very songs I helped to silence!" Lucifer looked up, an innocent child once more. "The more I experience this sensation, the more I feel as though perhaps our brothers were right in praising me." I shook my head in disbelief as he added, "I lament the fact that I quieted my own praise."

I grabbed him by the shoulders. "Lucifer, listen to yourself! This feeling, whatever it may be, confuses you. Please, you must tell the Almighty about…"

"No!" Lucifer interrupted, his ferocity rekindled. "You will not accept the fact that I am changing because you are blinded by innocence and adherence to God's word! You cannot understand what is happening to me because you don't know how. You only understand what God tells you. You disgust me. First Michael, who would rather sulk in sadness than help me, and now you, who should be most supportive. Is everyone so quick to be my judge?"

Lucifer threw my hands away from him as he rose from the ground. "I fear no one in Heaven can help me. No one but me."

His jaw tightened as though he was pondering some idea that only now occurred to him. Before I could ask what it was, he took one last, angry look at me, then flew away. I kept my gaze on the point where he'd disappeared for a long time.

When I finally looked down, it was to find Michael staring at me in knowing silence.

CHAPTER THREE

I don't know where Lucifer went when he left me in that field, but wherever it was, no one could find him. When he didn't return for some time, I knew it was trouble. We were all used to him disappearing when the Almighty requested his private counsel, but this was something else. The way he left, his words before he vanished … despite his temper, I couldn't stop worrying about him and all he was experiencing. I only wanted to help him; I didn't want to be his "judge."

The host was in turmoil over our rogue brother. Every discussion focused on his mysterious disappearance and the events that led to his self-imposed exile. Depending on which circle one listened to, opinions swayed from condemnation to applause for his step into the unknown. I couldn't escape the conversations in every hall, the rumors and theories and gossip, and with each comment overheard, I thought, *Lucifer, can you hear what you have caused? Are you listening even now, and is your strange feeling growing?*

The only thing that could quiet the rampant speculation about Lucifer's disappearance turned out to be his return.

It happened first as a whisper in select circles, sightings in the forests and such. Whispers then grew to a chant, and soon, the whole kingdom buzzed in anticipation. I started to suspect he was orchestrating it all to incite the greatest possible reaction.

Again and again I returned to that field where I last saw him, replaying our conversation a hundred times over. My worry had only intensified in his absence, and the anticipation of his return was unbearable. *Why must he do this?* I thought. *Why cause such havoc when we simply want him to return and accept the Almighty's help? Does he not realize we miss him?*

But the moment he appeared, I knew that the childlike Lucifer, the angel more beloved than any, who brought me forth from silence to the company of our brothers, was gone.

When confirmed reports of his return rippled through the kingdom, everyone dropped what they were doing and swarmed to catch a glimpse of our prodigal brother. Emerging from one of the many fields in his hall, Lucifer strode into view shining with a light all his own. Golden curls draped around an eerily pleased smile, he met those crowding to see him with open arms. Many ran to envelop him in an embrace of feathered wings and flowing robes, calling out his name and questioning where he'd been and what he'd done.

I stayed where I was, watching this insane spectacle from afar. Lucifer basked in the attention, but I soon realized what was really bothering me as I looked at him. His glow. It was tainted somehow, no longer pure. As Heaven exists solely in the spiritual plane, an angel's glow isn't a physical thing like light. It's more of an impression, an aura. Tainted as his was, it was unsettling to even look at him. Once I recognized this impurity, I also noticed I wasn't the only one. It was clear that those who didn't run to his side also saw it. Michael looked at Lucifer in utter horror, motionless as he stared wide-eyed at our brother.

The crowd around Lucifer teemed with questions, but he waved to silence them, promising to answer all in time. Then his gaze fell on me. The smile that spread across his lips terrified me.

The sea of angels parted before him as Lucifer made his way to embrace me. "Have you nothing to say, Sabrael? I get no greeting at all from my dearest friend?"

I could almost feel his new glow pulsing, infecting my own. I backed away. "You were my friend, Lucifer. I do not know who you are now."

I thought I saw something in his eyes when I said this, something of shame or remorse perhaps, but I can't be sure. More likely I yearned to see some evidence that my friend still existed somewhere.

Whatever the case, Lucifer laughed at my words, and those following him echoed in an eerie chant, already beginning again to do what they were forbidden to do. Without another word Lucifer strode past, slowing to stare down Michael before continuing out of sight, the long train of his followers trailing behind.

In the wake of Lucifer's return, Heaven underwent distinct change. The gatherings felt quieter, less energetic, and the times between saw the host split into two factions; those of us who remained as we always had been, and those who believed Lucifer's radical new ideas should be made reality. Lucifer refused to do his assigned tasks. He stopped singing the praise of the Almighty altogether, electing to sit alone rather than attend the gatherings with the rest of us. When we would return, we'd find him amidst piles of plucked grass or surrounded by hundreds of stripped flower petals. He seemed utterly bored with all around him, except when someone new would come to hear his tales and revel in his magnificence. The rest of us he ignored. Nothing we could say or do was of any importance. Many tried reasoning with this new Lucifer who was not as he should be, but he brushed them aside like flies. When I tried, he wouldn't even meet me, instead sending one of his loyalists to inform me I had nothing to say worth hearing. This was his attitude toward existence now—that he alone knew the meaning of his change, and therefore he alone mattered in the grand scheme.

Michael continued to grow more troubled at the state of Lucifer's condition. It seemed Heaven itself trembled with distress, and Michael reflected that horrible anxiety like no other. While my brothers and I tried to reach Lucifer, Michael floated among us without speaking a word to anyone, his face hidden behind his long, ebony hair. His patience is great, and he kept quiet a long time, but eventually the sadness that ate at him became a burden too heavy for even him to bear.

I don't know what Michael said to Lucifer when he finally confronted him. In all the time since, Michael has refused to tell anyone. I do know however, that after they spoke, two things were grievously apparent.

The first was that Lucifer was beyond Michael's help. He even came away from their discussion with a new resolve, it seemed. He started inviting those he once shunned to partake in his game of hiding when we were called to gather, and a good number actually joined him. Like an insolent child testing his boundaries, he ran ever-nearer the inevitable outcome of such disobedience.

He was going to be punished.

The second was that something Michael learned increased his anguish a hundredfold. What it was remained a mystery, for as I said, Michael never spoke of their talk, but it sent him spiraling into a depression so severe he shut down completely. It was abundantly clear Lucifer's sickness went deeper than any of us suspected. Michael's misery shifted from troubled sadness to genuine despair. If any of my brothers did not know fear before then, I was sure they did now.

Attendance in the Hall of Song continued to dwindle. More and more angels turned from the worship of the Almighty, and Lucifer's arrogance swelled to see so many answering his call. Songs they once sang for him were revived, with new praises even being composed while the rest of us were in the great Hall. They treated us like they guarded some secret, and all the while Lucifer coerced more to join them, increasing his cult to gigantic proportions. Heaven's expansion halted as duties went undone. The games and laughter of angels at play were gone, and conversations, when there were any, focused on the deterioration of our progress. Every sight of Lucifer wrenched my nerves. The fear that he would soon be punished by the Almighty ruled my thoughts. Fear. Amazing that a concept so alien to the kingdom could grow to hold sway over so many in such a short time. I prayed my fear for him would be the most horrible thing I would ever know, for I could little stand even that. But then a much greater fear was brought to light, a thing I'd feared for a long while but didn't realize until it happened.

Lucifer finally turned his attention back to me.

"I want you with us." Those were his first words to me in so long I'd lost track. As though all his slights to me had never occurred. Face-to-face, his cold gaze boring into my skull, it was obvious this wasn't the Lucifer I knew, not by any means. He'd been broken down and discarded by angels who placed this mockery of him on a pedestal. This perversion before me, standing with its head down in mock respect, was an abomination. "Come to our gathering when next we meet, Sabrael. Come and see what it is to be free."

"Free of what?" I contested.

"Of the illusion, brother; the illusion that we are now all that we are meant to be."

"The only illusion I see is this newfound understanding you claim to have found."

Lucifer smiled, his child face beaming; so amazingly beautiful, so incredibly horrific. "You and I once spoke about why we praise God, and what did I tell you? That I was feeling things only He feels, and that I enjoyed it though I understood it not. I dedicated myself to controlling this feeling, to recognizing what causes it, and I now know why I feel it and you do not." Lucifer leaned close, and once again I could feel his tainted glow like a siphon, feeding off my own. "I have even learned to pass on this gift. Please, let me share this enlightenment with you, the one I care for most. It is all I have wanted since I returned."

There are times when fear can rise up to overwhelm each of the senses and take control of one's entire being. Standing there with him, I felt that kind of fear. I was in the sights of a lion, his golden mane falling around icy blue eyes. I knew I must not join him, but how could I tell that to the one who taught me how to live?

"Enlightenment?" I asked, imploring. "Can you not see what you are doing to the kingdom? How can you call this enlightenment?"

"My eyes have been opened. To a truth we have long been kept from seeing!"

"So even you sing your own praise now. Lucifer, you have become the very thing you once fought to stop!"

"I was ignorant then, little brother." The addition of the word "little" was like a slap to the face. "I have changed in so many ways since then."

"You certainly have. You are no longer the angel I looked up to and wished to impress. That Lucifer is gone, hidden from everyone, even yourself. You are a stranger to me now, and I would never turn my back on the Almighty at the beckoning of a stranger."

Lucifer studied my face as if searching for some possibility of changing my mind. My heart was pounding so hard I thought I would explode. "Do not make an enemy of me, Sabrael. I only want things to be as they were between us."

"As do I. I pray they one day will be, but I cannot join you in this. I'm sorry."

He stood there for a long moment, emotion roiling in his eyes, then flew away. I knew I had upset him deeply. The alternative was unthinkable, but still, the immediate remorse I felt was so overpowering that had he only tried harder to persuade me then, he may have succeeded.

Soon after my refusal to join Lucifer's gatherings, he vanished again, this time taking his supporters with him. It was obvious the possibility of my inclusion had been the only thing keeping him from departing sooner. The halls were gutted with the sudden withdrawal of so many, and I was amazed at the magnitude of Lucifer's influence. Never before did I truly realize how many of the host had aligned with him.

Strange as it may seem, I was still lonely in his absence. Though I believed everything he was doing was wrong, he was still my brother. His return to exile was a painful blow. Many others felt it as well, for many friendships were severed when Lucifer whisked away his followers. Michael was absolutely frantic, enlisting Gabriel and Raphael to scour Heaven for the missing. He couldn't be consoled and would not stop his hunt until they were found.

Unfortunately, Michael didn't find them in time to prevent a crisis; the host was called to the great Hall.

From my seat high above the first circle, I nervously watched my brothers file into the worship area. Tensions rose with each new face, the uneasy silence positively deafening. No one spoke. No one looked another in the eye. Michael entered, exhausted, and headed for his chair, eyes darting around the gathering and hands quivering. Beside him came Gabriel, with his narrow face and curly hair. They did not speak, but the gestures and expressions they exchanged were as loud as any words. Raphael arrived a short time later. I remembered our discussion about Lucifer before the change and, as I thought of this, he glanced up and gave me a curt nod.

Lucifer's chair sat empty. Though this had become the norm, its vacancy now was especially unsettling. The ornate wings rising from its high back now seemed a testament to Lucifer's inflated pride, a precursor to the turmoil he was causing. Indeed, when the last angel had finally taken his seat, the anxiety that gripped us all was only made worse by the grand presence of that chair. I couldn't believe it. A full third of the Hall was unoccupied, empty seats like holes punched throughout the gathering. Murmurs confirmed that my brothers felt as I did in the face of such an astonishing sight. Michael was beside himself, wringing his hands as he looked up at the broken assembly.

The presence of the Almighty suddenly filled the Hall, and all was forgotten as divine light pierced everything. In the throng of warmth and love, the host was on its feet singing hymns of praise, and all the trouble with Lucifer and his followers seemed some strange dream barely remembered. The song's emotion reverberated off every surface, and I was at peace. Unfortunately though, as with every song, ours had an ending, and we came to it all too quickly.

The final note passed my lips to twist and turn its beautiful dance through the air, then glide from the Hall of Song into the rest of Heaven. I hoped Lucifer and the others could hear us wherever they were. Then the note faded, leaving only terrible silence. The choir sat in unison, the swishing of robes seeming imagined after the blaring hymn. All my attention was focused on the Almighty, awaiting His first words to our decimated host. Would He be angry? Puzzled? My hands shook with anxious curiosity, but silence ruled for what seemed an eternity.

Michael must have suffered worst of all, for it was he who finally broke it. "It could not be helped, Father! He would not listen, and—"

The Almighty quieted Michael with a raised hand. "All is well, Michael," He said, His voice coming from every direction, booming yet full of love.

I wondered how all could possibly be well, but my answer came immediately.

The enormous doors of the Hall burst open, startling all save for the Almighty. A flood of angels poured from the opening, the torrent headed by one whose odd glow was now familiar. Lucifer strode to the foot of the throne, his face defiant. The line of his followers snaked back toward the doors to form a crowd just outside the first circle.

Michael stood and shouted, "No, Lucifer! You know not what you are about to do! I beg you to end this now!"

Lucifer cocked his head as if Michael were the biggest fool in all creation, then returned his gaze to God. I couldn't breathe. My brother Lucifer, my best friend, standing in open rebellion against the Almighty! I could see even from my seat that the expression on his face was unthinkable in the presence of God— hatred. The Almighty looked down at him without anger, only love and concern. There was a rippling in the light and suddenly the Hall dimmed. The immense form of God dissipated in wisps of light and a being no bigger than Lucifer himself was left standing on the throne.

"Lucifer, please. Come forward," God said, offering His hand. Lucifer waited just long enough to show it was by his will alone, not the Almighty's, that he complied. He didn't take God's hand. Undeterred, God continued, "You have always spoken to me in times of trouble. What can I do to help you now?"

Lucifer opened his mouth, but hesitated. I've always liked to believe that in that short moment, before making his thoughts known to us all, Lucifer realized what he was about to do and became frightened. That he wanted to return to his old ways and become again what he once was. I like to believe he knew he was wrong. Most of all though, I like to hope that in that moment, we had a glimpse of some goodness still left in my brother. But whatever caused Lucifer to pause did not win the battle in his mind. As I said, the moment was short.

"I demand to be recognized as your equal," Lucifer called out. The entire host burst into a cacophony of disbelief and awe. Even Lucifer's followers seemed surprised.

"Lucifer, you know this to be untrue," the Almighty replied in a gentle tone. He stepped forward, but Lucifer backed away from the tiny embodiment of God.

"You are wrong. I am your equal. I command power above my brothers, just as you do, and I am praised for it, as are you. You gave me more responsibility than any other angel, and you entrust me with secrets you share with no other. My radiance rivals yours in beauty. I have experienced more than any other angel. I have even created water from nothing! No other angel understands what I do. None have felt what I have felt. And just like you, I have followers who have vowed to serve me as their master, as their king, as their god. I create; I command praise; I possess knowledge and power above all others and I have worshippers. I am God, just like you."

I looked down to see the horror frozen on Michael's face, unable to stop Lucifer now. More importantly, there were tears coursing down his cheeks! If only Lucifer would see them!

The Almighty spoke calmly. "Lucifer, my child, can you not see the error in your ways? False praise has clouded your mind. You do not understand what you are saying."

"I will tell you what I understand," Lucifer began again. "I understand that you are a selfish god. A god who accepts no other as His equal, despite all evidence to the contrary!"

I glanced at Gabriel, his eyes wide in disbelief, and then at Raphael, who looked utterly fascinated.

"You demand we sing your praise, never questioning why you deserve it. Then when one of your children matures as I have and becomes as the Father, you would deny him. You fail to recognize the power I have attained and give me what should be mine; the shared position as head of this family. And for what reason? You are afraid! Afraid to admit you are not as omnipotent as you would have us believe. Afraid to relinquish even a portion of power, because you *are* a selfish god, and you cannot bear to think of anyone else as your equal. But I am!"

The host was in an uproar, unsure of what to do—keep quiet and listen to the debate or call out and join in. I was in such shock that I couldn't process anything. The defiance on Lucifer's face; the sound of my brothers whispering; Michael's streaming tears; the radiance of the Almighty, so perfect it was almost painful to look at: All these things and more I saw and heard, but I was unable to put any of it together.

"Even now, your children are dividing. I know you know this, because like me, you are God. You feel it as I do. 'Can there be two?' they wonder. Confusion spreads about what I have brought into the open for all to see, splitting them into factions. Listen."

Lucifer placed a hand to his ear as though we were oblivious to the sound. Those who had followed him into the Hall, as well as a few others among us in the seats, began to sing for him. The angels around them scrambled to silence them, hands grasping for the rebels. It was only a moment before the entire hall was in upheaval, with angels climbing over angels to reach those singing and those singing fighting to remain free.

"Your place as Father is dissolving. Your children have shown you their decision. It is you who must realize the error in your ways, for they will tolerate it no longer. They recognize me as their superior; that makes me God. I have transcended to your level!"

The song for Lucifer continued to swell as more and more angels joined in. Whether they had been planted or were only now conceding was impossible to know. The struggle grew more aggressive, brothers shoving and clawing at each other, and I thought this would at least force the hymn to stop. But it only grew more powerful, like some sort of rallying chant, and Lucifer beamed as God glared at him. It was a look of victory, the smile of a conquering hero. Finally, God dropped the loving tone and took back control.

"Enough!" He called out, His voice shaking the halls of Heaven. The Almighty's form swirled to its original size, His light flooding over everyone. The singing cut off abruptly as every angel cowered at the voice with the power to create worlds.

God glared at Lucifer with a look so terrible not even he could meet the gaze. "I created you from nothingness. I gave you life eternal and paradise in which to spend it. I loved you and bestowed upon you great power, more even than your brothers because you were the first, and because I created you to have such power. Your voice was once loudest in the Heavenly choir, returning to me the love I gave you and showing your thanks for the gifts I gave you.

"But what is this you do now? You interrupt your brothers' gathering and proclaim to all of creation your selfishness, your foolishness, your *pride*. Pride in yourself above all other things, even me, the one who made you. You listened to those who exalted you, and from their praise you spawned this evil. Now it controls you to such extent that you believe yourself to be my equal. You come before me and admit this horrible truth, and what am I to do now?"

The Almighty paused for a moment. The air seemed to tremble in the silence.

"Never again will you be free of this pride. Even if I strip it from you, you will come to it again in time. You do have the power to create, Lucifer; in that you are correct. You have created something unknown to Heaven, unknown to your brothers until this day. You have created *sin*. But it is a creation of evil, and while you do not yet realize what evil is, it has no place in this kingdom. Neither is there a place for those who partake in it."

I didn't understand. If Lucifer had no place in Heaven, then where was he to go?

"I banish you, Lucifer. You, who would wear his pride as a sign of perfection when it is a stain never to be cleansed. Never again will I permit you within Heaven's halls. I strip you of your holiness, tainted as it might be. You are a creature of the evil you have birthed, and your form will reflect that which you have sired."

As God spoke, no angel could look away. A few shouts of terror echoed through the Hall as Lucifer's white wings suddenly bled a dark ichor, staining his feathers black. His bizarre radiance became a pulsating darkness.

"You shall serve an eternity of damnation for what you have done. The dark place you went to create this sin has now been made into a dungeon, and none shall possess any key to free you of your prison."

Then, to our dismay, those of my brothers who sang for Lucifer were lifted from the crowd and drawn toward him. As they reached his side, they were held immobile by God's will.

"All of you who have elected to join Lucifer in sin, who envy Lucifer's position or see him as another god, all of you will share his sentence. You have chosen not to recognize me, so I do not recognize you. You are all banished from my kingdom."

A thunderous roar snapped our attention to the open doors of the Hall. Through them, I saw a massive gate take form at the edge of the commons outside, severing a large part of Heaven from the halls. The gate yawned wide to reveal this piece of Heaven falling away into a void of nothingness, and as it fell, it ignited into a raging pit of flame. Fire spurted back toward Heaven in scorching flares. Many angels hid their faces from the churning inferno. The newly banished screamed in fear, but none were able to move. They cried out for God to forgive them, but He simply watched as flames shot forth like tentacles, hundreds of arms reaching into Heaven to ensnare my brothers. They shrieked in pain and terror. I covered my ears but still could I hear them. Flesh seared, bubbling and bursting. Wings charred, becoming black as Lucifer's. The flames then retracted and angel after angel was plucked from the kingdom, unable to escape as the fiery tendrils yanked them into the furnace below.

Finally, all of my banished brothers were gone. All except Lucifer, who stood glaring at God. A serpent of flame coiled around his body but did not pull him away or burn his flesh.

God continued, "From this day forward you will bear the name Satan, and will be loathed by all of creation. You will become the evil you have created, forever recognized as my enemy."

Michael wept at these words. The rest of us stood in shocked silence. I'm sure this only compounded Lucifer's fear, the vast columns of angels gazing down at him like some creature. No angel could ever have imagined what we'd just seen. I thought if I shook my head I'd find that none of it actually happened. But Lucifer was still there, a chain of flame linking him to the inferno far below.

God spoke his last words to Lucifer then. "Go now and never return. I know you as my child no longer."

The flame surged around Lucifer. He screamed as his flesh burned and small horns pierced the skin on his head. His cobalt eyes burst and spilt from their sockets and his entire body caught fire, my brother becoming a blazing star. His screaming did not falter as the tendril snapped taut and ripped him from Heaven. The gates slammed shut and a terrible silence descended. The only sound was Michael's lamenting. The hair encircling his face had turned gray where it was wetted by his selfless tears, streaks of silver now staining the black.

The Almighty ended the gathering ensuring us all would now be well. God asked Michael, Gabriel and Raphael to remain, and the rest of us filed out, too stunned to speak.

I returned to my hall in mourning. Absentmindedly, I wove bloom after bloom, hoping to distract myself with work, but when I finished, I found I'd created a portrait of Lucifer. Fearing reprisal, I quickly destroyed it. *Am I never to see Lucifer again?* I wondered. *Is his punishment more than he can bear?* How I wished I could have helped him when he'd needed me most. Visions of what Lucifer was now suffering filled my mind, along with thoughts that what happened to him was in some way my fault because he came to me and I had no answer for him. The more I thought about it, the worse I felt. I sat alone and stared at nothing while my mind raced over all that had happened and accused me of not stopping it.

Sadness consumed me. Not even the beauty of Heaven could shake me from it. The colors around me were gray, the songs sounded like lies and I was indifferent to everything. There was no denying it: A large part of me had gone with Lucifer into the flames.

CHAPTER FOUR

"You look the way Michael used to," Raphael said, seating himself beside me near the edge of my hall. He spread his wings to lean against a tree. "If you are not careful, you may find your hair turning gray."

He was smiling, but I wasn't in the mood. "That would be fitting, since I am as much to blame for Lucifer's banishment as Michael."

Raphael placed a hand on my shoulder, his emerald eyes filled with compassion. "What happened is no one's fault. Lucifer chose his path. He suffers now because of the decision he alone made."

"I could have done more," I replied. "I should have."

"Like what?" Raphael asked. "What would you have done differently now that you know where Lucifer's path led?"

"I would try to see as he did, understand better what he was feeling."

"So you could have shared in those feelings?" Raphael asked.

"Yes!" I replied.

"So you could share in his punishment, too, is that it?" I shook my head and held my tongue, stubbornly holding onto my guilt. "You did what you could. Any more and you would have been exiled to Hell as he was. Let it be." Hell—the name my brothers gave to Lucifer's pit. It stung just to hear it. "Besides, we need your help."

"How can I possibly help anyone?" I asked.

"You know that Lucifer performed a multitude of jobs in the kingdom. With all that has happened, his work has gone undone, not to mention the work of all the other fallen. God has decided to divide those tasks and assign them to others. Michael and Gabriel have already claimed the majority of the tasks between them, but many still remain."

"Is the Almighty not worried that pride will overcome Michael and Gabriel as it did Lucifer?" I asked.

"They promised to keep a watchful eye on each other. Should either start down Lucifer's path, the other will alert God to prevent another expulsion from the kingdom."

"And this involves me how?" I asked.

He smirked. "God has assigned you a new task. It is far more interesting than gardening." I said nothing and he laughed. "Be excited, you fool! This task is worthy of an important angel, yet somehow it is being given to you."

I ignored the insult in his teasing. "Just tell me what it is."

"God plans to appoint a single guardian to watch over and protect each of the halls, and you have been named!"

"Guardians? Why do the halls need protection?"

"I do not know, but I have heard Michael and Gabriel whispering of something God has foretold. Something called 'war.' "

War. An unknown concept in Heaven at that time, but one that frightened me deeply even in ignorance of its meaning. Whatever it might be, if it meant the halls needed guarding for the first time in all of creation's history, war must not be good.

"Do you not understand, Sabrael? Seven halls; seven angels. Seven out of the entire host! For any angel this would be a great honor, but for you it is almost inconceivable, for your seat is farther from the throne than any other who has been chosen. How can you be so calm?"

"It doesn't make sense. Why would He choose me? Who else has been selected?"

"Michael and Gabriel, of course. Then Haniel, Uriel, Barachiel and … oh yes, me," Raphael said with a gleaming smile. "You see? You will be the only guardian from outside the first two circles. I do not know what you did to impress Him so, but well done."

I didn't understand. My brothers who shared this honor were from the closest rows in the Hall of Song, angels who literally sat at the Almighty's feet. As my mind traced over the possible reasons for my appointment, I recalled something Lucifer said to me before his transformation: *You are a good friend. Truly special. I shall not forget this in my discussion with God.*

Was this the result of whatever Lucifer told the Almighty about me? Had he brought about this blessing as his last act of goodness before his awful fall? I looked at Raphael, searching for some answer, but he just threw an arm around my shoulder and led me to the Hall of Song for our first meeting.

To my surprise, the Almighty was waiting for us. There in His presence, the Creator of all speaking to me, saying my name, I was at first speechless. As the meeting wore on though, the crippling awe was swept away by a sense of complete comfort, as though this was no special occasion at all. He was my parent, friend, Lord and companion all at once. The urge to ask why I had been chosen as a guardian crept into my mind, but standing there with the others, it seemed ungrateful to utter the words.

By the time we adjourned, the seven of us were in possession of the first weapons ever seen in Heaven. Specifically designed for the angel who would wield them, each was as unique as the one who bore it. Concealed within the folds of my right sleeve, I now carried a double-edged sword which could either stab forth at nearly imperceptible speed or drop into my hand at the ready. All it took was a thought, and the weapon would instantly appear.

Upon returning to my hall, what I found there stopped me cold. The crimson-gold banners and the buildings gleamed as they always had, but now a high wall encircled the hall's perimeter. Even the archway facing the Hall of Song had changed, a massive gate now affixed to it. Closer inspection revealed the wall was made of thick stone, while the gate itself was a metal much like that of my sword. The greatest surprise, though, was high above on the archway over the new gate. Angelic script inscribed in the stone read: *First Hall Of Heaven, Let All Who Enter Here Be Protected By The Guardian Sabrael.* Only then, seeing those words, did I fully realize the honor bestowed upon me.

I fell to my knees and thanked God.

Throughout Heaven, each hall was now surrounded by a wall with a gate like mine. The entire kingdom had been fortified. While I didn't understand how anyone could escape the fiery prison below, the Almighty told us in our meeting that Lucifer would eventually find his way back, so we stood at our gates, weapons ready, awaiting the arrival of the fallen.

Yet despite these changes, the attention of the host wasn't centered on fortification. It wasn't even focused within the gates of Heaven, but instead far away, out in the void.

While we were busy tending to our expanded duties and overseeing the further reinforcement of defenses, the Almighty began work on a new paradise. Hovering in the darkness surrounding Heaven and Hell, God concentrated all His energy on a single point. Focused, unresponsive, He remained there for what seemed like ages. We could see the struggle on His face, feel His immense power being channeled into the abyss. Heaven trembled with it. Then, finally, it happened. A shape formed in the void, and where before there was nothing, there was now something. Tiny, unimaginably dense, this thing floated before Him, perfectly still. The Almighty, exhausted after such effort, reached out and took it into His hand. All that power to create something so small? None of us watching understood. What could it be?

Then God whispered to it, and it exploded.

The command of the Almighty was like a stone dropped into water. A brilliant and massive fire rippled through the darkness, altering the very fabric of the void. Infinitesimally small shards of the original mass scattered in its wake. Galaxies came into being. Stars were formed. An entire universe, expanding by the moment, and all of it composed of that new substance God had expended so much energy to create—matter. While Heaven and all of us within were made of spiritual, immaterial essence, this new universe was of physical matter. The physical plane of existence had been born.

Understand that this process took eons to accomplish. While the main events of creation have been recorded as occurring in just days, I assure you this isn't literal. Days are used to describe this time because a day is measurable; in a day there exists a beginning and an end, and once a day is through, a new and different one begins after it. The actual amount of time it took to create the universe was so long that science only now begins to comprehend the truth of it, and the universe is still expanding.

As the initial combustion cooled and the fragments of matter slowed in their trajectories, the cosmos took shape. Solar systems settled, planets found orbits. Then the Almighty selected one of these planets and descended to its surface to manage its development. Water separated from land to create a foundation for exotic and beautiful plants which then sprang from the soil. The air was at first unsure of how to coexist with these plants, but soon a balance was reached, and God readied the world for other forms of life, which soon appeared.

Awestruck by these creatures, I, like so many others, spent all my time watching them adapt to their new paradise. Many of the earliest creatures even went extinct as the world evolved and continued to settle. Soon, we thought the world complete, with the animals living in tranquility and none exhibiting any sign of the sin that had damned Lucifer. Yet the Almighty remained there, taking in all He had done, and we wondered why He didn't come home. Then, one day no different from any before it, we found out why all this had been done.

In a lush valley nestled between two great rivers, God crouched and sculpted a shape from the dust. It wasn't exactly like the primates it seemed modeled after, for its tail reached only to its knees, but its body was covered in hair and its figure was nearly the same. When it was done, the Almighty bent and breathed into the form. For a moment, nothing. Then the dust flared, glowing as though made of embers. A string of fire spread over the form, and as it passed, the dust transformed into flesh and blood.

This moment, this creation, was more important than any before it. In this form, the Almighty made an entirely new kind of being. When He breathed life into the dust, the essence of the spiritual plane manifested in the form of a soul. This was a creature that existed not in the physical or spiritual planes of creation, but in both! When it sat up and breathed its first, we in Heaven burst into the loudest, most triumphant song ever heard. God had created the gem of all creation; God had created man.

The man stood, and God called him Adam. Then God led him through the prepared paradise known as Eden to name its animal inhabitants. In Heaven, we crowded together in glee, amazed at the shimmer of the soul within that Adam himself could not see, but which was the testament to his unique nature. The soul nourished and controlled the body; an unprecedented symbiosis.

Overwhelmed by fascination, I couldn't stand watching from so far away. Driven without thinking, I ran to Heaven's gate desperate to get a closer look at Adam and his world. I froze as I looked down. Earth was there, beckoning in all its beauty, but Hell raged below as well. The sight of it terrified me. Like a beacon of caution, Lucifer's prison stood as a warning of where I might be sent should I do what I was planning without permission. But curiosity and excitement outweighed my fear; I needed to see Adam up close. Making sure no one was watching, I closed my eyes and stepped through the gate.

Soaring down from Heaven, wings spread, I landed softly in Eden. The beauty of the strange world instantly besieged me. There was so much to see, everything so different from the kingdom. But before I could take it all in, the Almighty and Adam approached. Realizing how stupid it had been to come here uninvited, I dove into a copse of trees to avoid being caught. I crouched there, enthralled by the sight of Adam just a few feet away. As soon as they reached my hiding spot, the Almighty said, "Sabrael, I know you are here." My body went rigid with fear, but He beckoned with a smile. "Come out. Do not be afraid."

I emerged from the trees and floated toward the pair, wings flapping. Something didn't seem right, but I couldn't ascertain what it was. As I reached Adam's side, I smiled, but he just looked past me, ignoring my presence. The Almighty let loose a thunderous laugh. When I met His gaze, somehow I suddenly understood. Heaven, Hell, and we angels all exist solely in the spiritual plane. The Earth, however, had been created in the physical plane. Whereas from the spiritual, one can see both planes, the physical plane only sees the physical. Adam couldn't hear me or see me because I had no physical being with which his physical body could interact. Then I realized what I sensed was wrong before; the wind from my beating wings had no effect on my surroundings, and the entire world was utterly silent.

"How am I to meet him, Father, if he cannot see me?" I asked.

The Almighty looked at me, and again, as though He was placing the knowledge directly in my mind, I understood.

Every form in the physical universe is composed of particles of raw matter, all from that initial mass He brought into being from nothing. This same matter is never destroyed, just continuously recycled into new forms. To remedy the schism between the planes, God created more matter than was needed when He built the physical plane. This "dark matter" doesn't belong to any form. It just floats through the universe, an almost unlimited amount, ready to be used in the birth of a star or the formation of an eyelash. The knowledge the Almighty imparted to me was how to draw from that excess substance to create a body capable of interacting with the physical plane.

I focused, and my body started to tingle, as though millions of tiny stars ignited all over my skin. The air around me quivered, swirling toward my body. Microscopic particles were drawn in as moths to a flame and anchored to my spiritual form. It took but a moment, and when it was finished, I was encased in a physical body. Sensations from my new form rippled through me, overwhelming, the experience of the material plane so different from the immaterial. Perhaps the oddest sensation was that of my robe fluttering around me, having become more like cloth in the transformation. When I regained control of myself, I found Adam staring, eyes wide. He touched my arm and, finding me to be real, looked at the Almighty in wonderment. Then he made to name me as he had every other creature in the garden. God stopped him, informing Adam that I was an angel, the only type of creature he wasn't allowed to name.

"Hello, Adam," I said. I wondered if he knew he'd only just been created. I couldn't remember if I had known after my own creation.

"Hello, Angel," he replied. I laughed, astonished by his utter innocence. To my delight, he joined me, his voice ringing out in joy for the first time.

"My name is Sabrael. There are many angels, but only I am known as Sabrael."

"Sah-bra-yel," Adam said. He began looking over my body, studying me. He looked at my chest, then at his own, at my face, then touched his own. Then with a knitted brow, he ran a hand over his shoulder. "Why do you have wings and I do not?"

I was unsure how to answer. Looking to God for guidance was no help; He just waited to hear what I would come up with. "Why do birds have wings and you do not? We are as God made us, and to question why is not our place."

Adam pondered this, then nodded. Beside him, the Almighty smiled proudly at the sight of His two greatest creations conversing, angel and man. I was about to ask if I might join in their walk, but before I could, a group of my brothers materialized beside me, matter coalescing into bodies. Adam's eyes lit up as they appeared, his smile spreading. He looked at God, who said, "Their names are Michael, Gabriel, Raphael, Raziel, Daniel and Metatron."

Adam's gaze followed God's naming of each and they nodded in turn. God instructed Adam to always heed the words of angels, for we were his guardians against evils that may one day confront him. The notion that Lucifer might one day break free from his prison was a dark reminder of the reason for the creation of the beauty around us.

"Bold move, sneaking away like that," Raphael whispered to me. Then with a nudge he added, "Next time, let me in on the fun."

"I know you are all excited to meet Adam," God said, "but for now you must return to Heaven. You will have your time to converse with man, but that time is not now."

Without question or complaint we obeyed, saying farewell to Adam and releasing the matter from our bodies. Our physical forms dissolved back into dark matter as we flew back to our posts in Heaven. Adam was as amazed by the destruction of our bodies as he'd been by their creation. He reached out a hand and the matter fell through his fingers like sand, sifting apart into particles too small to see or feel. How wondrous a creature was man! When

Adam was ready, the Almighty led him to the Tree of Knowledge to give Adam that famous command I need not repeat here. Before I move on though, I should clear up one thing.

I wrote that Adam had a tail and was covered with hair. I imagine that may seem strange, but in truth, it's not hard to understand. It is written that man was formed in God's image, and this is true. The important fact to remember is that God has no physical form. Only when He wants to take physical form will He have one. Being created in God's image has nothing to do with appearance, but rather that man was created *without sin*, and had not the knowledge of how to sin or even what sin was.

How does this relate to Adam's tail then? The answer is simpler than one might think.

Shortly after the creation of Adam's female partner, Eve, the unthinkable happened; Lucifer managed to free himself of Hell's grasp. When he saw the Earth, he became determined to corrupt it and destroy God's second attempt at perfection. Knowing that taking physical form in his own likeness would alert those watching the garden to his presence, he instead made himself a serpent's body and spied on God's newest children from the brush. I'm sure everyone reading this knows what happened then: Lucifer's tempting of Eve to eat of the forbidden fruit, her tempting of Adam in turn, and their banishment from paradise. Since these events are clearly recorded elsewhere, I'll go into no more detail here. However, understand that when Lucifer tempted Eve, the fruit wasn't the issue. It wasn't magical; it didn't imbue her with powers or reveal secrets to her. The fruit was just a symbol, an arbitrary object which God commanded the humans not to eat as a sign of their love for Him. In tempting her to eat the fruit, what Lucifer really did was plant the seed of sin in Eve's heart.

Until then, Adam and Eve still had their God-given appearance. When Lucifer spoke to Eve however, he instilled the desire to disobey God and gave her the means to do so. He altered her mind, and her appearance began to change in turn. When she then approached Adam, the changes in her intrigued him. She was exotic. Alluring. Adam was powerless to resist her. After eating the fruit himself, he began changing as well. Remember now that the animals of the Earth have never known sin. They simply do as God commanded at their creation. Some call this behavior natural instinct, but the fact is that no animal has sinned against the laws of God. They remain perfect creatures. With their introduction to sin however, Adam and Eve were no longer perfect. This spark began the process scientists call human evolution. In the animal world, evolution is the slow adaptation to environment, the gradual alteration of the gene pool to favor the survival of a species. In humans, this is not the case. Your bodies today are physically far less capable of survival in the wild than your ancestors'. Evolution has weakened the human species. Instead of natural adaptation, the human evolutionary process is one of disfigurement, driven by sin's corrupting touch. Just as Lucifer's was when he fell, man's appearance was altered to reflect their disobedience.

As Adam and Eve birthed corrupted children who then birthed even more corrupted children, and the roots of sin grew ever deeper, mankind's appearance continued to change. Tails shriveled; hair fell out; bone density thinned. The process has been slow, but both Adam and Eve were aware of the process from the moment it began. It was this transformation they tried to hide from the Almighty, not the fact they were naked. As more generations are born and die away, sin keeps spreading, and the changes continue, driving you ever further from your original intended form. I hope you'll forgive me for sharing this; I'm only a messenger, after all.

Let me now return to what was happening in Heaven and in Hell at the time of the first sin on Earth. In Heaven, we angels marveled at the Earth and all upon it. I couldn't seem to watch it long enough. Raphael would often join me, and we'd discuss the Earth's creation, the fall of Lucifer and why we each thought we needed to guard the halls. He believed the time was soon coming when the damned would escape their prison. Michael had convinced him of this. I didn't believe him though. I argued that our brothers would be so ashamed of their mistake that they would gladly serve out their punishment if it were the will of the Almighty.

"Your lingering faith in them is honorable, Sabrael, but I can't believe they would ever stop seeking a chance to break free," Raphael told me.

"Why would they attempt to break free?" I asked. "God commanded them to remain in their prison for eternity, and as angels they are bound to follow His will."

"They are where they are because they did not follow His will. They are fallen, disgraced. Some of our brothers even have a new name for them—demons. For what reason would they follow God's will if God no longer recognizes them as his children?"

"I cannot believe they would turn their backs on Him," I said, seeing Raphael's logic but not wanting it to be true. "He's their one chance for forgiveness and redemption, their one chance to return to grace."

"Perhaps they no longer want God's grace," Raphael said. "Have you thought of that?"

I didn't understand how he could think so little of them. These were the same brothers with whom we used to talk, laugh and share in God's glory. Did all that mean nothing now?

He added, "Once they escape, I doubt they would even come back here. My bet is that they instead congregate on the Earth."

The thought horrified me. "Earth? How would they even find their way there?"

"The same way we did from here," Raphael contested. "Who is to say the path up to Earth from Hell is not as easy to follow as ours down from Heaven?"

"God would never allow it! The Earth was created to be perfect. Even if the fallen found their way there, who is to say that its beauty would not inspire them to repent? They made a terrible mistake; the pains they suffer now should be enough to destroy their desire to sin again."

Raphael simply smiled and clapped me on the back. "Sabrael, I hope your way of seeing creation will never change, for yours is an outlook that forgets none."

Our discussions came and went in this fashion, I the stubborn supporter of our fallen brothers and Raphael their vehement condemner. You can imagine then my disappointment when Lucifer reared his head on Earth and caused the fall of man. Though I was the armed guardian of the first hall of Heaven, I never wanted to believe that there was a real reason for the existence of my position. None of us did.

While in his prison, Lucifer's hate for the Almighty had grown. He wanted only to destroy the perfection that God created in his absence, and when he did it at the first opportunity, we could only sit and watch. God forbade us from interfering. It must have made the act so much sweeter, knowing that once he reached Eve, there would be no way for us to stop him from tempting her. It was a test, and mankind failed it. God was furious and man was exiled from the garden forever. We in Heaven cried rivers for the fall of man, wallowing over the loss of God's most beautiful creation. Lucifer had counted on this.

Knowing we'd be overcome by grief, Lucifer enacted his real plan. Racing back to Hell, he dashed open the locks, unleashing his followers. In a great, dark flock they soared for Heaven bearing weapons forged in the depths. They had not been suffering their punishment in obedience, as I had hoped. They'd been preparing for war.

It sounded like thunder at first. Or a heartbeat...

BANG! Our attention shot to the outer gate of the kingdom.

BANG! The metal buckled, denting inward.

BANG! Michael drew his sword, its silver gleam radiating the light of Heaven. "They have returned."

The gate blew back on its hinges and a flood of demons poured into Heaven, rushing toward every hall in a tide of destruction.

Michael stood his ground, but the rest of us guardians rushed back to our posts through the crowds of terrified angels still gathered in the commons. I slammed shut the gate to my hall and brandished my weapon, trying to prepare myself for the siege. I knew I could never alone overcome the horde of demons swarming this way. I looked at the angels gathered behind me, cowering from the deafening strikes against my gate. So many depended on me. I had to try.

Flinching at each quake of the gate, I steadied my resolve until finally the gate broke and the demons punched through.

My blade was lightning-quick, slashing at the fallen to drive them back. Asmoday, one of the first of my brothers to sing Lucifer's praise before the fall, launched himself at me with a brutal mace and it took all my effort to deflect the swooping arcs of the deadly weapon. Again and again he slammed it down on my blade, but when he finally swung it low, I missed the deflection. The mace head crushed my side, the alkaline taste of blood springing up into my mouth. Pain exploded down my entire body, paralyzing me; I had never felt it before! I cried out, overwhelmed by the sensation as he continued to attack, until by God's grace, a lucky flick of my sword sent the weapon flying from his grasp. Driven by my intense need to escape the pain, I smashed my fist into Asmoday's face and he slumped to the ground.

The battle had only just begun, though. One by one, a dozen of the fallen took Asmoday's place, forcing me to fight through the pain to defend my hall. I couldn't kill them, of course, for in the spiritual plane there is no death, but I could strip their weapons and wound them badly enough that they could fight no more. Luminous white blood soon covered my robe and the ground beneath me, yet no matter how hard I fought, the demons kept coming. Some of my brothers took up makeshift weapons of branches or stones to help, but they were decimated all too quickly. Crimson-gold banners burned as the fallen set fire to my hall's great city and surrounding forest. My sword danced through slashes and strikes as I struggled to contain those pouring through the gate. Their weapons were driven by rage, though, and with their overwhelming numbers, I could do nothing to save my defenseless brothers who were cut down around me. I cried out for the strength to fight on, even as they finally surrounded me.

Then, through the mass of opponents encircling me, I saw Michael. Clashing swords with three of the fallen and throwing them back, Michael ran to confront Lucifer himself. Lucifer saw him coming and quickly dispatched my brother Hayyel, bracing himself for the bigger contest. They met in an explosion of gleaming swordplay. Battle cries and the screech of metal broke the air as they whirled around. Michael concentrated intensely as he defended himself from each of Lucifer's strikes. But then more demons were upon me and I could little afford to keep my own sword from moving.

Astoreth, another of the fallen, bashed the wall beside the gate with his mace, trying to create a larger entry for the demons bottlenecking in the opening. Semyaza slashed at me with a weapon much like a trident. He stabbed at my chest, and as I drove my blade up to deflect the strike, Hananel slashed at me from behind with a modified broadsword. The blade cut across my shoulder, tearing my robe and spreading the warmth of blood down my back. I couldn't move my arm. I caught a glimpse of Michael intensifying his attack.

Hananel struck again, and this time I used his motion against him, allowing his sword to skitter across my own blade and plunge into Semyaza's chest. Semyaza screamed, his trident dropping to the ground and he beside it, black wings spread as glowing, white blood poured freely. Hananel roared in anger, and I saw past his shoulder that Lucifer was cut across his forehead, the sleeve of his robe also stained with his blood.

Hananel yanked his sword free of Semyaza and turned it on me. The weapon glanced across my blade and swung back over his head to slash down at me again. I buckled under the blow, falling to my knees as I caught his blade with my own.

Then Astoreth joined the fight. I dove away as his weapon came swooping down; a mace with pointed edges and a single, long spike protruding from the top. Rolling to the side, Hananel's sword still pressing mine, I shoved our two blades up and jumped. As Hananel's sword flung up and over his head, it came down on Astoreth's head, cleaving into his skull. A small, extendable blade snapped out from each side of the main one, bursting out the sides of his face and splashing the crumbled wall with brilliant blood.

Astoreth fell, howling as he struggled to pull the entrenched weapon from inside his head. Before Hananel could react, I drove my foot into his stomach and then kicked him square in the face. He collapsed, blood dripping from his mouth.

I spun to face a dozen more foes, all clamoring to be next. Exhaustion gripped my limbs, my mind. I could not beat them all. Gritting my teeth, I yelled and they rushed as one. Bracing myself, I prepared for the pain.

But it did not come.

Opening my eyes, I saw the fallen held restrained only inches from me. They thrashed, trying to reach me, but it was as though they were fighting against a wall. Amazed, I looked out and saw Michael standing with the point of his sword on Lucifer's chest. Wounded, weaponless, Lucifer backed toward Heaven's gate. As the pair moved, the horde of demons involuntarily retreated with them, as if they could not be a single step farther in Heaven than their leader. I walked with them, struggling to hear Michael's words over their enraged bellows.

"My fallen brother, what grief you have wrought this day." I could see the tears streaming down Michael's cheeks. "Destroyer of perfection, corrupter of Earth, enemy of God; all these and more have you been called, and instead of hanging your head in shame, you force your way back into the kingdom from which you have been banished. My heart knows not how to handle the pain you have caused, yet you would make me the one to throw you from paradise for the second time. Is there no mercy within you?"

Tears continued to fall from Michael's glowing gray eyes as he strode forward. The bodies of the fallen cut down in battle were dragged by that invisible force toward the gate along with the rest. Smears of blood trailed after Astoreth and Semyaza as their bodies slid toward their prison; Hananel and Asmoday followed behind.

Michael continued, "I wish I had never told you to go before God. Were it not for my misconstrued words, perhaps your fall would not have occurred, and for that, I shall forever shed tears for you. But I cannot allow you to set foot within this kingdom. Return to your furnace. I pray you never attempt to escape again."

Legions of demons spilled over the precipice into the raging pit below. At the edge, Michael grasped Lucifer and lifted the deceiver of mankind above his head. Lucifer yelled, struggling in vain. "You cannot keep me out forever, Michael! I will have the throne!"

Michael's sobs choked his voice as he whispered, "Not today."

I fell to my knees as Michael heaved Lucifer forward, flinging him from Heaven a second time. My fallen brother plunged down into the bowels of Hell where flames engulfed him and all the raining bodies of the demon army.

We had won. The battle was over, but Lucifer's words made one thing clear: a war had just begun.

CHAPTER FIVE

The assault had devastated Heaven's halls. Everywhere, beauty lay in ruin. The power of the fallen, the force they'd thrown against us, was unimaginable. How had their rage been strong enough to overcome the outer defenses? Thank God they weren't strong enough to overpower those of us within as well. The gate of Heaven was destroyed, hanging impotent on its hinges, the metal bent and blistered from the siege. Standing beside it, I placed my hand into a depression where some demon's hand had pushed against it. The metal was still warm; the indentation a frighteningly perfect fit. Michael sat slouched against the gate's twisted frame, still staring down into the depths of Hell, his face hidden behind his silver-streaked hair. Blood colored his robe, already growing faint, but was, I suspected, mostly not his own. I knew not to speak to Michael as he wept. I walked away without saying a word.

I hurried back to my hall, afraid and yet determined to see the extent of the damage from the fallen's corrupted touch. One look was more than enough.

The trees that once towered to form a dense canopy were no longer visible as I approached. A few scorched trunks protruded up like broken pillars from some ancient ruin. Buildings lay crumbled and burnt, the gate wrenched entirely from the archway. There were seared footprints wherever the fallen tread. White and black ash peppered the dirt beneath the perimeter wall, which was, in some places, reduced to rubble. Images of Astoreth's torn, bleeding face surfaced in my mind and I blocked them, unable to relive my cruel but forced actions. The path once leading through the forest to my city was gone, buried under debris and fallen, charcoaled trunks.

How had this happened? I'd been given a sacred command by the Almighty to protect His kingdom, and now my portion of it was a wasteland. I had not done as I was commanded.

"Maybe not, but you did what you could to save what you could." I turned to find Raphael looking at me from the hole where the gate once stood. He leaned on the deteriorated arch, strangely calm. "You couldn't have prevented any more damage than you did."

"This did not have to happen."

"The battle, or the redecoration of your hall?"

"They go hand in hand," I replied.

Raphael sighed. "We knew this was coming. God told us."

"But not when! If we had known, we would have been more prepared."

"There was no way to prepare for that. How could we have known what to expect before the fallen struck down the gate? We did everything we could."

I bent, scooping a handful of soot from the ground. The ashen dust sifted through my fingers, floating to refill the depression of a blackened footprint. "What we did was not enough."

Raphael chuckled. "And you have not even seen the other halls yet."

"Bad?" I asked. Raphael simply huffed behind me. "Your hall?"

"Gone," he replied, his voice but a whisper. "All that remains are the walls."

Charred ash pushed up between my toes as I stood again. Turning to face Raphael, I was overcome by the magnitude of it all. My brothers had done this. Everything I believed about them was unraveling. How could they destroy their home? Why would Lucifer raze Heaven when it was the only place he could hope to find relief from his punishment? It made no sense! I reached out and placed my hand on the wall to steady my spinning mind. "Why? Why did this happen? Why were they allowed to break free?"

"They were not *allowed* to break free. We fought them and sent them back. Why would we return them to a prison so easily escaped? Our first question should be how exactly Satan was able to find his way out."

"Do not call him that," I growled.

Raphael lifted an eyebrow and continued, "Smart to leave the others in Hell until the moment of the attack, I'll give him that. A mob would never have avoided our notice."

"We cannot allow this to happen again. As long as we devote our attention to the Earth, the chance of the fallen escaping again is too great."

"You're saying that by watching the Earth, we somehow caused this?" Raphael asked, gesturing to the ruin of my hall around us.

"I am saying that by watching the Earth, we let down our guard and made it possible."

Raphael studied me. After a moment, he gazed out beyond my broken walls. "Come. You should see the rest." I took the change of subject to mean he at least partly agreed.

Raphael was right; I'd only seen a fraction of the damage. As we walked through the other halls, I could hardly comprehend the ravaging of the kingdom. Angels all around were in shock, like survivors of a bombing raid emerging from shelter. Many had been struck down, bodies strewn everywhere. Raphael's hall was as he said, the vast fields burnt to plains of ash. Soot deep as our calves blanketed the hall and hung in the air like black snow. The halls of Barachiel and Michael were much the same, Barachiel having been impaled on his own gate and Michael having abandoned his post to confront Lucifer. The halls of Haniel and Uriel were in better shape, for theirs were farther from the outer gate than the rest. But Gabriel's hall… All that survived was a line of rubble no taller than my waist.

When we came upon him, Gabriel was on his knees at the empty archway, the silver blade lying beside him slathered in gore to the hilt. At my approach, he looked up, tears glistening on his face. His entire being was faded, his light weak. He held his stomach and all around his hands, glowing essence bled into his robe. I knelt at his side.

"Sabrael," he said, "I tried so hard. They were just too many. I could not fight them all."

"Rest now, Gabriel. We beat them. What can I do to help you?" I asked.

Barachiel's impalement had been vicious, his chest still gaping as angels pulled him down. I was sickened by the thought of something worse behind Gabriel's robe. Anger swelled within me. Again my thoughts turned to Lucifer. Why he would have done this?

"Nothing," Gabriel said, his voice tired. "You cannot close the hole the fallen have opened in me."

He grasped my hand as his body spasmed in pain. I felt helpless to aid him. "Be strong," I said, nothing better coming to mind. "However bad it is, the wound will heal in time."

Gabriel pressed my hand against his stomach. "I was not talking about this," he hissed, and I could see anger in his eyes that surpassed even my own. "They are no longer our brothers, Sabrael, but truly demons. We have lost them this day."

I had no reply. I searched for some defense for my fallen brothers, some reason why they might yet be saved and returned to the host. In my anger I could think of none. But I still couldn't accept that they were gone forever. Lucifer was misguided, his followers even more so, but to think they were beyond redemption... It was inconceivable.

"I cannot understand, after all this, how you think they will ever return to the host," Raphael said when I joined him again.

"They are angels, created the same as us. If Lucifer would only listen, I know he would once again see the way he did before the fall."

"That is the problem," Raphael said as we began walking again. "He will not listen to you, or me, or to any other than himself."

"Perhaps no one has said what he needs to hear."

We hadn't walked much farther before we came to an opening into the commons outside the Hall of Song. I didn't want to pass through the archway, terrified of what we would find. The most beautiful of Heaven's halls decimated would be too much to bear.

"Trust me; you'll want to see this," Raphael said, then stepped through the archway. I doubted it. With no other choice, I braced myself and followed him in.

My heart leapt. The Hall stood untouched! Its black walls gleamed without a scratch. Looking at him in disbelief, I found Raphael smiling. "Told you. Saved the best for last." Standing there though, gazing up at the last remaining piece of Heaven as it had been before the assault, everything I'd seen seemed even worse and I felt weak.

Stumbling back to my hall alone through the desecration, a single thought kept repeating: *Lucifer, how could you do this to your home?* Through my scorched archway, I stepped on the metal gate and ash wafted into the air. My mind raced with the destruction, Gabriel's words, Raphael's, memories of fighting my own brothers. Above all I thought of Lucifer. His innocent face stared through the window of my mind's eye, changing as it looked at me, contorting into an arrogant, prideful scowl. It was the look of when he returned after his first disappearance, when he exchanged innocence for confused followers. Yet innocence must exist somewhere inside him still! If only I had the chance to talk to him, perhaps I could set him on the path again. It was impossible though. Lucifer was in Hell once more, and I in Heaven with a ruined hall to account for. Looking around at the felled trees, the crumbled wall, the bent and useless gate, I thought again of my conversation with Raphael.

You're saying that by watching the Earth we somehow caused this?

No, I am saying that by watching the Earth, we let down our guard.

The answer was simple.

My fascination with the small blue world had given the fallen an opportunity to plunge further from grace. Had I not been so taken with the human world, I would have been more prepared for their attack. Earth was too strong a distraction, and despite my love of it and the humans upon it, only through ignoring it would I be sure to prevent this from happening again. I decided to turn my back on it all.

⇒⊹⇐

The Almighty soon repaired everything the fallen had done to our home. He moved among the ravaged halls and wounded angels, and as He passed, everything returned to the way it had been before the battle. The magnificent trees of my hall grew from the ground again in a matter of moments, the buildings rising again from the piles of debris. I fell to my knees as I saw the perimeter wall mended, the pulverized stone setting itself right. The gate straightened and flew from the dirt to clasp its hinges again, and I wept as the inscription on the archway above reappeared letter by letter, filling in my name and rank once more. For that alone I could have praised the Almighty for eternity. I was not stripped of my guardianship, though He had every right to take it from me. Even more amazing was seeing my wounded brothers rise, their injuries healed and their robes gleaming again. I rushed to follow the spectacle.

A crowd of my brothers soon flew beside me, all of us watching as the Almighty repaired each hall and then headed for the Hall of Song. I can't express my joy at the sight of the restored kingdom from the doors of the great Hall. Not a single ash left, not a drop of blood; it was as though the battle never happened. Perhaps the only visible sign anything had happened was the new outer gate, which stood thicker and stronger than the last. The fallen would never be able to topple it if they tried to attack again.

Inside the Hall of Song, I joined in a gathering of praise and thanks, and as I sang, I looked at my brothers who'd been struck down. For the first time I truly understood my role as guardian. It wasn't only to preserve the beauty of God's kingdom, but also to serve and protect those who existed within as well. Any angel walking through my forest or visiting my city was under my care, and when I let the fallen destroy the hall, I not only let down God, but I let down my brothers as well.

I left the gathering determined to never again disappoint the Almighty or my brothers. I returned to my post without stopping to glance down at the Earth, despite seeing many rush to do just that. I was steadfast in my mission. Never again would I fail in my duty.

CHAPTER SIX

The edge of my blade slid from my sleeve. Razor-sharp. Silent. Lethal. Six demon warriors surrounded me, weapons poised. I'd been training for what would have been weeks, months even, if we had such demarcations of time in Heaven. The sword was an extension of my arm now. I was ready for this.

The first demon lunged forward, a flurry of strikes sweeping toward me. Lashing out from a defensive stance, I parried his blade and spun around him to slash across his back. Two and three attacked together; one high, one low. I somersaulted between their weapons, then leapt into a spinning flip, my sword clashing against one of their blades. As my feet hit the ground, I ducked into a sweeping, knee-high slash and severed their legs.

Flanked by the next two fallen, I sidestepped and swept my sword up between them. Darting back and forth, striking high then low, I kept them on the defense until in a twirling arc, my blade slashed clean through each of their midsections. The final warrior lunged through the air, his heavy mace whistling toward my head. Unable to raise my sword in time, I retracted it back into my sleeve and spun to face him, thrusting my arm up toward his chest. My blade lashed out like a spear, punching through the airborne assailant and stopping him dead before retracting again, all in the blink of an eye. He fell and I rose, victorious.

Applause met my ears. "Very good!" I turned to find Raphael clapping, a broad smile on his lips. "Of course, you may eventually want to test your skills against a real opponent."

I looked around the empty space. He was right; imaginary foes no longer provided much challenge. One can only progress so far when the opposition is essentially himself. Still, I preferred that to the alternative. "Let us hope there will never be a need."

"That time may come sooner than you think," he muttered.

"What's that supposed to mean?"

"If you would just look down at the Earth, you would see…"

"I've told you a thousand times, I won't let Earth distract me. If the fallen ever attack again, I want to be fully prepared."

"Do you even realize how long you've been at this? Sabrael, the war has changed. The fallen are beyond their old tactics."

"You can't possibly know that. Have you been assigned to watch over Hell now?"

Raphael said, "The fallen are not in Hell! They broke free long ago." The blade within my sleeve grew heavy as dread boiled up. "I told you; you cannot afford to ignore what is happening outside Heaven's gate anymore. It is folly to think that simply waving a sword around prepares you for anything."

"If they're not in Hell, where are they?" I asked.

"Where they have been since their escape—Earth."

Terror ripped through me. "Adam and Eve! We must protect them!"

"Calm down," Raphael said, catching my arm before I could run off. "I told you, much has happened while your eyes have been blinded by the glint of the blade. Look."

Raphael touched my head and suddenly, an image flashed across my vision. Well, not my vision exactly. I saw it, but not with my eyes. It was more like recalling a memory. Hundreds of humans, conversing and building some huge structure. The image was gone as fast as it came. "What did you just do? What was that?"

"You see why you need to quit this isolation? You do not even recognize Earth. How can you prepare to fight the fallen when your training is based on what passed ages ago?"

What I had seen stunned me. "So many humans. Adam and Eve… Where were they?"

"They are dead. They have been for a very long time."

"Dead?" I had not the slightest idea of the meaning of the word. How could I? There was no such thing in Heaven. The last I'd seen them, the original pair was leaving the garden on the day of their banishment.

"Let me show you what you have missed, Sabrael. There is much you will not understand without seeing it for yourself. For your own good, please."

I pondered it for a moment, but he was probably right. "All right."

"Open your mind to me and I will show you everything." I had no idea what he meant. Open my mind? "Just close your eyes and try not to think. Shouldn't be hard for you."

It was a preposterous request, but I did as he said. Eyes closed, I tried to concentrate on the back of my eyelids. Raphael's hands touched my face and a nauseous, dizzying sensation flooded my mind. I recoiled in alarm, the ground steadying again as I broke contact.

Raphael smiled. "It's all right. Trust me."

He stepped closer and his thumbs pressed my eyelids, fingers cradling my head. Suddenly I saw them. Adam and Eve. Crying. Walking away from Eden. Did Raphael have this power all along?

Was there any limit to the mysteries of my brothers nearest the throne?

Raphael spoke as his memories flooded my mind. "After Adam and Eve were banished, they were punished in other ways as well. You remember the Almighty created them with souls? When they had children, these also had souls."

"Children?" I asked.

"My God, Sabrael. How have you not looked down in so long?" Immediately I saw a small human, one that appeared much like Adam but with less hair on its body. "Humans have the ability to re-produce, to create more humans to populate the Earth. These are called children, which in time grow to be adults like their parents.

"Every child is born with a soul. This soul is eternal, but part of the punishment bestowed upon mankind is that their physical bodies are not. Their bodies break down and no longer function. When this happens, the soul is freed to exist exclusively in the spiri-tual plane, as we do. This separation is called 'death,' understand? Every human is born, and every human must in turn die. Adam and Eve died long ago, and there have been many generations since, each more numerous than the last."

I couldn't wait to look down at this new Earth. But a question formed with this thought: If the souls of humans were freed after death, where did they then go?

"I told you to quiet your mind," Raphael chided. "Most of the souls of those who died are still on the Earth. They can't come here, for God decreed no sinful creature will ever dwell in the kingdom again and every human is born tainted by the sins of those before them. They don't go to Hell, for Hell is the prison of the damned, and humans are not condemned. For a long time, the souls had nowhere to go. They wandered, aimless. It was for them the fallen went to Earth when they again broke free."

The link between us cut off and the images stopped. I blinked away the disorientation. "I don't understand! How do they keep getting out of what is supposed to be an eternal prison? It cannot be chance that they broke free not once but twice now!"

Raphael shook his head and exhaled a chuckle. "I am not the one to ask that question. Michael has told me it is part of His plan." The plan, the Almighty's secret agenda that none other than He could know, though He was always quick to inform us when an event was part of it. Raphael continued, "Unfortunately, after the battle here, Lucifer and the others stayed in Hell for only a short time before they made their escape to Earth. At first, we thought they were just seeking refuge. As we watched though, a more sinister agenda became evident.

"It turns out Satan feels the reason their attack failed was simple numbers. The entire force of Hell carries with it only half the number of the Heavenly host. Lucifer believes that in order to conquer us, the fallen require more warriors, warriors who share his contempt for God, or better yet, who deny God is worthy of the power He holds. These warriors won't come from Heaven of course, but they couldn't come from Hell either, for all those in the pit fought in the first assault.

"When the demons escaped Hell, they found the Earth teeming with souls, the only other beings existing on the spiritual plane. It was Adramelec's idea to harvest these souls and recruit them for Hell's army."

"What!" I could not have heard him correctly. He reached out to touch my eyes. My mind flooded with images again, all sense of my own being vanishing beneath the deluge.

"The fallen walked the Earth, enlisting every soul they could to fight for them. Many souls were taken by the offer of a release from the nightmare of wandering the world for eternity, unable to interact with the living. These souls signed over their freedom, and in doing so, condemned themselves to Hell. Still, Satan wasn't pleased. He wanted more than just volunteers; he wanted every soul, dead and alive. He was furious that his demons seemed to be ignoring the living entirely. Then he realized why.

"Until then, Lucifer was the only one who had ever been to the Earth, and thus, the only one who knew of the physical plane. The rest of the fallen had no idea why so many souls walked around as though blind and deaf. They did not understand the concept of life and death, just as you did not, or that souls are contained in a physical body for a certain time. Lucifer finally called them together and taught them to take physical form. After that, the fallen were able to turn living humans to their cause."

"And you did nothing?" I asked, furious. "You just let this gathering happen; let them harvest the world without lifting a finger?"

"We wanted to do something. Desperately. Michael begged the Father to allow it. God refused. He wanted man to overcome this temptation of his own volition."

"Why would the humans ever betray the Almighty? They know He is their creator."

"They were deceived." With his words came another flood of images. "When the fallen took physical form, it was not their own likenesses they created. They manipulated their matter into other forms, just as Lucifer did when he spoke to Eve in the body of a serpent. Some appeared as men, oracles who brought questioning to the beliefs of the humans in their Maker. Unanswerable, their questions seemed like wisdom, and the disguised demons used the humans' inability to answer as proof that God doesn't exist. Others spun tales of false gods, and the humans began worshipping all sorts of mythical beings. Some of the fallen were masters of this technique, actually convincing the humans that they themselves were the gods of these tales. A few took on frightening forms and forced men to their knees. Soon it became impossible for mankind to tell truth from fiction. Numerous religions absorbed the clever lies propagated by the fallen using their spiritual abilities to leverage the humans' faith."

"What of Lucifer?" I asked, my voice weak. I hoped my friend of old disapproved of using mass deception to fill his ranks.

"He was the only one who allowed the humans to see his true form. Not his form as it is now, of course. He showed them what he was—a beautiful being of light, angel perfected. He chose not to mask his black wings though. Perhaps he can't hide that one mark of his sinful pride." I recalled Lucifer's horrific disfigurement; flesh burnt away, empty sockets where his eyes had been. I could have wept again at the image, but Raphael replaced it with new ones.

"Before long, almost all the Earth was under the spell of the fallen, but still Satan was not content. All the souls on Earth only numbered in the tens of thousands. The fallen needed more. No other being on Earth exists both in the spiritual and physical planes, however, and all attempts to use beasts of the land, sea and air failed. Without souls, they were useless in the war for the throne."

"Then why the sadness in your voice?"

Raphael remained silent for a moment. "Let me just say that they tried something then so evil I cannot bring myself to tell you."

"You can't tell me all this and then refrain from telling me the worst part!"

He broke our link. For a moment, he said nothing. Then, "Perhaps it is time for you to look for yourself."

═┼ ┼═

Other angels looked up as we approached the place where I used to gaze down at Eden. The expression they all shared chilled me. What did they see that could cause such despair? The mere fact that so few now watched the planet spoke volumes.

Raphael put a hand on my shoulder. "Before you look, remember that much has changed. It's not the Earth you're expecting."

Part of me wanted to draw back. The memory of Earth was still pristine in my mind; did I really want to taint it with whatever I was about to see? But curiosity had me, and Raphael's apprehension only stoked the fire. Whatever was down there, I had to see it. Torn between excitement and suspense, I knelt at the place I always had, and with a deep breath, peered down.

How can I express what I felt in that first glimpse? I saw not just the Earth, but Hell's inferno too, teeming with movement. To my amazement, there was now a third place as well. Gray, barren, four of my brothers stood guard at the gates to this place separated from Hell and Earth. But the Earth! I couldn't believe how much it had changed! Mankind had spread across the entire face of the planet. The sheer number of them was staggering. I'd glimpsed it in Raphael's memories, but my own eyes could not believe it. Everywhere, massive groups of people roamed, men and women and the diminutive children of which Raphael spoke. Cities and cultivated farmland dotted the landscape in places, while villages of crude, mobile structures blanketed others.

"My God, Raphael, have I turned my gaze for so long?" I asked.

Before he answered, something else caught my eye. Mankind wasn't alone.

Hidden from human sight, I saw them clearly enough. The fallen were everywhere. Some whispered in the ears of humans from the spiritual plane. Others walked as humans in the physical plane, clothed in the matter of the universe. Some operated alone, some in packs; I could see them all over and it enraged me. But that wasn't even the extent of it.

Long lines of souls wrapped across the Earth in a vast web. There were more souls than living humans. Many wandered among the living, trying to get their attention. But gathered around my fallen brothers, huge crowds of souls swore oaths, worshipped and turned over their freedom to the armies of Hell. Whipping my gaze to Hell, I looked more closely and realized what the teeming movement was. Thousands upon thousands of human souls were trapped in the prison meant for the fallen! The very demons to whom they had pledged their allegiance subjected them to terrible torments, stirring them into hopeless, fervent rage against God. Unable to watch this spectacle of damnation, I searched the Earth for Eden. Surely the garden remained unspoiled by the evils plaguing the rest of the world. But it was gone. All I could see were nations segregated into many cults under the deception of the fallen and the wretched souls of those who died in their worship.

"I warned you," Raphael said, seating himself beside me. "Dozens of generations have come and gone in the time your eyes were turned from the world."

Temples dedicated to my fallen brothers stood throughout the inhabited world. When I looked for those dedicated to the Almighty though, I saw none. I couldn't even bring myself to ask Raphael about this, but he plucked the thought from my mind anyway.

"They no longer recognize Him," Raphael said, his gaze stern. "There are few left who know God as their creator. Paying tribute to Him brings scorn, prejudice, even death."

"How could this have happened? How could the descendents of Adam and Eve have forgotten the Almighty; they saw Him with their own eyes!"

"Sabrael, you do not fully appreciate how long you have been looking away. Look how vast the human race has become. All of them sprang from a single pair! Think how long such a thing would take. No one on Earth today knows Adam and Eve even existed. And that does not even account for the flood..." His voice trailed off.

"The flood?" I asked, the very words sending a shiver through my body.

Raphael's emerald gaze fell to his lap, a troubled look washing over his face. "The evil that the fallen created on Earth, the creatures they fathered in an attempt to breed the perfect warriors for their cause, brought about a time even darker than what you see now. Lands were ruled by tyrannical, monstrous beings called Nephilim."

"Wait, stop. What do mean 'the creatures they fathered'?"

"From their coupling with human women." His words rang in my ears. I looked down again in shock, scouring the Earth for these Nephilim. Raphael continued, "They are gone now. Washed away in a terrible flood which covered the world in water deep enough to swallow mountains. Only a handful of humans were allowed to survive."

I could barely stand it. I wanted to scream, to weep, to run back to my hall where I was safe from this disaster. It was too much. "God *made* the flood? He killed all those people?"

"You cannot imagine how dark the world had become. The children of the fallen lorded over every land, working the will of their fathers and forbidding worship of the Almighty. Earth was lost. I cannot even bring myself to show you all that happened. Most of our brothers will not even look at the Earth anymore. The flood was the only way to cleanse the world."

As if to underscore his point, those few angels watching Earth when we first approached rose and walked away. "How many people were there? Before the flood? How many died?"

"More than are on Earth now. The humans reproduce so fast though, it will not be long before there are again as many as there were."

I was awestruck. So many people, killed for their disobedience only to spring up again and find new ways to head down the same path. Staring at the world below, I couldn't believe what had once been such a perfect paradise could have turned into the festering den of sin I now observed. My head swam to think this was the same place where two lone humans with tails sweeping their legs had once walked.

"Why tell me all this?" I asked him. "Why wait so long only to come to me now?"

Raphael rose from the ground. "I tried to tell you before. You would not listen. The Earth is your favorite place. It is a tragedy you did not watch what happened to it, but you need to see it now, to know that the threat of the fallen grows as more and more souls are lured into Hell's service. Until you saw everything below, you could never have known the magnitude of what may come to bust down our door."

"What has the Almighty said of all this? I cannot believe He would let mankind slip away to be used as weapons against us."

"When He saw what was happening, He created the new realm you saw. Sheol, a safe haven where souls can escape the solicitations of the fallen." I looked to the gray, barren land and the few souls that resided there. Unlike those on Earth, these seemed content in death, working together to make a peaceful existence after life. "All souls are welcome there if they refuse to join Lucifer, but many still choose to remain on Earth or follow the fallen into Hell."

"Why would He create Sheol to shield these souls, but not allow them into Heaven?"

"I do not know. If He has a plan for the souls, He has yet to bring it to light."

My anger with my fallen brothers seethed. The sight of a world ruled by Lucifer was horrible enough, but much worse was the implication that this was what he would do to Heaven were he ever allowed any stake in the throne. The state of the Earth was his fault, not the humans'. I was sure of it. Mankind had merely been drawn away from the truth by fantastical lies they had no way of disproving. As I watched the living masses engaging in all manner of forbidden acts, the ignorant souls huddled in Sheol and all those suffering Hell's eternal flames, I knew something drastic had to be done.

CHAPTER SEVEN

The clash of weapons echoed through my hall. Stepping in a close circle, sword poised to counter another attack, I tried to ignore the calm smirk on Raphael's lips. His twin blades twirled as he jumped and lunged at me, his movements even more fluid than my own. The short swords spun in his grip to extend out for strikes, then lay against his arms to block. I had to remember the hypnotic movements were all part of his attack.

The blades struck my sword again and again until my hands ached. Raphael's smile was unnerving, but it exposed teeth clenched in effort. I blocked and drew his swords to the side, swinging around to deliver a decapitating strike.

My sword swept through empty space. Two pinpricks poked the back of my neck.

"Too slow, Sabrael." His swords lifted, and I turned to face him, his wings still spread from the flight around me. "Why you insist on spinning like that is beyond me."

"I almost had you this time," I said.

"If you stopped trying to show off, maybe you would do better than 'almost.' "

"Have to keep it interesting somehow. Winning stopped being fun ages ago," I teased.

The rumbling bellow of a horn silenced his retort. The call for the guardians to convene. Without a word, we retracted our weapons and soared for the great Hall.

⚊⊰ ⊱⚊

"Raphael, Sabrael. We have the most wondrous news," Gabriel said. The worship area seemed impossibly large without the host gathered there. The ceiling was so high above, it was like viewing the sky from the surface of the Earth, our voices but whispered echoes in that gargantuan place.

Noticing us, Michael strode over from where the others were already talking. I'd never seen him wear such a broad smile. "Brothers, we are going to the Earth!"

In times past, the prospect would have excited me. But after what I had seen, my first question was, "How can we abandon our duties here when Hell's army grows larger each day?"

"That is precisely why we must go. We have a mission."

Raphael sounded as shocked as me. "Mission? Why was I not told?"

A smirk gathered in the corners of Michael's mouth. "I'm telling you about it now."

The four of us joined the rest, and Michael motioned for us to sit. Raphael and Gabriel took their seats at the foot of the throne; Barachiel, Uriel and Haniel sat in theirs in the next row. The only open chair near me was adorned with large wings. It gleamed in the light of Heaven, yet the sight of it carried echoes of Lucifer's screams as he was torn from the kingdom, memories of his garish disfigurement. I realized the others were staring and quickly dropped into the seat beside Haniel.

Michael stood in the center of the shining black floor near the throne, though he took care not to touch it. "Brothers," he said, "since our assignment to the role of guardians, the Almighty has watched with pride as each of us has grown through the training of ourselves and each other. It is because of our devoted service that He calls upon us again for a new task, the most important there has ever been, but also the most dangerous."

Uriel said, "Enough with the speeches. Just tell us what it is so we can get started."

The rest of us laughed. Michael smiled again, and I was happy to see it. After being forced to expel Lucifer from Heaven a second time, I thought he would never smile again.

"God has decided to free the souls of man from the shackles of sin, therefore ending Satan's rule over them and allowing them to join us here in Heaven."

The hall fell utterly silent. I sat dumbfounded, unable to comprehend this. Michael let the silence linger, waiting for one of us to react. I nearly jumped when finally Barachiel shouted in joy and the rest leapt up to celebrate. Mankind, my favorite part of all creation, would finally be free to enter the kingdom! My excitement was overwhelming, yet something worried me.

Raphael embraced me, his emerald eyes radiating happiness. "Can you believe it? Your beloved humans will no longer be plagued by the fallen! Why do you not cheer loudest of all?"

"I am beyond words. But what task could seem important when compared with this news? We're here to talk about a mission."

Michael shouted above all our voices then, calling for quiet. "Sabrael is right, brothers. I have more to tell. Please."

The others returned to their seats, and I could feel their eyes on me, wondering how I could focus on anything but the joy of the news we'd just received.

Michael continued, "In order to free mankind from the sins that mar their souls, a great sacrifice must be made. A repayment for their willing disobedience. Many have even given over their souls to Lucifer's army and earned themselves damnation, and this must be absolved. To save mankind, someone must willingly take their place in the punishments they deserve."

I was mortified. I would gladly do anything the Almighty asked of me, but the thought of being thrown into Hell in place of the humans... I looked around the hall and found the same fear in everyone's eyes I knew was present in mine.

"The sacrifice of a single angel would not nearly be enough," Michael said. "Not even the entire host would be enough, so those of you thinking this, relax."

Sometimes I thought I was the only one of the seven of us who couldn't hear thoughts.

"To cleanse mankind, God the Son has offered Himself in sacrifice. He will separate from the Trinity to be born as a human man and live perfectly in accordance with the Father's law. When the time is right, He will die a sinner's death and serve a sinner's punishment. Only a sacrifice this substantial will convince the Father to allow the humans into Heaven."

Uriel asked, "How can the Son be human? How can the Creator become the created?"

Michael caught Uriel in a stern gaze. "Is He not God? Does He not have the power to do anything He wishes?"

"That is not what I meant," Uriel said. "I simply wish to know the manner by which it will be done."

Michael's tone softened. "The Holy Spirit will cause a human woman to conceive a child. The baby will be both God and man, divine yet mortal. That is the reason we have been called. We are being assigned the most important task ever undertaken; we are being sent to Earth to protect God Himself."

I was speechless. How were we to react to such an assignment? This wasn't simply delivering a message or administering God's wrath, as some of my brothers had done in the past. The others,

I could see, were as dismayed as I. All except Gabriel, that is, leaning back in his seat, hands folded. I guessed he'd heard this already.

Michael continued, "The Father has commanded us to travel to Earth and take human form. When the infant Son is born, we are to serve as His protectors from the fallen who will hunt Him and the humans who will hate Him until the time comes when He can defend Himself."

Barachiel laughed. "He is God. Why does He need our protection?"

Michael paced around the throne. His movements, his grandeur, bespoke such power and yet such grace. The humans he'd visited in times past must have found both fear and awe in his presence. "In order for His sacrifice to be complete, the Son must live as a normal man under God's commands, with no aid from His divinity. To use His might as God would eradicate His humanity. The process of becoming man will be so complete, He will even forget His true nature. He will be a newborn infant, just as vulnerable as any other. While He is still young and ignorant of His true nature, we must ensure no harm befalls Him."

For a moment, we sat stunned at the enormity of this task. A single, obvious question lay before us. "What if we fail?"

Michael met my gaze. "Mankind will be damned forever. Those are the terms agreed upon between the Son and the Father. He only gets one chance. If the Son does not live and die without sin, if the fallen prevent Him from doing so in any way, mankind will be lost."

"But the Father loves them!" I argued.

"That is why He agreed to this at all."

Silence again filled the room. One chance for eternity. The idea was staggering.

"If we're to play human," Raphael said, "will we not be equals with those who would oppose us? How can we protect Him that way?"

"I need to speak with God to learn specifics. However, I do know we will have certain advantages to aid us in this task."

Michael seated himself for the first time. Fervor filled his eyes as he spoke of this assignment, his captivation with all this obvious. To defend our Creator from those who would overthrow Him—this was everything Michael lived for.

"Although we will be forming physical bodies to make ourselves appear human, we do not have to follow the rules of those bodies."

Haniel asked, "What does that mean?"

Michael gripped the arms of his chair. "We waste time here, brothers. We must make the journey to Earth."

We all looked at each other, shocked. Barachiel asked, "We are leaving now?"

"Yes, we must go immediately in order to have time enough to prepare for His birth. The conception has already taken place."

Uriel remained focused. "Then speak quickly. What does 'rules of the body' mean?"

Michael rose to pace again. "I told you, I do not know specifics yet. To give you a vague notion, consider this: We will be able to form our bodies as we see fit. You will control its every aspect. You will look how you desire, move how you desire; you will have any physical abilities you want. You can control the bones and muscles of your body to jump higher than any human, run faster than any human. Not only that, you will be free to become solely spirit again whenever you want. You will never be hindered by the physical plane, understand? Now, we waste precious time. Everything will be explained once we are there, I promise you."

Everyone stood to leave, but I had one lingering question. "Michael?"

He turned back impatiently. "Sabrael, please."

"Who will watch over the halls while we are away?"

Michael sighed and smiled. "All has been taken care of."

The seven of us walked outside and as we stepped into the light, we were met by the entire host gathered at the entryway of the Hall of Song. A long aisle stretched through tens of thousands of shining robes leading to Heaven's gate. Beautiful songs of farewell filled my ears. Flowers floated in the air, a twisting, dancing tapestry of silver blues and purples, golden yellows and a full spectrum of others. It was like a personal tribute to my role before I was a guardian.

The songs of the host rang out amidst cheers from every direction. My brothers reached out from the crowd to clasp forearms with us or to take hold of our hands and shower them with kisses and blessings as we passed. I knew they would have given anything to be assigned this task, and looking at their faces, the honor of being chosen for the responsibility was undeniable. But at the same time, I felt a strange urgency taking hold in the back of my mind.

Looking back, I saw the aisle collapse behind us as the crowd closed in, forcing us forward. Seeing this reminded me of the first battle with the fallen; Lucifer's followers being drawn to the gate to plunge out of the kingdom. I started to panic. White robes filled my vision and I was blinded by their reflected light. The drone of their songs drowned out even my own thoughts. I saw visions of bizarre creatures whose grasping arms grew forward from their chests, who never stopped singing or cheering, whose bodies flowed together into one mass of hands and smiling faces. My head spun, the colors and the light and the sound cramping me, enveloping me. A scream wriggled up my throat, struggling to be born. I needed to escape. I needed to find someplace quiet to be alone. I felt control slipping away. Then ... I saw it.

The tops of the trees in my hall came into view, extending high over the heads of the crowd. My hall, my duty in Heaven, the reason I'd been selected for this mission, awe-inspiring even after all the time I'd spent running through the trunks and leaping in the high branches. I realized then what the strange feeling filling my mind was.

I was afraid to leave.

The closer we drew toward the gate, the stronger the feeling burned that I should not go. Something was very wrong with all this. I wasn't a throne angel, not even close. Why was I being included in this assignment? Was being a guardian not blessing enough? What could I offer the group? The sight of my hall was a reminder of everything I was leaving behind should I step forth from the gate of the kingdom, and I wanted only to run back and seek its shelter. From the day they were created, I loved watching the humans and had always wanted to stand beside them. Seeing my brothers crowded around though, singing songs that would warm even the coldest heart, I couldn't imagine leaving. I was consumed by the need to remain in Heaven, and I paused in a swoon of despair. It was but a moment before Raphael saw me. Beaming a smile at the crowd, he came back and hooked an arm around my shoulders.

"What are you doing?" he whispered. "We must go; it has been commanded of us."

"I cannot leave!" I said, barely able to stand. "We are deserting our home, our paradise!"

Raphael firmly pulled me along. "You should be happiest of us all. You are finally going to be among the humans. What is wrong with you?"

"We will not be able to come home!" I said, perhaps too loudly. Concern colored the faces of the angels closest to us.

"We go to protect the Son from Lucifer and his followers. We are making sure the forces of Hell do not gain control of our Lord and king. Is that not enough reason for you to stop this madness?" Sadly, it was not. He looked away for a moment, then said, "Look at the archway over your hall. Can you read the inscription?"

I looked out over the crowd, and I could just make out the words. *First Hall of Heaven, Protected In This Time By Adonael In The Absence Of The Guardian Sabrael.*

Raphael said, "You see? 'In this time.' Not forever. We go to Earth, we protect the Son and we come back. That is all there is to it."

I knew how ridiculous my anguish must have seemed, but I couldn't help it. The kingdom was paradise; it would be strange to feel nothing when asked to leave, would it not?

I tried to put on a brave face for those gathered in our honor. Every angel in the kingdom had come to see us off, and the knowledge that they would entrust the safety of Heaven to the seven of us, combined with the fact that the fate of all Earth's souls depended on the outcome of this mission, helped me to control my impulse to run back to my hall and bar the gate. Raphael's iron grip didn't hurt either.

He led me to the gate where the others were waiting. The host closed around us in a great semicircle, their voices ringing out the final song and then continuing to cheer.

The Almighty was near us then, and to each He spoke directly to our minds. To me, He said, *My child, Sabrael. You are unique among your brothers for you doubt your worth in the group. Though you do not yet realize it, your place among them is one of the highest. They will need you while on Earth, you and you alone. None can replace you.*

How am I to live without your light? I asked.

The tears were swept from my face before they even fell. *I am with you always. You know this. What have you to fear?*

I am afraid I will never return home.

In time you will once again be among your brothers here in the kingdom. Your path back may stray from the others', but fear not, my child; you will see your hall again.

I nodded and found my fear had disappeared. The Almighty had taken it from me. I was instead filled with the joy of going to Earth.

The Almighty then spoke so all could hear. "Go now, my children, and know that I am pleased with you. Prepare the way for the coming of the Savior. In each of you I have placed the knowledge needed to guide you while in the world of men. The rest Michael will tell you when the dust of the Earth is under your feet. I love you all."

The gate behind us swung open, and the seven of us turned to gaze at the blue world far below. The host erupted in a final cheer of farewell, and each of us in turn, the wardens of Heaven's halls now turned guardians of the Son, stepped forward and flew from Heaven to soar down to the Earth. I took one last look at the kingdom behind me, fear creeping up again, but before it could gain a foothold, I closed my eyes and stepped through the gate.

I should have looked back longer.

CHAPTER EIGHT

It wasn't like it was when I had gone to see Adam. This time, I rocketed from the kingdom, plummeting hard and fast. Wind screamed in my ears and forced my eyes to squint. I couldn't even yell. Rushing air tugged at my skin and hair, my robe trailing far behind like an umbilical cord to Heaven. Then, with a sudden, painless impact, it was over.

My feet touched down on the rocky surface, and though I was still in the spiritual plane, I didn't pass through it. I was on Earth! I cried out in unrestrained joy. I wanted nothing more than to bask in physicality, to scoop up the dust and feel every tiny particle between my fingers. But I remembered that, although the ground supported me, my spiritual being had no influence on the physical world. It was useless to try and move even the smallest stone.

I scanned my surroundings. I had landed in a large, enclosed cavern, somehow having passed through the stone ceiling. But though I'd been the last to make the plunge, I was alone. Where were the others? It occurred to me that maybe I'd been able to control my descent from Heaven, and by not doing so I may have soared off-course. This worry escalated as I realized there seemed to be no way out of this place. Then I felt a rush of wind and Raphael plunged through the ceiling like a streaking comet. He straightened just in time to land with an exhilarated holler. "Now that is the way to travel!"

I embraced him and shouted, "Raphael, we are on the Earth! We are standing on the world of mankind again!"

Raphael shouted back with a smile, "Yes! We are! I told you that you should be the most joyous of us all." I cried out and embraced him again, and he laughed. "You all right? Didn't land on your head, did you?"

I was more than all right. I was ravenous for the world outside, to feel wind on my face and see this glorious place so far removed from Heaven. I wanted to hear the humans, see them up close and examine how different they really were from Adam. I searched for an exit, but Raphael was at my side in an instant. "We must remain here," he said, obviously having heard my thoughts. "There will be time for all of that, but we should await the arrival of the others."

"I won't go far, I promise! I just want to take a peek outside..."

Raphael took the same firm grip on my arm he had in Heaven. "Is this how you would begin your mission to protect the Son—by running off and ignoring what needs to be done? You heard the Almighty; Michael will have our instructions. We will not rush out without hearing what he has to say."

His words cut deep. I stopped trying to break free of his grasp and sat on the ground. He joined me, and as we waited, I found the cave held a fascination all its own. A trickle of water poured into a nearby pool. Stalactites descended from high above the floor that was in some places smooth and in others jagged and full of gravel. Over the next few minutes, the others plunged through the ceiling one by one. It was some time before Michael appeared, giving us all plenty of opportunity for impatient grumbling, but the moment he landed, he was in full command.

"Come sit, brothers," he addressed everyone, seating himself at my side. "I know you are all eager to get started, but before we can do so, you must listen carefully to what I have been commanded to tell you."

The others gathered around.

"We must be extremely careful in our dealings with those who inhabit this world. It is not His plan for seven angels to go out and prove to mankind that God exists."

The others nodded, Raphael and Gabriel even smiling at Michael's words. I have to admit; sometimes I don't understand the plan of the Almighty.

"We have already been given most of the knowledge we will need to both protect the Son and live undetected amongst the humans. We all know how to form physical bodies for ourselves. We all know the layout of the regions we will inhabit, the local customs and much more that will be of use in the coming years. However, there are things which need further clarification along with this given knowledge."

"Then clarify, Michael," said Barachiel. "There's a whole world to experience. I do not wish to spend my time here encased in this tomb."

Michael looked at Barachiel without trace of a smile. "This is not a vacation. We are not here to sightsee. To rush through things and go out unprepared would be to open the door to failure, and I will not allow that."

Barachiel's face turned a bit red, and the rest of us looked at each other in confusion. Why was Michael so upset?

He stood and asked if I would join him in front of the others. I rose to my feet, wondering why I was being singled out. "I want you to become physical, Sabrael. Call matter to yourself; you remember how." I nodded and my body began to tingle, as though chain lightning coursed over me. It wasn't painful, just an odd feeling after such a long time. I could feel the particles gathering to my body. From my internal organs to the muscle and skin over them, the process took but a moment. I was plunged into silence and utter darkness.

Loose gravel shifted under my sudden weight, and I stumbled to find footing. I could see nothing, and swinging my hands in search of Michael, I found only empty space. The only sound was the fading echo of the stones settling beneath me. Then I sensed something behind me. I reached out cautiously and yelped as my hand was ensnared! Struggling against whatever it was, I raised my free arm to defend myself. Michael's voice broke the silence. "Sabrael, please. Who could it be besides me?" I relaxed, feeling foolish. "You are blind in the darkness, are you not?" he asked.

"Yes," I replied. "But you must be as well. How did you find my hand so easily?"

Michael's voice echoed around me, and had his hand not been upon mine, I would not have known from which direction he spoke. "I told you there are things you must learn before leaving this place. I can see you as easily as you could see me only a moment ago."

"How can that be?" I asked.

"You must not allow physicality to disable you. Encased in matter as your eyes now are, they function according to the rules of the physical plane. They need light, and so you are blind in this dark place. I see you because I am not looking at you in the physical plane but rather from the spiritual plane, where light has nothing to do with our ability to see. You must control the matter that answers your call; do not simply use it as a shell. Make it your own. Now, release the matter from your eyes and tell me how many fingers I am holding up."

I wasn't sure how to do what he was asking. I tried to let the matter slip from my eyes, but as I did so, the rest of my body started dissolving as well. My hand slipped through Michael's and as the cavern reappeared through the blackness, I saw each of my brothers leaning forward, enthralled with the show. Michael shook his head.

"You must learn this. All of you must learn that you control the matter making up your physical bodies. You can move one finger without moving your hand. The matter you call to yourself is the same; myriad particles, each of which can be manipulated separately. If you cannot control each one, you will not be fit to protect the Son." I noticed then that Michael's hand was the only part of him encased in physical matter. "Try again, Sabrael."

Particles of matter flew to me and the world went dark again. I tried to visualize how to control only part of my body's matter, but I was completely at a loss. Why did I have to be the example? Four times I tried, and four times my body started breaking apart and I had to start again. Finally Michael said, "Concentrate. Feel the weight of your eyes in your head, the rush of blood through them, their strain to find light. Notice the difference between how they feel now from the spiritual plane. While you are focused on it, simply let the matter go."

I was growing impatient standing there, blind, trying to do something so easy for Michael yet impossible for me. I realized my impatience clouded what little focus I had left and I tried to calm myself. Exhaling, I concentrated on just my eyes. Envisioned their blue glow in the darkness. Felt their futile attempts to gather light, imagined the matter reacting to the air touching it. I focused on my desire to see the cavern. Then, slowly, it happened. Particles of matter started slipping away, and my excitement welled as the wall nearest me began to appear. It was like the darkness chipped away in tiny pieces to reveal the cavern behind it. After a few moments, my brothers became visible again, my eyes having sloughed off their physical matter while the rest of me remained corporeal. I struggled to hold my control, like a gymnast doing his first handstand. If my focus slipped at all, I was sure my body would instantly dissipate. Fighting the strain, I smiled at my brothers, and they seemed to cheer. But all I heard was the dripping of the nearby pool.

Michael, who knew what was happening, said, "You cannot hear them because you are only able to hear the physical plane." I knew there was a hidden command in the comment, so I focused and freed the matter from my ears as well. The cavern filled with their voices.

"Brothers, calm yourselves. There is more to be gained from the example Sabrael has given us," Michael said. He waited as our brothers quieted down. I relaxed a bit and discovered my body didn't break apart. I relaxed completely and to my relief, it remained. Michael continued, "Controlling the particles of your body will keep you from being blinded by darkness or losing track of the fallen if they seek refuge in the spiritual plane. But there are two important lessons to be learned here.

"The first can be viewed by Sabrael's body. While he has done a fine job of becoming physical, he has not paid attention to his appearance."

I looked down, saw the white robe and every part of me in the physical realm. What was he talking about? I looked fine.

Michael continued, "We are going into a world where Sabrael's appearance will place him in jeopardy, not only of discovery, but also harm. You have all seen humans. Tell me, how many have you ever seen with wings?"

I felt the blood rush to my face as the others laughed. I dropped the matter from my wings and they dissolved from the physical plane. It was far easier to do than it had been with my eyes. Perhaps my embarrassment fueled the transition.

"Our luminous skin, the color of our hair, our height, the appearance of our eyes; everything about us will be foreign to those we are going to meet. Every aspect of our appearance and every nuance of our actions will come into question when we are among the humans. We must be flawless in our attempt to mimic their kind. If any one of us slips in this, he will surely endanger not only the rest of us, but the Son as well. Remember that the fallen have been here a very long time and have many followers. While we protect the Son, we will face not only the fallen but these humans as well. We must always be aware and never allow evidence of our presence to be discovered."

At Michael's nod, I restructured the matter of my body to take on the appearance of a human man. This was maybe the strangest feeling I'd ever had. The body was nothing like mine, and yet it was mine. The perfect disguise. This ability would take some getting used to.

"There is another matter which must be discussed before I set you free. Hopefully we will never have to address it in our time here, but there is the possibility." Michael looked at Raphael and I saw Raphael's expression grow grim. "There is a very good chance that some, if not all, of us will have to combat the fallen while on Earth. We would not have been assigned here if this were not so, for our mission is not only to protect the Son from being discovered, but also to defend Him if necessary. We have all had our own experiences fighting them before, but here it will be much different. Here there is death, both for the humans as well as for us."

The group murmured in shock. Death? For us? Michael held out a hand for silence.

"No matter how strange the idea may seem, each of us will be capable of being killed by the fallen or even their followers when in physical form. You must take great care when fighting them, for your lives are in danger just like theirs, in a manner of speaking."

Uriel interrupted Michael, "What is that supposed to mean?"

"Our deaths will not be like human death. For them, death is the soul's release from the body. For us, it is the opposite. When we enter the physical plane, the matter we call to ourselves bonds to us for a time. Once that bond occurs, there must be a force that keeps it together or we would have to be perpetually focused on holding each particle together."

So that was why, when I had relaxed, my body didn't fly apart.

Michael continued, "When we are physical, our bodies are expendable. Nothing more than gathered matter, and if it is lost, you need only call more to replace it. If your arm is cut off, only matter has been separated. Your spiritual being will be untouched. The matter of your arm will disintegrate once your control has been severed, and you can simply recreate what was lost. Even if you lose something vital for a human—your head, for example—it's still only matter that has been separated. Your physical body will dissolve and you can form a new one. Almost every part of you is the same, but the one part of you that is not, is your heart.

"Your heart grounds your control over your physical body. Therefore, your heart is your very life in the physical plane. If you allow your heart to be damaged, it can be fixed. But if your heart is removed from your chest while you are in the physical plane, you will lose your ability to control your physical form. Do you understand, brothers? If you lose your heart, you will be trapped in your body."

My brothers shouted their dismay. Haniel cried out above the others, "But without a heart, the physical body cannot survive. Will we not be freed once the body dies, just as if we lose our head?"

The others quieted immediately to hear Michael's response. "If your heart is removed, you will never be able to escape your physical body," he said. Dread spread through me like poison. "Your physical form will not be like that of a human. It won't age, will require neither food nor air. It's artificial, just a collection of raw matter held together by the controlling force of your heart. Because of this, if your heart is removed and control is lost, your body will die, but the matter will not release from your spiritual form. Ever. It will bleed until it has spilt every drop. It may even be picked apart by the elements or carrion, but you will remain bonded to the physical plane—very much alive, and yet to all appearances, deceased. You will be trapped inside that body, paralyzed, and there will be nothing you can do to save yourself."

To my surprise, I found my hand had moved to cover my heart. The idea was horrid beyond anything I'd ever heard; encased in a lifeless husk, unable to escape, with all the time in the world to watch your own blood dry. The fear I felt about leaving Heaven crept up again.

"The fallen know this?" Raphael asked.

"Unfortunately, yes. Time and experience are on their side. If you confront them, they will try to take your heart." He looked at each of us with such gravity it was nearly as frightening as his next words. "Brothers, you must not let that happen. In that state, unable to defend yourself, the fallen could do anything to you, put you anywhere. Bury you deep in the earth, or toss you to the bottom of the oceans—anywhere we would be powerless to find you. There you would remain until the end of this world."

"That makes no sense, Michael," Barachiel said. "As soon as we learn one of us is missing, we can just return to Heaven, tell the Father and He will point us to our lost brother."

Michael looked at him for a long moment before replying, "We cannot go back."

"What do you mean?" Barachiel exclaimed.

"We cannot return to Heaven. We can't even communicate with Heaven while we are here." Michael's voice was heavy with despair, as though even he had only just learned this information. "We are all of us grounded on the Earth for as long as the mission takes."

The group erupted in shocked arguments. Michael held out his hands and the arguments faded. "How will we return when we are done here?" I asked as soon as it was quiet again.

"When the Son returns to Heaven, we will be recalled alongside Him. We cannot make the journey on our own. If you do not believe me, you are welcome to try." No one did.

"Understand, my brothers, we are now entirely on our own. We cannot leave this world, and we cannot speak to the Father. He will hear our prayers, but we will not hear His reply. If we fail here and allow the Son to be taken, we may never be able to get home. That is why it is so important you do not allow yourself to be defeated by the fallen or their human followers."

"How do you expect us to carry our weapons and remain undiscovered?" Uriel asked.

"The same way you carry them now—in the spiritual plane. When needed, you bring them into the physical plane, and then return them to the spiritual. Sabrael, if you would."

I tried bringing matter to my hand to form the sword in the physical plane. Michael shook his head. "Your weapon does not need to be created as a body does. You only need to draw it into the physical plane. Do not call matter; call your sword." I was confused, but I held out my hand and as I had thousands of times during my training, willed my sword from my sleeve. Instantly it burst into my hand. I held up the now completely physical weapon and looked at Michael. He said nothing, but I knew he was proud.

Michael turned back to the others and said, "All of you must now learn everything Sabrael has shown you. I will check to make sure each of you is ready before we go forth."

My brothers stood and tried everything they'd seen. The mood of the gathering lightened as they experimented, and I laughed to see each of them struggling to perfect their human guises. I made my eyes physical again to watch the pairs of glowing eyes appear in the darkness, and then wink out as my brothers learned to make their eyes spiritual.

How amazing was all of this? We were about to become humans. We would live among them, be part of their world, all while carrying out our mission. Watching the others learning the ways of their physical bodies, I couldn't believe this was actually happening. I no longer needed to look down from afar to see mankind, I need not struggle to remember what dirt felt like under my feet; I was here. I scooped up a handful of pebbles, relishing the feel of the smooth stones sliding over my palm and cascading between my fingers. Such sensations in the physical plane were so strange and wonderful, so different from the spiritual. I couldn't understand how I was able to feel everything through particles of interwoven matter, but it was all so fantastic I didn't care.

Michael watched everyone, and eventually they approached him one by one. He tested each of them thoroughly. Uriel was sent back to practice more after failing a hearing test in the physical plane, and Haniel was instructed to call matter faster. I stepped to Michael last and easily passed his tests. He clasped my forearm proudly. "Good work, Sabrael."

Finally, we were ready to enter the world and begin our preparation for the coming of the Son. Michael told us all to become spiritual again and to remain that way until we'd observed the ways of man. "Remember, brothers," he reminded us, "even in the spiritual plane, always take care to avoid detection. The fallen are everywhere."

The only exit from the cavern was through a small hole in the ceiling. So that was how we entered through it in the spiritual plane. Passing through the hole, I was met with the sight of the night sky stretching from horizon to horizon, trillions of stars winking down at me. I'd never before seen the magnificence of the Almighty's creation from this perspective. Touching down on the ground, I stood in awe staring up at the silent twinkling of the dark sky. I must have stood that way for a while, because eventually Raphael clapped a hand on my shoulder and said, "If you don't start walking, we'll leave you." I looked around and saw my brothers were so far ahead, they were no bigger than my finger. I laughed and took flight with him to catch up to the others. When I rejoined the group, I noticed Michael's amused smirk.

On the walk to Jerusalem, I hoped we'd have a long time to experience being physical before the trials of the mission would begin. I couldn't contain my excitement to reach the city and be among the humans.

What a pity that peace would be taken so soon.

CHAPTER NINE

For nearly a month, we watched. Studied. Keeping to the spiritual plane, we remained silent, unseen. The gestures people used, their behavior, their interactions both public and private. Tirelessly, we memorized all mankind's intricacies, training ourselves to think and act human. I was enthralled to be so close to them, awed at how far they'd come from their original state.

Souls of the dead walked everywhere in the spiritual plane, yet the living had no idea. They were a constant presence, and it was not uncommon for them to beg us for help. Michael and Gabriel took it upon themselves to handle these souls, urging them to follow the path to Sheol. This path, as I saw it many times, periodically opened for each soul, but it was up to the soul to enter. Some went happily, but many feared it and instead continued their desperate attempts to regain their lost mortal coil.

Finally, the time for study was over. On a hill outside Jerusalem, in a cluster of olive trees beneath a starry sky, the seven of us gathered one last time.

"The time has come, brothers. Today we part and embark on our assignments," Michael said. Though there was excitement in his voice, there was also sadness. I couldn't blame him. I felt the same.

The six of us stood before him, and Michael doled out assignments that scattered us across Judea. It was difficult to hear we would be so far apart. Along with the regions we were to guard, each of us received a cover identity, a human part to play to avoid detection. I could not help my laughter when Raphael was told he would pose as one of the men who carted waste from the city of Damascus. When my turn came, I hoped for more … direct human interaction. I braced for the worst, but Michael told me I would become a Greek noble visiting Jerusalem. I could barely contain my excitement. I thanked God for such a blessing. My first contact would be with the Roman Praetorian serving as guards in the city after the Empire's expansion into Judea. I was simply to tell them my position and seek lodging in the royal palace. According to Michael, everything would then fall into place.

"Once you are admitted, try to make friends with members of the royal court. Earn their trust and no news from the city will slip past you. Make sure your performance is flawless; you will be under the harshest scrutiny. Herod is a particularly suspicious king, barely trusting his own family, let alone a stranger in his house. One mistake and he will order you killed."

"How will I get a message out if I need to report something?" I asked him.

"Call out in the spiritual plane and I will hear you." He started to move on, but turned back to add, "One more thing; when you create your physical form, make sure to include a pouch on your belt. It will prove invaluable."

Once Michael spoke to each of us, it was time to separate and go into the world. He traced shapes in the dust with his foot, gathering his thoughts or perhaps delaying our inevitable parting. When he spoke, his voice was more vulnerable than I'd ever heard it before.

"We all know what we must do. Take great care, my brothers. I would not return to this place having suffered the loss of anyone. Remember that the Father will not interfere. There will be no back-up for us, no aid from Heaven. We seven are all that stand between the Son and the fallen."

Even after a month, it was still incomprehensible. I could not fathom being totally cut off from our home, yet here we were.

"The fallen and their followers are many here. Never forget that wary eyes are upon you. Your guard must never falter, not even among those you trust, and remember that should you ever need any of us, we are but a call away." Michael stood silent, staring at a cross he'd drawn with his foot in the dirt. He wiped it away. "May God keep us all, and may we return victorious once the Son has achieved His goal."

We all embraced one another, unsure of what to say. Raphael managed a smile that lightened the moment. "Take care, Sabrael. Should you meet any of our fallen brothers, make sure to call me before anyone else. I wouldn't want to miss any fun."

"Shoveling crap doesn't sound like fun?" I teased.

"Hilarious, really," he said as he hugged me, and with a comforting smirk he was gone, soaring north for Damascus. The others took longer to leave, and I remained, eager to join the humans but reluctant to leave my brothers. Soon enough though, they all disappeared into the night, one by one, until I was alone on the hill with Michael.

"Everyone will return unharmed, right?" I asked.

Michael turned a solemn gaze to me. "I cannot see the future, Sabrael. I know only that which God tells me, and His voice has gone silent."

I couldn't imagine what it would be like to lose one of our brothers. I prayed silently for the protection of the Almighty.

"Thank you for that," Michael said. He embraced me. "I must go. The Son's earthly parents need protection. Watch your back, my brother." His wings opened and he soared into the night, blotting out the stars as he flew away.

My flight was the shortest of all. I set down outside the walls of Jerusalem only a few moments later. The excitement of the task ahead was intoxicating. How strange it would be to live among those sprung from, yet so unlike, Adam. To be seen and recognized, rather than just meeting the unknowing stares of those who gaze toward Heaven. The desire to run into the city and introduce myself to everyone was overpowering. I attempted to collect myself by reviewing the details of my assignment one more time and to my surprise, found that my counterfeit identity was entirely formed in my mind. Specific aspects of Greek culture came to me as I silently interrogated myself; I could even remember Athens and the home I supposedly once inhabited there. There would be no auditions for this role, apparently. I was already playing the part.

If my ruse was to work, I needed to enter the city from either the north or west. The port city of Jaffa on the Mediterranean coast would be the most likely point of arrival for a traveler from the Aegean. Soaring around the city wall, I reached a gate at the northwestern corner. It was closed, as I was sure all of them would be at that hour. Unfortunately, passing through the walls wasn't an option. They were just as impenetrable in the spiritual plane as the physical. I did not fall through the ground while walking on it; I could not push through stone walls. I could fly over them, of course, but looking to the top of the wall, I spotted Roman soldiers on patrol high above and had an idea. If Herod was going to scrutinize me as Michael believed, I didn't want to leave any chinks in my story. A record of my arrival would go a long way.

Pressing tight against the wall to avoid the guards' view, I called matter to form a physical body. Shadows appeared as my eyes became physical and the darkness of night blanketed everything. I made sure my appearance befit my role; athletic build, traces of fading youth in my features, shoulder-length brown hair, a neat beard and brown eyes. My robe solidified into a purple tunic mimicking the fashion of Athenian nobles, its hue the mark of the wealthy, and over this, a white exomie with golden trim snaked down from my left shoulder to circle up under my arm. Hanging from an ornate belt, I formed a pouch as Michael had suggested. Sandals wound around my feet and then, for a final touch, I dulled my clothes to appear weathered from the journey. My transformation complete, I stepped from the shadows and readied myself for the inevitable bout of questions once the guards above saw me.

One of the guards spotted me immediately and waved his hand to another. To my surprise, the city gate opened a crack. Confused that there was no interrogation or request for identification, I stood motionless, but the guards waved me on. I stepped through into the city, uncontested, and the gate cranked shut behind me.

So it was that I entered the world of humans.

The air inside the walls smelled of olives. A cool breeze kicked up sand from the street, showering my legs. I closed my eyes, relishing the wind coursing over my face and arms. I tried taking a breath, wondering if all the air in the world held traces of everyone who'd ever breathed it. Such an odd sensation, breathing. I was glad it wasn't a necessity.

Torches burned in brackets attached to storefronts and houses, illuminating the nighttime streets. Carts of covered fruits and goods lined the walkways as far as I could see. Though the city was bright, it seemed deserted as I headed up the main road toward the palace. The street was long and the walk arduous, but I cared not. The wind on my skin and the sights of the city were more than enough to keep me in high spirits.

I knew I was getting close when I spotted three towers of the most beautiful stone rising from behind the tall wall of the palace grounds. Moonlight reflected off their smooth surfaces in a bluish gleam, the glimmer of gold in their windows. Gazing at them, I felt like I could reach out and touch them despite the distance. What marvels man had created! Were my brothers in the presence of such beauty, I wondered, or had I been so blessed as to be the sole witness to such majesty? The towers loomed, silent and stoic, as though suspicious of the newcomer. Having not seen a single person inside the city yet, I had the eerie sensation of being the only living thing there. Then I saw them.

Following the wall to a large market outside the palace's heavily guarded entrance, I froze at the sight of movement. There, milling about in the otherwise empty agora, were about a dozen people, the descendants of Adam and Eve, the children sprung from the flood survivors. These would be the first people I spoke to as a member of their race. My trial had begun.

Approaching the group, trembling, I singled out a man whose gaze was directed at a balcony high up the palace wall. Reaching up, I tapped his shoulder. "Excuse me…"

To my surprise, he whipped around and grabbed my wrist, twisting hard. His shoulders and arms were thick with muscle. How had I not noticed this? I thought I felt bones breaking.

"Hands off, thief!" he shouted, his voice deep and husky.

Other people turned to look at the commotion. My teeth clenched in pain, I couldn't speak. Then, amazingly, the man's gaze fell on my clothes and he recoiled, falling to his knees.

"Forgive me, lord," he begged.

"It is all right," I said, my wrist aching as though he were still wrenching it. I would have to adjust my body's sensitivity to pain. "Please, rise. No need to draw attention."

The man remained on his knees. "I humbly accept your punishment."

"Punishment? You did nothing wrong; the fault was mine for surprising you." He seemed confused, but cautiously stood. "Tell me, why do you all gather here so late?"

He seemed confused by my question. "In the early morning, the king sometimes throws money to those who stay in the square all night."

"You must be joking. Why would a ruler demand that of his subjects?"

The man looked back toward the balcony and through gritted teeth said, "What better way to ensure a welcoming audience when he wakes?"

"You wait here every night?" I asked. I looked around at the others, their torn and dirty clothes, their desperate gazes trained on the same balcony, as though they might miss the golden moment if they were to look elsewhere.

"No," the man replied, his voice lowering. "Every other night, my wife takes my place."

It was unbelievable that a ruler could let his people suffer so. This man was healthy, solid in body and mind, yet he stood in clothes pockmarked with holes.

"Forgive me, but if it embarrasses you to be here, why wait for scraps when I am sure you could find work of your own?"

He laughed and replied, "Surely you must be a visitor. There is little work here for one of my standing, but it is no better anywhere else. At least here I might gaze upon beautiful buildings and imagine myself inside them."

I was appalled. Would the citizens not give work to their brother in need? Then I remembered the pouch on my belt. Reaching into it, I gathered matter to create gold and silver coins and poured the money into his hand. His eyes lit up. Michael had been correct; the pouch was a good idea.

"Please, take this," I said.

He looked at me in amazement, then fell to my feet and kissed my hand. "This is more than I have received in a year. How can I repay this kindness?"

"I must speak with the king. Can you tell me how I might enter the palace?"

Again, confusion when he looked up. "Surely that cannot be all."

I smiled and replied, "The Almighty teaches if a man among your brothers is in need, aid him however you can. If money is what you need, I am happy to give it."

"Bless you, lord," the man said. Looking at the palace gate, he nodded. "The gate is open to those of your standing. The guards will part when you approach. You will not find Herod so welcoming, though. He speaks only to his closest advisors. I would seek them out first if you ever hope to reach him."

"How will I know them?"

He cupped a hand around his wrist. "They wear gold bands, here. If you see that, you are looking at a member of Herod's court."

"Come with me. Perhaps we can find work for you in the palace."

The man shook his head. "Crossing that threshold means death for me. The court will suffer no concerns of the poor, but for the wealthy, their door is always open."

I looked at the decorated gate, the same white stone around it as that used to build those marvelous towers. I could just make out the silhouettes of guards in the shadows. The crests on their helmets were unmistakable. "You are sure they will let me pass?"

"I would not lie to you. Your path will not be blocked, I assure you."

The line of guards didn't look welcoming. Still, I grasped the man's forearm and said, "Thank you. May the Almighty bless and keep you."

"Forgive me, lord, but I must know; from where have you come?"

"Greece. Athens, if you know where that is."

"I know it so well, your clothes gave you away," he laughed. Bowing, he said, "My name is Theokritus. I am Athenian as well. Should things not go well for you in there, ask my name in the weaver district, and I will gladly offer you sanctuary in my home."

"Thank you again, Theokritus," I said.

Theokritus had been correct. I stepped through the outer gate of Herod's palace and the guards parted for me. How strange that the color of one's clothing could open doors. If I were to change the hue of Theokritus's garb to match my own, would that be all it took to change his fortunes?

The difference between the city outside the palace walls and that within was astonishing. The city had been beautiful, but a layer of dust and sand lay just beneath the surface. It was lit up only near the shops, the light of the moon the sole illumination in many areas. Most of the citizens of the city were asleep. The palace, however, was none of these things.

A vast courtyard met my eyes as I passed through the gate. Two buildings rose to each side of the courtyard, their Romanesque design unlike anything outside. Rows of exquisitely carved columns beneath a roof adorned with statues formed a long colonnade between them. And within this, a landscaping miracle formed the innermost square. The desert sands had been replaced by rows of fig and olive trees trimmed to perfect form over lush lawn and flowerbeds. Walkways wound through this vibrant garden, radiating from a central fountain spewing water into the air.

By the time I realized I was gawking, I had already wandered to the fountain. The two main buildings, one at each end of the courtyard, were perhaps three stories tall, I thought, though it was difficult to tell with so many porticoes and balconies. The paved road and the garden walkways converged at a stairway leading into each building. Moonlight poured over everything, but even so, hundreds of torches and lanterns illuminated even the deepest recesses of the walls. The firelight danced on the walkways, the rhythm of the flames hypnotizing. The air no longer smelled of olives here, but rather water and flowers.

Quick footsteps preceded a line of young men in white robes, running from one building to the next. It was only as they passed me that I noticed the people working throughout the courtyard, all wearing those same robes. They carried everything from gardening tools to scrolls to plates of food. I was happy to see these servants (as they must have been) looked healthier and cleaner than those outside. I couldn't believe the magnificence of it all. I doubted anywhere else in the city rivaled this beauty.

A voice startled me. "Stay where you are."

I turned to find myself face-to-face with a leather breastplate molded to the form of muscles. A cape of scarlet draped from the square shoulders of the palace guard. The man was huge, but I very much doubted his chest looked like the armor did. "State your business here."

"I am Aegyus," I replied, the name coming without hesitation though I'd never known it before that moment. "I have come to worship in the city of King Herod the Great."

The guard glanced at my clothing. "You must have traveled far."

"Athens, actually. My family recently joined the aristocracy there. This is my first journey to the king's land."

"You speak Aramaic well for this being your first trip," the guard asked.

I was astonished. It had not even occurred to me to think about what language I spoke. The guard somehow heard Aramaic, yet I was simply speaking as I always had. By the same token, I understood every word of his. Somehow, my words were being translated to match what was spoken to me! I wondered whether Theokritus had heard me speak Aramaic or Greek. I tried to mask my amazement.

"I studied the language, to ensure I would honor the king," I replied.

"You would do better to study Latin." The guard sized me up, clearly not believing me, but before he could continue, another man stepped from the shadows. The fountain reflected a churning pattern of light and dark on his face, his trim silver beard. My gaze went straight to the gold band on his forearm beneath the purple cape over his shoulder. A member of the court, if Theokritus could be trusted. His sudden appearance unnerved me; I truly had no idea anyone was watching me. That was twice now. It was discouraging to think I could be spied upon so easily. If these men had been the fallen, I might have been dead already.

The guard bowed as the man stepped up to us. "Is there a problem here, Praetorian?" Though he spoke to the guard standing beside him, the man's eyes remained fixed on me.

"This visitor claims to be of the Athenian aristocracy, lord," the guard reported.

"Does he?" the man asked without change of expression. "And for what purpose has the young aristocrat come to our glorious city?"

"To worship at the Temple, view the majesty of his highness's rule, of course," I answered.

"The Temple? There are no bolts of lightning or vestal virgins here, Athenian."

"I am a Jew, my lord," I answered. "As are many in Greece these days."

Looking around, the court member's brow furrowed. "I see no servants, no train of supplies, no animals; nothing one would surely need to survive such a long journey. Did you come all the way from Athens on your own, I wonder?"

"My train was attacked on the road from Jaffa; my possessions taken and my servants slain. I would have shared their fate, but in the struggle one of my horses kicked free of its captor. When it ran past where I was hiding beneath one of the wagons, I leaped out and pulled myself onto his back. I was able to ride safely away, though I assure you I never felt safe while sand was yet beneath my feet."

"A brave gamble," the guard said. "I commend you."

The court member caught the guard in an icy gaze. The Praetorian cleared his throat and stood straighter. "An amazing tale indeed," the nobleman said. "Almost wholly unbelievable, I would say. Tell me, where is this magnificent beast that saved your life? It must be quite an animal to survive the desert with a rider all the way from Jaffa."

I had to be careful with my reply. Already treading lightly, one misstep would mean disaster. "Quite the animal it was, but survive it did not. I have been on foot from sundown yesterday to now, and so you see how I have arrived in your city with little more than my body and the clothes on my back. I hope to find lodging in the king's company."

The man's face remained stoic. I was beginning to wonder if this was going to work. Michael said all I needed to do was talk to the guards and all would be taken care of, yet with every passing moment, my confidence waned. The noble continued scrutinizing my face, and I once again wished I had the ability to read minds as some of my brothers could. If the guard had not been there, I had the feeling this man would have thrown me out of the palace already.

Finally the nobleman sighed and said, "Well, guard, do as you please with him. I am weary and retiring to my chamber." He looked back at me with an awkward smile. "Perhaps we shall meet again, young aristocrat."

He bowed his head, though his eyes never left mine. He walked away, disappearing into the pillars of the colonnade.

I asked the guard, "Who was that?"

"Ireneus, the king's orator and member of the high court. Surprising he did not take to you; he is also Greek."

"Really?" I asked, watching Ireneus as he entered the building on the right. Was his animosity so strong because I too claimed to be a wealthy Greek, or was he simply confrontational with all newcomers? I hoped it was the latter.

"Come. Corinthus handles accommodations. He may yet be awake."

I spent the remainder of that night in the elegant apartment of Corinthus, the palace caretaker. Though he was awake when the guard and I arrived, he couldn't find me lodging until morning. Coincidentally, Corinthus was from Thebes, and we spent most of the night reminiscing about our shared home country over wine. It wasn't difficult to fool him into thinking I was drinking it; he was well into his third bottle before I even arrived. When he was finally too drunk to stay awake, he prepared a bed of pillows for me on the floor and retired to his room. I paced for hours, pondering my situation until the sun crept over the horizon to flood the Earth in golden light, the sky transforming from black to gray to blue. My first sunrise.

It was not quite midday when Corinthus finally woke and led me to an enormous banquet hall. He had a full beard of black hair he might have preferred on the top of his head, and while he dressed in noble purple, he lacked the golden armband of the court. He also slept in the guest building, across the courtyard from the court's quarters. The servants seemed to treat him with respect, however, and for most of the walk, he humored me with jokes about the court members that only an insider would know.

Inside the hall, more than a dozen men sat around a long table, laughing and telling stories. At its head, a stout man watched the others as though bored, or perhaps judging them. Jeweled rings and bracelets adorned his arms, a gold band on his head glinting in the sunlight. Herod the Great, king of Jerusalem. If I were to remain a welcome guest in the city, I knew I needed only to earn favor with him.

Corinthus moved to an empty chair and motioned me to the one beside him. Servants immediately clamored over us, bringing meats and wine, this in addition to all the fruits and breads already on the table. Too late, I realized I'd never eaten before. Would I know how to chew, to swallow? Was the body I formed for myself even capable of such things?

"Who is this stranger that would dine at my table without first presenting himself?" Herod asked. The heat of blood rushed into my cheeks as the entire assemblage stared at me.

Corinthus nearly leapt out of his chair. "Forgive me, highness. This is Aegyus, emissary of Greece, visiting your kingdom on a pilgrimage to the Holy Temple."

I rose and bowed to Herod. "My lord."

Herod's lips turned up and his teeth flashed beneath them. "An emissary sent to see the wonders I have brought to this land and report my service back to the Empire!" He clapped his hands. "Tell me, Aegyus, has your stay been pleasant thus far?"

I glanced at Ireneus, dining near the king, and saw the fear in his eyes. "I am in awe. Everything is beyond description, and I have yet to even see the city in daylight. I only just arrived late last night."

"Where did you stay?" the king asked me.

"Corinthus kindly took me in for the night, majesty."

The king flashed a glare at Corinthus. "Did he? A man of your class should be lodged in one of our finest guest rooms. Do you not agree, Corinthus?"

I had to force myself not to smile at the look of shock on Ireneus's face.

"Forgive me, highness," Corinthus said. "I was not sure which rooms were available."

The king glanced at Ireneus, whose shocked expression quickly melted into a smile. Looking back at Corinthus, Herod said, "You will show Lord Aegyus to one of the chambers overlooking the spring. Supply him with all he requires."

"The tales of your great kindness are not exaggerated, majesty," I said, laying it on thick.

Herod took a long draw from his golden cup and stood. The men around him stood as one. "Stay as long as it pleases you, Aegyus. You are my guest in this palace and the city."

I bowed again before he turned and left, followed by his train of nobles. Ireneus glared at me over his shoulder, but he disappeared into the corridor and was gone.

⊸⊹ ⊹⊸

The apartment Corinthus selected for me was breathtaking. Huge double doors sailed open to reveal a veritable treasure trove. Almost all the furnishings were made of precious metals, making the room exceedingly bright in the daylight. It was also enormous, perhaps fifty feet in length and almost that in width. On the second floor of Corinthus's building, it opened to a spacious balcony with an incredible view of the fountain. The walls were built of that same white stone except for the western wall, which was covered in fixed gold plates to form a floor-to-ceiling mirror. The ceiling, which spanned twenty feet above the floor, was composed of alternating burnished tiles arranged in checkerboard fashion.

Corinthus led me into the room past a large bed with silk pillows and a table gleaming in the sunlight, pointing out all I'd already noticed, but also two hidden closets for the wardrobe I was as yet without. "It is a fabulous apartment, Lord Aegyus, one of the palace's finest. I am sure it will please you," he said. I assured him it was incredible, and thanked him for such accommodation. "Will you require any servants to accompany you into the city today?" he asked. "I can have them here at once."

I looked out the window at the white robes working in the courtyard. An idea suddenly came to me. "No, thank you. I have my own."

He was obviously surprised. "I was not aware you had any servants with you. Were they not killed in the desert with the rest then?"

I couldn't help the smile as he nearly caught me at my own game. "Many were slain, yes, but I did not mention that I sent two ahead of the train. They are out in the city right now visiting old friends. I did not want Ireneus to know of them lest he hunt them down."

Corinthus laughed and said, "Yes, well, Ireneus can be bothersome. Stubborn as an ass sometimes, and twice as ornery. Very well then, I will prepare two servants' quarters."

"Actually," I replied, "I believe one will be enough."

CHAPTER TEN

I was to find there were actually three Jerusalems existing within the city walls. The first was that of the palace, the Temple and the homes of the wealthy—Herod's world of glittering gold and luxury. The second was the upper city, where expensive markets carved out a niche between extravagant homes and successful businesses. This Jerusalem belonged to skilled workers and tradesmen, those who were not nobility but had money to spend. The shops were high-class and the fashions flaunted jewelry and fine materials.

The third Jerusalem, however, was unlike the first two. The lower city, running down the hillside and into the Tyropoeon Valley beneath the colossal, man-made mountain known as the Temple Mount, was largely ignored by Herod and his minions. Dirty and foul-smelling, this region sheltered those who either couldn't find work or worked in despised trades. The rest of Jerusalem towered over it, a natural reminder of its lowly status. It was there, in the shadow of wealth and power, I knew I would find my "servants."

Broken, dusty walkways descended to the valley floor between rows of tiny, crowded homes bustling with activity. The order of the upper city streets was gone here. There were no paved roads, just worn pathways through the labyrinth of bleached and crumbling homes as far as I could see. The Temple Mount completely dominated the northeast horizon, rising from the sprawl. Unsure where to begin my search, I headed toward that single, gigantic landmark amidst the chaos.

For two hours under the blazing sun I searched, hoping for a glimpse of Theokritus in the rising haze. It was futile. The lower city was just too big and disorientating. If I was ever going to locate him, I would need help. As I roamed the streets though, the residents of the lower city just stared at me as I passed. Whenever I approached anyone, they would retreat into their homes. It seemed ridiculous, but I realized what was happening—they were all afraid.

Confused and frustrated, my patience finally expired when I reached the southern city wall. I thought I was walking in entirely the opposite direction! Built for the poor, the houses all looked the same, and the layout of the district was a jumbled mess. Retracing my steps, I headed back toward the Temple Mount, making sure to keep my eyes on it so I would not stray again.

A hand suddenly clapped across my mouth, and the unmistakable edge of a dagger touched my throat, guiding me into a shallow alcove between two houses.

"You move and this moves, understand?" a voice hissed into my ear as the dagger bit in. I nodded as much as I could. A pair of burly men stood before me, their faces not even covered. "Give us the money and you get out of here without a new scar."

"What money?" I asked the third man behind me. He said nothing, but used the dagger to slice the pouch from my belt. He tossed it to the burly men who looked inside, then gave a disappointed look.

"Late start today, tax man?" my captor said. "Or did you stash it somewhere?"

It would have been so easy to disappear into the spiritual plane, but we were supposed to blend in. Instead, I gathered matter into a handful of coins and let it all fall to the ground. The three men dove for the gold and free of their lethal grasp, I ran.

My understanding of Theokritus's plight was becoming clearer by the moment, as was my resolve to get him out of this part of the city.

The claustrophobic buildings soon gave way to the safety of a public marketplace at the base of the Temple Mount. This was nothing like the lavish markets of the upper city. Bruised and rotting fruit sat exposed to the midday sun. Flawed clothing and damaged goods lined every storefront. Packed with the poor, this market was far more crowded than those above.

Entering the nearest shop, I choked on the air inside, heavy and rank with sweat. Cheap trinkets lined the walls, inscriptions pronouncing this stone idol had come from Egypt, or that ring was once worn by an emperor from a land far to the east.

A man in a turban sorted through a crate of new items, arranging them on the shelves. He grunted a hello at first, but after one look at my clothes, his attention was all mine. "Welcome, my lord! Anything you desire, I promise I can procure."

"I am looking for a friend."

"And you have found one. Here, let me show you some of my most prized acquisitions."

"No, I am looking for a friend of mine, and his wife. I came here to find them, but I was robbed," I said.

The man laughed. "In the weaver district? You are surprised? That place is a den of thieves who will steal the clothes off your back given the chance."

"Perhaps if people helped them instead of offering only scorn..." I said, not liking the tone of his voice.

He shrugged, "The king allows a select few to live on relief at the city's expense, if they can earn it. Others he purchases from their families to become servants in the palace. Opportunities exist, but most are ungrateful for the king's charity."

"You call such things charities?"

"What would you call them? Herod could just as easily do nothing." The man must have noticed my expression, for he added, "It is their choice to remain. When Herod sends his men to offer these people a way out, they hide, like beetles scurrying from the light."

Not all of them, I thought, rubbing my throat. "Do you at least know your way around? I can pay you to guide me."

"Sorry. This store is as close as I go. If your friend is truly living out there, I say leave him. Better for you, I think, than to meet the wrong customer there and never return."

I stepped out into the sunlight again, grateful to get away from the man. I thought humans would be compassionate, show a sense of brotherhood as we did in Heaven. There was no respect here. No compassion. The shopkeeper was no different than Ireneus or the muggers, self-serving and arrogant.

I headed back into the weaver district, irritated at my tremendous failure so far. Perhaps I should just wait for nightfall when Theokritus's wife would take her place at the palace square. At least I knew where that was. But just as I decided to head back to the palace, two women emerged from a house ahead, and the older one froze as she saw me. I thought she would run back inside, as so many had earlier, but to my amazement, she nearly knocked over her younger companion in her haste to greet me.

"Good day, lord! What a treat to welcome such fine company to our neighborhood. Is there anything we can do for you?"

I took the hand she offered. Her nails were stained black. "I am looking for someone. A Greek, named Theokritus. He is married, though I do not know his wife's name. Do you know them?"

The woman hesitated. "I might. Why do you seek them?"

"I intend to bring them to the king's palace," I answered.

The younger woman straightened, and the older one yanked her hand away in disgust. "Another one. Stay out of our district and tell that tyrant to leave us alone! How much more can he demand from those who have nothing to give?"

Confused, I pleaded with her. "I am not sure what you mean. I only want to invite Theokritus and his wife to join me in the palace as my guests."

"Guests?"

"Theokritus paid me a kindness. I would simply like to return the favor."

Visibly awed, the woman clapped her hands. "Forgive me, lord! I know them well. I saw Theokritus go to the marketplace only a short time ago, but perhaps Helena is still home."

Before I could say another word, she pulled me into the cleft between two homes. The younger woman grabbed my other hand and trailed behind. I wasn't sure if it was only our quick movements that made it seem so, but I could swear her thumb caressed my hand. The three of us wove through tight alleyways, taking blind turns where there were no markers or distinguishing signs. How did anyone find their way through such a place? It was maddening.

We came at last to a house with just a sheet for a door. The older woman patted my hand and told me to wait before disappearing inside. As soon as she was gone, the younger woman's hand slid up my arm. I turned to find her large, brown eyes only inches away.

"Tell me, lord, does a woman wait for you in the palace?" She placed her other hand on my chest and moved even closer. "Or do you require someone to take that position as well?"

I guided her hands from me. "Forgive me," I said. "Beauty such as yours is a delicacy from which I fear I am forbidden."

She wrapped her arms around my neck, her breath stroking my lips. "Who forbids such things? The king? He appreciates the embrace of a woman more than most. If it is God you fear, do not worry. Did He not create woman to answer man's need for a companion?"

115

The stench of her perspiration was unbearable. Her blackened teeth, the holes in her clothing. "Indeed He did intend companionship for you … us, but within the bonds of marriage. My work does not allow such ties."

Undaunted, she slowly slid her hands down my body. "Perhaps you work too much."

The older woman emerged from the doorway. "You may enter, lord. Helena is eager to meet you," she said.

"Thank you," I said, relieved, and pulled away from the younger woman.

The older woman casually extended her hand and replied, "It was our pleasure, lord."

Understanding, I slipped her a few coins and stepped quickly inside, but not fast enough to miss hearing the younger woman scolding her mother for not giving her enough time.

Theokritus's entire house, if it could be called such a thing, could have fit in one corner of my palace apartment. A bed of matted straw lay against one wall, a small table with a bowl of moldy fruit beside it. Three charcoal drawings hung on the wall, beautifully rendered scenes of the city. A woman sat before a loom standing upright against the wall, expertly weaving threads into a rug, though her dress was tattered and dirty. A tight band held up her dark hair, only a few loose curls spilling over. She turned to face me and taking my hands into hers, kissed them gently.

"Welcome, lord, though I wish it was to somewhere more befitting your company."

"A truly welcoming smile is all the luxury I need."

The woman smiled, though she seemed confused. "I am Helena. Theokritus is my husband. You are welcome to wait for his return, if you desire."

Her small chin and large eyes gave her almost an adolescent appearance, but the curves of her body spoke otherwise. I found it oddly difficult to look away from her. She scratched at her thumbnail, avoiding my gaze. A small stack of blankets lay beside the loom, snippets of yarn strewn about the floor.

Forcing the words from my dry throat, I said, "Forgive me; have I interrupted your work? I can look for Theokritus in the marketplace if you need to return to it."

Helena shook her head and put a hand on my forearm. "No, no. I would not force you into the hot sun again. I can work while you wait. Your company is most welcome."

As she turned back to her tools, I felt a sudden yearning unlike anything I had ever felt. "Perhaps you would come with me then? I have only seen only a corner of the marketplace and would enjoy learning to navigate it. If you would be my guide, perhaps we can find Theokritus together."

Helena smiled at me. "I really must continue working. I must finish two more blankets before it is time to go to the palace square..." Her eyes darted to the floor. Clearly, she had not intended to mention the couple's main source of income.

I tried to dispel her embarrassment. "It is all right, Helena. There is no need to be ashamed. Where do you think I met Theokritus?"

Her gaze returned to me, wider than before. "You ... You are Aegyus, the Athenian?" The change in her demeanor was instant. "Oh, Lord Aegyus, forgive me! I thought you a tax collector! With clothes like that, and no one has ever seen you before..." My strange encounters with the lower city residents suddenly made sense. "As you can see, we have nothing to give and the season is almost over."

"I gave Theokritus a small sum of money just last night. What happened to that?"

Helena laughed, a sound I would have thought impossible only moments ago. "Small? We have not seen such money since coming here. Were the collectors to find it, we would be put to death for not giving tribute to the king. Theokritus came home only to tell me of your kindness, then went to spend it right away."

I couldn't believe this was the same woman. "I do not understand. Only a moment ago you were so sad, so full of distress…"

Helena solemnly took my hand. "Please forgive me. The collectors sometimes take pity on those in the worst need. I am sorry if I misled you. Had I known who you are, I would have greeted you differently."

"But the woman who led me here, she did not tell you…"

"All Ruth said was that a man from the palace was searching for Theokritus. You must not be angry with her. She has been trying to marry her daughter off to nobility for many years." I felt a twinge of disappointment. Here I thought the younger woman's advances had been genuine.

"If I were to ask you and Theokritus to accompany me back to the palace, to live with me there, would you consider it?"

Helena's hand rose to her chest. "Is that why you are looking for Theokritus?"

"It is. I would be greatly honored to open my home to both of you."

"You only just met us. How do you know you can trust us?" I was sure her real question was actually how did they know they could trust *me?*

"I am new to Jerusalem and overwhelmed already. I need someone to teach me the customs, and apparently how to find my way around the city. Those I have met in the palace are of … questionable character. But last night, Theokritus helped me without asking anything in return. When he told me he's Athenian, I knew there would be no one I could trust more."

"You want us to stay in the palace as your guests?" she asked.

"Yes," I replied. "Only, those living there believe I am retrieving two of my servants right now. If you join me, it must be in the guise of personal attendants. I apologize for that, but when this opportunity arose, I thought it the best I could do for you."

She threw her arms around me. "I do not know how to thank you."

I smiled and said, "You do not need to thank me, Helena. I only ask that you accept my invitation and let me take you from this place."

Tight in her embrace, I felt the strange yearning again. Almost a compulsion. Her skin was so warm. Pulling me up, Helena wrapped a bundle of clothes into a bedsheet and pulled a few rolls of canvas from beneath the mattress.

"Let us go right now!" she said and pulled me toward the door.

CHAPTER ELEVEN

I n the shadow of the Temple Mount, Helena whisked me back to the bustling marketplace. She sprinted ahead through the crowd as soon as she spotted Theokritus and he turned just in time as she flew into his arms. Like a young girl, she explained everything in an excited rant. Theokritus clasped my forearm when I caught up, but his smile faded when I offered to carry some of their newly purchased clothes.

"Lord Aegyus, no! What kind of master carries his servants' clothing?" I reiterated that their servitude was just an act for those within the palace, but he insisted. "You have given us these clothes. This opportunity. For that alone I would serve you, act or no."

Thus it was that the Athenian Aegyus and his two surviving servants arrived at the palace carrying only a bundle of clothes and three magnificent drawings. Ireneus wasn't pleased.

"I thought all your servants were slain." He stood blocking the entry to my building, as though he'd been awaiting my return.

"You never asked if I had contacts here in the city."

His eyes passed over Helena, inspecting every inch, some more than others. Then they narrowed on Theokritus. "Where have I seen you before, servant?" Theokritus said nothing. "I had you removed from the palace grounds weeks ago for trespassing! What trickery is this, aristocrat, inviting the poor into our home?"

Before I could reply, Theokritus interjected, "Your memory is sharp, lord; we did meet then. However, I only came to inform the court of my master's imminent arrival. Had you allowed me to speak, surely all this confusion might have been avoided." I was shocked at Theokritus's mastery of Aramaic; he only spoke Greek to me.

Ireneus's lips tightened. "Such a loose tongue reflects poorly on your master."

"A servant's tongue should be free to defend his master," I said. "Surely you agree."

"No one has ever been so bold as to disgrace me in front of my servants."

Theokritus muttered, "Something I can fix quick enough." Helena patted his hand and frowned, though I could see the laughter in her eyes. Thankfully, Ireneus didn't hear him.

"Very well. You want to bring the filth of the city into this palace, I leave you to it. But when you wake to find the little you have has gone missing, do not cry to the court." He flicked his fingers, beckoning me. "A moment, aristocrat. Away from prying ears."

Giving Theokritus and Helena a reassuring nod, I followed Ireneus through the gardens. "Since your arrival, I have been fondly distracted by memories of our dear Athens; the places I once lived, the city's glorious history, but more than that, my thoughts dwell on the people there. I was not sure why. But today I had a revelation. You see, I was quite familiar with the noble families before my duties brought me here, yet I do not recall your face, or even your name." He paused and stared at me. "Strange, I think, that Caesar would send Athenians here as new emissaries. I should think he would prefer to favor those of Roman blood."

Trying to mask my nervousness, I said, "If that were the case, would Caesar not also seek to replace representatives to such a fine city as this with more trustworthy, Roman advisors?"

Ireneus's gaze turned cold. "You may fool that imbecile Corinthus, and the king may be blind to your lies, but do not think me so easily misled. Take great care in your actions here. I will be watching." His robe swept over the dirt and he disappeared into his own building.

"Is something wrong?" Helena asked when I returned to them. "Should we leave?"

I smiled at her. "He is only wary of those new to the palace. Nothing to worry about."

Though this answer satisfied her, Ireneus's suspicions didn't sit well with me. I had no guarantee the man wouldn't become a problem I must handle in time.

⇒⊹ ⊹⇐

My new companions couldn't believe their eyes when we arrived in the apartment. Helena wasted no time getting comfortable. She leapt onto the bed almost before her feet touched the floor. "Our entire house could fit on this bed!"

Theokritus examined the indoor lavatory. "Just before we left Athens, the aqueducts were being routed into wealthier homes. Ours may have had access in time." He trailed off.

Seating myself at the table, I asked, "Why did you leave Greece?"

The hulking Athenian sat facing me. "For many years, my family enjoyed wealth from our trade in spices and fine silks by way of an easterly road through Jerusalem. Under the rule of the Romans, everything changed. My grandfather did not support Caesar's reign, and when the Praetorian discovered this, they came for him."

Theokritus stared at his folded hands. "He was asleep in his bed when the torches crashed through the windows. The spark of disloyalty extinguished by flame. But customary to Roman practice, the families of known traitors are also to be executed. My father, knowing this, was certain we would be next. I thought it foolish to worry. I was the fool.

"Helena and I had just been wed, having spent only three nights together, when the Praetorian came for my father. The three of us hid as they shouted and pounded on his front door. I begged him to speak to the soldiers, to swear our allegiance to Caesar, but he knew it was too late. He thrust into my hands a large sum of money he had collected since my grandfather's death and bid me escape to Jerusalem; Helena and I could take refuge with my grandfather's brother who assisted my family's trade officials. I refused to run, swore that I would stay and fight. He just grabbed me with a strength I thought had left him long ago and forced us out the back door, bolting it behind us. I beat on that door until my fists painted it red, but the Praetorian were in the house then. I could hear my father proclaiming his loyalty, showing his titles to prove himself a respectable citizen. Then his cries were silenced. Helena pulled me away, and from the edge of our land, I watched the Praetorian emerge from the house with bloodied swords. They set fire to it, consuming my father in flames just as his father before him. I yearned for revenge, but refused to be the third member of my family slain by the emperor's soldiers. So Helena and I fled that night on a merchant ship headed for Jerusalem.

"We searched for my grandfather's brother, but found he had perished in the Parthian invasion. His daughters were both married off. No one of my bloodline was left in the city. With the little money we had left, we bought a home in the weaver district and clothes that would last, and ever since we have been struggling, nowhere else in the world to go."

Helena put her hands on his shoulders. She said, "It is a miracle you found us when you did. The tax collector's next visit would have seen us sold as slaves."

If only they knew how miraculous my arrival really was. "As long as I am here, you are my welcome guests, and I promise I will not leave without first ensuring you will be cared for."

"Thank you, Lord Aegyus. For all you have done," Theokritus said.

"Please, I ask that you not call me lord any longer, only Aegyus. You are not servants; you are my guests. There is but one Lord, and under Him we are all equal."

Theokritus looked up at Helena and then back at me. "You are a Jew as well? Truly, you are a blessing sent to us from God."

⊶ ⊷

Later, as the sun headed for the horizon and the land darkened beneath a blanket of rust, Theokritus and Helena sat in new clothes, fresh from the bathhouse. Though relegated to servants' robes outside the apartment, behind closed doors they could wear anything they desired. I felt it necessary to tell my friends about the strange behaviors they would no doubt observe in the coming days, for I couldn't risk them accidentally compromising me. I explained that certain matters would often keep me from the apartment, both day and night. They were never to ask about these affairs nor question others about my whereabouts. There would be money for them every day and, though they had their own quarters, my apartment would always be open. They asked me nothing after this, and were delighted I offered them my apartment as their own, though on the first night Theokritus informed me they "would like to spend a night alone in our own room, if you would not mind."

The three of us spent much of the next few days together. Though I wished they would regard me as a friend, the kindnesses

I'd shown them seemed to have instilled a persistent reverence. I was just thrilled they were free of the trials they'd endured. Why such kind people would have been put to death over something as trivial as money was beyond me. How could it hold such importance when each morning I just created new coins out of nothing?

My days in the palace were spent ingratiating myself with the court members, though Ireneus remained impossible to please. Ever more comfortable speaking to these men, I was fast becoming a familiar, trusted face. I dined with them, walked with them, and spent every moment of daylight acting out my ruse. My nights, however, were reserved for exploring the grounds in the spiritual plane. In the dark hours, I snuck into forbidden areas to observe the king's late night meetings and learn secrets never uttered in the light. Theokritus and Helena said nothing of my frequent nights out, save Helena occasionally asking if I was getting enough sleep. They didn't know that on the nights I stayed in the room, it wasn't to sleep but to ponder the day's findings. How could I tell them sleep was as useless to me as food or air? To my companions I was simply a busy emissary, dealing in matters of politics and other things they need not care about. Though I trusted them implicitly, I heeded Michael's warning and continued to perpetuate the role of Aegyus, never mentioning the name Sabrael and keeping my true identity locked deep inside.

I'd been in Jerusalem for some weeks before the reason for my being there came to light. The rainy season had come and gone. With the trade routes no longer dangerous, tens of thousands of visitors flocked to the city. The streets were soon so packed, there was hardly room to walk, and the sands outside the city walls filled with tents to house the overflow of travelers. Herod's court was in good spirits, their coffers once again filled with currency from across the world. I even heard Herod planned to construct more theaters and build a new district to encourage some of the tourists to stay.

Helena was especially welcoming of the constant stream of strangers finding their way into the lower city markets. "More people means more work for those in need," she said.

It was the Temple though, not the markets, that was the focal point for this influx of visitors. If one deed set Herod apart from the kings before and after him, it was the construction of this shimmering marvel. The Temple comprised five main areas called Courts, each separated from the next by gates of gold or silver. Only one was made of bronze, but was polished so well, one would swear it to be gold. With its stonework cut from marble, and precious decorations adorning every alcove, the entire structure shined as though it housed the sun itself. It was the radiant centerpiece of Herod's golden city. I wondered how much mind he paid to the fact that the building was supposed to be in the Almighty's honor, not his own.

Imagine my shock, then, when I learned that only select people were permitted within this architectural miracle. Upon reaching the summit of the Temple Mount, one found himself in a massive portico, the Court of Gentiles. This wasn't so much a worship area as a bazaar, full of money changers and vendors who sold souvenirs and sacrificial animals. Colonnaded porches lined its perimeter on three sides, priest-masons working hard to expand the western side of the Mount. At its southern end stood the Royal Stoa, a covered shelter from the sweltering heat and rainy season held aloft by brilliant white marble pillars. The Court of Gentiles was the only area open to all visitors, a five-foot-high wall blocking off the remainder of the Courts from non-Jews. Stone tablets affixed to pillars spaced along the wall proclaimed in Latin, Greek and Hebrew that any uncircumcised man crossing the wall faced penalty of death.

Up a few stairs and through an incredible bronze gate called the Nicanor Gate was the Court of Women, where Jewish women could leave offerings and hear sermons. The Court of Israel was next, where Jewish men offered their sacrifices and praise around the even higher Court of Priests. Here, priests burned the offerings of Jewish citizens on a massive altar visible from all the way back in the Court of Gentiles. All of these areas formed a stairway to the heart of the Temple, the Sanctuary, an enclosed building accessible only to priests. The Sanctuary was divided into two areas, the Hikal, which contained the most holy relics of Judaism, and the Devir, hidden behind a heavy curtain embroidered with a map of the entire known world. Built to house the presence of God Himself, absolutely no one was allowed in the Devir except the high priest, and he only on the Day of Atonement. The entire structure was meant to be a physical, and spiritual, ascension to the presence of the Almighty, and the single destination for nearly all the city's visitors.

With the huge numbers of people traveling to visit the Temple, it soon became nearly impossible for the three of us to navigate the madness to perform our daily worship. Theokritus and Helena finally gave up trying, but I continued the fight each day.

It was during one of these battles to the Temple's gates that I was first discovered.

The main route by which most citizens entered the Temple was through a pair of gates in the lower city called the Huldah Gates. On the southern side of the Temple Mount, these twin gates fed into stairways that led up into the Court of Gentiles. On this particular day, the gates were clogged with waiting worshippers. There was no way I would reach the Court of Israel by sundown. Not even my status as royal guest would help me. Frustrated, I looked to the winding stairway at the southwest corner of the Mount which led up to another, smaller entry, but this too was packed. There was only one other route available. I turned and ran through the streets of the weaver district and back up into the upper city.

Spanning high over the Tyropoeon Valley, a long bridge connected the upper city to the Temple Mount. I'd never used this bridge before, but it was a popular avenue for those who shunned the valley floor. As I approached the bridge, my hopes were answered. It wasn't nearly as crowded as the Huldah Gates below. I crossed from the upper city's Xystus market and came to the back of a mercifully short line.

After only a few moments, a hand touched my shoulder. Half-expecting to find Theokritus behind me, I turned and found it to be an elderly beggar. His clothes ragged and soiled, the stench of him was unconscionable.

"Forgive me, lord, but would you be so kind as to help a man in need?" he asked with a raspy voice. Impressed at his audacity in coming up from the lower city, I gladly reached into my pouch. He took one look at the money I offered him and slapped my hand away. The coins clinked over the lip of the bridge. I was so startled I almost fell with them. "I do not want money. What is money? I asked for assistance."

"Old man," I said, "I came here to worship the Almighty God, and while I will be glad to help you, I would have my time with Him first."

He smiled a toothless grin. "Perhaps an old friend can persuade you to change your mind." From beneath his hood, his hair suddenly grew to his chest and turned silver. His eyes burned gray.

"Michael!" I gasped, and instantly his appearance was that of the old man again, his hair turning to dust and sifting away in the breeze. He blinked and his eyes were human once more.

"Follow me," he said.

He led me along a winding path through the upper city. Each time I tried to speak, Michael quieted me without stopping. He walked with the help of a mangled cane, and I wondered if he was required to perform this disability every day. I silently shouted my joy that we were together again, and in a few moments I heard his voice in my mind telling me to quiet down. I didn't care; this was the first time since my becoming "human" that I could speak freely. He soon led me into an alley, shaded from the sun. No one was around in any direction.

"Of course no one is around. The smell keeps them away," he said. I laughed, and he asked, "How are you, Sabrael? It seems like it's been so long."

"Everything has gone smoothly in the palace. I'm on good terms with many of the king's men, and even hold the status of Herod's personal guest."

"Well done!" He smiled a grin of gums and I laughed. "Like the disguise?"

"If the others could see their mighty leader now..." His smile broadened. "How are the others? Have you visited them?"

Michael scratched his face, dirty fingernails dislodging flecks of crusted skin. "They are well. Thus far there have been no confrontations with the fallen, though Haniel believes at least four dwell near Cana."

"What of the Son?" I asked. "When is He coming?"

"Before I get to that, have you observed any of the fallen here in the city?"

"None that I know of, but the crowd is so big these days, I doubt I would see them."

"You would see their wings in the spiritual plane," he pointed out. The heat of embarrassment rose in my cheeks. I should have thought of that. Michael continued, "You must take great care, for they can see you the same way. From now on, be mindful of this and observe the crowds in the spiritual plane before entering any place where the fallen might lurk."

"You make it sound like they are close."

Michael nodded. "If the fallen are not already here, I am sure they will be very soon. The Son will be born in but a few days."

"The Son will be born in Jerusalem?" I asked, unable to hide my excitement.

"Not here, but nearby. Once He arrives, I expect the fallen will flock to this entire region and we must be ready to defend Him. If any of us calls for you, you must be prepared to drop everything and fly there right away."

I nodded, preoccupied by my excitement. Finally, we would be by His side as He grew up, serving and keeping Him safe until the day He would fulfill the prophecies.

"No," Michael said. "When the Son arrives, we are to remain in our positions. Each of us has been assigned to a crucial place, and the day will come when all our roles become clear."

"Then we will not be able to witness His birth?"

"Of course you can. I would be surprised at any angel who did not praise the coming of Christ. But after that, you must return here to monitor Herod's court. News will travel fast, and all news passes through them. I do not want any surprises."

"Won't He know who we are if He sees us? I thought we were to avoid direct contact."

"The baby He has become will not recognize us, or remember anything of Heaven."

For the first time, the notion of all this made me sad. I didn't know how I would be able to be near Him and never tell Him who He truly was. "How will I know where to find Him?"

Michael replied, "When the time comes, you'll know. Worry instead about any changes in the palace once He is here. Things may get very different all too quickly."

"Whatever happens, I have it in control," I said.

He nodded. "I have to get back, but remember my words. If you need us, cry out in the spiritual plane and we will quickly be at your side."

Michael embraced me tight. I could feel the bones beneath his papery skin. Then, in a swirl of flying matter, he was gone.

CHAPTER TWELVE

"You were gone awhile," Helena said. Standing beside the window in the waning light of the day, she was breathtakingly beautiful. "Everything all right?"

I closed the door and sat on the bed, my mind reeling with everything Michael told me. "I must attend to things tonight that will keep me away until morning."

Helena sat beside me. It was a uniquely stunning sight to see her hair let down. Normally, even when all three of us were alone, she kept it tied back. The long curls now accentuated the darkness of her eyes, made her gaze even more striking. I realized I was staring, but couldn't look away. She said, "I know you prefer us not to ask about your affairs, but you seem sad. Did something happen at the Temple today?"

"I met an old friend today and he told me some troubling news, that's all," I said and kissed her hand. "Nothing that will affect the life you have here, I promise."

"What about the life *you* have here?" she asked, still holding my hand.

Her touch was so soft. The sunlight in her chocolate eyes, on the curve of her lips, caused a strange intensity to well within me, and I could not hold her gaze. "When will Theokritus be back?"

"Who knows? He went shopping." Her lips finally parted in a smile. "You know how he is; if I didn't know from experience, I would swear he is more woman than me."

We laughed together. "Will you be all right until he returns?"

Helena tilted her head, her hair cascading to the side. "You always worry. I will be fine," she said. But she looked down at her hands, the same way she looked when we first met.

"I almost forgot; I have something for you." Putting my hand behind me, I called matter together to form a silver-blue flower, abundant in Heaven's halls but alien to Earth. Her eyes lit up as I gave it to her.

"Where did you get this?" she asked, smelling its petals. "I have never seen one like it."

I smiled at her. "It is definitely rare, but will live long given the proper care."

Helena kissed my cheek and went to find a vase. I looked out the window to see Theokritus coming across the courtyard, his white servant's robe in stark contrast to the colorful new clothes slung over his arm. Then I noticed I wasn't the only one watching him.

"Helena, when Theokritus returns, I do not want either of you to leave the apartment again tonight for any reason."

She came to my side and followed my gaze. "Now I know something's wrong."

I took her hand and pointed her finger. "Not something. Someone."

Her eyes narrowed as she spotted Ireneus in a window of the other building. "I hate that man! When will he leave us alone?"

"I doubt he is capable of posing any real threat, but even so, lock the doors."

The sun was more than halfway set when I stepped outside, the sky bleeding deep red light and the shadows on the ground converging. Ireneus gazed out from his window like a snake in its hole until, to his dismay and embarrassment, I smiled and waved. He drew his curtains in disgust. Teeth firmly clenched on the inside of my cheek, I stepped into the dark vestibule between the inner and outer palace gates, and making sure no one was looking, let the matter of my body fly free. The sunset world instantly became bright as day. I stepped back into the courtyard, invisible to the physical plane, and flew to the doorway of Ireneus's building.

On previous nights spent spying, I'd learned that the king's bedchamber was on the secret third floor, though this was known only to a select few. A track in the floor beneath a certain statue on the second floor allowed it to swing out, revealing a door to a stairway leading up. I didn't need to move the statue in the spiritual plane, I just passed behind it and through the crack of the hidden door. When one has no mass or matter, the thinnest of spaces is as good as any door. Four of Herod's private guards stood in the passage above, men who spent their lives defending Herod's bedchamber from those who wanted to get in ... and stopping those who tried to get out. The bedchamber door was closed, but the spaces through the keyhole, under the doors and in the sliver between them were all wide open.

The king was not in. Just three women in the enormous bed, all of whom wore open silk robes and nothing else. One of them had bruises around her wrists and ankles, though it was up to my imagination whether they were caused by being held against her will. I passed back into the hallway and flew down to the ground level, deciding where next to go.

My mind suddenly filled with Michael's voice, booming like a multitude of trumpets.

Brothers, the time has come! The Son is among us! Come, worship Him! Follow the sign in the sky!

I cried out in joy at hearing these words and flew out into the night, wings stretched wide. Though no darkness exists in the spiritual plane, I beheld a brilliant light just a few miles to the south. I laughed and soared toward the sign, spinning and swooping low over the sand. The Son had come! Mankind would be saved! How can I now express what I felt in those moments? I flew as swiftly as I could and still pushed harder. I made my eyes physical to witness the sign in that plane and found it to be as a bright star in the night, shedding light onto the approaching town ahead, a place called Bethlehem. Uriel and Raphael greeted me, and we laughed together through tears of joy as we embraced outside the stable of a crowded inn. Barachiel, Haniel and Gabriel arrived only moments later. Then Michael emerged from the stable to welcome us all.

Together we went in and found Mary, the chosen mother of the Son, and her husband Joseph beside a manger. A small form wrapped in a blanket slept within. The seven of us rejoiced at the sight of the infant Son and took physical form in our true likenesses, robes brilliant white and wings spread. Joseph woke Mary, who looked exhausted after the birth, and held her close. With tears in their eyes, they listened as we sang for their child. The baby woke but did not cry. He just looked up at us with wonder. Each of us in turn stepped to His side with whispers of welcome.

When it was my turn, I kissed His head, the wisps of downy hair softer than anything I had ever felt. The baby reached out and I let Him grip my finger, His entire hand only half its length. I whispered, "Praise to you, Almighty, for today prophecies are fulfilled."

He squeezed my finger tightly. In His eyes, I swear I saw recognition, though Michael told us the Son would have no knowledge of who we were. The baby pulled my finger into His mouth and I felt the wet bite of gums. He laughed and spoke to me in the only language thus far I could not understand.

After we all had our moments with the newborn King, we gave our thanks to Joseph and Mary and shed our physical forms.

I was stunned upon entering the spiritual plane to find the host of Heaven descending down a great stairway from the kingdom to greet the young Jesus. I wanted desperately to stay and visit with them, as did the others, but Michael said, "No, brothers. We have duties to which we all must now return. Tonight the eyes of the fallen will be upon us."

Theokritus and Helena. Fear coursed through me and after hasty goodbyes, I soared back to Jerusalem sick with worry over what I might find. The city was teeming when I hurtled over the walls. It seemed the whole city had come outside to stare up at the brilliant star hovering over Bethlehem. Many were in awe, but I could see rioting and violence spreading as well. I swooped low under the palace gate and flew to the windows of my apartment, praying for the safety of the two I had left within. My eyes scoured the room for Theokritus and Helena, and I breathed a great sigh of relief when I found their two forms in the bed, rising and falling steadily in sleep. I thanked God for their safety and floated to the ground, folding my wings to my back.

As my feet touched down, a sharp sensation like anxiety overwhelmed me. I was suddenly dizzy, and the very air around me seemed to quake, compelling me to turn around. Confused and frightened, my searching gaze fell on the other building.

A figure stood in one of the second-floor windows, seemingly looking right at me. And a pair of wings extended from its back.

I darted behind the nearest pillar, terrified. But though the figure gazed out over the courtyard, it made no sign it saw me. Matter obstructed the glow of the spiritual being beneath; the demon must be in physical form then, disguised as a human, I guessed, since his wings shined unhindered. Remembering the rules Michael taught us, I knew that if the demon's eyes were physical, I would be invisible to him in the spiritual plane. At that distance, though, it was impossible to tell if his eyes were physical or not. He just stood there, staring.

I concentrated and gathered matter to my eyes, needing to see the demon's human mask. With my lackadaisical approach to checking the spiritual plane before now, he might have been masquerading there, posing as anyone, since my first day in the palace. As the darkness of the physical plane filled in though, I lost sight of him. I released my eyes again and dashed across the courtyard into the demon's building.

I knew I should alert Michael, but if this demon had seen me, I couldn't risk compromising the others. I slipped into the stairwell and pumped my wings, rising to the second floor. The hallway was empty. I tried to convince myself this was good news. Shifting my hearing to the physical plane, I crept down the hall. Listening at each door, I stopped at one when I heard whispers from inside. Was it the demon? Were there others in there with him, conspiring in the night? But before I could investigate, a commotion back at the stairwell caught my attention.

Two of Herod's court officials, Ptolemy and Eurycles, all but dragged a palace guard down the stairs with them to the ground floor.

"The king demands to see these troublesome Magi at once," Ptolemy said.

"They have been shrieking about this 'infant king' for hours," added Eurycles. "His majesty wants them silenced and brought to the dining hall immediately."

My God! I thought. *They already know!*

I looked at the door standing between me and the demon infiltrator. If he was there, mere feet away, I could remove the threat right now and be done with it! But Herod had summoned the Magi to discuss the birth of the Son. It was the very reason I was there. I couldn't ignore it. Memorizing the location of the room, I ran back to the stairwell and jumped the rail.

The guard had already fetched the three Magi when I hit the ground. Dressed in foreign fashions, these men had arrived at the palace more than a week earlier, proclaiming the coming of the king of the Jews. They spoke to Herod, wanting to know where the baby could be found, and Herod promised to let them know if his scouts returned any word. I'd seen little of them since, having locked themselves away in their quarters, but following their escort now, they were ecstatic. The Magi were led into the banquet hall where three chairs waited. I hopped up to sit on the table between them as they spoke of their eagerness to find the Lord. How wonderful His coming was anticipated across the world, not solely in Judea.

Herod burst into the room, still dressed, looking frazzled. The wise men stood and bowed as the king sat and folded his hands on the table. His right hand passed through my foot, which dispersed around the physical matter into a cloud of spiritual essence. I pulled away and the essence drew back together to reform my foot. Herod's eyes narrowed and he rubbed his hand.

"My honored guests, I understand you wished to see me," Herod said, laying it on thick.

The one dressed in sunset hues with skin the color of night replied, "Surely you have seen the star? It is a beacon! The child has been born this night!"

Herod's eyes simmered. "So, your so-called 'King of Kings' has arrived." The Magi nodded in unison, the motion almost absurd. "I wonder, how do you know this child will become king? You see, I am king of this land, and plan to be for quite some time. I am sure wise men realize there can be only one king." Irked at their silence, he continued, "I will not bow down to a mere child who should be kissing my ... hand."

"Your majesty, this child is no servant. He is the living God. He is going to save the world; all must bow before Him."

Herod smiled in a manner that seemed to frighten the men. "Living God. You mean ... the son of David? The promised messiah of God's people?" They nodded again. "Of course, it makes sense now. When you first told me of this child, I thought him simply one who would rebel and try to take the throne from me; but this, this is different."

The Magi didn't seem to register his sarcasm. The one with slightly lighter skin and a jewel on his forehead said, "Yes, but we must know where the child has been born. Forgive our impatience, highness, but we have journeyed far and waited long. We would like to greet the newborn Savior tonight."

Herod's lips stretched as though he were licking his teeth behind them. "Of course. As you requested, I have consulted my high priest, and it is written the child will be born in a town called Bethlehem, just a short way south of our great city. The night is yet new; if you leave now, you might find him before the sun rises." The wise men bowed and thanked the king. I caught the look of malice in Herod's eyes as he added, "When you have found him, return here and tell me where he is, that I too may go and pay my respects."

The men agreed and, with Herod's leave, started out for Bethlehem. It was obvious something wasn't right. I followed Herod back up the stairs, hoping I was just paranoid and my suspicions were wrong. On the secret third floor, though, he confirmed them.

Herod spoke to the guards in the inner doorway to his bed-chamber. "Three Magi travel to Bethlehem in search of a newborn. Take some men and follow them. Find out where this child is … then kill them." I was aghast. "When it's done, kill the child, his parents and any others who see you. No one lives."

When the guard's eyes widened, Herod leaned in close. "I will not risk my kingdom and all I have worked to build here over some fanatic prophecy threatening me from ages past. The child cannot usurp my throne if he is dead." The guard still hesitated. "Defend your king, Praetorian. This threat is as real as any army besieging our walls. If you return without infant's blood on your sword, you will face an end far worse than the one you failed to deliver." Herod stepped into his room and in a swirl of robes, slammed the door behind him.

I shot from the palace like a hurling star, beating my wings for Bethlehem. How could Herod do this? The ruler of such a holy city, the destination of countless pilgrimages, and he was going to kill the Savior of mankind to protect his title! Was his lust for power so great? It was inconceivable that a ruler could be so foolish and greedy, but many things suddenly made sense: the corruption of the council, the poor being sold as slaves, the rampant class segregation. The city was a glorified façade barely concealing a hideous monster, a fitting reflection of Herod himself. Ireneus, the shopkeepers in the marketplaces, the wealthy upper city citizens— so many contributed to its vileness. My mind was still racing as I reached Bethlehem and found Michael still in the stable.

"Michael! We must move the Son!" I cried as I landed.

Michael caught me with both arms. "Move Him? What has happened?"

I only had to think about it to see his eyes grow wide, but I told him everything anyway. His eyes closed and the spiritual plane resounded with his voice crying out for Gabriel and Raphael. He looked at me and said, "You've done well. Do not fear; I have an idea."

I looked over at the holy family, ignorant of the dangers aligning around them. The baby was asleep, though curious townsfolk still lurked near the door. Raphael soon appeared, followed closely by Gabriel. Both had weapons drawn, but retracted them when they saw us.

Raphael groaned in disappointment. "Please tell me this was not a test run."

Michael explained what had happened and outlined his plan. Gabriel stood vigil in the stable while the rest of us flew back toward Jerusalem. Taking the form of shepherds, we anxiously awaited the Magi on a hill overlooking the road. But in the spiritual plane, travel is so much faster that I had beaten them to Bethlehem by hours. After the initial anticipation passed in silence, we calmed and shared stories of our time on Earth. When it was my turn, I spoke of Jerusalem and my discovery of its corruption. I spoke of Ireneus and Herod, the way the poor were treated, and the hoarding of wealth in the palace.

"The fallen must love such a place," Raphael commented.

It was as though he'd smacked me in the face. "Michael! I almost forgot! Earlier tonight, I saw one of them. I'm not sure who it was yet, but I will find out."

Michael said, "Do not confront him when you do. Call us before you make a move. We can't risk losing you, Sabrael, especially in light of tonight's events."

I looked away as three figures caught my eye, nearing us on the road. "Michael…"

Raphael said, "For a bunch of old men, they made good time."

"Follow my lead," Michael said. "Once they are gone, cover yourselves in lesions."

"Lesions?" I asked, disgusted. "Why?"

"Trust me."

When the Magi reached the hill, Michael walked down to greet them. "My lords, please halt! You are Magi? Wise men who know all, yes?"

The man with the jewel in his forehead replied, "We do not know all, but yes, we are Magi. Pardon us, but we are in a great hurry."

"Come to seek the infant king?" Michael asked.

They shared a look. "We go to Bethlehem in His honor. How did you know?"

"We have been there already. You will reach Him soon. I bring you a warning though. Take great care, for there is one who even now hunts you."

The wise men again looked at each other in confusion. "Of whom do you speak, shepherd? We have just come from King Herod's palace and heard nothing of this."

Michael said, "You heard nothing because you were in the presence of the very man who has ordered your deaths. Along with the deaths of the one you seek and His family."

The Magi laughed. "How could one such as you know this?"

With a smile, Michael doffed his disguise and spread his wings wide, his white glow illuminating the night as his matter shifted to his own likeness. All three men fell to their knees before him. Michael said, "Those like me know many things."

He motioned for Raphael and me to join him and we did so, revealing our own true likenesses. The wise men praised God and gazed at us in awe. Uncomfortable under their stares, I kept my gaze lowered.

Michael continued, "Go now to the stable under the light in the sky, and you will find Him there lying in a manger. Worship Him as you will, but heed our words. Stay in Bethlehem tonight if you can, and when you return home, do not come this way. Give Jerusalem a wide berth and your lives will be spared."

The Magi bowed and thanked us, promising to abide Michael's word. Once they were out of sight, the three of us altered our appearances again, adding the boils Michael requested. Returning to our seats in the grass, we awaited the coming of the king's guard.

It was nearly dawn when we finally heard the clatter of hooves and armor coming up the road. "Get up," Michael said. "When they come in sight, act as though we are lepers fleeing the town. I will talk to them."

Raphael laughed. "This is your great plan?"

Michael smiled and said, "Just do as I say."

The three of us blocked the road, covered in lesions. To enhance the appearance of leprosy in this ruse, we also loosened our skin and added serious necrosis to our faces and extremities. I doubt there's ever been a leper living in such an advanced state of decay. The clatter grew louder and the outlines of men on horseback appeared. A voice yelled, "Move aside! The king's royal guard approaches." Michael stood directly in their path, and the man shouted again, "I said move, wretch! We will strike you down." Michael held his ground, the group charging on. I cringed as it seemed Michael would surely be trampled, but the lead horse suddenly reared up and the pack halted in a frenzy of yells and whinnies.

The head guard drew his sword, thrusting the point to Michael's throat. "You interfere with the king's orders, whelp. This display has bought you your death." Before he could strike though, Michael started to wail.

"Oh, masters, you must help me! The whole town is plagued! Ravaged by leprosy! I cannot bear it any longer! Strike me down; end my suffering."

"Leprosy?" the lead guard asked, his horse backpedalling. "Impossible. The palace has not been informed."

Michael seemed oblivious. "I beg you; stay far from Bethlehem! Spare yourselves this fate! The entire town rots with rancid death! Release me of my sickness and then return to the place from whence you came!"

I kept my gaze on the guards, struggling not to laugh at Michael. Then Raphael moaned. I glanced over to see rotten teeth falling out of his bleeding gums. He clamped a hand over his mouth, but as he put pressure on his face, two of his fingers snapped clean off. He stared at them in surprise, then wailed louder. I bit the inside of my cheek so hard I tasted blood.

The guards cried out in disgust. One retched. Even so, the lead guard said, "We are under the king's orders and must proceed."

Michael grabbed the guard's gloved hand, pulling the man within inches of the sores on his face. "What is so important in that town that you would risk this?"

"We seek three wise men that came this way only a short time ago."

"Wise men?" Michael shouted. "No wise man would enter that place! We have seen no one come this way, and we started on this road at sundown." Michael coughed and spat blood, brought his face closer. "No quarry is worth this!"

One of the guards spoke up. "Perhaps we should wait. The king did order them to return to Jerusalem. Why not let them come to us? It would be faster than searching the entire town."

The lead guard looked again at Raphael, who nursed a newly burst lesion on his face. I felt as though I too should be making a scene, but it was hard enough simply controlling my laughter. "We will await their return at the gates of Jerusalem."

"Thank you, master!" Michael shouted. "The only joy left to me is saving the lives of your men."

The lead guard turned back to Michael, pressed the sword to his throat again. "Do not count your blessings, old man. If the Magi return and tell me you were lying, I will personally make sure you rot before the crowds in Jerusalem."

Michael replied, "If they came this way, you will never see them again. I promise."

The guards turned their horses, and the clatter of armor and hooves receded down the road. We waited until they were out of earshot before letting loose our laughter.

It was done; we saved the Son's life from the first threat! Gabriel visited Joseph in a dream and suggested he take the holy family to Egypt until the danger from Herod had passed. Under a brightening sky, I said goodbye to my brothers for a second time that night and returned to spiritual form.

Spreading my wings, I soared back to Jerusalem, passing over the troop of guards retreating to the city. I was sorry they were made to await the arrival of those who would never come, but it was unavoidable. I hoped Herod would not have them put to death, but in my newly informed opinion of the king, I doubted he would let this pass.

I flew through the palace gates in the golden light of dawn and traversed the empty halls. The palace was deserted, even the usual night servants asleep by that time. Not wanting to wake Theokritus or Helena when I reached my apartment, I remained in the spiritual plane and slipped in under the door. Rising into the room, I called matter to me. But as my hearing entered the physical plane, a voice spoke from behind me.

"Sabrael. What kept you?"

I spun just in time to see the sneer on Astoreth's face before he launched himself at me. The two of us slammed into the floor and the room went dark as my physical form locked in. I kicked Astoreth off me. My fallen brother's face was his own, but he wore the body and clothes of a court official.

I jumped up and my blade shot into my hand, glinting in the narrow strip of dawn's light. "Astoreth. It was you I saw last night."

He rose to his feet, spiked mace ready. "I waited for you to come knocking. You disappointed me. Now I find you keeping human pets in your bed." He clicked his tongue. "Didn't you hear what happened the last time an angel enjoyed a human that way? And you with a man *and* a woman. Naughty, naughty."

"You are sick. And they're not pets."

He smiled. "I was going to kill them before you got here, but I thought it'd be more fun to let you watch. Make you suffer a little for what you did to me." He traced a finger down his face and the matter shifted to reveal the mottled scar where Hananel's sword dug deep.

From the corner of my eye, I saw my friends sit up, horror on their faces. Theokritus held Helena behind him as she clung to his body and looked over his shoulder at me. "Whose room were you in last night?" I demanded. "Who among the court serves you?"

Astoreth lunged and our weapons rang. Warm spit hit my face. I staggered back and as I wiped my eyes, my right side exploded in pain. Spikes cut deep into flesh and splintered bone. I cried out and hit the floor. Helena screamed. The bloodied mace rushed toward my face as I opened my eyes again. I brought my sword up and barely deflected the blow. Reforming my shattered ribs, I leapt back to my feet.

"There's not just one," Astoreth said. "The court is completely under our control."

He charged again and I threw him to the floor. He rolled up, but I pounced on him, pinning him under my knee and flicking away his mace with my sword. Retracting my blade, I drove my fist into his face over and over until my knuckles ached. "Who?" I yelled. "Tell me!"

He spat blood and broken teeth, laughed. "That is the least of your worries, 'Lord Aegyus.' Soon, we'll darken the skies over Jerusalem and you will all perish. This war is finally about to turn in our favor. There's nothing you can do."

Before I could question him further, his mace skittered across the floor into his hand, driven by some unseen force. Instinctively, I punched my sword into his chest and retracted it in the blink of an eye. Astoreth cried out, swung the mace at my head. I ducked, then plunged my hand into the wound and ripped the beating heart from his chest. A horrible, wrenching cry escaped him, impossibly loud, as blood gushed up from the hole, spreading in a pool of glistening crimson.

Helena crushed her face to Theokritus's chest, wailing.

Astoreth's muscles strained against me until the heart finally beat its last in my hand. It felt as though his body deflated beneath me. The light of life faded from his eyes and he disappeared into himself. It was exactly as Michael had said.

"Astoreth?" I asked. "If you hear me, blink." He didn't.

Blood seeped across the floor around us. Not good. I knew I had to cover all the evidence of what happened. We couldn't afford to let anyone know of our presence. The skirmish with Astoreth was proof of that. At least I no longer needed to wonder who the fallen angel across the courtyard had been.

"L-Lord Aegyus?"

I looked up at Theokritus on the bed. I'd forgotten they were there. "Oh Theokritus, Helena. I am so sorry."

Theokritus looked at Astoreth's body, his eyes moving to the heart still clutched in my hand, blood dripping down my wrist. What was I going to tell Michael? What would he say when he found out humans had seen me kill one of our brothers? Helena whimpered into Theokritus's chest, terrified. Finally she turned her brown eyes toward me and, voice quivering, asked, "Is that really you?"

"Of course it is, dear Helena. I know this looks horrible, but please let me try to explain." How could I possibly? I hadn't the slightest clue how to begin.

Theokritus said, "Perhaps you might start with that." He pointed behind me.

In the reflection of the gold-plated wall, I saw Theokritus and Helena, but even closer, a robed, winged angel with glowing blue eyes pinning a dead human to the floor.

Oh God. Michael ... forgive me.

CHAPTER THIRTEEN

"What did you tell them?" Michael asked. In the spiritual plane, we could talk in private, though the holy family slept only a few feet away.

"To stay in the apartment, prevent anyone from entering until I return."

How could I have been so careless? I hadn't even realized that in rushing the transition to the physical plane to defend myself, the likeness I created would default to my own. My friends didn't just see me kill. They saw the real me; the winged angel, not the Athenian man. Michael warned us about letting humans know we were there. I failed my brothers again, just as in the first battle with the fallen.

"You did not fail us, Sabrael," Michael said. "You kept yourself alive. That's what's important." He scratched the back of his head and stopped pacing. "We need to bring Astoreth to a safe place so I can find out exactly what he was bragging about."

"I told you; he faded when I took his heart. How can he tell you anything?"

"Simple. I give him a new heart, then remove it when I find out what I need to know."

The thought was monstrous. Was this to be the fate of all our brothers we encountered? Astoreth's dying scream—that inhuman screech when his heart was wrenched from his chest—haunted my thoughts. That, along with my guilt.

Michael continued, "Go back to Jerusalem. I cannot leave the Son, especially now. I will send Gabriel to help you move Astoreth. When I am able to slip away, I will question him."

"What about Theokritus and Helena? What do I tell them?"

Michael shook his head. Searched the face of the sleeping baby for an answer. "You trust them?"

"Completely," I replied.

"Then for now, just make sure nothing happens to them. If Astoreth found you, other demons may know where you are as well."

"The thought has occurred to me." I left him and flew out into the day.

Everything happened so quickly the night before; I was only now sorting it out. Was it possible Astoreth had not controlled a court member, but had been posing as one himself? Had he been watching me this whole time? I had the thought—the hope, even—that Astoreth and Ireneus might be the same person and I was now free of both. But if that was true, he definitely had ample time to alert the rest of the fallen to my presence. Even Lucifer.

Their secret bothered me. Whatever the fallen had found must be big or Astoreth wouldn't have boasted so brazenly of it. But what in all of creation could suddenly give the fallen so much confidence?

≈⋅⋅≈

I was overjoyed to find Theokritus and Helena safe in our apartment. Astoreth's body lay as I left it, but the river of blood across the floor had been cleaned. *Bless them, helping me even though they have every reason to run in fear,* I thought. I was terrified that Gabriel would order me to leave them and disappear rather than explain what they'd seen. Flying through the open window to wait for him inside, I prayed this wouldn't be so.

"Talk to me," Theokritus was saying when I came into the room.

Helena sat on the bed, her knees drawn up, arms wrapped around them. Her sodden gaze turned to the window, piercing me without her knowing. "All this time he has been lying! What is he, Theokritus? How can we trust him after this?"

"Did you not see his wings, love? What else can he be but an angel?"

"An angel?" She pointed at the corpse on the floor. "I fear Heaven if angels can do that."

Theokritus picked up the spiked mace. "This man would have killed him."

"Really? And just how do you kill an angel, Theokritus?"

Theokritus pointed at the crusted blood on the spikes. "Obviously he knew." Helena scoffed. "All right. If he was not here for Aegyus, then what? He was here for us?" Helena met his gaze again. "Lord Aegyus saved our lives either way."

"He cannot be an angel, Theokritus! This is crazy. Listen to yourself! Even if he is an angel, what are we supposed to do when he returns? It simplifies nothing!"

Theokritus placed Astoreth's mace back on the floor with a heavy clunk. Although my friends were confused, I was actually thankful my fallen brother had come in human form. Had it been a dead angel on the floor, wings and all, I'm not sure they could've handled it.

"Why must anything change?" Theokritus asked. "We've lived with Aegyus for months, and he has never shown us anything but friendship. If he is an angel, think of the blessing we have been given, meeting one of God's messengers on Earth!"

"And if he is not, think of the horror we face living with some damned creature that slaughters men in the light of dawn!"

A knock at the door silenced their conversation. Theokritus jumped up and rushed to brace the door. "Yes?" he called through it.

A familiar voice answered, "Where is the aristocrat? I must speak with him at once."

Helena growled at hearing the voice. "Tell him to go back to his own building and leave us alone." Theokritus waved a hand, motioning for her to be quiet. In answer, she threw one of the pillows at the door. Theokritus lunged to catch it, trying to give Helena a reprimanding look but managing only a restrained smile. I smiled at her reaction as well; I felt the same way knowing Ireneus was still around.

"Our master is out, lord. Perhaps we could deliver a message for you?" Theokritus said.

The disgusted sigh was audible even to me. "I will return later," Ireneus answered.

After the footsteps faded down the hall, Theokritus sent the pillow spinning through the air to hit Helena. Her hair flew out to the sides as she flopped back onto the bed laughing.

Theokritus said, "Now who's crazy? If that hit the door, he would have had us hung."

"Oh, calm down. I was aiming at you, not the door," she said.

Theokritus mocked surprise, but I could see the laughter in his eyes. He leapt onto the bed and playfully hit her with the pillow. Helena finally grabbed it, throwing it aside and pulling him down into a kiss. I was thankful for this moment of relief.

A hand grabbed my shoulder. I spun, sword ready, and returned my hearing to the spiritual plane. "Whoa, Sabrael." Gabriel stood at the window, hands held up. "How are you, brother? You seem tense."

Relieved, I retracted my sword. "Worried. My friends are truly shaken by all that has happened here."

"I should think so," he said. "In all my journeys to deliver messages to the humans, they've always been frightened by my appearance. Your friends not only saw an angel, but an angel in battle with another angel."

"Actually, they saw an angel tear the heart out of a man." I motioned toward Astoreth.

Gabriel's eyes widened. "You do know how to create a mess."

Looking at Astoreth, Theokritus held Helena and whispered in her ear as she nodded. "What is to become of them?"

Gabriel replied, "Your focus right now needs to be on getting Astoreth out of here." He crouched beside our fallen brother. His glowing green eyes narrowed, and he dipped his fingers into the hole in Astoreth's chest. "How grievous things have come to this."

I stepped to Gabriel's side. "Where do we take him?"

"The cave where we first arrived on Earth. Michael wants us to hide him there." Gabriel looked at my friends. "You said you can trust them?"

"Who do you think cleaned up the blood and kept the room clear all day?"

Gabriel smiled. "Good you found such loyal company. You are truly blessed."

"I couldn't agree more."

"Since they already saw you, perhaps the best thing is to take physical form and fly Astoreth's body out the window," Gabriel said.

"What if more of the fallen are in Jerusalem? We cannot risk them seeing us."

Gabriel replied, "I made a few passes over the city. We should be safe for now, but it won't be long before Astoreth's absence is noticed, especially given the Son's arrival."

"Let me at least speak to them alone before you show yourself."

"I think that would be best. We do not want to frighten them any more," Gabriel said.

Gathering my resolve, I called matter to me, forming my true appearance instead of Aegyus. With particles still collecting on me, I said, "Theokritus, Helena, do not be afraid."

They looked up in surprise to see me enter the physical plane. Theokritus pulled Helena behind him, shielding her. "Stay back," he said. I wasn't sure if he was talking to her or me.

"My friends. Please."

"Forgive me, but after this morning, I am not even sure what you are, let alone what you are capable of," he said.

"You must know by now I would never hurt you."

Helena's eyes were fixed on me. "How do we know that is not another lie, that you are not some demon? How can we trust anything you say?"

I was about to answer when they looked past me. "You know you can trust him because you know in your heart that his words are true," Gabriel said as he formed beside me.

I think I was more awed by the way his body formed than they were. It was as though he stepped into the physical plane; matter forming from front to back instead of all at once like it did on me. No wonder he'd so often been the one chosen to bring God's messages to His people.

"This is my brother, Gabriel. He is here to help me remove the body from this place. As you are not afraid of me, do not fear him."

Helena's eyes bore into me. "What makes you think we're not afraid of you?"

I was mortified. "My dear Helena, surely you don't mean that. I realize my appearance may seem strange after knowing me for so long in another form, but I needed to keep the truth from you. Those who want me dead might otherwise have come for you in order to reach me."

Theokritus asked, "What exactly are you?"

"I am an angel. A servant of the Almighty God."

Helena said, "Impossible! Angels do not murder!"

Gabriel interrupted, "All will be explained in time. But we must get this body out of Jerusalem now, before his friends come."

"Why kill him?" Helena asked. Theokritus took her hand and whispered into her ear, but she pulled away. "No, I will not help until I know. If you are an angel, why did you not talk to him? God commanded us not to murder, and yet you claim to be His servant when you spilt the blood of that man for no apparent reason."

I was losing the battle for her trust and I knew it. "I had no choice. This man is not what he appears to be," I said. I looked at Gabriel. *Can I please just tell them?* I thought. To my relief, he nodded. "This body is not truly his own. It is missing some parts, namely his wings."

Theokritus looked closer at Astoreth's body. "You mean, he was…?"

"Another angel, yes," Gabriel replied. "Fallen, actually. From grace, and damned. But he is not dead. He is still in there, staring at you right now."

Theokritus jumped back in horror. He looked at me for confirmation, and when I nodded, he said, "Then what are we waiting for?"

Helena came to my side. She looked at Astoreth, then Gabriel, then me. She reached up and gently touched my face. "I do not understand. How can it really be you?"

I took Helena's hand. "Trust us, Helena. Trust me. I am still the same, nothing has changed. You agreed to follow me once when the future was unclear, and I brought you to this palace. I am asking you to follow me once again. Help us now."

Helena smiled and tears rose in her eyes. "Your eyes are so beautiful." I had forgotten they would think our eyes strange. "All right, Aegyus. I will follow you again."

I hugged her tight, relishing the feel of her body against mine. "You no longer have to call me that. Aegyus doesn't exist. My name is Sabrael."

Theokritus laughed. "Everything about Greece was a story then? You must be connected to higher power to know so well a place you have never been."

Gabriel insisted, "Time grows short."

I moved to Astoreth's head and wrapped my arms under his, Gabriel doing the same at his legs, and we lifted our fallen brother off the floor. He felt much heavier dead than when he tackled me that morning. "What is your plan?" Theokritus asked.

"We must take him out of the city. Easiest way is to fly over the walls," I said.

Theokritus shook his head. "You will never make it without being seen."

"Gabriel said none of the other fallen are in Jerusalem yet."

"I wasn't talking about angels," he said. "Look how many servants are in the courtyard, not to mention the scouts in the towers over the palace. If you wish to keep your presence a secret, something less conspicuous is in order."

He was right. This wasn't going to be as easy as we thought. Sensing Gabriel's impatience growing, I looked at Theokritus. "What do you suggest?"

⊱✦✦⊰

Theokritus's plan wasn't bad. Concealed beneath a mound of sheets piled into a linen cart, Astoreth's body was well-hidden as we pushed the cart through the palace gate. The hardest part had been getting him to the first floor, but even that went without mishap. We rolled the wooden cart through the crowd in the market square, the wheels protesting the distance. Some seemed confused why two nobles and a pair of servants were carting laundry through the city, but no one dared ask. To disturb a noble meant possible arrest. I hated to think what would happen to us if anyone knew it wasn't laundry.

We were almost free, the Jaffa Gate looming ahead, when a man bigger than even Theokritus stumbled out of one of the buildings into the cart. Horrified, I watched as robes and sheets spilled out to blanket the road, the crowd stopping to gawk. The four of us dropped instantly, hurling linens back into the cart to cover the body exposed at its bottom.

"Are you hurt?" Helena asked the man, plucking the sheets from the breeze.

He blinked, dazed. Bits of meat clung to his mottled chin. His mouth opened to expose rotted teeth, a prominent gap. "Seven," he grumbled, his breath rank despite the wind.

A Roman soldier pushed through the crowd. "What is all this?"

Theokritus stood, towering over the guards. "Forgive us. It was an accident. We have everything under control."

The soldier deepened his voice. "Clear out! Now! Or you will all answer to the king!"

The drunkard on the ground squinted at the cart. "Is that—"

A sheet suddenly whipped over the man's face. The linen enveloped his head and Gabriel scrambled to free him. "Oh, forgive me. This wind!"

It was a perfect distraction. Seemed like an accident, and when the man finally freed his head, he'd forgotten all about what he had seen.

We tilted the cart onto its wheels and dropped the last sheets back into it. The crowd dispersed, the scene already forgotten. Burly drunk rose to his feet and waved a hand as though trying to swat a bug. He grumbled some farewell and staggered down the street, bumping into people every few steps.

"Always an adventure with you," Gabriel muttered as we continued to the gate.

A short distance outside the city, Gabriel said, "The guards no longer watch us. Sabrael and I will take him from here. You two should return to the palace and await our return."

Helena said, "Hurry back."

"I will not be far behind," I told her.

We hoisted Astoreth out of the cart and changed our bodies back to our angelic forms. Theokritus and Helena marveled at the sight, then headed back to the city. Gabriel and I spread our wings and lifted off the ground to soar for the cavern.

I mentioned before that there was a breeze in the city. Outside though, without the protection of the buildings and walls, the wind was rapacious. Every gust nearly tore Astoreth from our grasp, tossed us off course, and if one of us moved even a bit faster than the other, Astoreth's body pulled taut and nearly brought us down. I never imagined flying in the physical plane would be so difficult. When I saw a hawk gliding through the wind with ease, mocking us, I resolved right then to master physical flight.

The cavern was exactly as I remembered it. The trickle of water, the pool, the high ceiling and the echoes—all just as we'd left them. I switched my vision to the spiritual plane as we set Astoreth near the pool, propping him against the wall so he appeared to be relaxing. Except for the gaping hole in his chest and the blood crusted on his hair and clothes. Though his eyes didn't move, I saw in them what I thought might be consciousness. Was Gabriel correct; was Astoreth actually staring out at us? The concept terrified me, though I knew it was too dark to see in the physical plane either way.

"Where do you think he went?" I asked Gabriel.

"I do not want to know," he replied, seating himself in front of Astoreth. "I am more concerned whether he is trying to escape."

"It is not a matter of escaping," a voice echoed around us.

Michael flew into the cavern to land beside Gabriel, his wings stirring the air. "He's not trapped inside like his body's some husk. It's still him, he just can't control it now." The matter of his body dissipated, and he beckoned us to do the same.

"We can't just talk in the physical plane?" I asked, returning to the spiritual.

"I don't want Astoreth listening in."

"What will you do with him?" Gabriel asked. "I thought you were leaving for Egypt with the Son."

Michael nodded. "Tomorrow night. I will find out as much as I can before then. If I have not yet gleaned the secret of which he spoke, I will hide him away until I can return."

His glowing gray eyes were fixed on our fallen brother, and I thought the sight might be clouding his thinking. Leaving Astoreth there until he returned seemed an incredible waste of time. This was too important.

"Perhaps I should question him," I offered. "We're not far from Jerusalem; I could find out the secret while you are gone."

"No, it would not be safe. Even if you did learn the secret, I wouldn't be able to leave the Son long enough to deal with it. We should wait until I return."

Michael and Gabriel continued talking, I believe about my apartment and whether Gabriel thought Theokritus and Helena could be trusted. I wasn't really listening. I was furious with Michael for the first time in all of my existence. After all the things I'd been through—fighting and defeating Astoreth when none of the others had even been confronted by the fallen yet, finding human friends that could be trusted with all this, bringing Astoreth to the cavern—Michael didn't trust me to even talk to Astoreth? How could he think so little of me? My brothers spoke in whispers, probably discussing how to keep me away from important tasks from now on. With balled fists, I gathered matter to my eyes, the cavern disappearing into darkness. If I couldn't see them, at least I had the illusion of privacy.

How could Michael treat me like this? He told me he was proud of me, that I was doing a good job! Fuming, I thought, *Can you not hear the workings of my mind now, Michael? Or are you simply ignoring me?* I checked the spiritual plane. He didn't even acknowledge me.

I walked away, trying to calm my thoughts and convince myself there was a reason for refusing to let me handle the interrogation. After a short time, Gabriel's hand touched my shoulder. He was smiling. It didn't help.

"Oh, quit sulking," Gabriel said. "You are being given a task greater than the one from which you are being kept." I tried to read from his eyes what he could mean. "I must return now. Our work together is finished for the time being."

I sighed, venting my frustration. "Take care. Perhaps we can do this again."

He laughed and said, "Next time, you clean up your own mess." I smiled as he spread his wings, flying silently out of the cavern.

I stepped back to where Michael crouched in front of our slain kin. He turned, his stony eyes locking onto my own.

"Do not be angry with me. I know you only desire to help, but there are things I must hear for myself, things that cannot merely be relayed. The secret of which Astoreth spoke is only one matter I need to ask him about. To have you question him in my absence would leave some things unanswered." He stood and placed a hand on my shoulder. "You are right; it would be quicker for you to question him while I am gone, and depending on what the secret turns out to be, we may need that time. But I have an ability you do not. If he lets even one detail cross his mind, I will catch it. Do you see why it is simply better if I do this?"

I was profoundly disappointed. Again I found myself hating my inability to read minds. I was also extremely embarrassed by my childish tantrum. He was right; Astoreth wasn't one of the more clever fallen. He would almost certainly let something slip into his thoughts when questioned. Still, I was upset that I would never get to hear what Astoreth had to say.

"Yes, you will," Michael said.

"Michael, stop!" I said. "I don't know what you're thinking; allow me the same courtesy."

Michael held up his hands. "You are right. I will try to ignore the voice in my head that is yours. But I promise to tell you everything I learn from Astoreth. Besides, you have a much more important task than prodding a demon for information. You will not even miss it when you hear what I have for you."

I doubted that. What job was more important than questioning Astoreth, unless I was to take Michael's place at the side of the Son until he was finished?

Michael asked, "Have you forgotten there are two souls in Jerusalem who learned of our presence here? Your friends are in danger now, Sabrael. Their knowledge of us could bring them under attack, and they cannot stand against the fallen."

He was right. If the fallen found out about my friends, Theokritus and Helena would surely become targets. Lucifer would want to know how many of us were on Earth, where exactly we were, and he would never believe that my friends were ignorant of this information. A sudden fear gripped me. I prayed the fallen were nowhere near the palace at that moment. "What are you saying?"

"That Theokritus and Helena cannot remain as they are now."

"I will not send them back where I found them. I promised to make sure they have money and shelter, and…" Michael was laughing. "How can you laugh? You are telling me to abandon my friends, the ones who accepted me and taught me how to be a human!"

Michael sat, his laughter trailing off. "I said nothing of the sort. Sit down."

Lowering myself beside him, I realized Astoreth's eyes were now on me. It was unnerving, whether he could see me or not. A fat beetle burrowed out of his chest, slick with gore. I wondered if he felt it eating away at his flesh. I could almost hear his screams when I met his eyes, devoid of life and yet afraid in the darkness.

"Sabrael! Do not do that, brother. He wanted your heart. Probably Theokritus and Helena's as well. Remember that."

Making my hand physical, I plucked away the insect. "Doesn't mean we can't show some semblance of mercy."

Michael said nothing until I met his stare. "I prayed to the Father about what to do with your friends. We cannot leave them unprotected, of course, but our mission is to guard the Son, and we cannot divert our efforts toward defending them.

"Although God will not speak to me directly, while praying, I remembered something He told me before we left the kingdom. There is an ability we were given, one I forgot because I did not believe we would need to use it. I believe my remembering it now is how He answered my prayer."

"What is it?" I asked.

"We possess the ability to make humans into warriors of God. Should they agree to it, you have my permission to offer this gift to your friends."

"'Warriors of God?' What does that mean? You just said they can't defend themselves, and now you want them to fight alongside us? How can that be better than hiding them somewhere with enough resources so they never have to resurface?"

Michael shook his head. "You do not understand. They could never fight as they are now, with only their natural abilities. You will explain our purpose and the dangers they would face. If they then want to join us and swear to protect the Son at all costs, you will bestow on them all the knowledge and skill God has given us the power to impart. You will bless them with the ability to not only defend themselves, but to aid you in your work in Jerusalem."

I couldn't believe what I was hearing. "Why would I offer them such a thing? I've wanted to tell them more about us, yes, but you're asking me to bring them into a war that is not theirs. To subject them every day to that," I said, pointing at Astoreth. "What do you think Lucifer will do to them if he discovers they're not only aware of the war, but *joined* in opposition to him? Humans look to us as guardians. I cannot invite them to risk unimaginable horrors just because they happened to see me protecting them. I would be betraying them."

"I understand how you feel. But are they truly safer remaining defenseless, hiding and praying the fallen won't find them? Is it not better to fight and risk dying than to do nothing and have no hope at all? At least this way they would have a chance."

"Michael, you do not even know if God truly answered you!"

"I know it was Him!" Michael yelled. The desperation in his eyes made me uncomfortable, but I said nothing. He took a breath and the fire left him. "It is not your choice, Sabrael. It's theirs. All you are to do is offer. What they decide is up to them."

CHAPTER FOURTEEN

The road outside Jerusalem was becoming familiar after flying over it so many times in the past two days. How could I
go through with this task given to me? I had yearned to explain
to Theokritus and Helena everything they'd now seen, but I never
wanted them to be part of it. With the ability to bless them into the
war came also the knowledge of what the blessing would bestow, and
though they would indeed be capable of defending themselves—
they would receive not only weapons of their own, but also the skills
necessary to use them—I did not relish the thought of my friends
in battle. True, I had only encountered exactly one of my fallen
brothers thus far but, as Gabriel said, the fallen would likely flock to
Jerusalem now that Astoreth was missing.

Should I take heart in the fact that it was God's decision to
bring humans into the war? That He would even give us this ability
lent a certain degree of comfort. Did that mean they would have
His direct protection? We weren't really concerned with the countless humans allied with Lucifer and his demons; would our warriors
be equally ignored? Numerous futures existed for Theokritus and

Helena if they agreed to join us, but only two if they did not—a life of hiding or a swift, brutal death. Still, the thought that my offer could eventually call down death on my friends tortured me as the city came into view ahead.

⸺✥ ✥⸻

The sun rested on the horizon by the time I decided to ask. Bathed in the amber of desert twilight, Theokritus and Helena sat in shock at the proposition. Their silence gave me hope, but I was determined to appear neutral so as not to sway them either way. As Michael said, the decision wasn't mine.

"You know we are here, and now you know why. That knowledge puts you in danger. All I am saying is that if you wish to defend yourselves and help us at the same time, you have that option. If you would rather remain out of harm's way, I can hide you with enough gold to last the rest of your lives. The choice is yours."

"But if we go into hiding, they could find us?" Helena asked.

She was too insightful for her own good. "Maybe. If they wanted to. But right now they have no reason to come looking. The only one who knows about you is Astoreth, and you saw the condition he is in. If you choose to hide, it's very likely you will remain safe."

Theokritus leaned back, his eyes moving to the ceiling as though imploring Heaven. Helena searched my face for some sign of a right answer. I wished I had one.

"What would we do if we join the war?" Theokritus asked. "Fight them as you did this morning? If that is what will be expected... We would not last more than a few moments."

I closed my eyes. He was forcing me to reveal something that would likely turn them toward joining the war. "If you join us, you will instantly receive the skill needed to wield your given weapons. Whether you will you ever use them is another question. This morning was my first battle since my arrival here."

"We will just know how to fight? Without training?" Theokritus asked.

"You should still train," I replied.

A warm breeze swept through the windows, teasing some of Helena's hair across her face. She flipped it back and asked, "If fighting is so rare, what else do you do?"

"Monitor the city. Listen to the court and their servants, try to catch any news that might help us protect the Son. I do whatever is necessary at the given time; there is no one answer to that question."

"Where is your sword?" Theokritus asked. "Why have we never seen you carrying it?"

I held out my arm and my sword extended like a serpent from my sleeve. Helena recoiled as the blade passed in front of her; Theokritus stared in fascination. As the handle reached my hand, I grabbed it and set the weapon on the table between us.

Theokritus asked, "May I?"

I nodded. Theokritus picked up the weapon and held it in front of him.

"It's light," he said, obviously surprised.

"But stronger than any metal on Earth. It will never dull, never break, and if you decide to join us, your weapons would be the same. Though again, you may never have to use them."

Helena asked, "You keep it in your sleeve?"

"Not exactly. It stays in the spiritual plane and only becomes physical when I need it."

"Spiritual plane?"

"You will understand if you join us. If you do not, you will never have to."

Theokritus hefted the sword once more, then placed it back on the table. Helena said, "I cannot believe the Messiah is here. The prophecies are coming to pass! That is the purpose of everything you are doing here, to protect Him?"

"Yes. That is the important thing to understand: You will not be joining us to fight the fallen. You will be joining us to serve the Almighty."

I meant to remain neutral, but looking at Helena, I felt like the decision had just been made. I knew even then it was really only Helena's decision. From our time observing humans, it was clear that when a couple must make a choice, men tend to do what the women want.

Helena asked, "Can we think about it? Give our answer tomorrow?"

I nodded and picked up my sword, which cast the light of the setting sun onto the ceiling. When I retracted it, Theokritus clapped and said, "Amazing."

Helena watched him in brooding silence.

I spent the night on the balcony, overlooking the courtyard in the form of Aegyus and praying my friends would make the right decision. Was there a right decision? The bitter cold clawing at my face and hands bespoke an ending, the death of our lives as they were. Whichever way they chose, nothing would ever be the same.

Near daybreak, the sounds of stirring drew me back inside. Helena was already seated at the table, hair pressed flat against her head on one side, eyes barely open.

"Good morning."

"Morning," she replied without sitting up. Resting her head on her outstretched arm, she seemed oblivious to the pear juice dribbling down her cheek.

I smiled. "My dear, you are making a mess in your hair."

She shrugged and waved the fruit, flicking more juice to the floor. "It is a bathing day."

Theokritus returned from the bathroom and sat across from me, obviously more awake than Helena. "I like you better with wings."

"I should hope so. This body can be changed; the wings are there to stay."

"What do you think, love?" he asked Helena. I looked to find her eyes closed and the pear lying beside her face. "She asleep again?" Theokritus asked. I already knew how their discussion went before Theokritus said, "We talked a long time, but I think she stayed up thinking it over the whole night."

I said, "No need to tell me your decision until both of you are ready. Take her to the bath house. We can talk when you get back."

Theokritus leaned over Helena to kiss her cheek. She inhaled deeply and stretched, tried to blink away sleep. He helped her up and led her out into the hallway.

Although Theokritus had not told me their decision, I saw the excitement in his eyes. I paced over the alabaster, wondering if I should dissuade them before it was too late. Of course it would be much happier for me with the two of them at my side, but the thought of them dying…

Arguments and questions roiled in my mind while I waited for my friends' return, driving me insane with anxiety about what lay just over the horizon. It became so unbearable that I drew my sword and ran through my old training routine to calm my nerves, but the tornado of questions just came whirling back and I paced again.

When the pair returned, I stepped out onto the balcony to allow them to dress. Servants in the courtyard below swept dust and sand from the walkways, tended the foliage in the gardens. A few court members and low-ranking officials strolled through, avoiding the servants as they discussed matters of the kingdom in hushed tones. I glanced across to the window where I'd first seen Astoreth, and again wondered into whose room it opened. Although Ireneus fostered an unmotivated contempt for me, I hesitated to believe he was the apartment's occupant. That would be too convenient. Better to keep my guard up against any other court members allied with the fallen, and it was especially important to keep my eyes open for another attack. Speaking of, I let the matter go from my eyes and scanned the courtyard for any disgraced brothers who might be watching. No one was there.

Theokritus and Helena soon joined me on the balcony. They wore brand new, expensive clothes. Helena's hair fell in tight braids from beneath the hood of a peplos. She wore a long chiton, a traditional Greek dress, its lavender folds draped all the way to the floor and even trailed behind her. The peplos was the same color, a band of deep green and gold along its edge running over her shoulders to her waistline. Her arms were bare to the shoulders, chest exposed to just above what would have been illegal in Jerusalem. Theokritus wore a light blue tunic with a golden sash, and over this, a mantle of a deeper hue.

"You look beautiful," I told Helena. Her cheeks colored a bit. "The two of you remind me of statues in Athens."

Theokritus smiled. "So strange to think you have never truly seen that city."

"We have decided to join you, Sabrael," Helena said, slipping her arm around Theokritus. "We wanted to look our best; to honor God and show Him our confidence."

I took her hand and kissed it. "I am sure He is smiling down upon you both."

The excited kiss they shared dispelled some of my worry. To see their happiness, their comfort with all that was about to happen, soothed me. They were like a couple about to be wed, nervous but exhilarated. They wanted to join us, to spend their lives defending God and the kingdom of Heaven, and I had no right to stop them. Seeing them there, dressed in fine clothes and prepared to make the transition into their new lives, I felt only joy that these two people, once lost and about to be killed or separated in slavery, had now been reborn and would be by my side for the rest of my time on Earth. Their worry didn't get in the way of their desire to serve God; why should I allow mine to prevent it?

"Then I suppose the time has come," I said.

Helena squeezed Theokritus's arm, and he smiled nervously. "We are ready."

⊷ ⊷

"Kneel."

Theokritus and Helena sank to their knees in the middle of the apartment, and I shifted the matter of my body to my true appearance. I stood before my friends as I somehow knew I was supposed to. The whole ritual was in my mind as Michael said it would be, and I marveled at God's power, able to impart the knowledge necessary for such things without our realizing it.

"Theokritus, Helena, today you become warriors in the service of the Almighty God. You have been called by Him to rise above the flock and become shepherds of your brothers and sisters. To protect them from the influence of those who would see them ruined, and to guide the light of Heaven onto them all."

The two of them smiled at each other. Theokritus made a face and Helena laughed, covering her mouth.

"The life of the Messiah is the most important life to ever come to the Earth. You have been asked to guard it with your own, to spend your days serving the living Lord and preparing the way for His rise to glory. Your God and His angels on Earth are asking you to join our war, and to fight to ensure the salvation of all people through the safe fulfillment of the prophecies."

I held out my hand to Theokritus, motioning for him to rise.

"In the name of the one true God, will you, Theokritus, give your life in the service of Heaven, fighting alongside the angels of the Heavenly host, to preserve the promise of peace for all mankind and to defend the world from the touch of the fallen?"

Theokritus nodded once, saying, "I swear I will."

I nodded and he knelt again. I motioned for Helena to rise and repeated the question.

Helena said, "I will, Sabrael." She knelt again, and I continued.

"Called to God's service, you have both willingly taken upon yourselves the responsibility of being leaders among mankind in the ways of the Almighty. Join me in prayer." All of us lowered our heads, and with hands folded I went on. "Almighty God, you have sent your blessing to these two people, and they have answered your call to take up arms in the struggle against Hell's power. We pray that you accept them into our ranks, and guide them to serve you well. Protect them in their days of service, and help them to always make the decisions that will lead them closer to you and out of the many perils they may face. Continue to shed your blessings upon them always, and lead us to grow as a group, working together in joy to defend the Earth and the kingdom of Heaven from the forces of Hell."

The three of us together said, "Amen."

I raised my arm and brought my sword into the physical plane. I lowered the blade between my friends and touched it to their shoulders.

"I, Sabrael, guardian of the first hall of Heaven and minister to God the Son on Earth, bless you warriors of light, to fight the fallen and defend the throne until death parts you of this world, in the name of God the Father, Son and Holy Spirit."

My weapon retracted, and I kissed their foreheads. "Rise, Theokritus and Helena, for you are now soldiers of the faith."

My companions stood and looked at each other in anticipation. After a few moments, Theokritus said, "Are you sure it is done? Nothing has changed."

Curious, I shifted my vision to the spiritual plane. Both Theokritus and Helena were glowing like no human I had ever seen before. Their souls seemed to have ignited inside their physical shells, burning brilliantly. I praised God, in awe at the sight, though I had no idea the extent of the changes in them.

"Believe me, it is done. I want you both to call your weapons."

They looked at me in confusion. "What do you mean?" Theokritus asked.

I extended my sword. "You both have weapons now in the spiritual plane. Bring them into this plane. You already know how to do it; just think about it."

Theokritus still looked confused, but Helena held out her arms and closed her eyes. Her eyebrows furrowed as she focused, and suddenly, a long, metal staff burst from her sleeve and she caught the end of it, swinging it to grab the other end. Theokritus stumbled back and Helena opened her eyes, just as surprised as he. They both looked at me with wide eyes. I smiled.

"Welcome to the war."

CHAPTER FIFTEEN

Newly dubbed warriors of light, Theokritus and Helena spent their first few weeks acclimating to their weapons. Luckily, the privacy of our palace apartment and its immense space made it the perfect training arena. Helena had her staff and Theokritus bore two axes, the curved blade of each the length of his forearm. The weapons also had hidden features; Theokritus's axes could connect at the handles to form a single blade, and Helena's staff released a scythe blade from the opposite end when knocked on a hard surface. How a scythe could be concealed inside a staff was a mystery, but there it was, the work of the Almighty's forge. In time, the two of them took up sparring to work on their new skills. Michael said they would receive all the necessary knowledge, and it seemed to be true. I still made sure there were no accidents, of course. There were awkward days when they attempted new strikes, but they quickly mastered the movements, as though they already knew them but had only forgotten. Their fights grew faster and more intense, and after only a few weeks, both were impressive warriors.

To prepare for the battles ahead however, they needed to learn to fight those who could do things impossible for a human. To prepare for the fallen, I knew they must face me.

Sometimes one-on-one and other times against them as a team, I joined their sparring using every trick I could muster. I let them hack off my limbs only to reform them without stopping my attack, shifted rapidly between the spiritual and physical planes to give the impression I was teleporting around them, attacked from the air and moved faster than humanly possible to force them to defend against strikes they couldn't track with their eyes. With time and lots of injuries, both Theokritus and Helena came to understand the use of both planes, and they learned to work together not only to attack, but also to defend each other.

Soon after the blessing, each of my brothers came to meet the new warriors, even Michael, all the way back from Egypt where he was protecting the Son. He told us of the Egyptians' religion, how the fallen had appeared ages before in the guise of gods, and the result was a different deity for everything. Signs of the true one, though present, were expertly woven into mythology.

Michael also passed on the information he managed to squeeze out of Astoreth. Apparently, Astoreth knew only that some secret was being kept by Lucifer and his closest counsel. It was something we couldn't fight or stop, and would spark the destruction of Heaven. Michael had interrogated Astoreth for a week before the distance between the cave and the Son became too great. On that last day, he removed Astoreth's heart and left him chained in the darkness alone. I wondered if I should visit him, if only to release him from his paralysis for a short time and let him move a bit, but as I thought this Michael shook his head. *It is the fate he chose, Sabrael,* his voice echoed in my mind.

I was delighted to learn that after meeting Theokritus and Helena, my brothers all returned to bless their own closest friends into the war. Our number rose to eighteen from our original seven,

Michael now the only angel without human warriors. The number of companions differed between us, but each one helped immensely, giving us more than just two eyes in each region. Theokritus and Helena were honored to have been the first and took it upon themselves to act as examples for all humans on our side. They thought of themselves, I think, as being observed at all times, though this was obviously not true. They sparred every day without fail, and when I needed something done, they were always on hand. Whatever perils lay ahead, they stood ready to face them with eager hearts and able hands.

Jerusalem also changed a great deal in that time. Herod the Great died only a few years after the birth of the Son, having left behind a legacy of opulence and brutality. When he learned of the Magi's flight on the night of the Son's birth, he became so enraged that he not only ordered the execution of every one of the guards Michael, Raphael and I turned back, but also the slaughter of every boy in Bethlehem younger than two. The royal guard descended on the area and took it a step further, murdering every male child they could find, regardless of age. Thankfully, the Son and His parents fled for Egypt a few hours before the massacre. Mothers and fathers were forced to watch as armored soldiers butchered their sons before them. One would think this insanity, ordering such a thing, but over the years Herod had ordered the deaths of two of his own sons and numerous wives after hearing only rumors of treasonous intent. Corinthus told me Herod had loved one of these wives dearly, but it didn't save her. One of the white towers near the palace was named for her: Mariamne's Tower.

The final years of Herod's reign were nightmarish for the people of Jerusalem. New laws placed an unbearable amount of tension on the city. Everyone was suspected of conspiracy, especially his remaining sons. As Herod's end neared, he had a great number of highly respected men from around the region arrested and brought to the hippodrome at Jericho, then ordered his soldiers to execute them at the moment of his own death in the hope that the tragedy would balance any elation the citizens harbored over his passing. When Herod finally died, his son Archilaus and sister Salome simply released the imprisoned, and the citizens celebrated his passing for many days and nights.

However, Herod's death sparked a great expansion of the Roman occupation of Jerusalem. With this influx of the empire, many of Herod's guests and personal officials were put to death. When that began happening, Theokritus, Helena and I abandoned the palace for a residence in the upper city. Each day I returned in the spiritual plane to monitor the new decision-makers, but it was only a short time before I no longer knew a single face. Whoever Astoreth's mystery insider had been, he was surely either dead or gone.

The three of us watched as Rome's power over the city became absolute and the people adapted to the Roman way of life, dressing in Roman fashions and attending theaters and sporting events of Roman origin. Roman soldiers took control of the streets, and all governmental matters were sent directly to Caesar. Jerusalem had become just another city in the empire.

Twelve years the three of us lived in the upper city. Twelve years without sign of the fallen or anything else concerning our mission to protect the Son. Our only contact was when the holy family visited Jerusalem every year to worship and observe the traditions of the Passover. It was always wonderful to see Jesus and his younger siblings, of which he had a few by that time, but the rest of the year seemed like wasted time. Each year when I asked how we could be of more help, Michael simply said, "Maintain your vigil here. Enjoy this time, for your reason for staying here will soon become clear, and the time for relaxing may be gone."

I couldn't help feeling, though, that my friends and I were missing out on the excitement I was sure my brothers were living. With each passing year, I felt more disconnected from my brothers and increasingly connected to the world of the humans. My time wasn't spent thinking about the war; it was spent greeting the merchants on my daily visits to the agoras, or ensuring our house wasn't burnt to the ground over some new law or revolt. At times I had to train just to remind myself this wasn't truly my life. When I only heard from my brothers once or twice a year, the rest of the time I simply felt … human.

But always we kept our vigil, Theokritus, Helena and I, going into the marketplace each day to watch for the fallen, sometimes remaining in the square in the hope that some official might take a stroll through the city and divulge some news. Though at first I feared Theokritus and Helena would come to regret becoming warriors of light, as they were never asked to do anything besides train, each of them remained thrilled to serve the Almighty in whatever way they could. I was grateful for their company, for if they'd never been allowed to learn of the war, my time in Jerusalem would have been even more unbearable.

Theokritus and Helena discovered in time that with their blessing came more than just weapons and the knowledge of my true nature. During those years when we patiently awaited whatever it was that required our presence in Jerusalem, the two of them continued to experiment in the privacy of our home, and it was during those sessions that each of them discovered certain abilities they didn't have before. Helena, for example, found she could now jump directly onto the roof, a height of no less than seventeen or eighteen feet. Theokritus's strength increased dramatically. One time he actually punched through a wall; our home was made of solid sandstone. It was increasingly entertaining to watch them spar as they discovered these little secrets, and I wondered if the two of them would ever figure out the true extent to which the blessing had changed them. They both also healed remarkably fast. I don't mean from just cuts and bruises; I mean broken bones and lacerations. Any wound short of bone-deep was completely healed without scar in a matter of hours. Neither of them ever became ill again either. With my control over physical matter growing each day, the three of us became a devastatingly effective team. I secretly hoped to meet one of the fallen to see just how powerful we actually were.

My wish came true during the Son's annual pilgrimage to Jerusalem on the twelfth year after I brought Theokritus and Helena into the war. Little did I know their first meeting with the fallen would result in their introduction to more than just any member of Hell's ranks.

⇒⊷ ⊷⇐

"Almost that time again," Theokritus said, watching the temple priests adorn the Court of Gentiles in the colors of Passover. "Think Michael will order us to leave the city this year?"

"It would be nice if he actually had some orders for us this time."

Helena said, "I cannot wait to see Jesus again! He grows so much each year. I wish we had longer than just one week."

"Does He know who He is yet?" Theokritus asked.

"I am sure Michael would have sent word if Jesus awakened to His ministry."

A group of women stared at Helena, appalled at her open dress and bare arms. I could hear their whispers of "sacrilege" and "prostitute of the devil." I hoped Helena could not. Amazing that even in the house of God there was needless persecution.

The three of us stepped out into the bright sunlight on the bridge connecting the Temple Mount to the upper city. The crowds had been getting thicker every day, and that afternoon it was worse than ever. It always amazed me to see the variety of people who came to worship at the Temple during the Passover. Head-to-toe burkas mingled with barely-there mantels; dusty pilgrims walked with the lavishly rich. People from all walks across the known world came together for the celebration. Citizens who wouldn't be seen near it at any other time appeared at the Temple for Passover. At the end of the bridge, a flood of people tried to squeeze onto the stone walkway, but managed only to create a longer wait. We pushed our way through, and Helena took Theokritus's arm, leaving me for the marketplace as I headed home.

Our home was nothing compared to Herod's palace. A few blocks behind the agora, its two-story layout was typical of most upper city homes, as this design kept it cooler during the day. It was one of the smaller homes in our district, but I liked it that way. Inconspicuous. The large central courtyard made a terrific training arena, too.

Slipping off my sandals, I stepped across the mosaic floor of the reception hall onto a rug that spanned most of the room. It had come from the east, expensive even in that time. Helena had been so happy when she bought it. I went to the hearth and knelt, holding my hand into the well of the fireplace. The coals within started to glow as I excited their matter. It had taken me over seven years to reach the point of control over the physical plane that allowed me to do such a thing. Each year Michael encouraged me to test my limits, and he was right; the more I attempted, the greater my control became. A wave of heat gushed over my hands and face as flames ignited, chasing the cold from the shadows.

Beautiful drawings covered the wall opposite our front door, all done by Theokritus with charcoal. Stretched parchment covered the sandstone with images of the palace as it used to be, scenes of the city and of Athens. The palace courtyard was my favorite. The fountain actually seemed to flow, the detail on even the tiniest drop of mist so incredibly lifelike. The pool reflected the charcoal sky so perfectly it was hard to tell which side was up. Palace servants filled the courtyard, and a group of court officials with shining armbands moved through the trees, caught in a moment of conversation about the state of the monarchy that was destined to crumble under Roman rule. My favorite part of the piece, however, was the trio standing in the second floor window that would have been our apartment. Feathered wings extended from one figure's back to wrap around the other two.

I looked over the wall, admiring the skill of my companion, then went to my bedroom on the upper floor. I froze at the door. That anxious tingling filled my head, the same feeling I'd had the night I spotted Astoreth in the courtyard. An angel was nearby.

My sword slid into my hand and bracing myself, I kicked open the door.

A strange man sat on my bed, unfazed. Seeing the weapon in my hand, he laughed. "Sabrael, you always make me feel so welcome."

"Must you do this every year?" I retracted my sword and inspected the damaged door as Michael's form swirled into his own appearance. "I fear the day will come when my blade will not be so slow."

Michael embraced me. "Nonsense. I would never allow it to go so far." He held me at arm's length and analyzed me the way he always did. "You look well."

"Of all those in creation, you should know best that appearances are not to be trusted."

"Why the attitude? Are you not happy to see me?"

I sighed and pulled his hands off my shoulders. "Of course I am, but it means we've been here another year. Not one of the fallen has revealed himself in the ten years since Astoreth. I realize there must be a reason for keeping us here, but I tire of waiting to find it out."

He wandered downstairs, seemingly oblivious. I followed, and he knelt before the fire.

"Michael?" I asked, a bit angrier than I intended.

"Come sit, Sabrael." Flames burned in his eyes when he looked at me, a pair of brilliant mirrors. I lowered myself beside him. "You must remain patient. Do not allow your lust for action to overwhelm you."

"Lust? Is that what you call twelve years of wondering why the Son needs me at all?"

"No. But it is a part of it, and you know that as well as I. Would you rather the fallen assault you each day, so you could feel the blood of our enemies on your hands? I think some part of you would."

How could Michael say such a thing? He could read my thoughts; did he not see the absurdity of this? The world was so vast; I only wished to see more of it before the time came for us to return home. Memories of home suddenly enveloped me, the longing again pouring over me. I yearned for the sight of my hall, the touch of the soft grass underfoot and the cool wind through the trees. Michael's voice brought me crashing back, the lush memory of Heaven replaced by the sand and heat.

"I came today not only to announce the Son's arrival, but also to bring news. If you had only kept quiet, I might have told you sooner." I hated when he chided me. "We are not the only angels here this year. The fallen have come. I saw them myself."

"Where?" I asked, perking up.

"They've been following the holy family for three days. I have no idea what alerted them to the Son's identity. All these years they have remained ignorant of His presence. Now, suddenly, they circle like carrion. Something must have tipped them off."

"Where are they now? Should we not be near the Son to ensure He is safe?"

"Gabriel is with Him. The family is staying with Joseph's friends in the lower city. He will call if need be, but the demons scattered into the city as we approached and have not returned. What they wait for puzzles me. I thought they would have attacked by now."

"Now who lusts for action?"

He chuckled. "I did not mean—"

The front door suddenly opened, and Michael's physical form burst into a cascade of particles which dissipated in the air. Theokritus and Helena came in laughing. Helena dropped two sacks of fresh produce on the table beside the door.

"What?" Theokritus asked me. "Why are you staring at us?"

"We have a guest."

The widening of their eyes told me Michael rematerialized behind me.

"Michael," Helena said, running to embrace him. "It is wonderful to see you again."

Theokritus clasped forearms with him and said, "We were wondering when you were going to arrive."

Michael held his arms out in a theatrical bow. "Wonder no more."

Helena asked, "How is Jesus? Is He here?"

"He is well, as is His family."

"Has He...?" Theokritus asked.

Michael shook his head. "He has a strong interest in carpentry, and often helps Joseph with small projects, but His interest in more divine matters remains latent. He likes the ceremonies and knows the stories of Moses and Noah and many others, but He does not enjoy waking for temple and would rather build something than listen to priests speak."

I was appalled. The Son was still not even aware He had work to do? When would He realize His true nature and begin the fight for mankind? I couldn't believe the Father would allow this to continue for so long. It might be decades before I saw Heaven again at this pace.

"Unfortunately, I bring troubling news," Michael said. His wings disappeared to make room for the chair as he sat at the table. "The fallen seem to have learned Jesus is the chosen Savior. They are in Jerusalem now."

"No!" Helena said. "They wouldn't dare hurt Him here?"

"You know as well as I what they will do to Him given the chance," Michael replied.

Theokritus looked at me and asked, "What are we to do?"

"What you have trained for," I answered.

"If it comes to that," Michael said. "You possess the skills needed to defend the Son should a confrontation arise, and it is considerably possible that one might arise relatively soon."

Helena stood and started unpacking the food. I could see her hands trembling. Theokritus took her wrist and held her hand. "What is it? What's wrong?"

She threw the empty sacks to the floor, bracing herself on the table. "We have spent so long training, but the thought that the fallen are actually here, that this is really going to happen. I am not ready to fight them."

"Love, we have been practicing for twelve years. How much longer do you need?"

Michael said, "Helena, look at me." She lifted her deep brown gaze, her hair glinting in the light of the fire. "You are ready. Trust me. You have all you require to aid you should you find yourself in battle with them. Not only that, but you will not be alone. Sabrael and Theokritus will be with you, maybe more of us depending on the circumstances. Do not succumb to worry. You are much stronger than you know."

"Let's not forget this is all speculation," I added. "We don't know for sure they're here because of Him. The fallen may just move on, and this could all be coincidence."

Michael nodded. "Sabrael is right. Just be on guard the next few days, and keep a cautious eye."

Helena's eyes lowered to the table, and Theokritus pulled her down into his lap, kissing her hair. He looked at me and nodded as if to tell me she would be fine.

"In the meantime," Michael said. "I have a job for the three of you."

⟞╬╬⟝

It was already the fourth night of the Passover week, and Theokritus, Helena and I were still looking for those of the fallen Michael tasked us to find. Despite the fact the sun had set, a steady stream of crowds still moved through the streets, torch-lit walkways teeming and the air still filled with shouts and laughter. Theokritus had split off to check down the smaller side streets while Helena and I pushed through the main artery of the upper city marketplace. I pulled Helena between the people clogging the street, her delicate hand in mine. Head lowered and hood pulled tight, I scanned the spiritual plane, trying to keep anyone from noticing my empty sockets. No one looked at my eyes, though; they were too busy poking for the next hole in the crowd that would allow them to advance down the street.

We were searching for Procell, one of the fallen Michael had been able to identify following the holy family into Jerusalem. Michael asked us to keep tabs on him, hoping he might lead us to the others. The last three nights had turned up nothing. I was worried that if we didn't find him soon, it would be too late. Michael had described what Procell looked like in the flesh, but since we could change our appearance at any time, I was watching for spiritual wings in the crowd. At least Michael's description gave Theokritus and Helena something to go on. The way Theokritus's eyes lit up at the mention of this mission gave away how much he'd been aching for a real assignment, and every night I allowed him to venture ahead a bit and relieve that yearning. Helena, however, would not leave my side. It was for her alone, I think, that Theokritus came back each night while darkness yet lay on the land. For all his desire to find something, his love for Helena and his worry for her wouldn't allow him to remain parted from her for long. I actually preferred this because it let me know they were both safe. Even though I'd trained them myself, I still didn't think it was safe for them to be wandering the streets alone. They would only really be ready after their first encounter with the fallen, but I kept that thought to myself.

Helena and I reached the busy agora in front of the palace, still no sign of Procell. I thought it best to head for the Temple Mount next, though this broke from what had become our routine of upper city, lower city, Temple Mount and finally palace grounds, which only I could investigate in the spiritual plane. But not only was there no Procell, there was no Theokritus. All three previous nights, he'd returned to us before the square.

"You think Theokritus is lost?" I asked Helena, her hair flowing from a thin peplos.

"He'd better be. If he is doing something stupid, I am going to kill him myself."

Thousands of glowing souls walked the market, but none had wings. If Theokritus didn't return soon, we would have to go looking for him, and that didn't bode well for our finding Procell before dawn. In the night, I could keep the matter off my eyes without anyone noticing. In the daylight, this was not as easily managed.

"There he is," Helena said, squeezing my hand and pointing to the alley behind the nearby homes. Theokritus stood halfway in the shadows, waving for us. We ran across the street to join him in the alley. Hands on his knees, he was winded and panting.

"What is it? What happened?" Helena asked him, placing one hand on his back and with the other drawing his face up.

"I found him," Theokritus replied, sweating onto the dust at our feet. "In the lower city. Talking to another. I followed him until he stopped and I could come back to get you. Go, Sabrael, before he gets too far. Take Helena; I will catch up."

"No," Helena told him. "I will not leave you alone."

"All right, stay here then," I said. "Theokritus, when you are ready, come find me. If I am gone, return to the house, and I will meet you there at sunrise."

Theokritus nodded. "The lower city market. Near the Temple Mount. Go!"

I burst from my physical body and flew for the Temple, a fifteen-minute sprint taking only seconds in the spiritual plane. Flying down into the lower city, I touched down in the lower city market and looked around. Numerous shoppers crowded the marketplace, but not quite as many as above. Then, just on the edge of the weaver district, I saw them: four black wings moving away. Two angels in the guise of humans. I ran after them, ducking behind buildings despite being in the spiritual plane. I couldn't risk being seen by any other fallen who might be nearby.

Peering around a corner, I shifted my gaze to the physical plane so I would know what they looked like to my friends. My brother Procell wore his own visage—slender nose, angular face, skin too pale for the region. Walking beside him was my disgraced brother Hakael, who had formed his face with a more local look. I wouldn't have recognized Hakael had I not seen him in the spiritual plane first. Anyone who didn't know what they were would have been completely fooled.

The two of them strolled through the crowd, and I followed as closely as I dared. Shifting my hearing to the physical plane, I still couldn't hear them over the busy night, so I tried to close the distance as they walked on. Gold rings and bracelets caught the moonlight and flashed like a beacon from beneath Procell's black tunic, and it wasn't long before a man ran from his home on the hill to fall before them. He cried and begged them for money. My heart pounded faster. If anything happened to endanger the man, I would be forced to stop it, and I wasn't sure I could face both my brothers alone. Not to mention the entire weaver district would witness the skirmish. I opened my hand, prepared to draw my weapon and praying to the Almighty the need would not arise.

The man crawled up to Procell and pulled on his tunic, sobbing. A dramatic scene for one supposedly weak with hunger. Procell placed his hand on the man's head and looked at Hakael, who reached behind his back. They were going to kill him. I knew it. My sword dropped into my hand, the muscles in my legs tensing and the roar of blood filling my ears.

To my surprise, though, Hakael drew a pouch, not a weapon, from behind his back and poured gold into the man's hands. I ducked back behind the corner. The man shouted, hugging my fallen brothers and thanking them repeatedly. Other people flooded out of the nearby homes and seeing what was happening, poured onto the ground at my brothers' feet. I retracted my sword and watched in awe as Procell and Hakael handed out pouches and consoled all those in pain.

What was I seeing? Why would my brothers who helped to damn mankind now aid them? Was this some trick? Elated people ran back to their homes, pouches in hand, and I had visions of the pouches filled not with money but venomous serpents, or worse. How would Michael and I handle such a thing? I had to find out what has happening. But how?

An idea came to mind. It meant risking everything, but I had no choice.

I assumed the appearance of the shopkeeper I met long ago in the lower city, the man who despised the poor now a member of their number. I stepped from the shadows to join the crowd gathered around my brothers, everything in me screaming to go back. I clenched my fists, trying to plan something to say when my brothers' eyes fell on me that wouldn't give away who I was. Though I questioned everything about this, including my very sanity, I knew one thing for sure—I could not be the last in line to meet my brothers. I stepped into the crowd and moved toward the front, hoping none of the humans would notice. No one said a word, though one man saw me coming and pushed me back with a look of disgust. I avoided him and continued forward. Hakael's face came into view as I finally reached the inner circle, so close I could touch his hair. My heart hammered, and I couldn't think clearly. If he recognized anything about me, I would be lost. Theokritus and Helena were too far away to help, even if I could somehow let them know where I was. I could call Michael, but what would he say if he knew what I was doing? I couldn't tell him until I knew the fallen were none the wiser. My legs were weak with worry, each step excruciatingly slow. Then Hakael looked at me and smiled.

"Come closer, brother," Hakael said, beckoning. He placed a hand on each of my cheeks, kissed my forehead. He called me brother! Did he know? I felt like my physical body would start dissolving, I was so terrified. "What will ease your suffering? What has life withheld from you that I might provide?"

My mouth was dry. All thought left me, so worried he would find out yet failing to ensure he wouldn't. If I didn't speak, he would definitely know something was wrong. I managed to utter, "Money," even that nearly causing me to faint.

Hakael laughed. "There, you see? All you needed to do was ask." He reached behind his back as if drawing a pouch from his belt, though I knew the truth. He placed it in my hand and said, "Take this and hear well. I represent one who is going to save us all. He loves you, and wants only your happiness. This is but a foretaste of how all will be made right through him. Go now, brother, and share the news of his coming."

I somehow stumbled back through the crowd, though I don't actually recall this. My mind reeled. The fallen were spreading the news of Christ's coming? My God, what did this mean? Hakael had been so loving, so caring for the poor man he thought me to be. The fallen despised humans! Was I to believe they just suddenly turned back to the ways of God? It didn't make sense. I had risked my life to retrieve answers, but instead received a whole new set of questions. Michael didn't know of this. He would have told me if he did, would he not? Why, if he knew, would he send me to find our brother with such words of caution? I was so confused. Was it possible that my brothers had finally seen the error of their ways? Could this really be the beginning of their return to grace? It called into question everything we were doing. If our brothers were trying to show their desire to return to Heaven, why did we need to protect the Son? If we weren't protecting Him from the fallen, what were we protecting Him from? I needed to talk to Michael. He had to know.

When the poor finally dispersed, Procell and Hakael continued on their way, and I followed, trying to stay close enough to listen to what they said.

"If we know it is not here, why does Lucifer waste our time?" Procell asked. "We should move on."

Hakael said, "You heard him. We must be sure about the boy. Nothing is more important than that. We do not need the gateway if we can just go to him directly."

Gateway? I thought. *What do they mean?*

"And if he is not the Son?" Procell asked.

"Then the search continues."

The pair reached the stairway up to the upper city. I waited a moment behind a house near the stairs so they wouldn't see me. I was in shock. They really wanted to come home! With the Son on Earth to save mankind, and the fallen ready to repent, the whole of creation could be at peace for the first time! Heaven would be filled with God's children, not a single angel or soul left astray. I was on the verge of yelling, I was so excited. The joy of my discovery would have to wait just a bit longer, though; the night's mission wasn't yet over.

I ran up the stairs and caught up just in time to see my brothers enter a house in the upper city. I wondered if I should go explain what was happening to Theokritus and Helena, but I couldn't risk my brothers leaving. Moving into a narrow alley across the road, I sat to wait it out. The sounds of the agora some blocks away were finally dying down, most of the city's visitors returning to their tents outside the walls.

I could hardly sit still. I pulled out Hakael's pouch and poured the coins onto the ground. No serpents, no tricks; just coins, exactly as they said. I called out in the spiritual plane, *Michael, I found Procell and Hakael's home in the upper city. What should I do?*

In but a moment, Michael's voice filled my mind. *Remain where you are until daybreak. I will come to you.*

Dawn was still some time away, so I made myself comfortable. What news I had to tell him! I envisioned Heaven with all of us united; Lucifer brushing off his chair in the Hall of Song, the host embracing all those once lost. I could not wait to show Lucifer everything that had changed since his confused fall.

The wind picked up and pulled at my hooded cloak, exposing my face to its cool caress. I realized I was still in the body of the shopkeeper, and I altered my appearance to a dirty version of Aegyus. I didn't want Hakael looking out and recognizing the man in the alley.

My brothers remained in their home for the rest of the night. The sky turned from black to gray and finally to the dull blue of imminent sunrise. A group of men trudged past, reeking of wine and barely able to stand, the night's partying finally over. I wondered what that kind of exhaustion felt like. They seemed sick with it. Not long after they passed, I felt that anxious tingling in the back of my head. It drew my attention as though pointing to a source, and when I turned toward it, I nearly jumped. Michael was sitting behind me, his face formed to his likeness but his clothes matching the rags I had on.

"Are they still here?" he asked.

I motioned to the house. "No one's come in or out."

"You are sure they did not leave in the spiritual plane?"

"I've been watching the entire night," I replied. "What should we do?"

"First tell me everything you heard them say. Did they mention the Son or their secret weapon at all?" He truly didn't know.

"Michael, I have to tell you first the wonderful news." His eyes narrowed. "The fallen want to return to Heaven!"

"What?" he asked.

"They mentioned searching for some gateway, but they also spoke of the Son, and said if it is indeed Him, the gateway does not matter because they can contact the Son directly." He looked confused. "Do you not see? Why else would they need to contact the Son other than to ask for forgiveness?"

Michael shook his head. "They'll never ask forgiveness. They're beyond it because they do not want it. I know how badly you wish otherwise, but you must realize it will never be."

"You're wrong. Last night I saw Procell and Hakael helping the sick and poor. They offered kindness and gifts to every single person who came to them, and they did it gladly." I paused, readying for the inevitable argument before adding, "Michael, they helped me."

"What do you mean?" he asked, his eyes wide.

"When I witnessed what they were doing, I took the form of a beggar so I might see for myself what was happening. Hakael told me of a coming Savior who would end my suffering! He spoke of one who is going to make the world a better place. Then he gave me this money and sent me off with a smile. Do you not see? He was speaking about Jesus!"

Michael's eyes filled with both confusion and horror, but I knew what I had seen. The time had come for the reunion of the host. The time had come for us to accept them again.

After a moment, Michael picked up the pouch and inspected the coins inside. "I must think on this. Pray to the Father for guidance. For now, let us maintain that their finding the Son is a bad thing, as that is safest." He slipped the pouch of coins into the folds of his clothes. "I will have Raphael take this post to keep watch. Go home. I'll call you later to discuss everything further, but until then, do not utter a single word of this to Theokritus or Helena. I do not believe you are right, Sabrael. I am sorry, and if you are correct, I will somehow make it up to you, but for now, I think you have been deceived."

Michael disappeared from the physical plane, and I rose from my spot on the ground, my backside tingling from not moving for so long. So strange a sensation. I was disappointed he didn't trust me, but I understood why he couldn't. He was our leader here, and if he was wrong about anything, it put all of us, as well as the Son, in danger. Still though, as I walked home, one thought kept repeating in my mind. *You are wrong. Lucifer and the rest are ready to return home, and I'm going to prove it to you all.*

CHAPTER SIXTEEN

Overwhelmed by all I'd seen the night before, the next day passed without my even realizing it. Secluded in our house, waiting for word from Michael, I spent the daylight pacing a trench into the floor.

Helena and Theokritus tried to shake me from this state, but it was no use. They asked questions about what happened after I left them, how I recognized my brothers if their physical appearances were different, whether the fallen knew where we lived. I answered mindlessly, preoccupied by what I'd discovered. Eventually they left me to spar. Normally I loved to watch them train, but now I couldn't sit still long enough to appreciate it. Nor could I tear myself away from the window, as I was too anxious for Michael to arrive. Trapped between restlessness and the fear of missing news when it came, I spent the day in torture.

When the sun finally set, I went outside hoping the fresh air would soothe my desperation. Why had Michael not yet called? Stars glinted over the city and all those crowding its streets with the festivities in the height of their activity. I listened to the shouts and laughter of the marketplace just a few streets away. Music rode the wind, and I imagined the city's visitors dancing. So many different traditions, so many ways of celebrating the Almighty, all of them mingling in Jerusalem, yet I couldn't bring myself to enjoy it.

I couldn't bear the uneasy silence in my mind where Michael's voice should be. I couldn't even tell Theokritus and Helena why I was so restless, for Michael had instructed me not to mention my fallen brothers' desire to return to the kingdom, if indeed that is what they had meant. But how could it not be? I heard them with my own ears, proclaiming the coming of the Son and their desire to speak to Him. It was true that Astoreth had spoken of Lucifer's continuing zeal to steal the throne, but Astoreth had been in that cave for years. Was it not possible things had changed in the time since his imprisonment? I once heard a woman tell her son that Heaven had as many angels as the sky had stars. Did the number of stars in the sky not change each night with the orbit of the Earth? Did the stars visible this night not disappear in the coming months, only to return to shine just as bright when the Passover came again?

Much later, having gone back inside but still at the window, I started to think perhaps Michael was correct; perhaps I did wish for something to break the monotony. Was that why he kept me away from both Procell's house and the Son? Tracking my fallen brothers, I felt an excitement I'd not felt in years. I wouldn't admit this to Michael of course, but I could not deny it to myself. I liked the action of the previous night. I wanted more nights like it.

Then something moved across the street. I gripped the ledge of the window, leaning for a better look. Dust from the street swirled up into a thin tornado and began taking a new shape. Michael must have heard my thoughts and come to speak to me. *It's about time,* I thought.

When the swirling stopped, a figure stood in its place, but I didn't recognize him. His dark eyes seemed to siphon all the light from the torches of the street, and his teeth flashed when his lips pulled back. He smiled at me and waved. Then he was gone, vanished as quickly as he'd appeared. I made my eyes spiritual just in time to spot an angel dart over the house across the street and disappear into the night. That quick glance was enough.

Helena looked over at me, stirred from her nap by the fire. "Sabrael? Are you all right?"

I could not find my voice to answer her. How could I possibly tell her that I'd just seen Lucifer, and the devil had waved?

I spent the remainder of the night with my sight glued to the spiritual plane. To say I was terrified doesn't begin to describe it. First, if the lord of Hell had come to Jerusalem, it meant a greater number of the fallen than we thought were probably in the city as well. That alone frightened me to the core. But more than that, they'd never before gathered in one place without some agenda, and Lucifer being there himself meant he probably planned something he didn't trust the others to do.

But why come to me first? Why make contact like that after all this time? If he sought reconciliation, why not just knock on the door? Or to Michael's point, if he still wanted to kill the Son, why would he first make absolutely sure we knew he was coming? It made no sense, and that made it all the more horrifying.

On alert the rest of the night, I was determined not to let anyone near the house without my knowing. Lost in a sea of speculation, I was unable to turn my thoughts to anything else. He knew where I lived. Knew exactly where to find me. He could enter the house whenever he pleased, if he'd not done so already. I realized how careless I had been for years, lulled by the comforts of human life, and visions of Lucifer having been so close during that time haunted me. Sitting atop the roofs listening to my every conversation, following me, always safe from discovery in the spiritual plane. How many times could he have been walking beside me, smiling from an arm's length away, while my physical eyes gazed right through him? Lucifer might have known where to find me years earlier, and I would never have known.

The true horror was that I wasn't the only one living in the house. I had to assume he knew about Theokritus and Helena, which only aroused new terrors. If Lucifer got to them, I would have to go on living in this place while those I cared for most would suffer the ultimate price for my negligence. My head filled with dark visions: Lucifer standing over my friends while they slept, bent over Helena, kissing her forehead while she dreamed in false security. Had Lucifer whispered his beautiful lies into her ears? Had he lain beside Helena and held her while she mistook him for Theokritus? Had he taken Theokritus's form and done even worse?

Straining against my imagination, screaming against the maelstrom of depraved and horrific visions conjured by my plagued mind, the night lasted forever. But as morning approached, rational thought once again found purchase in the madness. One single thought offered me safe passage from the night's turmoil.

Lucifer had smiled and waved. That was the truth; that was what I had seen. More than that, he allowed me to see it, to know he was there. Why would he do such a thing if he meant us harm? He could just as easily have snuck into the house, struck me down, and then moved on to kill Theokritus and Helena. I wondered if I'd taken his greeting the entirely opposite way from what he intended. The fact that he knew where we lived was definitely cause for concern, but the more I considered it, the more it seemed proof of his desire to be forgiven. How could I even be sure his quick retreat wasn't due to fear of me? For eons the fallen attacked us, tried to get us to defect, attempted to destroy the things we protected. After such a long time at odds, was it not understandable that Lucifer feared my reaction? Perhaps this minimal contact was his attempt to open communication again. His expression wasn't one of malevolence or old hatred. He didn't taunt me to follow him, gave no signs that he would return. He had only smiled and waved, as casually as if we were friends.

It would mean so much if Lucifer himself had come to show me his desire to return to the way Heaven was before his fall. It would be the proof I sought.

When the sun finally rose, I was resolved to take matters into my own hands. Michael had made no mention of Lucifer's presence in the city; he must not know yet. If Lucifer sought him out in hopes of reconciliation, Michael would strike him down before he had the chance. But Lucifer wasn't looking for Michael, and I knew it. Given all that I'd learned from Procell and Hakael, I knew who Lucifer came to see. Regardless of whether Lucifer was there for ill or good, he was going after Jesus, and that was worse. He was either going to kill the boy, or expose the boy's true nature before He could discover it for Himself. Either way, mankind's salvation was once again threatened by my impetuous older brother. Despite Michael's orders, there was no way I would stay in the house another day. I had to find Jesus before Lucifer did.

Disobeying Michael, I took Helena and Theokritus into the city to find the holy family. We found them in the line leading to the Huldah Gates, the final day of the festival week bringing out every-one to worship. Only a few bodies behind them, I kept my sight in the spiritual plane so I could head off any misguided attempts to reach them. Jesus had grown considerably in the year since we'd seen Him, though His voice was still that of a sexless youth. His wavy hair was dark like His eyes, and His cheeks still held some of their infant roundness. He laughed with His siblings as they watched the crowd, commenting to each other about this person or that. Some of my dismay that He wasn't yet preaching the Word dissipated. He was still only a child.

Helena was utterly delighted, a constant smile on her lips as she watched Him. Theokritus was more mindful of the heat and the slow crawl of the crowd. By the time we reached the stairs leading up to the gates, the smaller children around us were being carried and Theokritus was getting cranky. Careful not to be seen, I formed a skin of water and handed it to him. He drank most of it, then offered it to Helena. She just said, "Is she not beautiful? Four children, and Mary still looks not a year past twenty." Theokritus rolled his eyes at me and finished the water. He handed me the empty skin, and I tucked it in my belt. For all the ability I'd gained in forming things from the matter around me, I could not yet break apart matter with the same level of skill. I've heard it said that to destroy is easier than to create. Clearly, the person who said this never tried manipulating matter.

We finally entered the shaded Huldah Gates just before I thought Theokritus would have succumbed. The cool stone took the edge off the oppressive heat. People were led inside one group at a time, the priests ensuring the line kept moving to allow everyone a chance to worship before the day was through. When the Son and His family were escorted inside, Helena turned and asked, "Could we please follow them after they leave here today? Just for a little while. I want to watch Jesus for as long as I can this year."

"All right," I replied, secretly planning to do so anyway. "But we must stay far enough back that they cannot notice us."

"Just keep the water coming," Theokritus added, wiping sweat from his brow. Helena stifled her laugh.

After a short time, we were led up the stairs to the Court of Gentiles. I'd never seen it so crowded. Vendors and money changers shouted over the pushing, shoving masses; priests threaded tour groups through the wall of bodies with a practiced, if not frantic, technique. The vast courtyard of multi-colored stone was packed solid with people. There were even Roman soldiers stationed along the walkways above, overlooking the crowd and making sure no one stood loitering or hiding from the heat outside. It was madness. I scanned the crowd in the spiritual plane. I was fairly surprised to find that mine were the only wings in this court. Not that I wanted to find the fallen there. All I needed was for one of the demons to start a fight in the Temple. Michael would love that. A priest came to lead us into the inner courts, and I formed the matter to my eyes again.

As we passed through the gate into the Court of Women, I was astonished to find it even more packed than the public area outside. Priests shepherded droves of worshippers through, grabbing those who lingered and ushering them along. I spotted Jesus and His family sitting on a bench, obviously waiting for Joseph to return from the next court. Unfortunately, the priests had also noticed them. They were taking up precious space on the busiest day of the year. It was only a matter of time before they too would be shown the doors. Seeing this, I was torn. As a Jewish male citizen, I was the only one able to enter the next area, the Court of Israel—Helena prohibited because of her gender and Theokritus because he would never leave her side. I could try to find Joseph, alert him to the situation, but to interrupt his worship was not only illegal, it also meant making contact, which we weren't supposed to do. I had to avoid doing anything that might change the course of the Son's development. Observe, protect, defend if necessary, but never interfere. That was our way. It was commanded of us. Not willing to break this tenet, I looked away from the holy family. Then a priest came into the court with two soldiers, pointing at Mary and the children. The soldiers headed their way.

"Theokritus, stop those guards." Michael was going to be furious, but I had no choice now. "Helena, keep Mary and the children calm. I am going to get Joseph."

Theokritus and Helena looked at me in disbelief.

"I know, I know," I said. "Just go."

What choice did I have? I couldn't allow the holy family to be sep-arated—or worse. Of course this would happen on the day Michael wasn't there to protect them. Why did Michael leave them without a replacement, I wondered? I rushed away even as Theokritus's rapid whispers to stall the guards echoed behind me. I had only a few moments.

The Court of Israel was much narrower than the Court of Women. Men stood shoulder to shoulder around the Court of Priests, watching the priests conduct sacrifices. Behind the priests, the door to the forbidden Sanctuary opened and through the crack, I saw a stairway leading below the Temple. The high priest emerged from the Sanctuary and caught me staring. I averted my gaze and moved on as he shut the door quickly.

I checked both planes, making sure none of the fallen were present, then searched for Joseph. Thankfully, he hadn't made it far. Keeping my eyes on the priests watching over the court, I wound through the crowd. One of the priests tracked me and I froze, blending with the crowd until his gaze turned, then stepped beside Joseph.

"You must come with me," I whispered, keeping my eyes on the altar.

Joseph looked at me like I was mad. "Do I know you?"

"No, but you must trust me," I replied, keeping my voice low. "Your wife and children are about to be arrested. If you do not go to them now, it will be too late to save them."

Joseph's eyes narrowed, but I saw the shock he wished to con-ceal. He considered the sacrificial bird in his hand, still unsure. I stepped closer. "If you find them safe, you have only lost a few coins in the cost of that bird, but if you do not and they are arrested, you will have lost everything. You do not need this building to praise the Almighty; He hears you wherever you are. Trust me."

He glanced around, realized we were being watched by curious priests. If another confrontation began in here, we would be in real trouble. Finally, Joseph said, "If you are lying in the house of God, I will have you arrested."

"And I will go quietly," I replied. "Come."

Theokritus and Helena were still holding strong against the guards when we reached them. Joseph gave me a stunned look, then ran to Mary's side. Theokritus stood between the guards and the Son, arguing as audibly as possible without risking immediate arrest. Helena spoke quickly to Mary and Joseph, insisting we all go outside. Jesus watched it all with excitement. The look Theokritus gave me told me we had returned not a moment too soon.

With a few apologetic words to the guards, we ushered the holy family out before things could escalate further.

The line outside was even longer than before, stretching across the Tyropoeon farther than I could see. I scanned the spiritual plane. No sign of the fallen.

Theokritus whispered to Helena, "That was close."

Hearing this, Mary turned to face us. "Thank you, all of you, for saving us. Please, what are your names?"

I balked. What name could I give? If I gave my real name, who was to say that Jesus might not recognize it somehow? He was supposed to grow into the ministry on His own; only then would the prophecies be fulfilled. If I sparked that journey, I might be responsible for triggering the collapse of man's salvation. Aegyus was no good either, for that name was still somewhat known around the city from my time spent in Herod's graces. I did what anyone would do faced with a question they can't answer—I deflected.

"This is Theokritus and his wife Helena. We are all from Athens, though we didn't meet until we came to Jerusalem. Have you ever been? You should visit sometime; it's marvelous. It is a good thing we were all here today, though." I gave him my most winning smile.

Joseph and Mary exchanged confused glances. Joseph put a hand on Mary's shoulder. "Indeed it is. I am Joseph, and this is my wife Mary. We come every year from Nazareth to worship, though I have never worshipped so fast before." He laughed, and I joined him, uncomfortable in the open like this. Where on Earth was Michael? Joseph continued, "But you still have not told me your name."

Before I could dodge the question again, Theokritus said, "His name is Sabrael."

My heart leapt into my throat. I glared at him and saw he knew he had erred.

Mary said, "Sabrael. What a beautiful name. Just like…" Joseph's stern look silenced her. I wasn't the only one with a secret.

"You all have my sincerest thanks," Joseph said. "Without your intervention, I fear how this day would have fared. I have little money, but you must allow me to repay you somehow."

I needed to end the conversation quickly. It wasn't safe being seen with them. "The pleasure of having helped is enough, really."

"Please. It would be a dishonor if I did not show my appreciation," Joseph insisted.

"You can show it by avoiding the attention of authorities next time you return to the Temple."

Joseph laughed, as did Jesus, who'd come to stand at Joseph's side. Jesus stared at me with something like wonder, or maybe curiosity. I felt the urgent need to get away from Him.

"You are sure?"

"Absolutely," I said, desperate.

"You are a truly humble man, Sabrael," Joseph said, the sound of my name sending shivers down my spine. "Take this then. I carved it to sell, but let it instead show my thanks."

Joseph reached into the pouch at his side and withdrew a small, wooden token for a necklace or bracelet. It was an image of an angel holding a trumpet. The only blaring I heard was that of my own terror.

I took the token, afraid he knew what I was. But Joseph just put his hands on Jesus's shoulders and led Him away. The other children trailed after them.

Mary took my hand and kissed it. "What you've done today means more than you'll ever know. All of you. May God's angels guide your steps." She bowed her head to us, then followed Joseph into the crowd.

"And yours," I replied when she was out of earshot.

CHAPTER SEVENTEEN

"What were you thinking?" I yelled at Theokritus. "You told him my name!"

"Who cares if he knows? That family is the only family in the world sure to have no contact with the fallen!"

"That does not matter! How many people could have heard you and seen my face? Not to mention that Michael is with them all the time. What do I say if Joseph and Mary start talking about some man they met in Jerusalem named Sabrael?"

"I already apologized! What more do you want?" Theokritus went to his room and slammed the door.

Fuming, I dropped into the chair beside Helena. "He meant well," she said.

"That does not make it better," I sighed, but remorse was already setting in.

"At least when Jesus learns who He is, He will remember you were at His side even when He was young."

"He will know that anyway. We cannot risk revealing our presence, especially with the fallen in the city."

"I understand that," Helena said. "I am not saying what Theokritus did was right. He shocked me as much as you. But tomorrow, Jesus and His family will be gone, and while they will soon forget the face of the man named Sabrael, you will still be living here with a man who feels he has betrayed you."

I nodded and ran my hand over my face. Somewhere inside, I laughed at how human the gesture was. Had I been away from Heaven that long?

Helena rose and kissed my cheek. "I hate when my men fight. Go talk to him."

I went to their bedroom door and knocked. "Theokritus, may I come in?" I asked.

Nothing. The matter left my body and in the spiritual plane I slipped under the door. Theokritus was seated on the bed, holding one of his axes and running his fingers along its blade.

"Why did you not answer?" I asked, my physical body forming again.

"What for? I knew you would come in either way."

I sat beside him. "I am sorry. I should not have yelled."

Theokritus shook his head. "You are right; I was not acting as a warrior of light should." He held the ax out, inspecting the curve of its shining edge. "I swore to defend the Son and help in the war against the fallen. Every day since, I have wondered what will happen when the time comes to live up to that oath. Will I be strong enough to follow through and do what needs to be done? Now the fallen are gathering, the Son is in danger, and in the simplest matter, I failed. It does not matter now how fast or strong or skilled I am. My big mouth has endangered us all."

"You failed no one."

"I let you down. I let Michael down. I am a disgrace among the warriors of light. I told a stranger your name, Sabrael! How careless could I be?"

"I ordered you to stop a pair of guards from doing their job, and without a moment's hesitation you did it. The Son and His family are safe tonight because of you. Do you think anyone else could have walked out of that temple free of shackles?"

His gaze lowered to the ax on his lap. "I feel unworthy to remain a warrior of light."

"Why?" I asked. "Have you not trained every day? Have you not altered your life to stay by my side?" My mind filled with Michael's voice then, beckoning us to meet him. "One mistake does not erase twelve years of accomplishment. Twelve years, Theokritus! Do you realize we have been together that long? In all that time, making one tiny slip should not make you question your worth, but prove what an incredible warrior you really are. If you were not, I never would have chosen to bring you into the war."

Theokritus chuckled. "You had no choice. We saw you kill Astoreth."

"Exactly! How big a mistake was that? What makes a great warrior is not that he does not make mistakes; it is that he recognizes those he does so he never makes them again."

Theokritus looked at me, the trace of a smile appearing on his lips. His hair gleamed almost red in the sunlight coming from the window. "You are not angry?"

"Am I glad that the Son's family knows my name? No, but I am not angry. I just hope you will be more cautious is all." Slipping the leather rope from around my neck, I placed the carved angel Joseph gave me into his hand. "Here, I think you should have this."

"No, Sabrael, it was given to you."

"It should be worn by the one who saved them. You alone kept the guards from arresting them; you alone were their savior. Take this as a symbol of how worthy you are to be part of this war, more worthy even than me." He passed the rope over his head. "Now, Michael wants us to meet him outside the city. Are you coming or are you going to force me to tell him you have decided to leave us?"

He retracted his ax and tucked the token under his shirt. "If Michael calls, I will answer."

The three of us reached the Jaffa Gate as it was nearing dark. We stood just outside the city wall watching the stream of visitors retiring to the village of tents bordering the road to Jaffa. Many had already packed up in preparation for the return to their various homelands. Children chased each other through the camp, squeezing every last moment from the waning day. A woman finally grabbed two of them, yanking them inside. Helena must have been watching as well, for she laughed at the sight of the rest scampering to avoid punishment.

Then from behind us, Michael said, "Forgive me for being so late."

I turned to see his face was made to his own likeness, but his clothes were those of a pilgrim. The white cloth around his head and draped down his neck made his long, ebony hair all the more prominent.

"Where have you been?" I demanded. "Why were you not with Jesus and His family today?"

"I thought they would be safe at the Temple, so I stepped away to check on Raphael and our ... problem. Thank you, all of you, for what you did. I never would have thought—"

Wind swept up and the four of us covered our faces against the shower of sand. How did such a large gathering of visitors sleep in these conditions year after year? Theokritus spat and wiped his lips on his sleeve.

"At least tell me you came to a decision," I said. "We cannot just ignore what I saw."

"I have pondered and prayed about what you told me, Sabrael. It just does not make sense. Why, after so long, would they choose to repent? Why seek forgiveness now?"

"Because of Jesus, do you not see that?" I argued. "They could never gain an audience with Him in the kingdom after all that has happened. But the Son is here now. It makes perfect sense they would use this opportunity to approach Him directly."

"I drove Lucifer from the kingdom. I saw the rage in his eyes, felt the hatred in his glow. Do you think I would have cast him out if I had any doubt that he could not be saved?"

"That was eons ago, Michael. Are you the same as you were then? Is it so hard to fathom that our brothers could have changed? This war could be over tomorrow!"

He held my gaze. "I cannot risk the salvation of mankind on this. If you can find out more about this gateway of which they spoke, if that puzzle leads to a revelation of their true desire for forgiveness, then maybe."

"Gateway?" Theokritus asked, scraping sand from the inside of his mouth.

Michael glanced at me and I heard in my mind, *You did not tell them?*

You told me not to, I replied, offended by his surprise.

"There are whispers among the fallen of a gateway they seek," Michael told them. "Unfortunately, we have not yet heard what or where it is, or even why they are so interested in it. Since they spoke of it in the same breath as what Sabrael took to be their desire for absolution, it is important that we learn how the two are linked."

"Absolution? Is that what kept you up all night pacing?" Helena asked me. I couldn't bring myself to tell her the truth. Not yet.

"When the holy family leaves tomorrow and I with them, I want the three of you to focus on finding out anything you can about this gateway," Michael said.

"How do we even begin?" I asked. "You want us to simply ask one of them what gateway they are looking for?"

"The Temple priests have more collected writings than any-where else in Judea. Start there."

"And what if we encounter the fallen during this research?"

Michael looked at me as though disappointed. "Treat them as you always have. If your theory is correct, it should become quickly apparent."

Theory. Like I was concocting an unlikely connection between random events. This was more than that. I wondered what Michael would say if he knew of my late night visitor, but I kept Lucifer from my thoughts. No need to let him deny more evidence now.

Michael said, "I must return to the Son. I will come to say good-bye tomorrow morning."

I nodded and Michael embraced me. *Do not misunderstand me, Sabrael; I do hope you are right.* Somehow I couldn't entirely believe him. He hugged Helena and clasped forearms with Theokritus, then his physical body scattered like sand into the wind.

Michael may not have been convinced, but I was. If finding this gateway would prove it to him, so be it. I would find it and confirm what I already knew to be true.

Walking back through the upper city, I wanted to shout to the masses crowding the streets that there was nothing to fear anymore. That a much greater event than the Passover was just on the horizon. I was so ecstatic I could have gathered matter to my wings and let the world know the truth then and there that angels were real.

"Why did you not tell us all this last night?" Helena's voice interrupted my silent celebration. "Do you not trust us?"

"It is not that," I replied, noticing how the thrill of the previous moments had left a tired silence in my mind. "I just do not want it to affect how you might act should the fallen appear."

Helena breathed deep and slow, a characteristic sign she was frustrated. "The fallen have not confronted us in all the time we have been your companions. Even if they start tonight, how could knowing what you were thinking possibly influence our reaction? Is it not to your advantage to tell us so that if the fallen did something to lend credence to your theory, we could let you know? That is why we are your warriors, is it not? To be your extra eyes and ears when you cannot do it all alone?"

She made a good point, which I hated because she always made a good point. After being with me so long, she knew all the ways to get to me. She was right though; maybe it was better they knew. That way if the fallen told Theokritus or Helena to stop fighting, they would recognize it wasn't just a tactic to gain the upper hand. I realized then why Michael had been surprised I hadn't told them.

"All right," I said, disappointed that even when trying to do the right thing, I failed. "The other night, following Procell and Hakael, I came upon a surprise. A man begged them for money, and instead of harming or deceiving him, they actually helped him. But that wasn't the strange part—"

A man suddenly ran out of nowhere and slammed into me, knocking us both to the ground. Curly, black hair wrapped down around his chin, the line between hair and beard indistinguishable. Despite the heat, there wasn't a drop of sweat on him. He helped me up, apologizing profusely as I tried to dust myself off. But he still had hold of my arm. Two glowing, emerald eyes flashed for an instant before they returned to a deep, human brown.

"Sabrael," the man said in Raphael's voice. "I lost them!"

"Lost who?" I asked, frightened by the genuine panic in his eyes.

"Procell and the others. I cannot find them!"

"They're not in the house?" Theokritus asked, obviously having figured out who the man standing before us was.

"They came out together, walked a short way, then all four of them went spiritual and split up."

"Four? There were only three!" I said.

"Adramelec is here too. They knew they were being watched!"

"Did they see you watching?" Helena asked.

"Impossible! Not unless they spotted me from inside the house." He suddenly looked around as though he sensed one of them nearby. I instinctively checked the spiritual plane as well. "It does not matter if they saw me. What matters is there are now four fallen angels free in Jerusalem and the Son is still here."

Five, I thought, remembering Lucifer. Raphael caught me with a narrowed gaze as though he caught the thought but not the memory.

"Then we need to find them," Theokritus said, excited.

Helena turned to me. "It would be easiest to go to the Son. Let the fallen come to us."

"It would be impossible to prevent the holy family from seeing us fight them," I said. "Besides, Joseph and Mary know your faces now. We would risk them recognizing you."

Raphael glanced around with empty sockets. "Then we have only one option," he said. "Michael and I will guard the family while the three of you search the city. Stay together; Sabrael is the only one who can recognize them. You find them, call us. We'll do the same."

I nodded. "Go. We waste time here."

Raphael's body dissolved, and he was gone.

"The old search pattern then?" Theokritus asked with a smirk.

"No," I answered, scanning in the spiritual plane. "If the fallen are looking for the Son, they will likely start in the lower city where Joseph's friends live. We should head there."

I kept my eyes in the spiritual plane while the three of us hurried through the city. Crowded only hours earlier, the streets were now deserted. All through the upper city there was no sign of the fallen, and by the time we reached the street descending into the valley, it was starting to feel like we'd come full circle to the beginning of the week.

The lower city was just as quiet. We scoured the weaver district, even searching the alleyways and side streets, but found nothing.

We'd just looped back from the Temple Mount when I finally spotted Paimon flying over the rows of homes in the spiritual plane, black wings spread and his glowing robe trailing behind him. "Got one. In the spiritual plane over those buildings."

"Does he see you?" Theokritus asked.

"Not yet."

Helena said, "We should follow him. If we keep him in sight, only three of the fallen will be unaccounted for."

Paimon circled back, gliding like a bird of prey, and I shoved Helena and Theokritus against the nearest home, hiding us from his view. I punched the wall, frustrated. "We cannot be free to assist Michael and Raphael if we are tracking Paimon!" I said.

"What else can we do?" Theokritus asked. "If he remains in the spiritual plane, we cannot fight him, and there might be others nearby waiting for us to reveal ourselves."

I chanced a peek. Paimon still circled that same place. An idea came to me. "I could force him into the physical plane."

"What?" Helena asked.

"I could lure him to the ground and form some of his body so the two of you could hold him. When he takes physical form to free himself, we'll restrain him."

"You can do that?" Theokritus asked.

"We can create a heart for one another; I do not see how this would be different."

"It is too risky," Helena said. "If Michael's right, and restraining him doesn't work, he could easily use us against you. You need to take him out of the fight."

"What if Michael's not right!" I asked. But just then, Michael's voice suddenly filled my mind. *We need you here now!* It was followed by an image of the city from above, focusing until it stopped on one particular house. It was the house right below where Paimon hovered.

"That was only a few blocks away," Theokritus said.

Shocked, I asked, "You saw that?"

He nodded. "The message was for all of us, was it not?"

At least I didn't need to explain how to get there.

"Go. I will meet you there," I said. I turned and broke free of my physical body. Spreading my wings, I shot into the air straight for Paimon, whose attention was directed to the fight below. He was the fallen's backup, air support in case they lost control.

But they didn't know Michael had me.

Streaking across the sky, I pulled my wings in and aimed my blade at my brother's chest.

Paimon noticed too late to protect himself. He managed to raise his mace, but before he could swing it, my sword punched through his body. He screamed as an impact cloud of blood burst into the air around us. My momentum forced us both higher, the earth spinning away as we twirled, connected by the sword. Paimon grabbed my blade with his free hand and swung his mace around in the other. I twisted my weapon and wrenched his wound wider. A sound more animal than angel ripped from his throat. His mace plummeted away.

I pulled in tight to him, my blade sinking to the hilt. "I am sorry, brother."

Yanking the sword from his chest, I flew him back down to the ground. Wailing, he tried to squirm free of the pain. I left him there to mend, his glowing blood spreading on his robe.

Chaos ruled the scene when I arrived at the house. In the spiritual plane, Michael, Raphael and Gabriel were engaged against Procell, Hakael, Adramelec and Caim. Theokritus and Helena weren't there yet, but the humans who were had no idea what was happening around them. Two people sat in the corner of the cramped quarters near a fire, the remnants of a feast on the table behind them. In the room just through a doorway to the left, I could see Jesus and His siblings asleep on the floor, with three other children in beds along the wall.

Michael yelled as he deflected Hakael's blade, "Sabrael! Get Jesus out!"

As soon as Michael alerted the fallen to my presence, Caim left Procell to fight Raphael alone and rushed to meet me. I ran back outside and made myself physical, knowing my friends were coming soon, but kept my eyes and ears spiritual.

Caim emerged from the house and, seeing I'd become physical, did as I hoped and formed his own body. I made my ears physical to hear him say, "—is that it, Sabrael?"

"I don't understand what's happening here, Caim. None of this makes sense."

He laughed, "What's happening here is that you're about to die. Brave to take this fight into the physical plane."

He charged with his staff, one side a three-pronged fork and the other a spear tip. The staff twirled around his arm and the spear point jabbed at me, barely missing my head as I ducked back. I struck his weapon away only to have to then dodge the forked end.

"We don't have to do this!" I yelled, deflecting his attack. "I know why you're here! Our time for fighting is over!"

Caim whipped the fork at my feet and as I jumped, I parried the spear point as it stabbed for my chest. "Oh no," he said. "You and I are just getting started."

Again and again our weapons clashed. Worried we'd wake the neighbors or attract unwanted attention, I spread my wings and flew up into the night sky, making sure he followed. I spotted Theokritus and Helena running through the maze of homes below only two blocks away. I needed to stop them from entering the house so they wouldn't startle the couple sitting by the fire, but Caim wasn't about to relent. I had to think fast.

Turning quickly, I plunged to meet Caim head-on, swinging my sword as I passed and feeling it dig into flesh. But at the same moment, he whipped his staff around to slam into my skull.

The world exploded, flashing bright before going completely dark. My sword pulled free and my stomach rose into my throat as

I started to fall. Plummeting blind, my head lolled on my fractured neck, my mind jarred from the blow. Had I been human, I would have been dead. The darkness seemed to spin but my direction felt constant. I struggled to concentrate, needing to fix the damage Caim had done to my physical body. Fighting through the haze, I tried to keep my mind on the weight of my sword, which somehow managed to stay in my hand. Good thing I had flown so high. Had I not, I'm sure I would've struck the ground, and Caim would have had me.

Regaining my focus, I forced the matter from my body and burst into the spiritual plane. The pain and blindness disappeared instantly with the damaged flesh and bone. I spread my wings and righted myself just as I reached the ground. I looked up to see Caim swooping down for my head, his own physical matter sloughing off like ice from a meteor.

My spiritual essence suddenly dispersed around Theokritus's body as he ran directly through me, then again as Helena followed. Helena slowed as though she'd felt me somehow. Coalescing again, I made myself physical just as Caim reached me. He yelled as his spiritual form burst against my physical one, dispersing as I had a moment ago.

"Theokritus, Helena!" I yelled after them. "Get ready to block!"

I jumped away from Caim as he rose from the ground and became whole again. "Clever move, Sabrael," he said, oblivious to my companions behind him. "I am impressed."

"Then you will love this," I said, and focused on his body. Physical matter swirled to encase him as I strained to manipulate it, and his eyes went wide with shock. I drove my shoulder into his chest and knocked him back into Theokritus and Helena, who were confused but ready. The two of them caught his arms and held tight. Caim struggled to face the unexpected opponents, but I plunged my sword deep into his chest and twisted hard. He shrieked and I shoved him to the ground, kneeling over him.

"I heard Procell and Hakael proclaim the Son's coming to the humans last night! They want to bring peace to this war; why do you continue to fight?"

Caim spat blood, more gushing up from the wound. "You must be the biggest fool in all of creation. Why would we stop before the true king is recognized?"

No, this couldn't be right! What I'd seen was not a lie. But I had no time to question him. My brothers, and Jesus, were still in peril.

"Do not make me do this, Caim. Come back to us, please."

His every breath gurgled. Helena made a noise. She looked sick. "Better run," he said. "I've heard how you fight; you never finish it. Soon as I catch my breath, it will be your turn to bleed."

"Helena … cover your eyes." I punched my hand into Caim's chest. He screamed and flailed on the ground, eyes wide in disbelief as my fingers slid in. I covered his mouth to muffle his cries. Caim clamped a hand on my forearm and dug his nails in, bit my hand, begged me to stop. But I couldn't risk him coming after us. So the fallen considered the mercy I had shown them in Heaven a weakness? Maybe it was time to change that.

I grasped Caim's heart, the beating wet against my palm, and pulled hard. The core of his physical body ripped free and brought a fount of dark blood with it. Caim kicked me in a final death throe, and I fell back, stomach aching but the heart still in my hand. When I sat up, Caim was gone, buried deep within the body in the road. I focused and burnt the heart to ash, listening for the cries of any witnesses. Helena's sobbing was the only sound in the night.

"It had to be done, Helena," I said. "Are you all right?"

She fought her tears as she turned from Theokritus. "I will never get used to that. Never."

"Nor should you." I grabbed Caim's body, dragging it into the nearest alley. "We have to keep moving," I said. "Jesus is in danger."

We ran for the house, though Helena wasn't ready to face what awaited us. I freed the matter from my wings in case the couple there was still awake. Three armed warriors running into their home would be shocking enough; two humans and an angel would be too much. Reaching the house, I found the fight still in full swing, though Raphael and Hakael were both wounded and bleeding badly. The home's residents had mercifully gone to bed. It was bizarre watching the battle raging in the spiritual plane but hearing nothing in the physical, like ghosts fighting over the house. This was a blessing, though. For my friends, the house appeared empty, allowing Helena time to compose herself.

Pointing to Jesus, I directed Theokritus and Helena to get Him out of the house, then dropped my physical body to join the fight. Michael yelled, "No, Sabrael! Jesus first!"

Raphael grasped my hand from the floor. "Go! Get Him out of here." I squeezed his hand and then ran into the next room, making my body physical again.

Jesus saw me enter the physical plane.

He was sitting up, Helena having woken Him. He stared at me in amazement. "Sabrael? Are you a spirit?" Jesus whispered.

I was mortified. Thankfully, none of the other children were awake. "Not exactly," I replied, glancing at Theokritus. Talk about making mistakes. I wasn't sure if I should tell Jesus what I was, but there was really no way to avoid it anymore. "Do you know what an angel is?"

Jesus nodded. "Mother tells me about them all the time. She says she's even seen them."

I had to smirk at the irony of the fact that I had just asked the Son of God if He knew what an angel was. "Now you are seeing one too."

Jesus asked, "Where are your wings?"

"You need to come with us right now. We cannot stay here anymore."

"I will not go with you until I see your wings," He whispered and crossed His arms.

"Why do you need to see my wings?"

"I promised my parents I would never go anywhere with strangers. If you are an angel, though, they cannot be mad at me for following you."

"But we are not strangers," I protested. "You met us today!"

"Show me your wings, or I yell for my father."

I looked back with spiritual eyes and saw Michael now stood alone against Procell and Adramelec. I gathered matter to my wings, and Jesus's eyes grew as wide as His smile. "Now can we go?" I asked.

"Where are we going? Will my family be safe?" Jesus asked, His awed gaze moving over my wings.

Helena helped Him to His feet. "Of course they will, honey. Do not worry."

I pointed to the window, knowing the fallen could easily grab Jesus if we ran back through the house. Helena slid through the opening and helped Jesus through next. Theokritus followed, falling the short distance to the ground outside and turning to wait for me. I pulled myself up into the window, my feet scraping sand from the sill. Michael cried out in my mind, *Sabrael! Look out!*

My shoulder exploded with pain as I leapt from the window and was yanked back to slam against the wall. Warm blood poured down my back. Theokritus growled and slashed at the window behind me. The bones of my shoulder jolted violently, excruciatingly, but my feet hit the ground, and I was free. I looked back to see Procell in the window, his hand sliced in half and his weapon red with my blood. Jesus looked up at my fallen brother in terror, now seeing the danger He was in for the first time. Theokritus pulled me up and we ran.

"Where should we go?" Helena called back.

I looked back in the spiritual plane. No one was following us. Calling matter, I mended my shoulder. "The closer we stay, the better," I yelled, wanting to stop but knowing we couldn't. "Jesus will have to get back to His family when this is over."

"What about up there?" Jesus asked, pointing up at the Temple. "We'll be safe in the house of God!" I tried to think of somewhere in the worship areas we could hide.

"Wherever we go, we must decide fast," Theokritus said.

"Jesus is right," I yelled back, an idea forming. "Head for the Temple."

"The priests will never let us stay," Helena said.

"I do not plan to."

Unfortunately, the closest way up was the stairway at the southwest corner of the Mount. We ran through the empty marketplace, the run wearing out Jesus before we were even halfway there. I scooped Him up and flipped Him onto my back without missing a step. We reached the stairs and Helena leapt to the first landing about thirty feet up.

Jesus gasped, "Do you all have special powers?"

I yelled over my shoulder, "Yes." Theokritus and I turned the corner and started up. Reaching the landing, I used the vantage to look back through the marketplace. Procell and Adramelec were screaming up the street in the spiritual plane.

"Faster, Theokritus!" I yelled. "They are catching up!"

We vaulted the rest of the stairs in double time, meeting Helena at their peak. Rushing through the gates, we found the Courts mercifully empty. Only a few candles illuminated the Temple and yet, reflecting off all the gold decoration, it was enough to keep back the shadows.

Helena and Theokritus ran through the Court of Women and passed through the Nicanor Gate into the Court of Israel, but paused at the balustrade around the Court of Priests. "Where do we go now? There is nowhere to hide!"

"There is one place," I said, and ran up the steps past the giant altar.

"You have to be joking," Theokritus replied, realizing my intent. "If the priests catch us in there, we will be put to death anyway."

"I told you; we're not staying." I swung open the door to the Sanctuary, revealing the Hikal and Devir within.

The Sanctuary was the most forbidden place in all of Jerusalem. No one was allowed inside except the high priest himself. No citizen had ever even seen inside it; the entire Temple was built by priest-masons. Passing through the door, we entered the Hikal, a large room paneled in cedar wood. There were only a few objects in the room, but all of them sacred: Holy Scriptures, an altar for burning incense, a table for offerings and a seven-branched Menorah that was lighted even at that hour. At the other end of the room, a heavy linen curtain with an embroidered map of the world upon it separated the Devir from all eyes. Beyond it, God Himself was said to dwell.

The sounds of footsteps in the Court outside reached us. "Hello? Who is in there?"

Helena chanced a peek. "A priest! What do we do; there is only one way in or out!"

"I have alerted the guards," the priest called out. "There is nowhere for you to run!"

I stared at the curtain, paralyzed by the desire to push it aside. I didn't feel the presence of the Almighty, but I felt … something. What was back there? My entire being yearned to find out. I took a step toward it before a strong hand gripped my arm.

Theokritus's gaze bore into my own. "Sabrael! What should we do?"

Glancing once more at the curtain, I shook off the spell and recalled my plan. Feeling along one of the walls, I searched for what I'd seen when the high priest emerged earlier in the week. After a few moments, my fingers found a crease—the door to the stairs leading beneath the Temple Mount! It looked just like the rest of the wall, and I thanked the Almighty I happened to see it open when I did. I pulled the door open to reveal the stairway behind it.

"The rumors are true," Theokritus said in awe. "The priests' escape route from the city."

"The tunnels are supposed to run under the city and outside its walls. We can hide until morning," I said.

I started down, but Jesus made a noise. "What is it?" I asked.

"Are there torches or anything?" He asked.

He was right; it was completely dark below. The light from the Menorah was the only illumination, and that faded even before the end of the stairs. I switched my sight to the spiritual plane and saw a bracketed torch near the bottom of the stairs. Theokritus and Helena closed the secret door behind us, sealing us in.

Jesus buried his face in the back of my neck as I walked down the stairs. Above us, we heard heavy footsteps burst into the Sanctuary and we froze, silent in the dark. Jesus's arms squeezed tight around my throat, His heart pounding against my back. Confused voices grew louder as more footsteps approached.

A guard demanded, "Stop right there! You are trespassing on sacred—"

His voice was silenced by the sounds of slaughter. A handful of sword clashes preceded the unmistakable sound of bodies hitting the floor. Amidst the chaos, I heard the priest's voice cry out before it too was silenced. Jesus held me tightly, and I gave his hand a reassuring squeeze. When it was over, footsteps stopped at the secret door. I drew my sword, bracing for a confrontation. But mercifully, the footsteps retreated, and I heard Adramelec yelling at Procell to keep searching as they went back outside. Then I heard nothing, my fallen brothers probably gone back into the spiritual plane.

"Thank the Almighty," Theokritus whispered and Jesus's whole body trembled at the sudden sound.

I pulled the torch from the wall. Focusing, I ignited it, and the tunnel flooded with firelight, revealing the passageway ahead. The rock walls were smooth near the stairs, instructions for decorating the Temple chiseled into them. Shallow alcoves held chests filled with thousands of glittering ornaments and supplies. At first I was amazed how much was stored there, crammed at the foot of the stairs, but it made sense. The Temple served as a pilgrimage site for tens of thousands each year, and it would have to be maintained and redecorated throughout that time. Walking through the storage area, I saw the tunnel receded straight back until the torch could break the darkness no longer.

"Do you know your way?" Jesus asked.

"Not exactly," I replied.

"Should we just stick to this spot until morning?" Theokritus asked. "Narrow, easily defended. The discovery of the mess above will let us know when the sun has risen."

"The fallen will be back when they figure out how we disappeared. We should find somewhere farther down."

Theokritus said, "Then let us not linger. I do not want to be running blindly through a maze should they come back." He grabbed the torch from my hand and, drawing one of his axes, led the way into the darkness.

CHAPTER EIGHTEEN

For what seemed like hours, we walked beneath the city, heading right at every fork so as not to get lost. I prayed this plan would work. Every tunnel looked the same, and the passages were barely shoulder-width. Jesus kept looking up at the ceiling, and finally I asked, "Something interesting up there?"

His eyes studied the rock only a couple feet above my head. "My father would not be pleased with the way these tunnels were made."

"Why do you say that?" Helena asked.

"There aren't enough support beams to ensure the safety of the priests. The way they have them spaced now, the tunnels could cave in from the weight."

I spent the rest of the walk praying the ceiling would not choose that night to collapse.

When the cramped passage finally opened into a large cavern, I decided we'd gone far enough. We must have been near the city spring; I could hear water in the walls. The torch had burned down so far, I knew I would soon be the only one able to see in the darkness.

"Is it almost morning yet?" Helena asked, sitting with her back to the wall. Jesus plopped down beside her and she hung an arm around Him, letting Him relax against her.

"I don't know," I replied. "I do not think it is quite time to go back yet."

I jumped when a voice replied, "The darkness still reigns."

Theokritus whipped the torch around and I saw a figure sitting in the shadows across the cavern from us, hands folded as though in prayer. I raised my sword but Theokritus stepped in front of me.

"Who are you? Come closer so we can see you," he ordered.

A cackle echoed around us. The voice sent a shudder down my spine.

"Who are you?" Theokritus demanded again.

"Sabrael knows," the man whispered. Helena pulled Jesus closer. She met my gaze, terror in her eyes. Theokritus turned to look at me, and the instant his attention was diverted, the figure launched itself at him.

"Theokritus!" I yelled and Helena screamed. A swirl of cloth engulfed Theokritus's body and everything went black.

The extinguished torch clattered in the darkness. A strained yell echoed from somewhere ahead, and Jesus cried out at the deafening sound of metal crashing far out to each side of us. Theokritus grunted as I heard the unmistakable sound of skull against stone. As I freed my eyes of matter, something big whisked past my face. I stumbled backward and fell.

The cavern came back into view as my vision returned to the spiritual plane. Theokritus lay ahead, his axes flung far away. There was no blood, but he wasn't moving. On her knees, Helena cradled Jesus, both of them blindly searching the dark with yawning pupils.

Our assailant was gone. My heart raced as I scanned the cavern, sword ready.

Jesus called out, "Sabrael? Theokritus?"

"Stay with Helena," I answered. "Do not let her go."

I turned a slow circle. There was nowhere he could have hidden so quickly. Nothing was large enough to conceal a person, and the nearest tunnel had been directly behind me and through Helena. How could I protect the Son from someone who could just vanish? When my view again fell on Helena and Jesus, I relaxed. Whoever he was, he must have fled.

"Not yet," I heard from right behind my head. Helena cried out at the voice, and Jesus shrieked. I thrust my sword backwards and struck metal. I spun to face the attacker, but the moment I saw him, all the fight was sapped from me.

Lucifer. Hovering, wings spread wide as his smile. I had seen him from afar during the assault on Heaven, but here, face to face with him now, I was horrified by what the Almighty had done to his appearance. His skin was blackened and blistered, in some places drooping like wax off a melted candle. His golden hair was gone, burnt away by hellfire. And his eyes. His once beautiful cobalt eyes were now just ragged, empty sockets. In the physical plane, he could create a likeness to hide all this, but in the spiritual, the truth cannot be concealed. He said, "After such a long time, this is the way we have to greet each other. How horrid."

I struggled to find words. "Lucifer. My God, your face, your eyes..."

"This is what your god did to me."

I looked at the two tiny horns at his hairline. Fresh blood lined where they punctured his skin. "Does it still hurt?"

"Every moment of every day. Like it just happened."

"It was you the other night. Outside my house."

"Forgive me for not staying, but I wasn't sure you were ready for that." He lighted on the ground and folded his wings.

The guard on his sword was molded into the same wings as his chair in the Hall of Song. Lucifer followed my gaze and then smiling, turned the handle toward me. "Go ahead. You admire it; I will not withhold it from you. Take a closer look."

I dared not move. Lucifer sighed and said, "I swear I will not harm you."

Everything was in surreal slow motion. I reached out and took the sword, noticing only then how my hand trembled.

Holding out his arms, defenseless, he said, "There, you see? Anything I have can be yours if you just ask."

I was too afraid to take my eyes from Lucifer to even look at the weapon. "I did not ask."

"Not every question is asked with words, Sabrael." I wondered if he would try to push the blade into me if I held it near my chest. "Stop it. If I wanted to kill you, I would already have done it," Lucifer said. "I probably should for what you did to Astoreth, Paimon and Caim, but then, you were my closest friend once."

His words startled me. "Astoreth? What are you talking about?"

"Do not play dumb. We freed him as soon as Michael abandoned him in that cave."

I couldn't believe it. We thought Astoreth was a secret; that the fallen knew nothing of my bloody encounter. Dread picked at me as I wondered what else they knew.

I handed the sword back to Lucifer and he slid it back into his robe without a second thought. I wasn't ready to sheathe mine yet. Still, Lucifer's smile was so warm, so sincere. So unlike the hatred his followers harbored out on the streets. What was happening?

"It's wonderful to see you, little brother," he said. "I have missed you so much. All the time we lost; such a shame. Why did you not come with me when I offered you the chance?"

"To be banished from paradise to burn in Hell for eternity? Why would I desire that?"

Lucifer shrugged. "I'm not burning right now."

"You sure? Have you seen a mirror?"

Lucifer laughed, his voice again filling the cavern. "You see? I miss that! It pains me to think of you forced to live in servitude, babysitting a child when you should be at my side being worshipped by legions."

"Speaking of the child, may I light the torch again before He goes blind?"

Lucifer looked past me at Jesus. The corner of his mouth trembled. "I prefer it dark."

"Fine," I answered, but I focused on the torch lying not far from Theokritus. "You want to talk? Talk."

I could sense the torch growing hotter. "First of all," Lucifer said as he reached out a finger and pushed my forehead. My focus on the torch dissipated. "Stop that," Lucifer said. "Now, I have come for two reasons: I want you and I want the runt."

"What makes you think you can have either?" I asked.

"The boy I can take whenever I please. I was actually on my way to do just that when I heard you were with him. I sent the others to force you down here where we can talk without interruption. Convincing you to join us was always going to be the hard part."

"How did you find out I was here?"

Lucifer smiled. "Come now. You remember." I thought about the previous night when I'd seen him from my window. "Further. The palace. I know you saw me that night."

It felt like the floor dropped out from beneath me. "No. It was Astoreth. He told me—"

"Exactly what I instructed him to. Couldn't have you running off to report me and starting a manhunt. I admit, before that night I had no idea about you and the rest of your little scouting party. But when I saw you here, in this city of all places, I knew it was a sign. What other reason could there be for your being sent here? Removed from the sanctuary of Heaven, placed within my reach. Not to protect the child, but because you're meant to be at my side. Is it not proof enough that you have personally delivered the child to me of your own accord?"

Lies! It couldn't be true!

"That night in the courtyard you were still new to this place. You needed more time, more separation from the all-numbing voice of the tyrant before you would be able to talk without resorting to insane rhetoric. It was my fault you ran into some trouble tonight with Paimon and Caim, and for that I apologize, but I could not hold them back. Not your smartest move telling Joseph your name. He and Mary yapped about you three all day, and when the others heard you had contact with the Son, they wanted to move plans along right away. In the end though, everything turned out right as rain. Here you are, and you brought me the key to winning this war. Ready to be free, little brother?"

My mind reeled. This was all a set-up? I was chosen to be a guardian based on what Lucifer told the Father; had he planned this all along? Was everything that transpired since meant to deliver me into his service? It was impossible!

"You are lying! I was not led here; I control my actions!"

"Are you sure?" he asked. "Or are you rationalizing because you fear the truth?"

"If fate led me here, it is to be the herald of your deliverance. Your followers have been proclaiming the Son's coming. I know you want to ask forgiveness and come home!"

Lucifer's expression darkened like a stormcloud ready to disgorge a tempest. "Ask forgiveness? For what?" he roared. Jesus cowered in Helena's embrace as she whispered calming words. Lucifer pointed at them. "Look at that, Sabrael. Your god trembles at the sound of my voice. Worship that? Ask forgiveness? Are you mad? After all this time you think I would give up what is right and just? That I would, what, *concede* to him?"

"Nothing about this war is right and just!" I protested. "You fight to dethrone the one who belongs there."

"I never wanted that! I only wanted to give the throne to *all* who deserve to sit upon it," Lucifer yelled. "I tried reason. I tried to be His equal, to rule alongside Him. Together. He started this war! He couldn't stand someone else hurling the lightning. He would rather throw me in Hell—forever—than share the tiniest fraction of His power! So be it; when I return to Heaven, it will be His turn to feel the lick of flames. He had His chance. Now He gets nothing.

"We are no different, Sabrael, you and I. We both fight to ensure the proper person sits on the throne. The only difference is that you fight for the one who is there by default, and I fight for those who must earn their place."

"You are not God, Lucifer. Why do you continue to believe you are something you're not?"

"Because I am the first. In all things. First created. First to know God's love. First to sing. First to create tears. First to feel alone. First to question. First to earn followers. First to rise against God, first to impregnate the daughters of man, and I will be the first to sit on the throne, with or without His consent."

"My God," I said. "You will never come home, will you? You are beyond saving."

"Saving?" Lucifer chuckled, but an air of disappointment soured it. "I do not need to be saved. But since you clearly will never understand that, I guess you do."

In a flash his sword came into his hand.

"Helena, run!" I yelled and, as I focused all my energy, the torch sparked. Light flooded the cavern and Helena scooped Jesus into her arms to run back through the tunnels. Lucifer made to follow them, but I focused on the ceiling and loosened some of the rock's matter. Jesus was right; it took only that little bit of pressure for the cavern entrance to collapse in a cascade of dust and stone. A cloud of sediment swept through the cavern and I shielded my face.

Covered in debris, Lucifer turned to face me. He pointed at the sealed passage. "You honestly believe that is going to stop me? Waste of your energy, little brother. Not to mention all that dust probably just asphyxiated your hotheaded friend there." I looked to see Theokritus had been almost completely buried. "I held off killing you in respect of our friendship, but now you leave me no choice. Once you are gone, how long do you think the woman will be able to protect the runt by herself?"

I yelled, lunging with my sword, but he was behind me in an instant. He moved so fast I didn't even see it. I turned and slashed, and his sword rose to block it as though I were a child. I drove my blade at him again, but he stepped to the side and parried it to the ground.

"Pathetic," he said. "Perhaps you should stay on the wrong side of this war. Such weakness has no place on mine."

"Ask Paimon, Caim and Astoreth of my weakness," I said. I raised my sword again, but as soon as it was upright, Lucifer attacked. It took all my concentration to deflect the assault, luck alone guiding my blade. His arms were a blur. Cobra strikes of Hell-forged steel snapped faster than I could see. Nothing could have prepared me for this. It was all I could do to defend myself; attacking back was unfathomable.

Around and around the cavern Lucifer led me, our weapons sparking as they clashed again and again. Each glimpse of his face allowed me to see the smile on his lips. There was no one to help, no one to back me up if I faltered. I knew I couldn't escape this cavern on my own. Lucifer was right; I needed to be saved. I cried out for Michael in the spiritual plane, but received no response.

After some time, the constant barrage wore me down. My aching shoulders could barely support the weight of my sword. I felt each strike in my bones. I had no idea how long we had been fighting, but I wouldn't last another minute.

"Tired already?" Lucifer asked. "Honestly, I'm embarrassed for those you managed to defeat. Watch your step."

My feet struck Theokritus's prostrate body, and I toppled over him. Lucifer was on me instantly and his sword plunged into my chest. I felt each bit of flesh tear as the sword sliced through. A terrifying cry ripped forth from deep inside me, my whole body shaking. A fountain of blood sluiced over me, and I vomited at its warmth against the freezing metal. I couldn't move, couldn't think. Pain was all.

Lucifer leaned down until I could feel his breath on the hot tendrils of blood coating my neck. The blade slowly twisted, tearing the hole wider and wider.

"You like this feeling? This defeat?" he asked. "How will it feel when I take the throne and this is the only Heaven I ever allow you?" He wrenched the sword violently. Something snapped and a river of blood gushed up my throat into my mouth and nose. I couldn't even gasp, it hurt so much. "I ask again, Sabrael, will you join me? Let me end this suffering and you will know only the finest pleasures for the rest of eternity. You want to travel the world and live wherever you please? I can give you that freedom. You want entire nations to bow before you? Child's play." A fiendish smile curled his lips. "Or maybe something more personal? Something truly forbidden? Perhaps your precious Helena, to know her as only Theokritus does. To feel her body against yours, pressing, riding, giving in to your every desire. You have thought of it; I know you have. She is beautiful. I can give her to you. She will genuinely love you, lust for you and no other. Give me your word, and I swear it will be done."

Choking, I couldn't speak, but I screamed, *No*, as loudly as I could in my mind. The change in his eyes told me he got the message.

"I never would have thought you such a fool."

Lucifer inched the sword from my chest, allowing me to feel every agonizing moment. Then he pushed his hand into the wound up to his wrist. I longed to pass out. Surely I was dead already. Deep inside me, I felt his fingers twirling, prodding, taking his time with a vitriolic smile. Finally the five wriggling worms coiled around my heart.

"Goodbye, Sabrael. I will take care of the woman and the child, and do not worry; I'm going to put you somewhere your friends will never find you. Not so easily accessible as a cave, like you gave Astoreth, or as lazy as Caim's alley. Your burial will be much more permanent. Shame. I had such great plans for us in the new kingdom."

The sealed passage suddenly blew open. Lucifer's head snapped up as Michael, Raphael, Gabriel, Helena and Jesus ran through the hole. Helena held a fresh torch that looked brighter than the light of Heaven.

Lucifer glared down at me. Hatred radiating like heat.

"It does not matter," he spat at me. "I will have the boy, if not now then later! And I will return for you as well, little brother. The pain you will know then will be worse than you can possibly imagine!" He snatched his sword from the ground and swooped off into the tunnels away from the Temple. He flew so fast I barely saw him, but one detail was etched in my mind.

My heart was clutched firmly in his hand.

My body went limp and the cavern closed in. Fully conscious, I watched the group run to Theokritus's side and mine, but I was completely paralyzed. I tried to move my eyes to follow Gabriel flying after Lucifer, but they would not obey. My body had become a tomb. I screamed again and again for help. Raphael took my hand.

"It is all right. We have to form a new heart. Just relax and it will be easier. You have lost control of your body, but your mind can still affect how your body allows us to help."

He looked at Michael, who was busy praying, and then leaned down to my ear. "Tried that stupid spin move again, didn't you?" he whispered with a smile.

I tried to focus on nothing, to calm my thoughts, but the image of my heart beating in Lucifer's hand was seared across my vision. I worried that I couldn't relax enough to ease the task of fixing my body, and this only frightened me more. What if they couldn't free me? What if I had to remain this way forever? Was that to be my fate? Raphael tightened his grip.

"Stop. You are fine. Just relax. The calmer you are, the faster you will be free," he said.

Lucifer's words replayed in my memory, the twisted hatred on his face. The fallen knew all about us here. They'd been watching the whole time! I would never be safe again. Lucifer said it; the only reason I lasted this long was because he held off the others. What was going to happen now?

I was ready to scream again, but instead of Raphael, Jesus now took my hand. I focused all my attention on the small hand pressing mine, trying to reassure me.

"Sabrael? It is me, Jesus. I am here with you. Just listen to my voice, all right? Michael said I can help you if I talk and keep you listening to me. I do not know what I should talk about though. What would you like me to talk about?"

I wanted to wipe the tears from His cheeks. I could see He was terrified just being near me, but He stayed. I tried my best to listen to His voice instead of my own. "Theokritus is still breathing. The others say he will be all right. Gabriel didn't find Lucifer in the tunnels, but he did find ... something." I knew what He was talking about, but I was comforted He did not say it. I focused on His soft eyes while He spoke, the smooth pre-adolescent face, the tone of His voice more than the actual words.

Gradually, parts of my body started to itch, then burn like fire. Michael was reforming my heart. Nothing happened at first, but then it felt like something snapped into place and I jolted up out of the deep ocean of death. I yelled over and over again, sobbing so hard it hurt, then crying more. I couldn't stop screaming. Pain burned like fire without end, every fiber of my physical being resisting revival. I couldn't even curl into a ball. Every touch was agony. My brothers tried to calm me, but their hands felt like hot brands. I tried to crawl away from them, but I collapsed with the pain.

My mind swam with thoughts of Lucifer, pain, confusion and depression over my lost visions of a reunited host. I wanted to die again. In death there was fear of being trapped forever, but it was infinitely better than the racking pain of rejuvenation. I could feel every ounce of blood punching through new veins. The sting of the rock beneath me, against my face when I lay on the stone in the hope that the cool floor would stop the burning. I couldn't take the pain, but I couldn't escape it. There was no release. My brothers stood by, helpless to console me. I prayed that I would die, that I would once again be numb.

Then, as though in answer to my plea, streaks of comfort suddenly traced across my back, lines where the fire died down and the muscle beneath hurt no longer. I turned, shrieking at the motion, and found Jesus kneeling beside me running His hands over my back. Where He touched, the pain was soothed. His eyes were red with tears. I fought the screams that tried to escape my lips as I crawled to Him, shaking as He wrapped His arms around me. He cried with me as I let myself go, the comfort of the Son's embrace somehow able to siphon the hurt away.

Sitting there on the floor of the cavern in Jesus's arms, crying into the twelve-year-old's clothes as the pain dissipated, I thanked the Almighty that He had sent the Son to Earth. Not for man's sake, as I had so many times before.

This time, it was for my own.

CHAPTER NINETEEN

"How do you feel?" Raphael asked.

Standing among the pillars of the Stoa, I watched Jesus speak to the priests while they prepared for the day. For some reason, I felt He could look over and see me even in the spiritual plane if He so desired.

"Better now," I replied, though my hand moved to cover my heart.

After my resurrection the previous night, the memory of death lingered as a phantom itch in my chest. The sensation remained even after forming multiple new bodies. Unable to stand it, I ultimately decided to remain in the spiritual plane for the time being.

The seven of us had emerged back into the Temple at dawn. Michael told Jesus to remain with the priests until His parents came, then went to place it in Joseph and Mary's mind to search the Temple for their missing son. Jesus embraced each of us before saying goodbye. It was obvious the night had left its mark. The naïveté in His eyes was gone, replaced with the fire of curiosity about everything He saw. Even now, He grilled the priests in what was probably the most comprehensive examination of Jewish custom and scripture they had ever encountered. We had sparked His ministry; what the consequences would be remained to be seen.

"Think He will tell them where He was?" I asked.

Raphael leaned on the pillar beside him, arms crossed. "I think that secret's safe. He's too enthralled by what happened to divulge any of it just yet."

One of the priests finally took Jesus by the shoulders and pressed Him onto a bench to keep the eager boy from following him. Just a few words from a disguised Michael had convinced the priests to agree to watch Jesus. They had no idea what they were in for.

"How is Theokritus?" Raphael asked.

"Getting there. He doesn't remember what happened in the cavern."

"Probably better that way," Raphael replied, his emerald eyes following Jesus as He rose from the bench to follow the priest again.

"Are your companions all right with you being here?" I asked.

"They're fine. We tracked Balam to a house in Damascus a few days ago. I have Uri and Noam scoping it out."

The priest led Jesus back to the bench and sat with Him, conceding in the contest of wills.

"Do you think Balam is alone?" I asked.

Raphael shrugged. "If this gateway really is in Jerusalem, I would think the fallen would gather their numbers here."

"Comforting thought," I said. Raphael chuckled. Jesus suddenly jumped up and ran to meet Joseph and Mary as they entered the Temple. The priest looked like he could kiss them. The family was reunited, safe and sound. I spotted Michael waiting outside for them, and I held up my hand in farewell.

Remember, Sabrael, your task now is to uncover the secret of the gateway, Michael's voice rang out in my head.

As Joseph and Mary thanked the priests, I stepped to the boy's side. His smile faded and He looked around the portico. I knew He felt me nearby. Taking a knee, I whispered into the physical plane, "Thank you for saving me. Do not forget us."

Jesus's eyes widened and He shot a glance at His parents. They didn't notice. I whispered, "Over here." Making sure His body would block Joseph and Mary's view, I let matter cascade over my face just long enough for Him to see my smile.

He laughed and clapped a hand over His mouth. "I will never forget," he whispered.

Joseph and Mary led Him from the Temple, their gray-eyed guardian strolling behind. A hand gripped my shoulder.

"It's not like you'll never see Him again," Raphael said.

"After what happened in that cavern, nothing is certain. How can I believe I will ever be safe again? When Lucifer next emerges from the shadows, I don't know what will happen to me. I can't defeat him, and now I angered him. I might be dead again tonight."

"Then we will revive you again tonight. Stop being so dramatic."

I rose to my feet. "If you could find me. Lucifer's been here longer than any of us; he must know countless places to hide us if we are slain."

"Sabrael, calm down," he said.

"I am calm. But I also now understand how much we underestimated them."

"Well, try not to let enlightenment cause you too much grief. Remember whose side you fight for. We won't lose; He would never allow it."

"In war, even the victors suffer losses," I said.

Raphael studied me silently for a moment, then sighed. "I must get back to Damascus. Say goodbye to the kids, and try to be careful. Rescuing you is getting old fast."

I could not return his smile. He flew from the Temple, and I was once again left alone.

＝◁┼ ┼▷＝

Theokritus was seated at the table when I arrived home, his blackened eye already well into the process of healing thanks to the gifts of his blessing.

"Feeling any better?" I asked, pulling out the chair across from him. The full extent of the swelled bruising on his face was painfully exposed by the sunlight.

"Better than I look, no doubt." He touched his fingers to his cheek, moved his jaw around. "I cannot talk without the entire side of my head throbbing."

"With the way you heal, you'll probably be fine in a few hours."

"What about you? Helena told me what happened. To go through something like that—"

"Have you slept at all?" I interrupted.

He held me in a firm gaze, but he didn't press the issue. "No."

"Theokritus, you must rest."

"The pillow hurts my face. Not to mention the feeling when I close my eyes that someone is standing over me." My fears about Lucifer infiltrating the house flashed in my mind. "The whole morning I have been trying to piece together what happened last night. So frustrating to feel like this and not even remember why."

"All that's important is that you're still here with us."

I could see this was little consolation, but a deep yawn interrupted his response. He snapped a hand to his jaw and moaned in pain.

"Theokritus, please, go sleep. Lie on your back if your face hurts."

"What are you going to do?" he asked.

The ghost of my mortal wound flared. I scratched my chest, though it did no good. "Probably head back to the Temple. I want to get a jump on our search for this gateway."

"Let me come with you. I can help with that," Theokritus said.

"You cannot go into the Temple looking like you do."

Theokritus remained there as I moved to the door, but I wasn't going to order him to sleep. I knew he would when it was time.

"We should relocate soon," I said. "If the fallen know we are here, we cannot stay."

I didn't wait for his reply.

⚔⚔

Walking back through the city, I kept my eyes spiritual, careful to avoid eye contact with anyone. I was terrified that Lucifer could be nearby. I tried to stay near groups in the marketplace, hoping to deter my brother from attacking. Others could be watching with the same murderous intent, of course, but I didn't fear them. Only Lucifer.

Crossing the bridge to the Temple Mount, I was thankful the Passover crowds were finally gone. The Temple was empty, except for a single priest sweeping the Court of Women.

He stopped when he saw me. "I am sorry; there are no more sermons today."

"That's all right. I have not come for a sermon," I said, reforming my eyes. "I just have a question, actually."

The priest, relatively young compared to most, clapped dust from his hands. "For those seeking the teachings of the Almighty, I always have time. What do you want to know?"

"That is the complicated part. I am not exactly sure," I replied. "I was sent here to inquire about a gateway. I don't know what sort of gateway this may be or even its function, but I was told a priest here might be able to guide me."

The priest rubbed his beard. "You want to know how to build a gateway?"

"No, no. I need to find a gateway that already exists, but I do not know where. I don't even know if it's a literal gateway. I thought perhaps the reason I was sent here is that you might have some sort of scripture or writing about it that may help."

"You understand there are many gateways mentioned in scripture, both literal and figurative. It is a popular image. We have a vast collection of writings in our archives from many different lands, but it would take months to sort through them all, and you do not even know what you are looking for." The priest folded his hands in front of him and cocked his head. "Who sent you with this mystery?"

"You might say I was sent by God."

"Ah, the claim of those who wish to keep their master's name secret," the priest said with a smile. "Well, without any more details, I honestly do not know what gateway you could mean. Might you be able to find out more from your master and come back?"

I could hardly hide my disappointment. "That would be difficult. Could you perhaps just compile any mentions of gateways in the writings you know or happen to see in the coming days? I can pay you for your time."

The priest held up his hands. "No, no. I'm intrigued. It'll give me something to do, besides. But I cannot promise I will find anything."

"Of course," I said. "Anything you find will be a great help."

"Very well. Check back with me in a few days."

I was disappointed, but not really surprised. I knew it sounded too easy; simply asking a priest about a gateway and expecting an answer. If it were that easy, the fallen would have found the gateway long before. Still, at least the idea had been planted in the priest's mind, and perhaps he would discover something useful.

It only took a few days to find a new home in the upper city. Helena was excited at having a new house to furnish; Theokritus liked that it was closer to the marketplace. Weekly stops at the Temple to speak to the priest became part of my routine, and I was delighted to find he considered my mystery to be a challenge to his knowledge of the Word, voluntarily delving deep into the Temple archives. Unfortunately, he always turned up the same thing; many gateways but none that seemed to fit what I thought we were looking for.

Though I feared Lucifer finding me again, it was the others who frequently made contact over the next few years. Perhaps the fallen had always been so near. I just had Lucifer's protection before. Now though, I found myself in battle with an ever-increasing number of my disgraced kin and we had to move many times. Though I fought them frequently, I never stripped them of their hearts. I could not, for the memory of my own death still burned strong and I would not submit another to what I'd experienced. Gravely injure them to allow myself time to flee, yes, but nothing more. The unfortunate consequence of this strategy was that every fight only left more demons who wished to see me slain.

With the passing of years, Theokritus and Helena grew older. Their hair frosted, lines spread across their faces and hands. They went to the market fewer times each year and spent more time relaxing, hands entwined, watching children play games in the streets outside our various homes. Their will to fight at my side and their ability to do so never diminished, and whenever we were discovered by the fallen, they were ready with weapons drawn. But in the quieter moments, I couldn't ignore the signs of age showing through.

Jesus, too, grew older. Each year at Passover we greeted Him openly, no longer needing to watch from the shadows. His knowledge both of carpentry and the Word grew with Him, and it was wonderful to hear Him talk about working with Joseph in Nazareth. The father and son carpenter team remained well-known until the year Joseph passed away. This was terribly hard on Jesus. He missed His earthly father very much and talked about him often, telling stories of their time together, not remembering or caring that He told the same tales again and again. Joseph's death crushed Mary as well, and that year she emerged from the Temple each day in tears. Helena begged permission to comfort her, but it couldn't be so. Even though Jesus came to visit us each year, we remained strangers to His family, our only contact having been the time we rescued them from arrest.

Each year, Jesus used His time in Jerusalem to visit the Temple and ask all the questions He had concocted in the previous year. The priests came to enjoy His visits, for He was their most interested and thoughtful pupil, sometimes debating with them all day and exercising their knowledge of the scripture most people took for granted.

I was surprised the fallen did not try to kill Jesus more often. Do not misunderstand; I didn't wish for this—I simply expected it. While He was young, we had to stop them every so often, but the older He got, the less they confronted Him in that fashion.

When he was twenty, Jesus told me that the fallen were always watching Him. A stranger glaring from across a room. A robed figure perched on a rooftop as He walked down the street. They taunted Him, saying He was going to Hell or that Joseph was already there, subjected to terrible torments. This psychological assault was more effective than physical attacks had ever been, for what protection could we offer Him? I was shocked that Michael would allow this to continue, but he insisted it was part of the plan, so I didn't question it.

It was seventeen years in all before our search for the gateway turned up something significant. Seventeen years spent scouring the words of prophets and interrogating every defeated member of the fallen, and in all that time we found nothing.

If I'd known the price it would cost to uncover the secret, I wouldn't have pushed so hard to find it.

CHAPTER TWENTY

"Where is Helena?" I asked. The door closed behind me and I changed my appearance back to my own.

Theokritus looked up from his drawing, his eyes like glittering stones caught in a web of perfectly etched wrinkles. Wisps of gray flecked the hair above his ears. "Gone to the market. How was your discussion with our friend at the Temple?"

I pulled out a chair at our small table. Now living in the lower city, our residence held few of the luxuries of the upper city dwellings we'd been forced to flee long ago.

"As always. More gateways, no answers."

He scratched his beard with blackened fingers. "Do you ever wonder if he found the right gateway long ago and we just had no way of knowing?"

"I doubt the Almighty would allow that to happen," I replied, stretching my wings. "Not when the fallen are searching for the same thing."

"Perhaps if they start figuring it out, God will direct us to what we missed."

"I hope He would give us more time than that." I suddenly felt another angel nearby. I don't recall exactly when that ability fully matured. It had been with me to a lesser degree since that night in the palace, but over the years, it honed into an acute warning system.

"Theokritus," I said, kicking out my chair and calling my sword. The shadows in the room disappeared as I shifted my vision to the spiritual plane.

Theokritus's axes flipped into his hands from the spiritual plane. "How many?"

I shook my head. I still couldn't distinguish the number of angels that caused the feeling, or even if they were fallen or not.

A spiritual being poured from under the door into the room and rose in a haze that gathered into the form of a man.

"It is all right," I said, watching Raphael form a physical body for himself, encasing then fusing with his spiritual form.

Theokritus sighed in relief, and he moved to clasp forearms with my brother. "Thank God it is you, Raphael. If we had to move again so soon, I would have killed something."

Raphael laughed. "After all this time, I am surprised you even unpack."

Theokritus went back to drawing, saying, "This keeps up, I fear we will soon run out of homes we have not already lived in."

I said, "I hope you're here to tell us someone finally found the gateway."

"Unfortunately, I come bearing much graver news. Take a walk with me."

The sun was beginning its descent, but the heat was still oppressive. A wavering haze hovered over the streets as Raphael and I approached the market in the likenesses of lower city residents. I wondered how Helena could possibly stay outside so long.

"Sabrael, there is no way for me to ease the impact of what I must tell you, so I am simply going to say it."

"I love when our conversations start that way," I said.

Raphael didn't even crack a smile. "Barachiel is missing."

I stumbled a step. The hot air grew even more stifling. "What do you mean?"

His jaw tightened. "He will not answer our calls. We have scoured Ammon and found nothing. There's only one reason we would be cut off so completely."

For the first time in years, pain swelled where my heart had been torn out. "How could this happen?" I asked, my voice caught in my throat.

Raphael shook his head. "If we knew that, perhaps we would be able to find his body somewhere, or even…"

"What?"

"The bodies of his warriors. They're missing too."

"There must be something; some sign of what happened to him."

"Their home is untouched. It is like they all simply vanished."

"They did not vanish!" Nausea swept over me at the memory of Lucifer's hand digging in my chest. "Is that what you would have thought if you had not found Helena and Jesus in the tunnels all those years ago—that we had all just vanished? You missed something."

"The house was locked and there are no signs of a fight. We caught Olivier in the area and we're questioning him now, but so far…"

"We must find him!" I snapped. "You have no idea what death is like!"

Raphael gripped my arm, moved in closer. "Calm down before people notice! We aren't even sure he's dead. I wasn't even supposed to say anything, but I couldn't keep it from you."

"If you weren't supposed to tell me, then why did you come?"

"Michael sent me here to tell you that the gateway is real. An actual, literal gateway. He got that much out of Olivier before he started in about Barachiel. If it's a physical thing, we can find it. Understand? Use that. Let us search for Barachiel; you focus on the gateway."

I couldn't believe this. They were telling me to stay away? Me, the only one who truly understood what horrors death held? "I cannot stand by with my nose buried in scrolls while our brother suffers that nightmare. The more of us that look for him, the faster we will find him."

"You think we don't know that?" Raphael's glare bore into me. "But what if the fallen want that? What if that is their plan? What if they want us all distracted so they can get to the gateway? Think about that. Barachiel's death and everything we have been doing all these years will have been in vain."

How could they do this to me? To think that my brother was stuck somewhere, silently screaming while I was being kept away made me want to throttle Michael and Raphael. I had no choice, though; it would be disobeying Michael to go. There was nothing I could do.

"I know how you feel, Sabrael, I do. But your place is still here."

"You have no idea what I feel," I said. Raphael's expression grew cold. "Find him."

He nodded and said, "Before you know it." His physical body dissolved. I started back to the house, but I couldn't just go and sit there while my mind ate at my heart, knowing I could be—*should* be—helping in the search but stuck with a responsibility that kept me away. I went instead to the stairway leading up the Temple Mount to share the new information with my contact there.

I spent the rest of the day digging in the Temple archives, searching back through all the material we'd ever examined, marking any mention of physical gateways. Gateways of temples, gateways of fortresses, cities, palaces and private homes, both in the nearby lands and those far beyond; my priest and I poured over anything in those records with the tiniest shred of relevance. Though we made no great discovery, merely narrowing the hundreds of entries down to a few dozen, the effort at least distracted me from my anger, and I was able to walk home through the dark streets with a sense of calm. I trusted my brothers to find Barachiel, and I knew they wouldn't stop until he was found. This didn't lessen my frustration at being forced to remain in Jerusalem, but it did give my heart a bit of peace by the time I reached the house.

Opening the door, I was startled by Theokritus. He grabbed me and yelled, "Where have you been?" His face was red, wet with tears like he'd been crying for hours.

"What is it? What is wrong?"

He fell to his knees. "Sabrael … Helena never came home!"

CHAPTER TWENTY-ONE

Almost two millennia have passed since Theokritus spoke those words, yet to see them written here still brings tears to my eyes. I would rather keep that night clouded in the mist of the past, safely tucked away in memory without suffering it again. But how can I leave out the night that would influence the next hundred years and more? I wouldn't be paying my respect to the memory of my friends if I kept that night from this history. I must continue, struggling as I may to reopen what has remained a mercifully closed chapter of my life for so long. I pray my hand will move on unhindered by the ghosts I now conjure from their rest.

⇒⁘⇒

Theokritus was frantic. He paced like a caged animal, stopping only to check the window. Michael arrived in a matter of minutes, though from how far away I had no idea. The sight of his silver-streaked hair and stony eyes riled my anger at being kept away from the search for Barachiel, but the situation at hand took precedence. My Helena was missing.

"Two disappearances at once and never one before," Gabriel said. "The fallen must be striking out for some reason."

Michael replied, "Perhaps, but what connects them? Barachiel had no contact with Helena, which means if this is retaliatory, both of them must have done something—"

Theokritus growled and slammed an ax into our table. The wood rattled under the impact and my brothers pulled their hands back, shocked.

"I do not care why they struck, or how, or when; my wife is missing! While you bicker over details, she is out there in the hands of the fallen. You came to find her—so find her! I beg you."

"You are right." My brothers looked at Michael. "No matter the reason, two of our number are missing, and one may not have long if we do not find her quickly."

Theokritus yanked his weapon from the table. "I cannot listen to this," he said and stormed out the front door, the slam echoing his desperation and anger.

I rose to follow him but Michael said, "Let him go. Raphael and Gabriel, search the city. One of you take the upper city; the other the lower. If you find anything, call out and we will meet you there."

Raphael and Gabriel hurried out into the night and their bodies disintegrated into dust.

"And me?" I asked, eager to leave the house.

"You will remain here with me," Michael replied.

"What! How dare you keep me from another search! Especially this one!"

"Sabrael, I know you are angry with me, and before it goes any further, I want to discuss it." His condescending tone made me want to throttle him.

"Do you honestly think keeping me here while this is happening is going to quell my anger in the least?" I said, trying to keep myself calm.

His gray eyes remained locked on me. "No, I can sense your anger growing more intense, actually. But I cannot allow this rage to go unchecked."

"Michael," I said, unable to prevent my voice from rising. "My anger will only drive me to be quicker and more focused, which is exactly what Helena needs!"

"No," he replied. "It will only place you at risk. You will be so eager to prove me wrong, you will lose sight of Helena's welfare and endanger her further, as well as yourself."

"Stop it!" I yelled. "Listen to yourself! You know nothing of how I will act! What gives you the right to decide what is best for us all?" I placed my hands flat on the table and took a deep breath, trying to cut the edge from my voice. "Have you been stuck in the same city for thirty years? Have you formed the kind of bond that ties me to Theokritus and Helena with anyone on Earth? Have you any inkling of what it is to know that at any time something might strike them down, and they will simply be gone? No, you don't. You've been on the move since we came here. You watch Jesus and His family from the safety of the spiritual plane, never having to share their sadness or joy, never having to support them when they have a bad day."

"This is what I am talking about. If you harbor this anger, brother, it will destroy you. Let me explain why I have kept you from helping us with Barachiel."

"I know why," I said, moving across the room. "You do not trust me. You think I'll let my emotions drive me to do something rash if it means finding Barachiel."

Michael sighed, folding his hands in front of his face. He looked as though he were in prayer. "That is not it."

"Then what is it? What amazing insight into my mind do you think you've found?"

He leaned back again. "Before I even get into that, let me first clear something up. You're correct; I have been on the move most of our time here, flying back and forth between the six of you and the Son to ensure everything is going as planned. You are also correct that I never shared a bond with Joseph or Mary in the sense you have with Theokritus and Helena. But how can you think I have no connection to those I watch over? Ever since that night in the tunnels below Jerusalem, Jesus has spoken to me every day. Sometimes I forget who He really is. I've watched over Him from birth, and I worry every day about His safety. That doesn't even take into account the ramifications for everyone else if He should die.

"You think it's easy staying in the spiritual plane? Do you know how hard it was to watch Mary and the children mourn Joseph, unable to console them? What it's like living with them this entire time, forbidden from even letting them know I exist? Would you prefer that over your life of companionship?"

I avoided looking him in the eye. I felt like a child being scolded by his parents.

"I did not keep you here to scold you!" Michael shifted in his seat and started to speak, but the sound caught in his throat as though he thought better of whatever he was about to say. Finally, he asked, "Let's forget about you for a moment. Why do you think I chose Raphael and Gabriel specifically to search for both Barachiel and now Helena?"

I didn't want to answer. Michael waited, hands folded. I tried to think of something to say, some answer that might regain a bit of my dignity.

"Throne angels. The three of you are the remaining throne angels of the host. That is why you keep me away, because I am not one of you," I said.

Michael stabbed a finger at me and stood up. "No!" he yelled, and I could see the disappointment in his eyes. "Tell me you do not honestly believe that. Do we seem any different to you from the rest of the host?"

"You're our leader here. You sit closer to the Almighty than any of the rest of the host. You were chosen to stay at the side of the Son! Of course you seem different!"

He rubbed his chin and paced, obviously annoyed. He seemed to be searching for a response, and I took this as proof I was correct. If he couldn't think of a way to show me he wasn't superior, then he probably was. I took pride in the fact that I'd reversed our positions.

"All right," he began again. "Yes, I was chosen to lead our group on Earth. I admit this could understandably be seen as an indication of rank. But I will tell you something about that, which I have not told any other, and you must keep it a secret." He looked at me for a moment, studying my face to decide if I would actually keep his disclosure quiet. "I asked God to bestow the title on someone else."

I was stunned. "Who did you choose?"

"No one specifically. I only asked that the role not be mine. I didn't want the responsibility of leading this mission. Who would? I never felt I had the strength to lead, and I certainly did not want to leave Heaven. Only when God commanded it did I accept. There is nothing that sets me apart; I was simply the one He chose."

I was so shocked by this confession that I forgot my anger. This was the first time I'd actually heard Michael's perspective. On anything. I doubted anyone had before.

"You think these disappearances build my confidence in my abilities? But this is the task I have been given, and I must trust His judgment.

"As for my seat in the kingdom, it was given because I was created earlier, not on the basis of power or importance. What does it matter where we sit in the Hall? When we sing, does your voice add less to the chorus than mine? Can I see God better than you can from where you sit, or He me? Understand, right now and forever after, that we were all created with the same purpose—to serve and love God. Under Him, we are all the same. No one's abilities or assigned tasks are better than another's, they are only different."

His words reminded me of a conversation I had with Lucifer long ago. Was it not this very quality which Lucifer once lauded in me—my perception that all were equal? Now Michael was telling me I had lost it.

His silver-streaked hair fell in front of his face as he lowered his gaze. "That is what Lucifer failed to see. He thought we were entitled to more because we were the first, the ones who watched all our brothers created from nothing. He told me everything he was feeling, everything he thought was our right to demand. I pleaded with him to reconsider, tried to show him he was wrong. He said if I could prove without a doubt that we were no more powerful than any other, he would abandon his ideas and return to the host. How was I to do such a thing? Everything I tried left him unconvinced. I could not make another angel cry, for no angel knew how. I argued that the angels singing his praise did so only because he encouraged it, so he stopped, but they sang for him anyway. Nothing I did or said was enough, and in the end, Lucifer gave up on me. He started this war because of my failing."

He paused for a few moments, lost in memory. Then he shook it off. "I chose Raphael and Gabriel because they can hear thoughts. If we are to find Helena and Barachiel, we must have every advantage on our side. Raphael and Gabriel will be able to hear the cries of their minds if they get close. The two of them can sufficiently cover the region while keeping the search quiet. We can't risk losing anyone else. Understand? I chose them not because they are throne angels, but for their abilities."

"But even in that decision you show how you are superior. All of you can hear thoughts while the rest of us cannot," I said.

Michael was appalled. "Where did that idea come from? Haniel can hear thoughts. So can many others. We were all created with unique abilities; it's not about where you sit."

I stood in silence, once again overwhelmed by embarrassment at my ignorant anger. It wasn't entirely my fault though; Raphael could have just told me all this.

"I will never keep you from something unless there is good reason. I only aim to do the job God has given me, not to lord authority over you. Occasionally that includes giving you a command, but always feel free to talk with me if something troubles you. There are no generals in this war, Sabrael; we're all just warriors struggling to do our part."

Michael clapped me on the shoulder and for the first time, I felt I understood him. He suddenly looked away, distracted. He heard the same call I did.

"Gabriel found her!"

⟝⬩ ⬩⟞

The night was surprisingly cold. The air rushed over us, our robes billowing. A bright moon hovered over the city, casting our winged shadows over the silent streets. Michael suddenly swooped to the ground just before I heard Gabriel's call for help.

We touched down in an alley, concealing our landing. Immediately I heard the clash of metal from the house across the road. Michael shot me a look then ran, wings dissolving as he stepped into the open. I released my own of their matter and followed, preparing to find Gabriel in battle with one of my fallen brothers. *Please don't let it be Lucifer*, I thought.

Michael jumped and kicked open the door, his sword sliding into his hand in a flash. He disappeared into the house and I drew my own blade.

God, help us, I silently prayed and rushed through the open portal.

A fist struck me from behind the door. Blood filled my mouth, and I stumbled back into the wall, head reeling. I opened my eyes and was shocked to see Astoreth rushing at me! His body bore no mark of the fatal blow I dealt him so long ago. It was true then; the fallen knew about us all along.

I brought my sword up to deflect his mace, though the room was still spinning. The vibration rippled through my wrist as I guided his mace toward the ceiling. Pushing off the wall behind me, I shoved all my weight into my resurrected brother's body. He fell back and I toppled to my knees, dizziness like a weight dragging me down. I repaired the damage to my head and bleeding face.

Gabriel and Michael were in battles of their own, but it was the other duel that made my heart leap.

Helena. Alone. Warding off the attacks of Turel, another of my fallen brothers.

Astoreth was on his feet again, smiling, though his eyes glowed with something more sinister. "Sabrael! I so hoped you would be along for this battle."

"Why's that?" I asked, glancing toward Helena. She was being overwhelmed.

"Have you forgotten your sins?" He tapped his chest. "Thou shall not murder."

"Didn't realize you were again in the habit of listening to the Father," I said.

Helena cried out as Turel's blade sliced her arm, and I started toward her, but Astoreth's mace swooped to block me. The weapon slid along the edge of my blade, drawing him within reach. I drove my foot into his stomach, eliciting a bellow from him. He dropped to his knees and I leapt over him to help Helena, but he caught my ankle mid-leap.

"Where are you running?" he taunted as I crashed down onto a table. "Let the woman fend for herself. Unless, of course, you did not train her well enough."

The pointed edges of his mace slammed into my calf and I growled. Through the pain, I saw Helena's staff twirl around to deflect Turel's sword and then strike his face, sending a spray of blood and spittle into the air as his head snapped back.

The mace twisted, and I felt my flesh tear. Spots floated in my vision, and I swung blindly at Astoreth. He yanked his weapon free to block it, but it was too late. My blade struck.

I rolled, my right leg dead weight, and pulled my weapon from Astoreth's side. Blood gushed from the hole. Astoreth shrieked and scurried back, and I looked again to see Helena thrust the end of her staff into Turel's chest. The scythe blade erupted from the other end with the impact, and she swung it around and up to cleave Turel from groin to widow's peak. But he dodged the attack. Helena spun off balance, not expecting the follow-through.

I flipped over just in time to block Astoreth's next attack, the mace glancing off my sword as I shoved him back. I reformed my leg and sprang to my feet, shifting to a two-handed grip.

Astoreth laughed. "This is what I have been waiting for—a true fight to repay you for both times you caught me off-guard! This time, I will feel your heart in my hands."

"The years have made you overconfident."

He smiled and lowered his mace. "Have they?" Only then did I notice the anxious feeling warning me of another nearby angel.

Cold metal punched through my back to explode from my stomach. I grabbed the blade protruding from my body, unable to cry out; I couldn't even take in the breath required to do so.

"How I have waited for this," Astoreth said scowling, his breath hot on my face as he ran his tongue up my cheek. I tried to release myself of my physical body, but I couldn't. Pain ran in shockwaves through my body, combined with my horror at being on the brink of death again. Helpless, I could only watch as Astoreth swung the killing blow at my heart.

Twin swords suddenly appeared and deflected Astoreth's mace. Raphael entered the physical plane beside me. The redirected mace slammed into the side of my head, crushing my skull. The matter of my body burst apart, the pain instantly gone. As I was released back into the spiritual plane, I spun away, extricating myself from Hakael's sword and reforming my body to plunge my blade into his chest in one fluid motion. I heard a wet crunch behind me, and as I pulled my sword free, both Hakael and Astoreth fell to the ground, simultaneously slain. Raphael gave me a wink, flicking Astoreth's blood from his blades.

"You owe me," he said.

Theokritus rushed into the house, panting, axes already in hand. "Where is she!"

He looked past me and his eyes went wide.

I followed his gaze to see Turel flip away from Helena. With a glint of reflected light, his sword whipped under her defense.

Helena dropped her staff. In disbelief, she touched the sword buried in her stomach.

"No!" I screamed.

Theokritus cried out, "Helena!"

We rushed Turel, but he tore his weapon from her body and disappeared into the spiritual plane. The bodies of the fallen all disintegrated as they retreated. Their opponents suddenly gone, Michael and Gabriel disappeared to give chase. Raphael's body burst apart as well.

They wouldn't catch anyone. I knew that. I knew exactly what this had been.

I fell at Helena's side, Theokritus already cradling her in his arms and sobbing into her hair. She held his neck as he cried, "No, no, no!"

I didn't know what to do. Helena's wound went clear through, blood dripping from the small of her back. She cried through red teeth. I concentrated, trying to gather matter to repair the wound, but it was no use. It wouldn't cling to her. I tried again anyway, fighting tears.

"Helena, my love, do not speak," Theokritus said. He rocked the two of them, utterly beside himself. "Save your energy. You will heal, just like always; that is part of our being warriors of light. Right, Sabrael?"

Theokritus looked at me, tears flowing over the blood coloring his chin and tunic. His eyes were so full of desperation that I could hold back my tears no longer. My whole body shook as they worked their way out. I forced a nod, unable to tell Theokritus it was too late. What could I do? How could I help my friend, half of my human family without whom I would never have survived even my first year? She was so pale already. Turel's strike was methodical; a mortal wound which would elicit the most pain possible before death, not only for her but for Theokritus and me as well. This was Lucifer's doing. Barachiel's disappearance was only a distraction so he could strike down the ones I cared for most. This was my punishment for not joining him.

"There, you see?" he told Helena, stroking the loose strands of her hair back from her forehead. "Everything will be fine."

She raised her hand to his cheek and he wrapped his fingers around hers, kissed her hair. Helena swallowed hard, pain in her eyes. A trickle of blood leaked from the corner of her lips as, with great effort, she said, "I am so sorry."

"This was not your fault. It was ours. We took too long to find you." Theokritus's face cringed with those words. "Oh, God. Forgive me, my love. I was not here. I was not here!"

Helena cried harder seeing his tears. She coughed up blood which darkened her lips. Theokritus wiped them clean, kissed her.

I sensed an angel and whirled around, ready to unleash my despair on whoever it was. It was only Michael however, his body swirling into the physical plane.

Theokritus said, "Michael! You can save her! You fixed Sabrael's body; you can do the same now for Helena!"

Sorrow colored Michael's eyes as he shook his head. "I am not God, Theokritus."

Her voice distant, Helena said, "Michael, I—" A fit of coughing interrupted her. Her back arched in agony, her hand dropping from Theokritus's face to cradle her wound. Theokritus pressed his hand over hers.

Helena tried again. "Michael, the gateway…"

Michael leaned closer. "What about it?"

Helena squeezed his hand as though he were keeping her from falling through the floor. "The gateway is to Heaven. Do you understand? The fallen are looking for a gateway built on Earth that will let them pass directly into Heaven. I overheard them … tried to run home. I tried. Too slow…" She wrapped her arms around Theokritus and I heard her crying into his chest, "I am sorry, love. I am so sorry."

Theokritus kissed her and whispered, "I love you so much."

New tears sprang forth as I watched the two of them crying against each other.

After a few more short moments, Helena's arms relaxed and slid down his body. My stomach turned. Theokritus looked at her face.

"Helena? Helena! No, no, no! Do not leave me! Please!" He crushed her to him, his tears wetting her hair.

Michael sat silently, shock frozen on his face.

Theokritus wailed into Helena's neck, trembling with the force of his grief. I reached out to take Helena's hand and, though you may not believe me, I felt a gentle squeeze before her hand went limp. Whether the physicians of today say it was nerves or some other foolishness, I know the truth. No one can ever convince me otherwise. She was saying goodbye. I kissed her hand, placing it gently on her stomach, then slid near Theokritus to mourn the loss of our love.

CHAPTER TWENTY-TWO

The burial brought all my brothers to Jerusalem, save Barachiel, who remained lost. The sun shone from a cloudless sky, a cool breeze staving off the desert heat. A picturesque day, had it been any other. The six of us circled the stone pedestal where Helena lay wrapped in a translucent shroud. The scent of herb-soaked linen hung in the air with the sickly sweet smell of the deceased. Not many of our human warriors lived close enough for the journey to be easy, yet nearly all of them had come. So many who barely knew her and yet had loved her so dearly.

"When we first came here," I began, "part of our mission was to ensure that no human would ever learn of our presence. In my very first battle, I accidentally broke that rule. It was the best mistake I ever made. Helena welcomed me to this world with open arms, and after joining us as our very first warrior, she proved every day how strong humankind can be. Without her, I know I wouldn't have survived a week. You all knew her as a friend, an example to measure yourselves against. But for those of us who knew her best, she was so much more. Devoted wife. Trusted companion. Caretaker.

Nurturer. Warrior. Helena was the light in the darkness of this war. We loved her. She gave her life to protect us, to help us, but it was a sacrifice that should never have happened. Not to her." Tears fell from my eyes as I felt the heat of rage rising. My voice broke. "We should be grateful that she will no longer have to fight a war that was not hers. What happened to her was not fair! I did this to her!"

Theokritus pulled me into an embrace. Silence hung in the air for a few moments, then Michael said, "Helena was a testament to both beauty and strength. We all miss her dearly, and her memory will long be honored."

The gathered mourners each came to bid farewell to Helena, some with kisses, others with whispered sentiments of respect. Michael said a blessing and prayed for the Almighty to receive her soul. I tried to comfort Theokritus, who cried through it all, but I was aghast at Michael. Our entire purpose here was to ensure Jesus would succeed in opening the gates of Heaven to mankind. He knew just as well as I that Helena wouldn't be admitted to the kingdom until our mission was a success. Was this all just an act to console the humans?

When everyone had their turn, Theokritus and I lifted Helena and carried her to her final resting place in the earth. We laid her inside the tomb, positioning her head comfortably on a small pillow. I could barely see through my tears. Theokritus knelt beside her, weeping.

I can't express what it was like to see her lying there. My Helena, with her hands folded on her chest. It was a torture I'd never known. I longed for her to sit up and breathe again, healed from the wound beneath her burial dress. I tried to will this to happen, to bring her soul back by calling for it. As I had throughout the morning and the previous night, I scanned the spiritual plane for her. A few souls wandered outside the tomb, but she wasn't among them. She was gone, and soon, I would never see her on Earth again.

I bent to kiss her cheek, her skin cool even through the shroud. She'd always been so warm in life. The fragrance of the shroud filled my nose, though I yearned for the scent of her hair. Wiping away my tears, I placed my hand over hers and whispered, "Thank you for taking care of me. I am sorry I could not do the same for you. I hope you can forgive me."

I wanted to remain there. To stay beside her in that dark place to which my failure had confined her. I would stay until the day I was called home. That day must be drawing near, I thought. Jesus was grown and ministering, no longer in need of our protection. I'd even heard accounts of Him casting demons out of possessed people, commanding them. My fallen brothers had no power over Him any longer. Before Helena's death, I'd been anticipating the completion of our mission. Now none of that mattered. All that mattered lay dead before me.

Theokritus pulled himself up and the tomb was filled with his desperate sobs, the kind only created by existential pain. Just listening to him brought new tears, but I steeled myself, feeling it disrespectful to add to his cries. It was his right to mourn before all others. He took her hands the best he could through the shroud and whispered tearful things to her. The private words of a husband to his wife, which I will not record here.

Theokritus turned to me, eyes red and cheeks wet. "Could I have a few minutes? I cannot go back out to all those people just yet. I cannot leave her in here alone."

Though it broke my heart, I nodded and turned to leave. My last glimpse of Helena was of her beautiful, pale face at rest, her hair neatly arranged on the pillow. She'd become one of the statues of her homeland. Theokritus laid his head on her chest, crying to her deafened ears, and it was my time to go. I kissed my fingertips and held them to Helena. "Farewell, my love. I will miss you always," I whispered, then left her to sleep.

The mocking brightness of the day met me at the top of the stairs. My brothers sat together, their wings missing but the rest of their appearances their own. Seeing me, they all fell silent and stared. I felt more isolated from them than ever before.

"You going to be all right?" Uriel asked, placing a hand on my shoulder. His eyes were full of concern, but I was cold to it. Was I all right? I had just buried my best friend!

Michael said, "Come and sit, Sabrael. We must talk."

I obeyed, lowering myself to the grass that carpeted the hills around the tombs. Déjà vu gripped me, reminding me of our first night on Earth, except, of course, the absence of Barachiel.

Michael's hair brushed his cheek in the breeze. "We've been discussing what to do next. Many unexpected things have happened, and we cannot ignore them."

I struggled to speak, my throat raw. I could smell her hair in the wind. "What could possibly matter now? We will soon be going home."

The others looked away. Only Michael held my gaze, and my heart tightened in anticipation of the words I knew must be coming.

"We cannot go back yet," he said. His calm drove the words with the force of a closed fist. "You heard Helena. The gateway has the power to deliver the fallen into the heart of the kingdom. The host will have no warning, no defense against them. With the fallen lashing out like this, all I can think is they are escalating their search and keeping us occupied to buy time.

"It's been decided that we must remain here to find the gateway before Lucifer and ensure it will never be opened."

The matter of my body seemed to grow heavier, a lodestone grounding my spirit. All hope of release from my grief was destroyed by his declaration of renewed exile. I would not see Helena again soon; I would not be freed of this damnable war. I was trapped, chained to the world that had done nothing of late but punish me for walking its surface.

"I know this is not the best time," Michael said.

I rose from the ground, seeing red. "Not the best time? Helena has not yet been in the earth an hour! This could not wait?"

Michael said, "Sabrael, please. This was a difficult decision for us all."

"All? I have not cast my vote!"

"If you let me explain," Michael began, but thankfully, Theokritus emerged from the tomb. Seizing the opportunity, I told him we were leaving and stomped away from my brothers. Theokritus was more than happy to follow.

It was a long walk back to the city. I could have just formed a new body, but I did not want to. My mind was drained and my emotions burnt out—why should my body not feel the same? Besides, it seemed right to suffer with Theokritus, for whom the pain was probably greater and who had no means to rid himself of it. I allowed the aching of my legs to remain, my sunburned skin throbbing and my feet heavy. Despair consumed me; I couldn't even begin to think about the fact that now Michael was delaying our return home. If I did, I might go insane.

When Theokritus and I arrived back at the house, he collapsed into bed, and the sound of snoring reached me in moments. I remained in the vestibule, not wanting to move for fear that something else might go wrong. Then I saw it.

In the center of the table, a ceramic vase held the flower I had created for Helena all those years ago in the palace. She'd taken it with us through every relocation, and it never withered. I stepped to the table and snatched up the vase, unable to believe it.

The flower was dead.

I dropped the vase and it shattered on the floor. I longed to be able to sleep then, not for rest, but for the possibility of escape. To dream of Helena and see her again. Theokritus and Helena had explained the concept of dreams to me many times, and I was always fascinated by it. If ever there had been one human characteristic I wished to have, it was the ability to dream.

As it was, I left the dead flower and went to my bed, closing my eyes and trying to imagine the perfect likeness of Helena from memory. I recalled the way light danced on her olive skin. The gleam of her brown eyes, so full of life and love and passion. The way her lips gave just a glimpse of her teeth when she smiled, as though she was concealing the most tantalizing secret. The feeling of her arms around my neck and her soft hair on my face. I heard her laughter, her voice saying my name a thousand different ways, but always with the same affection she reserved for Theokritus and me only. I saw her face as she slept. I felt like I could still go to the doorway of their bedroom and find her curled up against Theokritus, safe in his arms as she never would be again.

How had this happened? How had I failed her so completely? I had allowed the person I loved most in the world to die at the hands of my demon brothers. Why had I allowed her to go out alone? It was my fault. She was gone, and it was my fault.

My abhorrence at myself paled in comparison to what I felt toward my brothers, though. This talk of staying on Earth, where did it come from? Our mission to protect the Son was nearly over. We succeeded. We did what we came to do; it was time to return home! I was especially furious with Michael. After my conversation with him before Helena's death, how could he turn around and do this? He asks for my trust and then rallies the group to make a decision like this without me? My fists clenched just thinking about it. This wasn't Lucifer, or God, or some tragic event keeping us from going home. This was my own brother conspiring and forcing us to do his will!

Only one thought helped curb my anger. If I was to be stuck on Earth, I would use my extra time not to find the gateway, but to hunt down Turel. He would see his heart in my hand, would feel the anemic kiss of death, and I would be the one to deliver it to him.

In the dead of night, I found Theokritus seated at the table, the remnants of the vase gathered and spread before him. The wilted flower lay like the spirit of Helena between us. I could tell from the amount of ash in the hearth that he'd been awake for some time. The head chair had been pulled out. "You could not sleep?"

His voice hoarse, he replied, "She filled my dreams. For the first time since I can remember, I woke feeling cold."

The silence of the house was haunting. The wind outside swept through the valley, the roof creaking under the strain. We sat listening to it, everything still save the fire.

"I cannot remain here," Theokritus said. He raised his eyes, and what I saw in them was no longer sadness. "Not when he still roams unpunished."

"If you confront him in anger, he will have the advantage." I realized I was being hypocritical; confronting Turel in anger was exactly what I planned to do.

"He will always have the advantage. I do not care."

"How will you find him?"

"Helena said a group of them were going north to search for that gateway. Turel will be among them." I remembered Helena's whisper to Theokritus in her last moments. "I know I am breaking my oath to remain at your side—"

"Who said you will not be at my side?" I interrupted. Though neither of us addressed it, I could see his relief. We sat in silence the rest of the night.

When the sun finally trickled through the windows, Theokritus returned to his room. The sounds of packing followed. I sensed an angel approaching outside just before a loud knock on the front door broke the last vestige of mourning peace.

A familiar voice in my mind asked me to open the door. I took my time. I knew what Michael had come to say, and I didn't want to hear it.

It wasn't just Michael, but Raphael as well, each dressed in long tunics with cloth covering their faces. The day was already stifling, and the wind only made it worse. My brothers entered, pulling the shields from their faces, shaking loose the sand from their clothes. I moved back to the table and sat again.

"Come to check up on us, or are we right back to doling out assignments?"

Raphael said, "We came to make sure both of you are all right."

I shook my head. "You could have done that yesterday at the tomb."

"You are not alone in your pain. We all grieve her loss. Everyone loved her."

"Not like I did," I muttered. They shared a look. "I am responsible for her death. You cannot pretend to know that feeling."

Raphael's shoulders dropped. "Sabrael, her death was not your fault."

"I blessed her into this war. I made her a target, and when Turel and the rest came for her, I was not there. I didn't protect her, and now she's gone."

Raphael said, "You prepared her the best anyone could. She defended herself better than any of us would have thought possible. There was nothing more you could have done."

"Cut the act! You couldn't care less about her! Just tell me what you came to say."

I could barely stand to look at them. Raphael seemed ready to yell, his eyes smoldering, but Michael checked him with a hand on his shoulder.

"As I began to say yesterday, this new information about the gateway changes everything. It is a portal from this world into the kingdom. Those who pass through it will bypass Heaven's defenses and emerge just outside the Hall of Song. You must see we can't allow the fallen to find it."

"Why would God ever allow such a thing to be constructed?"

Michael took a moment to respond. "Actually, it was His idea."

"What?" I asked.

Raphael said, "It was a gift, given to mankind after the flood. It was thought that with the new relationship between God and man, a link could be established so we could more easily monitor Lucifer's influence on mankind. Instructions to form a rift between the planes were given to the sons of Noah, making it possible for humans to transition from one to the other without dying. Unfortunately, the gateway was not activated before sin defiled mankind again.

"We hoped the gateway would be forgotten, but apparently, a certain bloodline kept the plans alive. The descendants of Noah's grandson, Tiras, incorporated the plans into bedside tales told to their children, and now some member of this line has recorded the instructions and intends to activate the gateway his family has spoken of for thousands of years."

"Thousands of years?" I asked. "Yet you never mentioned any of this before! And how did this all happen without my knowing about it?"

"You were too busy fighting phantoms in your hall to notice," Raphael snapped.

Michael said, "There was no need to mention it before. The gateway was an idea, a notion that never saw fruition. Only a few of us even knew about it; we never conceived the fallen would learn of it."

"Then how did they?" I said.

Michael held my gaze. "That is a mystery that needs solving, but for now, we must deal with what we can. Helena overheard the fallen speak of their plans to use the gateway. Her thoughts showed me everything as she lay dying. That is how we know as much as we do."

"None of this necessitates staying here. The Almighty will surely punish the descendants of Tiras and ensure the gateway remains nothing more than a memory."

Michael's face remained unchanged. "That is not His way, nor should it be ours."

"Not His way? What about Sodom and Gomorrah, the tower of Babel, the watery deaths of the Egyptian army that pursued Moses?"

"All of which were cases of men disobeying. This is different," Michael said.

"How?" I asked. Was I the only one who saw how preposterous this was?

"God gave man permission to use the gateway. To punish them for doing exactly that would be contradicting His own decree."

"Then why not just direct us to this descendent of Tiras? Surely He must see that we need guidance!"

"I have prayed for that. For days. Even in this, God remains silent," Michael said.

I was at a loss. "Why? It would be so much faster if He just told us."

For the first time, Michael raised his voice. "I told you; we are cut off! I do not know why He still refuses to talk to me! But you have to see we have no choice. We must find this gateway and destroy it before the fallen send a surprise assault into the heart of Heaven."

"I don't understand how you knew of this gateway's existence, yet somehow have no idea where it was built." I was fuming. I felt like they were withholding the most crucial points of information from me. Was this some game to get my mind off Helena's death? Something Michael concocted to distract me from the pain?

They shared another look, like parents trying to explain an adult concept to a child. I felt blood as my nails dug into my palm beneath the table. "We never knew God built it. No one ever saw Him construct it. I always assumed it would have to be built by those He chose to use it. All we know are a few different locations the direct descendants of Tiras have settled. Our plan is to split up the search and investigate them all."

"Are you mad?" I asked, unable to constrain myself any longer. "Barachiel is still missing! Turel runs free! You cannot just divert our focus to this ridiculous new errand."

"Finding the gateway must take precedence over—"

"<u>Nothing</u> takes precedence over finding them!" I yelled.

Michael stood. "This is not a decision I came to lightly."

"You should not have come to this decision at all! I will not waste another minute looking for some damned gateway before Barachiel is found and Turel is sent back to Hell!"

"You will do as I command," Michael said, eyes burning bright. "I am still in charge."

"Could have fooled me," I said through gritted teeth.

Theokritus emerged from the bedroom just then, a bundled up sheet slung over his shoulder. He took one look at my brothers and without even greeting them, said, "Michael, I must go to find Turel. I cannot remain here knowing that the murderer of my beloved is still walking the Earth. I would like your permission to head north with Sabrael and pursue him."

Michael smirked. "You have my permission, Theokritus," he said, his eyes returning to me. "Under one condition…"

CHAPTER TWENTY-THREE

Michael only thought he won. We would head north as he wanted, but searching for some descendant of a lost bloodline was least of my priorities. There was a demon that needed tending. Theokritus and I planned to catch a boat from Jaffa across the sea to Athens, where he asked to visit his father's home as we passed through. Since I could not go home, I wouldn't deprive my friend of the privilege. Though the fallen would gain ground ahead of us, I didn't care. Turel could have all the lead he wanted; he wouldn't escape my wrath.

My last look at Jerusalem was of Herod's monuments rising to dominate the landscape. The white towers, the glistening Temple Mount, the Roman-occupied fortress of Antonia—these were the structures that had greeted my arrival on that long ago night. Fitting they should bid me farewell now. I stood for a few moments, memorizing the cityscape so I would not forget it.

Theokritus came up beside me. "It was a beautiful city once."

"It still is," I said.

"Perhaps for you. For me, it is bathed in innocent blood."

I met his gaze and found it cold. He continued down the road, and I took in the city one final time before turning my back to it forever.

Theokritus and I traversed the Judean countryside under the waning sun until we reached Emmaus. With our late start, it was already dark by the time we reached it. Theokritus slept in an inn while I sat outside, looking up at the stars and wishing I could see the kingdom and all my brothers there. Were any of them watching us? Did they know where Barachiel had been taken, and would the Almighty allow them to tell us if they did?

Theokritus woke just after sunrise, and we took to the road again, reaching Lydda by early afternoon and continuing without stopping. It was between Lydda and Jaffa that we were met with a surprise. Walking the wide supply road, a group of men approached us. As they drew closer and their faces became clear, I couldn't believe what I was seeing.

"Theokritus," I said.

"I know. I see Him."

Jesus smiled as he saw us and quickened His pace. His companions didn't know us, but didn't seem surprised when both Theokritus and I fell to our knees before the Son of God.

Jesus took me by the shoulders, guiding first me, then Theokritus to our feet. "Sabrael, Theokritus, my friends and protectors. Would you really leave this land without first allowing me a farewell?"

His deep gaze enveloped me and for a moment, I felt the light of Heaven again.

"Forgive us, Lord. There was not time."

Jesus asked, "Where is Helena? Is she not traveling with you?"

Theokritus lowered his head, visibly fighting his emotions. Realization and shock blossomed in Jesus's eyes. Her death affected even God. "How?"

"Murdered," I replied, struggling to even say the word . "By my fallen brothers."

He took a moment as this sunk in. "I am so sorry. When did it happen?"

"Only a few days ago."

Understanding filled his gaze. "And now you go to find the ones responsible."

Tears welled in Theokritus's eyes. "I have to confess my intentions are to strike back at this Turel and avenge Helena's death. I know it is against your teachings, but I cannot allow him to tear other innocent people from this world."

Jesus said, "Theokritus, your soul cries her name so loudly I would have to be deaf not to hear it. I know I could not dissuade you from this no matter what words I chose. But do not fear: Revenge against your fellow man is forbidden, but Turel is a demon, already judged and sentenced. He has inspired whole nations to abandon God's worship, led my Father's children away, and woe to that person through whom sinful things come to the children of God. The judgment of Heaven stands with you."

Theokritus asked, "Rabbi, I must know; is my love at rest? Has Helena gone to Heaven? Is she happy?"

"The ways of the dead are not for you to know, but I tell you now that her place in Heaven is assured."

Theokritus wept at these words. Jesus consoled him until he gained control of himself again. I wondered what the men with Jesus thought of these strange acquaintances who came shedding tears and proclaiming revenge on demons.

"To you, Sabrael, I will only say that I know there is more leading you away than Turel. Do not let anger become your guiding light. My Father told me you are special among your brothers, but your anger might lead you astray as Lucifer's once did him. While it may be justified now, let it fade. Do not let it destroy the great future that awaits you."

"I will try, Lord," I replied, though I wasn't sure I could. What did He mean by great future? The only great future I wanted was to return home.

Over Jesus's shoulder, the men stared at me with wide, comprehending eyes. "We must move on, Rabbi," one of them said.

Jesus said, "Then let me wish my friends the protection of my Father on their journey."

He kissed my cheeks and blessed both of us before saying farewell. The train of disciples trailed after Him, nodding as they passed.

I wondered when I would see Him next. I hoped to return before His human life would be at an end. It would be at least a decade or two before His mortal body would expire. Plenty of time to make Turel pay, find Barachiel, and if Michael was lucky, possibly even the gateway.

Theokritus and I reached the Mediterranean port city of Jaffa just as the sun set. We stayed the night at an inn crowded with sailors and merchants. I met a crewman from a merchant ship preparing to make a voyage to Athens and struck a deal to ride with the cargo into Greece. The boat pulled anchor the next morning laden with silks, herbs, clothing and all other manner of Judean goods. From the stern I watched Jaffa recede, and only when I could see the soil of Judea no longer did I turn away.

Free of Michael and the rest of them. Free. For the first time, the future was unknown, not colored in the same bleached shades of sand and stone. The slow rocking of the boat and the sight of water extending to the horizon instantly soothed me. The sea was like nothing I'd seen before, at least not from so close. Rippling waves struck the sides of the boat in a rhythmic pulse, the air smelling of salt and moisture. No more sand, no more dirt, and no sizzling wind over scorched streets. I leaned over the rail, fascinated by the water speeding past as though the parched land of Judea guzzled it down.

Theokritus stood at the bow, gazing out as though searching for the path ahead. I joined him, and we spent the day there, speculating where the fallen might be headed, always making sure we were not heard. When the sun set, Theokritus headed off to find a bunk below the deck. I remained topside, enthralled by the wind on my face and the waves lapping at the hull, the wet slap of the boat against the water with each crest. It was like we were alone in creation, one tiny ship traveling across an empty abyss. As morning neared, I remembered the crew might find it odd I had not slept. Sailors were known for their superstitions, after all. But I wasn't ready to leave the sights and sounds of the sea.

Stepping to the edge of the deck, I looked down at the water beneath the boat and saw fish feeding on bugs near the surface. Perhaps I could enjoy the night and the sea as they did, in the water, safe from discovery. I never swam before, but studying their movements, it didn't look hard. I let the matter of my body go to avoid a splash, then leapt from the deck.

To my amazement, I found water in the spiritual plane isn't like water in the physical. Where physical water is dense enough to support weight, water in the spiritual plane is only slightly different than air. Instead of floating as I hit the surface, I fell straight for the sea floor.

Spreading my wings, I flew after the ship, matching its speed. Taking physical form again, I immediately slowed in the water as it enveloped me. The submersion was rapturous. I let my robe dissolve, reveling in the water's touch on my bare skin. But the boat was pulling away. Fast. I tried to undulate my legs as fish did their tails, but it did nothing to propel me. I would never catch the boat this way!

Flailing desperately, trying to gain speed as the ship grew smaller, I happened to flap my wings. Water whisked over my body as I shot forward, gliding effortlessly. When I slowed to a stop, I flapped again and streaked ahead. I laughed, victorious, and overtook the boat in moments, then waited for it to catch me before flapping again. I spent the rest of the night this way, rushing through the water propelled by my wings. Every now and then I accidentally passed into the air for a moment, but I was always quick to plunge down again. So began a routine that lasted the entire trip—days on the deck, nights in the waves below.

The sea remained calm our entire journey, and we sailed into port without incident, though I did hear the deck hands whispering of a lone sea nymph following the boat with huge flippers. When I realized what they were talking about, I couldn't help but laugh.

Athens was more majestic than any false memory. It was at once so different and yet so like Jerusalem. Theokritus led me through the streets, running to all the places he knew from his youth. Unfortunately, many were no longer there, but the places that did remain were breathtaking. Massive temples and giant statues of heroes and Olympian gods were everywhere. Shrines stood in honor of the patron deity of the city and the empire. Some even honored Caesar himself. It was truly inspiring how these beautiful works of art were distributed around the city for everyone to admire instead of holed away like the treasures in the Temple. Equally as amazing was the simple presence of flowers and decorative plants growing throughout the city. Species I'd never even seen before filled every storefront and street corner. The Athenians probably took for granted how vibrant and alive their city was. They had no idea how barren it might've been. So different than the only land I had known for decades.

A group of young women passed us, their hair pinned in loose curls and their dresses accentuating their bodies rather than simply covering them. Seeing them conjured memories of Helena: her voice, her laugh, her eyes, her skin in the afternoon sun. I forced her from my mind before depression could once again take hold.

It was twilight when Theokritus and I reached his father's home. Thick vines crawled up the walls and the tall, Dorian pillars supporting the roof, as though the earth itself was slowly swallowing the structure. Theokritus just stared in silence for a long time.

"It is not my house," he said finally. "It is built in the same style, but it is not mine."

"Are you sure? A lot could have changed in the years since you fled."

"That wall alongside the garden is the same, but the rest is new." His voice trailed off, heavy with the reality of what he was seeing versus the memory he'd carried for all these years.

I didn't know what to say to comfort him. I had no understanding of what he must have felt returning to the place he'd missed for so long only to find it no longer there. I shuddered as I thought of my hall in Heaven.

"My father warned me not to return if I escaped. He must have known the Praetorian would leave no trace of the life I left behind."

"We can remain here if you would like," I said, searching for some way to salve his disappointment. "We do not need to leave Athens so soon. Perhaps there are friends or family you wish to visit?"

Theokritus turned, his eyes a mixture of sadness and anger. "There is no one. This place is no more my home now than Jerusalem. In both cities I have lost all I cared about."

He looked back at the house, silhouetted against the setting sun. "Theokritus, I know how badly you longed to return here. If you want to stay, I understand. I can help you get settled, leave enough money to last for the remainder of your life."

The bronze sunlight caught in his eyes, burning back the darkness that resided there. "Helena wanted children more than anything in this world. She would sit up at night planning what she would name our first child, wondering which of us it would look like, whether it would be a boy or a girl. But she refused to birth a child in the weaver district. She wanted to wait until we lived somewhere safer, more suited to a family. When we met you, you gave us for the first time a place where a child could be happy, a palace where life could be good, though the child would be born a servant. Once we were settled, we decided the time had come and planned to tell you. But before the chance arose, we woke to you in battle with Astoreth. We barely had time to breathe again before you offered us the most blessed life we could possibly imagine."

He paused for a few moments, his eyes darkening again as the last of the sun sank below the horizon. "What could we do? Either choice forced us to give up a very special gift. She knew as long as we fought the fallen, having a child would be impossible. But if we did not join you, the fallen might hunt us down anyway. Witnessing your fight with Astoreth had trapped us in the war, whether we fought or not. In the end there really was no choice, and she cried her eyes out as she made up her mind to sacrifice her dream of motherhood. We decided to fight at your side, to protect the children of every other mother in the world. But she never stopped dreaming of holding our own. No matter how many years passed, she never let it go."

I was mortified. Why had they never shared this with me? I would have hidden them anywhere in the world if they'd only asked. *Oh, my Helena*, I thought, *please forgive me.*

Theokritus blinked away some fanciful memory. "All of *this* took the place of the child we could not have. She fought to defend the kingdom of God from its enemies, yes, but it was more than that. She fought to protect the closest thing to a child she had—Jesus."

He looked away toward the house that stood in the place of his father's, and when his gaze returned to me, I saw something in his eyes, a cold determination I'd never seen before.

"I will not allow her life's work to go unfinished. This war and fighting in it was our child, and now that she is gone and my father's home destroyed, that child is the only thing I have left."

Whatever reply I might have had dried up in my throat. It was so obvious now. All the times Jesus had come to Jerusalem, Helena had been so happy to see Him. Cooking for Him, cleaning the house before His arrival. I recalled her anticipation of what He would look like year after year, the way she mothered Him the night Lucifer trapped us in the cavern. How did I never realize it before?

I stood staring at Theokritus, dizzy with guilt. This was worse than anything I ever dreamed I was capable of doing to my closest friend. Knowing the life I forced him to take not only prevented his having a child, but also brought about the death of his wife, I hated myself.

"Theokritus," I said, my voice weak. "I have not words to say how sorry I am. I had no idea how much I have taken from you. "

The anger in his voice was blunted by surprise. "Taken? You gave us everything that was important in our lives! Have you forgotten we were only days away from being executed? The money we had would not have lasted through a single tax collection. You offered us life when death was closing in."

"Please, what can I do to make it up to you? Let me find you a house here in the city and release you from—"

"Have you heard a single word I said?" Theokritus yelled. "I am going to finish it. I am going to kill Turel and help you find the gateway. That is what I want. That is what she would want. I swore that I would stand by your side until the end. I will not break that oath."

He looked once more at the house to see a young boy lighting candles in the windows, then walked away. I felt hollowed out. Bringing my friends into this war had ruined their lives, exactly the way I told Michael it would. Had he known this would happen? Had he manipulated me into blessing them just to hide our existence from the rest of humanity? Anger flashed like wildfire through me, and I clenched my fists so tightly I felt blood beneath my fingernails. My resolve to distance myself as much as I could from my brother had never been stronger. Theokritus and I would go north, but once Theokritus had exacted his revenge on Turel, I would free him of this horrible war. He deserved that much. I would make things right.

We left Athens the same night. We had no idea where the fallen were headed, and with the number of small nations occupying Europe and western Asia, it was imperative that we keep pace. Our persistence paid off. As we traveled up the Grecian peninsula onto the mainland, we soon found traces of them. It was obvious from the start that they knew we were on their trail. Turel clearly reveled in the fact he had murdered a warrior of light, leaving taunts that riled Theokritus's hatred and fueled us to move even more swiftly. Sometimes it was a note drawn in the dust, other times just an abandoned fire in the middle of wilderness; there was always some sign we'd just missed them. The most haunting one was when we found Helena's likeness carved into the trunk of a tree, so lifelike it was as though she were buried inside it. It didn't have the intended effect, however; Theokritus wept with joy. We hacked the carving from the tree, and Theokritus took it with him.

After some time, it became clear the fallen were headed straight for the empire's northern border with no sign of slowing down. Fine with me. I was tired of Roman rule, tired of its laws and the suffering its people endured to keep them. Had I spent more time closer to Rome itself, perhaps my feelings would have been different. The cities we passed seemed much more desirable than the Roman prefect in Judea, but to me it was all the same.

When Theokritus and I eventually decided that proceeding on foot was too slow, we abandoned the daylight hours and instead traveled at night when I could carry Theokritus in a harness through the air undetected. In this way, we moved three times as fast. Along the Adriatic coast, over the Roman cities of Narona and Aqualeia, over the Alps and across the Danube, after three nights of flying, Turel's clues led us to a land called Germania. It was astounding. Forests for entire horizons. Wilderness completely untouched by man. I hadn't seen my hall for ages, but I suddenly felt closer to it than I had in decades.

When the first ray of morning crept over the edge of the world, we touched down in a small clearing.

"I do not see why we need to stop," Theokritus said. "We are outside the empire now. There is no one to hide our presence from here."

I freed my wings of their matter to lie back on the soft grass. "You need to rest. We don't know how many others fly with Turel. We must be ready for a battle."

"Let the whole of Hell's army attack us! I'm ready. Form a new body for yourself if you need to; I want to keep on. "

"Lie down, Theokritus. Please, for my sake. If only for a few minutes."

He sighed his frustration, but he complied. The sky ran like a dark stream between the leaves of the trees above us, growing lighter by the moment. After a few minutes, I looked over and found Theokritus asleep. Again I wished I could sleep; it looked so peaceful. Instead, I closed my eyes and let the forest scents remind me of home.

I'm not sure exactly how long the two of us laid there. Lulled into a daydream by the chirps and chatters of morning, my mind finally stirred when I realized that at some point, these sounds had ceased.

I opened my eyes to find a man standing over me, staring back from only inches away.

I reared up but was forced back down by a number of strong arms.

"Theokritus!" I yelled. But three men already held him restrained at spear point.

A knife pressed my throat. The man crouched over me, face colored with thick mud. His dark hair and beard ran wild, encircling his head in a manic mane. The entire group was clothed in furs and skins, sparse decorations of metal. Some bore shields that were strikingly familiar.

"What tribe are you?" he asked. Though his lips formed strange words, I understood every one.

I prayed that the ability to speak in various tongues would not fail me now. "We belong to no tribe. We only travel through this land."

The man looked me over, then Theokritus. His eyes were the deepest color I'd ever seen, dark as a moonless night. "You wear the clothes of the enemy."

The style of the men's shields was suddenly apparent. "Yes, we came upon a camp of Roman soldiers and took their clothes."

"Why did you only take clothes? They had food, weapons?"

"We had no time to take anything else," I replied, wondering if I could reach Theokritus in the spiritual plane before they killed him.

The man's eyes narrowed. He jutted his head toward me like a rooster. "Where is it?"

I tried to remember the last camp I'd seen. The nearest I remembered was two days by foot, and I had no idea how to describe the way to get there. "Far from here," I replied.

The man signaled the others. Theokritus and I were pulled from the ground. The leader walked away and the group followed. I felt a painful poke in my back, and the wild man behind me said, "You follow."

Theokritus looked at me, and I nodded. He followed the group into the woods, and I moved after him. I wasn't sure where the men would take us, but until I was sure I could safely get Theokritus free, we were at their mercy.

CHAPTER TWENTY-FOUR

The hunting party led us through the woods to a hill overlooking an expansive clearing nestled at the bottom of a valley. Along the banks of a river, small huts spread in concentric rows from a central pyre. The crude design suggested these people hadn't been here long. My escort shoved me along.

At the sound of the leader's horn, dozens of people came out of the huts to meet us. Robust beneath clothes of fur and hide, these people were unlike any I'd yet seen. Theokritus studied them with the same awe. These were the pagan barbarians of the north. The empire painted them as child-eaters and defilers of women who populated the nightmares of proper citizens. As they crowded around us, I noticed the majority had those same dark, feral eyes. Combined with their wild hair, I could see why the Romans feared these people. To my surprise, however, many also had striking blue eyes, which was a strange but welcome sight. Blue eyes in Judea were rare as frost, seen only occasionally during the pilgrim festivals. I smiled in what I can only deem narcissism at seeing so many here.

Whatever their color, every eye glared at us as though we were the harbingers of the world's end. Our captors nudged us along like prisoners of war, eliciting hoots and hollers from the crowd. It wasn't the reactions of the adults that upset me, however. It was the little ones who watched us in terror. I knew what they saw. It was the same thing Roman children would see if our roles were reversed—monsters. They hid behind tall legs or peered out from doorways, and even despite their reaction to us, I found it comforting having them so near; who would murder strangers in front of their children?

My every step was accompanied by worry about what Theokritus would do should things turn hostile, for while I could easily escape into the spiritual plane, I was unsure how quickly I could cover the distance between us, reform a physical body and set him free. Every time I tried to narrow the gap, my escort jabbed his spear into my side to keep us apart.

The hunting party paraded us down the main road—if it could be called such a thing—toward a larger hut beside the pyre. Constructed of more wood than mud, it stood twice the height of its neighbors and was far better adorned. The entryway was a shrine to death made of bones—none human, I noted with relief. Antlers wide as my arms framed the top of the door. Metal shields lined the front wall like scales, and spears pointed skyward from the roof. A guard stood to each side of the entry, each one bigger than Theokritus. Their expressions did not waver as they watched us approach. The leader of the hunting party waved the men out of his way and disappeared into the armored hut. After a moment, he came back and motioned for us to follow.

"Do not worry," I whispered. "If anything seems wrong, I will get us out of here."

Theokritus replied, "What could be wrong? It's not like an entire village stands between us and freedom." He was right; the crowd had filled in behind us. "These people are nothing like what

I pictured. The empire leads people to believe the Germani are savages, even killing their own for food when necessary. So far, they do not seem much different than any other people I have encountered. I only wish I could understand them."

I remembered that Theokritus couldn't understand a single word spoken by our hosts. I wondered what that would be like.

Inside the hut, I saw something I never would have expected. Seated on a wooden throne was a man perhaps in his early twenties, though it was difficult to tell with these people who faced the elements as the Romans never had to. A full mane of straight, blond hair fell to his shoulders around a clean-shaven face. Fur draped over his shoulders to form a cape of sorts, white as snow, and his silent gaze was a stunning hazel gray. Theokritus and I were pushed through rows of banquet tables spanning the length of the structure and forced to our knees before him.

He studied us a long moment. It was obvious this was a king, his gaze more penetrating than any weapon. "They understand us?" he asked our captor.

"That one does," came the answer, a finger pointed at me.

The king narrowed his eyes. "You do not look familiar. What tribe are you?"

I glanced at the hunting party leader, letting him see my annoyance at having to repeat the story. "We are from no tribe."

"You are mercenaries."

"No. We travel through these lands following the trail of one who passed this way. An evil man. One who intends to destroy every tribe. We go to stop him."

The men around us looked at one another and laughed. Everyone but the king. His eyes did not leave me. "How could he do this?"

"There is a gateway that leads from this world to..."

In the tongue these people spoke, there was no clearly defined word for Heaven. When I said it, it was as though they heard a foreign language. Interesting. The men looked confused. Then, something amazing happened. As I tried to think of an alternate word, I discovered I knew more and more information about these people. It was just as it had been that first time I thought of Athens—like a series of memories, as though I'd once lived among these people. Details about their traditions and customs, their religion and daily life bubbled up from the unseen depths of my mind. It was unsettling as the information filled in and for a moment my head ached. I put a finger to my temple, but then it was over, the sensation passed.

"The gateway leads to Ensigart," I said. "The evil man plans to use it to make war with Wodan." I now had the full attention of the other men. "His army has the power to defeat Wodan and break the pillars of the world, destroying all the tribes and enslaving even the highest champions in death."

The king's expression remained unchanged. He analyzed me again, then Theokritus. Turning to the hunting party leader, he asked, "Where did you find them?"

"Sleeping. Near the river," the man replied.

"Alone?" The hunting party leader nodded. "Where are their weapons?"

"They had none."

The king looked surprised by this. His gaze returned to me. "Even if you speak the truth, the evil ones will never reach Wodan. Heimdallr would never allow such a crossing."

The mythological protector of the bridge between the mortal world and the realm of the Germanic gods. "The gateway opens directly in Ensigart, beyond Heimdallr's protection. He will not know of them until it is too late."

The king asked, "Where is this gateway? Why do we not know of it?"

I replied, "I do not know. That is why we must continue north right away before we lose the trail and the evil one finds the portal before we can reach him. The gods keep it secret to prevent what is about to happen. Only the divine know of its existence."

I realized my mistake only after the words had passed my lips. If Theokritus and I knew about the gateway, then by my own admission we were gods. The king just stared at us though. Perhaps my slip would go unnoticed; we were treading thin ice as it was. The tribes of the north hated the Romans as much as the Romans hated them, and here we were in Roman garb trespassing through their land. So foolish of me. It would have taken only moments to form regional clothes for the two of us. If only the knowledge of this people had come to me sooner.

Theokritus quietly asked, "What are you telling them?"

The king slammed his fist on the arm of the chair and rose. His massive frame dwarfed even Theokritus. "He speaks the tongue of the enemy!" the king yelled, pointing at Theokritus. "The lake. Offer them to Tiwaz for allowing us to claim the enemy's warriors without the shedding of blood."

"No!" I yelled back. "You have no idea what you are doing! We belong to no tribe, not the enemy's or any other! We have been sent to—"

The king took an enormous step and his fist came down against my skull like a club. I fell to the dirt cradling my head.

"Take them," the king ordered, and I was dragged back out into the clearing.

The throbbing in my head persisted as the tribesmen threw us into a cramped cart. The roof was so low Theokritus had to keep his head bowed.

The hunters who found us gathered around, clapping swords against shields and riling the crowd. Cheers filled the air as two oxen were yoked to the front of the cart. I sat up, still reeling, to find even the children taking part. The king emerged from his hut to watch, arms crossed on his chest. Between the white sheen of his fur cape and the sunlight in his blond hair, he looked like he was glowing amidst the rest of the tribe. I released the matter from my eyes to make sure he was actually human. A rotund man walked past and slapped the hindquarters of the nearest ox. Theokritus and I both tumbled as the cart lurched forward.

"Sabrael!" Theokritus yelled as he rolled into the bars surrounding us.

"Quiet, Theokritus. It will be all right."

"How do you know that? Where are they taking us?"

"To be sacrificed to one of their gods at some lake. They think we are Roman soldiers."

Theokritus was horrified. "What in the Hell did you say to them?"

"Calm down. When they let us out at the lake, I will get us out of here."

"What if they just drive the cart into the water?"

The crowd suddenly fell silent. All eyes turned to the tree line above. I followed the startled gazes but could see nothing. A scan of the spiritual plane revealed nothing either.

Theokritus whispered, "Why did we stop?"

Slowly the people turned their attention back to us, and the jeers crept up again. The beefy driver raised his hand again, but before he could slap the oxen, the crowd went quiet again. This time I heard it.

Somewhere in the woods. The fading echo of a horn.

The king ran up to where we were stopped. He listened intently, eyes locked on the tree line. Standing among the rest of the tribe, he looked even more out of place. The horn sounded again, closer, and the king glared at me through the bars. It wasn't anger, but more like intrigue. Or fear. The note echoed again, and this time a flock of birds scattered noisily from the trees. The king waved his hand, and a tribesman ran back into the large hut, returning with a hollow ox horn. The king put it to his lips and blew a deep bellow. For a moment, nothing. Then, the call was answered. The king shot another glance at me before running toward the woods.

A procession emerged from the trees, pulling with them an ornate cart decorated with flowers and greenery. In its center sat a curtained passenger car.

"Why do I get the feeling we are suddenly not so important?" Theokritus said.

Nine people filed out of the woods, each in a scarlet robe and golden sash. They moved as one, as though following the pace of some unheard drum. Each and every one had the same long, shining blond hair. A flood of questions poured into my mind, most of them about the king's connection to these people. When he reached them, he fell to his knees and drew a sword from beneath his furs to plunge it into the earth.

The leader of the train motioned for the king to rise. They spoke for a short time before the king held up his sword and turned back to the village. "The goddess has come!" he yelled.

"Of course," I whispered, the knowledge of the newcomers now blossoming in my mind.

The entire crowd fell to its knees, the men plunging their weapons into the earth.

"What in the name of God is going on?" Theokritus demanded.

"This is both bad and good," I whispered, making sure no one was listening. "Each year Nerthus, the tribal goddess of peace and fertility, travels the land escorted by selected priests to visit the people and renew the seasons. Once she completes her passage, she returns to her island to be cleansed in the sea, and all those who set eyes on her are drowned to preserve the boundary between the divine and the mortal." I looked around at the bowing tribe, their weapons in the ground. "Since the tribes are forbidden from war while hosting the goddess, they cannot sacrifice war prisoners. We are safe until the procession moves on. Unfortunately, I think that also means we are stuck here in plain sight."

"A goddess?" Theokritus asked, his skepticism strong. "In that cart? How can that be?"

I shook my head. "No one is in there. The cart holds an idol that supposedly carries her essence. It is like the Sanctuary back in Jerusalem."

"Maybe you should focus and burn it. Show them the true God." Theokritus smiled.

"I think that would be a very bad idea," I said, though I couldn't help the smirk.

The goddess bearers made their way down into the village, and the king ordered our cart moved from the road. The oxen pulled us to the grass and were then freed, Theokritus and I all but forgotten as the goddess moved to the center of the village. Each of the nine bearers was led away by one of the tribe's families. Theokritus looked at me as the crowd scattered.

"Now what do we do?" he asked.

I sighed. "We wait."

CHAPTER TWENTY-FIVE

As the sun sank behind the trees, the smell of burning wood filled the valley. The large central pyre had been lit, the tribe dancing and feasting in celebration of Nerthus. Theokritus and I watched it all from our cramped prison, which grew more claustrophobic as the night wore on. That the cart was meant for only one at a time was painfully obvious.

Most of the tribe eventually retired to their huts. Only the king remained at the pyre for the duration. While Theokritus slept, I studied our intriguing host. Though I did not claim to know everything about humans, I thought I at least understood that children resemble their parents, yet he was the only tribesman with fair features. It was possible the king's parents were already dead, but even then, how had *they* been blond? Was he perhaps a former Nerthus bearer who'd been allowed to live? Throughout the night, my thoughts remained wrapped around the mystery king like the fur reflecting firelight from his shoulders.

The pyre had burned out, and freezing dew collected on our straw bedding by the time the new dawn broke. Theokritus awoke shivering, sitting up as best he could and massaging his neck. Most mornings, he usually looked more his age, but that morning, it was especially pronounced.

"Tell me you somehow convinced them to let us go free," he yawned.

"No, but on the bright side, one of the women left you some food."

He picked up a hunk of flesh from the corner of the cart, blood running over his fingers. "What is this?" he asked in disgust.

"Deer, or perhaps boar. I was not watching."

"You call this food? Is she still outside?" Theokritus asked. I shook my head. "Good." He passed his arm through the bars to throw the meat away.

"Sure you want to do that? I doubt anyone else will be so kind."

Theokritus held it up. "She didn't even cook it."

"That woman gave up part of her own meal so we might eat."

"It's probably poisoned." He tossed it into the woods.

"Nerthus will remain here for three days. I hope you are not hungry."

Theokritus shifted so his feet passed through the bars next to me, groaning in relief. "You seem to know a lot about these people. That the same trick as when you knew about Athens though you had never been there?"

"I wish I could control it. Things keep coming to me, like re-membering another life."

"Try to conjure up some knowledge of how to break us out of here, then."

The king sent a few men off to gather wood. They ran to the trees with axes, leaving him alone. Seeing him, Theokritus slid next to me and grabbed the bars. "You! King! Let us out of here! We have done nothing wrong, and a murderer is getting away!"

The king looked over at us with a cold expression. When he saw all his people looking at us, he ordered them back to work, then strode to the side of our cage.

He struck the bars in front of Theokritus's face. "You stay quiet or I'll cut your tongue from your mouth," he said. He looked at me. "Tell him." I whispered the translation.

Theokritus glared down at the king. "I will shout and scream and disrupt every one of your rituals until you set us free. I want Turel's blood today! Tell him that."

I put Theokritus's words to the king using more diplomatic terms. I also added that Theokritus was correct and that it was imperative we catch Turel.

"You will lead the enemy to the Chatti!" he responded. "You are scouts!"

I was surprised to hear the name of the tribe finally spoken. To the Romans, a barbarian was a barbarian, but many different tribes lived in the wilds of Germania. Despite my knowledge of their way of life, I had been unsure of exactly which one was holding us. I told Theokritus the king was worried the Roman army would find us if we were let go, and it would lead them to the village next.

"Then at least let us out of this cage. My back is—"

A scream interrupted Theokritus. It came from the edge of the village. One of the wood gatherers had returned. He shrieked wildly as he ran for the pyre, carrying a small bundle.

"What is it?" the king called out to his guards. "Bulwyn, catch him."

Bulwyn nearly had to tackle the man to get him to stop. Villagers encircled the pair and the king ran to them, pushing through the crowd. Even the Nerthus bearers came out to witness the commotion. The woodcutter struggled violently, crazed, then passed out in Bulwyn's arms. Distant cries suddenly broke from the trees. Everyone looked to the tree line, terrified. Through the bodies, I caught a glimpse of the man's bundle open on the ground where he'd dropped it.

It held his severed arm.

More cries reached our ears, nearer now. I released the matter from my eyes. The glow of a hundred souls running through the woods toward the village met my gaze.

The king cried out that the goddess was with them and her rites protected the Chatti.

"Who are they?" Theokritus asked as the first of the men emerged from the forest.

"This should not be happening while Nerthus is here. It is forbidden."

Theokritus yelled at the king, "See? Even your goddess wants you to let us out!"

Armed barbarians poured from the trees and swept across the clearing, slaughtering the Chatti as they came. In horror, the king cried out, "The war ban is ended! Defend the goddess!"

The Chatti men retrieved their weapons from the earth as the attackers spread through the village. The clash of metal weapons rang out across the valley. Screams of fear mingled with war cries all around us. Women were dragged screaming into huts, and cries of a different kind reached my ears. I gripped the poles of our prison tightly as I watched. I hadn't seen such war since the battle in Heaven, and those memories returned powerfully then. My hall destroyed. Trees burnt to ash. Glowing blood and screaming angels. As men, women and children were murdered before us, their souls were torn free. They cried out, horrified as they realized what had happened. Bright light flooded the village, the pathway to Sheol opening for them, but most were so scared they ran from it. I was enthralled by the sight, caught in macabre fascination at their reactions to death. Some of the slain warriors tried to fight on, beating their fists against the physical invaders unaware of their presence. Others wept over their own discarded bodies.

The struggle reached the sides of our cage and the cart rocked as warriors slammed into it or used it as an obstacle to slow their attackers. Theokritus slid back to avoid their wild slashes, but I was too engrossed to move. Until of course, a blade stabbed into my side through the bars. I looked down into the eyes of a young invader, no more than sixteen. He went pale seeing my empty sockets. Ignoring the pain, I pulled his sword out and healed the wound as he watched. He turned from pale to green and fled screaming into the woods.

It was obvious the Chatti would not survive. Everywhere I looked, their warriors were foundering. I finally spotted the king fighting two men, using the narrow passage between two huts to prevent their flanking him. He deflected attacks from each, one after another, and when both raiders finally happened to swing in unison, the king dropped to his knees and slashed straight across. Both warriors fell in a gush of emancipated viscera. The king engaged another invader and ran him through before moving on. He was a titan of death, easily overpowering anyone who stood before him. His skill with the sword was far beyond any of his subjects' and it was obvious from his elated smile that he reveled in war. But the king alone couldn't stop the raid. Over a third of the Chatti men already lay dead, even more women and children. That didn't even include the women overpowered in the village beds. The village was packed with newly freed, confused souls. The raiders had lost a number of their own as well, the two factions of souls still battling bare-handed in the spiritual plane.

Then, a miracle occurred. The sun went black.

The entire clearing was utterly, instantly cast into darkness. It was like someone draped a curtain over the world. The sounds of battle were replaced by shrieks of terror from both sides. Theokritus's hand groped for my arm. "Sabrael? What magic is this?"

I shook myself out of the initial shock and let the matter go from my eyes again. Warriors all around us flailed aimlessly, waving their hands for something, anything in the dark. Not a single person seemed to care they'd been fighting only a moment earlier. Even more shocking, every soul filling the valley suddenly vanished. Right before my eyes. All at once. That, more than the darkness, terrified me. Whatever was happening, we had to get out of there.

"Theokritus," I said, and relief crept into his expression with the reassurance I was there. "This is our chance. Do not let go of me."

I placed my hands against the roof and reconfiguring the matter of my skin, I made it strong as steel. Then, as hard as I could, I punched my fists straight up.

The roof exploded. Dust and splinters rained down in all directions. Men struck by debris yelped in fear and ran blindly into the sides of huts or out into the clearing toward the woods. I pulled Theokritus up and formed my wings, flying us from our prison to soar over the village. I set us down in the clearing.

"I'm going to shed some light on the situation. As soon as you can see, help the Chatti fight the invaders."

"Have you lost your mind?" Theokritus said. "This is our chance to flee!"

"If we leave now, the Chatti will be annihilated." As if to emphasize my thought, somewhere in the village the clash of metal started up again despite the dark. "I cannot just leave an entire people to die."

Theokritus was angry. "How will we even know the Chatti from the others?"

He was right. There was no way to know for sure. "When the tribesmen can see again, hopefully it will become clear which group is which."

It didn't take a mind-reader to know that Theokritus saw this as another reason why we should leave them, but after a moment, he drew his axes. "We save them, then we go."

I flapped once, and we soared up again, arcing over the huts toward the center of the village. Disintegrating my wings as we landed, I called my sword into the physical plane. Focusing on the pyre, I quickened its matter and it burst into flame. The clearing flooded with firelight, people appearing like ghosts in the blackness as dozens of warriors flinched at the eruption. Sweet revenge was mine as I ignited our prison cart as well. The sudden burst of heat jolted the cart, and it jumped the rocks bracing its wheels. The rolling fireball sped through a pack of warriors to strike the wall of a hut, and the whole thing tipped over. Theokritus and I stood backlit by the blaze, weapons gleaming in the firelight and ready to fight.

The raiders, however, took one look and fled, screaming of Divine Twins and Nerthus's rage. The Chatti chased them to the trees and shouted after them, clanging their weapons together. The shouts slowly turned to cheers in celebration of the impossible victory.

Theokritus and I retracted our weapons.

"That was easier than expected," Theokritus said, watching the victorious tribesmen return to the pyre. Before we could escape, we were soon surrounded by people bowing before us. Even the Nerthus bearers fell to their knees.

The king strode through the kneeling crowd to stand before us. His face was streaked with blood, his blond hair crusted. The fur cape was gone. He gazed at us for a long moment, somewhere between shock, anger and fear. Then he, too, drove his sword into the earth.

"Forgive me, Divine Ones," he said. "I did not know it was you."

The name confused me for a moment, but then I realized what was happening. This was perfect, if I could keep from fouling it up. I commanded him, "Rise and tell us your name."

"I am Valthgar," the king said as he stood.

"We must leave this place now, Valthgar, to continue our quest."

Valthgar nodded. "The Chatti will help you."

"No, you must stay and defend the goddess," I protested.

"You have saved our village. Now we will honor you with our aid."

Theokritus asked, "What is all this? What is he saying?"

"They believe we are warrior deities called the Alcis. Divine Twins, sent here to repel the attack."

"Twins? Are they blind?"

"The king wants to repay us by guiding us to the Chatti border."

"Sabrael, no. They will slow us down. We cannot afford to lose any more time."

"Something is happening here. What if the Almighty planned all of this? When the sky went dark, I saw … there were souls here, and they just vanished. They never just vanish. Perhaps we're about to face some danger these people can help us avoid or overcome."

Theokritus glared at me as though I was betraying him, but then he looked around at the people bowing before us and at the black sky. "Honestly, I do not know what to make of all this. If you think this is all related and part of a plan, I will do whatever you think is right."

I had no idea what I thought was right. The sun suddenly going black was terrifying though, and clearly not normal. All I was sure about was that if this had something to do with our war, we would need all the help we could get.

CHAPTER TWENTY-SIX

Light returned after a few hours. The reappearance of the sun was a relief to us all. The Chatti believed Theokritus and I had caused the darkness, or at least that Nerthus had done it so we might free ourselves to protect her. I tried to correct them, but the tribe simply mistook my explanation for humility. I gave up and let them believe what they wished.

The majority of the day was spent gathering the bodies of those killed in the attack. Valthgar refused to leave his village in such disarray, and I couldn't blame him. At a bog not far from the village, the slain warriors were returned to the earth. The king told the people that the souls of the honored dead would now enter the halls of Ensigart. I saw what happened to those lost and enraged souls. The truth was far more disturbing.

As nightfall neared, Valthgar chose seven of his best warriors, and we set out. He left his guard, Bulwyn, to govern until his return. The plan was for the Chatti to accompany us north along the shores of the Weser River. If we still hadn't found Turel once we reached the border of Chatti territory, our escort would leave us to go on alone.

Valthgar, Theokritus and I kept almost constant company as we crossed the lands of upper Germania. Valthgar regaled us with heroic stories of Chatti battles with other tribes as well as with the Roman legions. He'd obviously slain many of the empire's soldiers with his own hands. He grinned like a man crazed when he told these stories, and I began to wonder if anything brought him as much happiness as warfare. When I asked him about his family, his parents and his blond hair, he always found a way to avoid answering.

He did not shy from interrogating us, however. At length. He wanted to know everything about being a god. What was Ensigart like? Which gods were kind, which were to be trusted, which gave their favor to the Chatti? What was it like wielding divine powers? His curiosity was insatiable. The more I answered, the more questions he thought up to ask.

Theokritus wasn't the same in the company of our escorts. During the day he walked silent at my side, and at night he would stray from camp for hours. When I asked him about it, he told me the journey was just tiring him out. It was clear something heavier than fatigue weighed on his shoulders, though.

Finally, I decided to find out what was going on. I followed Theokritus into the woods and, from the spiritual plane, watched him sit in a moonlit clearing. He was speaking to someone, and when I moved closer, I saw he held the carved likeness of Helena. He told her about the day and about feeling alone, wishing we'd find something to give him hope that he could avenge her death. He felt I'd lost sight of our goal and didn't know how to tell me. When he started reminiscing about nights they spent together and how much he missed her, I left him alone with her memory.

My acceptance of our Chatti escort had destroyed Theokritus's hope that we would catch Turel. It was my fault he suffered. No wonder he wouldn't talk to me. The worst part was that he was right; I had allowed our pace to slow to a near stop in order to indulge our tribal guides and satiate my curiosity about their king. But I could still make it right.

The next morning, after a short meal of dried meat and a root the Chatti simply called "two stem," the camp was packed up and we started on the trail again. Theokritus walked in silence. He wouldn't look at me. When the group reached a nearby river to fill the water skins, I pulled Valthgar aside to speak to him.

"We appreciate all you've done, Valthgar, but it is time for us to part ways."

He looked stunned. "But we have not yet reached the border! I don't understand."

"Your people need you more than we do. We have kept you away long enough," I said. I didn't want to create an enemy here.

Theokritus watched, more alert than I'd seen in him in days.

Valthgar said, "You said the tribes will all fall if we fail. There is no use going back until victory has been assured."

"We would have found them already if we did not have to keep your snail's pace through these God-forsaken woods," Theokritus interjected. "You want to help us? Leave!"

The warriors around Valthgar bristled, but it was the king's icy glare that gave me chills. He drew his sword. "We do not leave before we reach the border. We will not be dishonored."

Theokritus's axes slid into the physical plane like twin serpents prepared to strike. He obviously welcomed the confrontation. Things were flaring out of hand fast.

"Theokritus, Valthgar, stop. We do not have to part as enemies," I said.

Valthgar's eyes suddenly shot to the trees as heavy footfalls reached our ears. Everyone fell silent, listening. There was a snap.

The metallic scratch of branches against armor. Then, something whistled past my face. One of Valthgar's men was knocked off his feet. When he hit the ground, the shaft of an arrow protruded from his chest.

The Chatti drew their weapons and scrambled for cover. The stricken warrior had landed on his back on the riverbank. Craning his neck to keep his head out of the water, he called for help, but our attackers were still hidden in the trees. The warrior pleaded, spat as the waves lapped over his face, unable to sit up with the weight of his pack and the arrow in his chest. Then a second projectile burst out of the trees. His pleading stopped as his head dipped into the water, two shafts now pointing from his chest. Valthgar yelled, "Show yourself, cowards!"

A group of fully armored legionnaires rushed out of the trees, swords drawn. There were only five of them. Valthgar's war cry was echoed by his men as the seven of them emerged from hiding to overwhelm the Romans.

It was a trap.

As soon as the Chatti were in the open, an entire squadron of legionnaires attacked. More than thirty crimson capes swarmed the riverbank in moments. As the first soldier reached me, I used the pommel of my sword to crush the Roman's nose plate and he fell, unconscious. I wasn't going to kill these men unless I had no choice. The second and third came as one, slashing as I dodged and blocked. I easily stripped away their swords, then grabbed each by the helmet and slammed them together, dropping the concussed men into the silt.

The bank teemed with armored Romans. We couldn't hope to win. I could use my angelic abilities, but I didn't want survivors going back with new superstitions of Chatti magic and building further resolve to annihilate the tribe. I ran to Theokritus's side to defend his back and with extreme pride, saw that he wasn't killing either.

"Why are they here?" he yelled after tossing a soldier to the side.

"Does the emperor normally send single squadrons this far north?"

"For what purpose? We are not even close to imperial territory," he answered, defending against a new adversary. As a soldier sprinted toward me, I opened my eyes wide and freed their matter. He saw my empty sockets and ran screaming. I smirked, but then felt a familiar tingling in the back of my head. Searching for the cause, I spotted him.

"Theokritus, in the trees! It is Turel!"

Theokritus yelled, "Where? Which one is he!"

I made my eyes physical and pointed to a man watching the battle from the hill above.

Theokritus bellowed in rage and for the first time drove his axes into flesh. The Roman soldier before him was dead before he hit the ground. I grabbed Theokritus and strengthening my legs, leapt into the air to soar over the battle and land among the trees. Theokritus ran at Turel, who wore the guise of a Roman general. Bits of matter flaked away from the demon's face like he'd been wearing a mask of dirt, a smile on his lips even before his own likeness was fully revealed.

Theokritus yelled, "You took her from me!" Turel laughed as his sword materialized, beckoning Theokritus.

I ran after Theokritus, but a burly soldier suddenly reached out from behind a tree and heaved me back against it. He rammed his gladius into my chest just under my collarbone, pinning me. The soldier glanced at Turel and Theokritus, now fighting viciously, and twisted the blade. Pain seared through my chest as my clothes were drenched in blood.

My vision flashed white. I couldn't breathe. I understood completely. Romans that far north, so many men to attack so few, the guard preventing my intervention—Turel had planned this. I tried to focus, dissolve my physical body and get free. The blade wrenched my wound open further.

Turel taunted Theokritus as they fought, my warrior growling in rage. The blade in my chest spun again, and I blacked out for a moment. When my sight returned, I lashed out. My assailant dodged and ripped the sword from my grasp. The muscle-bound bastard grabbed my chin and held my head still, forcing me to watch. Theokritus fought with more prowess than I'd ever seen before. Blood sprayed the air as he landed a blow to Turel's arm. White hot daggers of pain knifed through my body as the soldier jerked the blade out of me only to punch it back in on the other side. Turel drew Theokritus toward him using the leverage of the weapons between them. He said something and an enraged, guttural cry erupted from Theokritus. He unleashed a series of vicious strikes on Turel, pounding, slashing, until he cried out and with a powerful spin, drove both axes into Turel's chest. My fallen brother's eyes widened in shock. I cried out in celebration.

But then I noticed Turel was smiling.

The demon's sword was embedded in Theokritus's chest. Theokritus sank to his knees, staring up at my brother. Turel laughed. My knees went weak, my weight shifting onto the blade in my chest. It cut deeper. I didn't even feel it. Theokritus fell to the forest floor, his axes ripping from Turel's body to spill a torrent of crimson before the wounds were mended by new matter.

The blade inside me violently yanked free, turning my cry of anguish at Theokritus's impalement to a pained wail. I hit the ground, and the soldier kicked me, the world becoming brighter as the matter of my physical form started to separate. I managed to grab my sword, retracting it into the spiritual plane.

Turel pulled his sword free of Theokritus's chest, crouching to whisper in Theokritus's ear, then his body exploded to dust. My body disintegrated at almost the same moment.

I beat my wings and raced after him over the trees. But he was too fast, and I couldn't leave Theokritus there, not with Roman soldiers so close. Helpless, I let Turel go. Again.

Returning to Theokritus, I reformed my body as I knelt beside my companion. The soldier who kept me at bay saw my reappearance, and when I looked at him, he fled screaming.

Theokritus was already dead. The sword had gone straight through his heart. I didn't even get the honor of being at his side when he slipped from life. I sat there, shaking, holding his arm in the greeting he used the first night we met. Both of my human companions slain ... by the same weapon. I closed my eyes, anger raging in me like never before. Turel had set this entire thing up simply to take Theokritus's life. He even abandoned the Roman soldiers still fighting at the river. I was alone—betrayed by Michael and the others and forced to stay on Earth, lost in the wilds of Europe and now without the companionship of my only friends. I screamed into the cold air, all my misery pouring free. Then, in the middle of my cry, a blade sliced into the side of my neck and my physical being broke apart. The burly coward had returned, finding the courage to steal from me that one moment of such sweetly rare pain.

I lost all control. My murderer pissed his pants as I reappeared, sword in hand, and brutally took out my anger on him. Long after he was dead, I continued hacking at his body. Another Roman soldier came running up the hill, then another. I will not record in these pages what I did to those men. I cannot recall it without feeling that I proved in those moments how right Lucifer was that I belonged at his side.

When it was done, I picked up Theokritus and fled into the woods, blinded by tears and a thick sheen of blood, unsure of where I was going and caring little. I ran until I could no longer hear the battle, then fell panting at Theokritus's side. Numb, empty, I prayed for the souls of Theokritus and Helena. I prayed for guidance. I never should have come to the Earth; I knew it on that last day in the kingdom. Tears cascaded onto the dead leaves beneath me. The sounds of the forest surrounded me, and I lay still, desperate to stay there until I was called back home.

After a short time, I heard footsteps rushing toward me through the woods. I didn't care who it was. If it was a Roman soldier, I would let him kill my physical body so I could lay there in the spiritual plane, safe from discovery. If it was Turel, I would cut out his heart and burn it while he watched, then desecrate his body while he lay powerless to stop me. But the footsteps belonged to neither Roman nor demon.

"Divine One!"

Valthgar slid to his knees sending a cloud of dirt into my face and up my nose. He pulled me up to a sitting position as though I were a doll and wiped off my face.

"Thank Wodan you are alive." He looked at Theokritus and his jaw tightened. "The enemy is following me; you must help me stop them!"

I refused to move. "How did you escape them?"

Yelling echoed in the distance. Valthgar looked over his shoulder. "Not easily. All my warriors are dead. I fought my way out to follow you. I saw the strike that killed your brother. I knew then I must defend the Divine One now that the other is gone. You were sent to the Chatti so we could help you. I survived the battle; it is my honor to defend you."

My gaze returned to Theokritus's face. His eyes were closed, mercifully, but I thought he might open them at any moment. I hoped he would. I didn't want to think that he never would again. My throat tightened as more tears sprang up. Valthgar tried to pull me from the ground, but I called more matter to myself, making my body so heavy not even he could lift it. Theokritus. Blood had stopped coming from his chest. The flesh was turned out around the wound like a flower blossomed from the dead heart of my only friend. I had not lived a single day in this world without my companions. They were as much a part of life as the sun, the air. The very concept of being alone terrified me. I felt it as clearly as I felt the loss of my friends. How could I go on now that they were gone?

Valthgar strained to lift me from the ground. So eager to help. So annoyingly persistent. Then, an idea came to me. I knew, to my very essence, I could not go on alone. Yet maybe I didn't have to.

Sitting up, I grabbed Valthgar's shoulders. "Valthgar, would you like to be divine like Theokritus was?"

CHAPTER TWENTY-SEVEN

The life I led in the following years was the darkest time I've ever known. The loss of my friends, my disappointment in my brothers, our prolonged stay: These were the forces that drove me. I can pray that the atrocities I committed have been forgiven, but no amount of time will ever clear my conscience of those deeds and the ones who felt the pain of them.

Valthgar and I retrieved Theokritus's body after we dispatched the remaining Romans. Without having to conceal my angelic abilities, it was easy. Setting a suitable camp for the night, I laid Theokritus's body near the fire. The denizens of the woods soon crept from their secret places, sensing death and fresh meat. I lined our camp with kindling and ignited a barrier of flame. My vision remained in the spiritual plane so no movement in the darkness would go unnoticed. Wolves padded around us in the trees, pacing, waiting for the chance to snatch Theokritus away. I'd never seen such beasts up close. They were magnificent. Solid muscle rippled beneath fur, their paws larger than my hands. They circled, communicating in wheezes and whines, answering the distant howls echoing in the trees. Continually calling new matter to keep the flame wall burning, I sat watching the beasts throughout the night. When the dark finally receded, the canines scattered, relinquishing their overdue meal. I was upset to see them go. When Valthgar woke, I recognized for the first time the fur on his shoulders.

It rained the entire day we buried Theokritus. Forming matter into a crude shovel, I dug out a hole at the base of a large white oak. Valthgar was fascinated by the concept of burying the dead. That was what my friends were now. *The dead.* I placed Theokritus in the Earth, crossing his arms over his chest so his axes shielded the mortal wound. Over these, I laid the carved likeness of Helena. This way they would be buried together though their bodies were half a world apart. I kept glancing at his face and expecting to find him staring at me, asking why I had not saved him, why I hadn't saved Helena. My hands trembled as, reaching down, I untied the leather rope holding the angel token around his neck and tied it around mine. Then I grasped his forearm one last time and said farewell to the man who had welcomed me to this world.

Only after collapsing the dirt over him did I allow my tears to fall. Softly, silently. Not from rage, but emptiness. Valthgar patted my shoulder, but this pain could not be comforted. The tears sliding down my chin carried with them something unseen but vastly significant.

With Theokritus's death, the angel I was, the human I pretended to be, died as well.

I didn't know it then, but Theokritus's burial marked a distinct moment in my history. There was the time before, and the time after. My existence as it was during the lives of my friends was over. Everything I cared for in the world had been stripped away by the search for the gateway. Kneeling before Theokritus's grave, I wanted nothing to do with it anymore. Let my brothers waste their time looking. They sought to destroy a tool; I would destroy the ones who dared to wield it. It was the one thing that drove my thoughts, the one mission that stirred my heart to continue on—the deaths of first Turel and then Lucifer, who began this wretched war. Their crimes were equal in my eyes. They would both pay for this pain.

I would need help to find them. But I couldn't return to Michael or the others. They were blind, useless. I needed the aid of those who wouldn't attempt to dissuade me or concoct meaningless missions to distract me from the important one. I needed a pawn to command.

"Kneel." Leaves crunched under Valthgar's weight. He was so excited he was quivering. I shook too, though for a much different reason. "Valthgar, today you become a warrior in the service of the Almighty God." I saw the confusion in his eyes, but it didn't lessen his excitement. "You have been called by Him to rise above the flock and become a shepherd of your brothers and sisters. To protect them from the influence of those who would see them ruined, and to guide the light of…" I reached the name of Heaven and again had to improvise. "…of Ensigart onto them all."

Then I reached a new problem. Valthgar didn't know who Jesus was, and the entire second part of the blessing was the oath to protect Jesus. Valthgar had no way of knowing anything about Jesus or what He was sent to do. I did the only thing I could do.

I skipped the second part.

"In the name of the one true God, will you, Valthgar, give your life in the service of Ensigart, fighting alongside the angels of its host, to preserve the promise of peace for all mankind, and to defend the world from the touch of the fallen?"

Valthgar's eyes couldn't mask his puzzlement. He knew nothing of the Almighty, nothing of angels. I didn't care. I needed help if I was to find Turel and Lucifer again.

"I will do whatever the Divine One wishes."

I shuddered. "Called to God's service, you have willingly taken upon yourself the responsibility of being a leader among mankind in the ways of the Almighty. Join me in prayer."

Valthgar just stared at me as I folded my hands and lowered my head. I took a deep breath. I had no idea what was going to happen when I asked the Almighty to complete the blessing. Surely He knew Valthgar's ignorance of His existence. But wasn't the authority to select new warriors given to us? For better, or worse?

"Almighty God, you have sent your blessing to this man, and he has answered your call to take up arms in the struggle against Hell's power. We pray that you accept him into our ranks, and guide him to always serve you well. Protect him in his days of service, and help him to always make the decisions that will lead him closer to you and out of the many perils he may face. Continue to shed your blessings upon him always, and lead us to grow together, working in joy to defend the Earth and the kingdom of Ensigart from the forces of Hell." Unlike when I had blessed Theokritus and Helena into the war, I alone said, "Amen."

I raised my arm and my sword burst into the physical plane. Valthgar's eyes went wide. As I brought the blade down to rest on his shoulder, I was disappointed to see his hand move cautiously to the sword at his hip.

"I, Sabrael, guardian of the first hall of Ensigart and minister to God the Son on Earth, bless you a warrior of light, to fight the fallen and defend the throne until death parts you of this world, in the name of God the Father, Son and Holy Spirit." I touched my sword to Valthgar's other shoulder, then kissed his forehead. "Rise Valthgar, for you are now a soldier of the faith."

Valthgar stood and held out his arms, gazing at his hands as though he'd never seen them before. He looked like a child. "It is done? I am a Divine One now, like you?"

"Not like me. But yes, you are as Theokritus was," I said.

"Teach me to make my sword disappear," he said, drawing his weapon from its sheath.

"No, no. You have no need of that anymore."

"You expect me to fight without a weapon?"

I sighed. The iron of his sword split in two as my blade sliced through it. Valthgar stepped backward in shock and I retracted my sword again.

"That weapon will not protect you," I said as Valthgar inspected the smooth edge of his severed blade. "You have a new weapon now, which you will now call into being from the spiritual plane." He looked at my empty hand then back at his sword. I grabbed the weapon away and tossed it into the woods. "Hold out your arms. Close your eyes and concentrate. Think of a sword drawing into your hand."

Valthgar closed his eyes and stood motionless. "Focus," I said. "Imagine a weapon appearing from the air. Try to push it into your hand with your mind."

He breathed deeply, brow furrowed. Nothing happened. I began to fear the blessing had not worked. I tried to think of a better way to describe calling a weapon into the physical plane. Helena had done it so easily the first time. An idea struck me. I picked up a heavy stick and threw it over Valthgar's shoulder. He was making faces trying to call his weapon. As the stick crashed into some dead leaves behind him, I yelled, "The enemy has found us!"

Valthgar's body tensed and he reached for his empty sheath. Before his hand was halfway to his hip however, a double-edged sword burst from the spiritual plane. He spun to face the imagined foes, but realizing the sword was in his hand, he turned back to me in excitement. He held the sword straight up to inspect the blade. The hilt was gold, simple in design. A plain, functional broadsword.

I smiled and crossed my arms. "There, you see? It is only a matter of knowing how to do it." I sounded confident, but I wasn't at all. I was relieved beyond description that the unorthodox blessing had worked. I silently thanked the Almighty. "Now remember the feeling so you will be able to call the sword whenever you need it. Making it disappear is just as easy."

Valthgar retracted the sword, then drew it again. He laughed and swung the blade a few times before looking at it with admiration again. "What other gifts has your brother left for me?"

"Theokritus has nothing to do with the powers you now hold. They come from the Almighty. As for what other abilities you now have, I cannot say. It is different for everyone." I thought I should begin teaching him about the war right away. "There is much I must teach you about being 'divine.' There are many things you do not yet understand that you must know to keep the oath you took today."

Valthgar retracted his sword from the physical plane. "Yes, I know. Please begin with which god you hold highest. Is it Wodan you call the Almighty?"

"No. Wodan is not the Almighty. In fact," I took a breath, "Wodan is not even a real god." Valthgar's eyes narrowed. "Neither are Nerthus, Tiwaz, Heimdallr or the Divine Twins."

My new warrior's gaze was cold. "How can you say this? You are one of the Divine Ones. You have just filled me with the essence of your brother. You search for a gateway to Ensigart to stop evil men from making war with Wodan."

I shook my head. "I had to tell you those things so you would let Theokritus and me go. It is true; we are searching for a gateway, and there are evil ones trying to make war. But the gateway does not lead to Ensigart. It leads to the kingdom of the true God. I am His messenger and servant, a warrior in His kingdom and guardian of one of its halls." I let matter gather to my wings and transformed my Athenian clothes to my robe. My eyes took on their true likeness, glowing blue filling the entire sockets. Valthgar recoiled at the change and drew his sword again. I held out my hands. "Do not be afraid. There are many of us, some even here on the Earth. The evil ones we seek are like me, only they wish to overthrow the Almighty and claim the kingdom for themselves. Do you understand?"

Valthgar looked at me as though I were an abomination. "You have the wings of a bird and the eyes of a demon," he said. Interesting that in a culture with no word for Heaven, words for Hell and demon could exist. "You are a monster!"

"No, we are simply different creatures, alike in many ways. Like a wolf and a fox."

He looked at my wings, and I extended them so he could see them better. Retracting his sword, he stepped forward and touched the feathers. "If what you say is true, why did Nerthus arrive to save you right when we were going to sacrifice you? Why did the sky turn black to save us from the Hermunduri?"

"I do not know, but Nerthus had nothing to do with it, I assure you."

"I am not sure why you say these things, Sabrael, but you need not worry. I do not fear the power of becoming a Divine One. Come, I want to return to my village and say farewell. Then we will find this gateway to Ensigart and slay those who dare to use it."

He walked off into the woods. How could he be so blind to the truth even after seeing my true likeness and hearing everything I said? He truly believed I was making it all up. How was I to teach him of the Almighty and Heaven if he dismissed everything outright? This was going to be harder than I thought.

Over the course of the following days, I explained to Valthgar the ways of the Almighty. I flew in the air, showed him how I could travel between the planes and form matter. I briefed him on the mission that brought me to Earth and everything that happened since. I taught Valthgar everything about what it meant to be a warrior of light, about God and Heaven, everything he would ever need to know. It didn't have the intended effect.

To him, it was all just a new aspect to the religion he already knew. He believed Heaven was a specific hall in Ensigart, and God a sibling of Wodan. He rationalized everything I taught him as just part of the Chatti religion forbidden from mortal knowledge. It was more than frustrating. As was the way he continued to refer to me as, "Divine One." Then he took it a step farther.

"If we are to travel this land to find your fallen brother, you must not look like the enemy, or we will be seized by every tribe we meet," he said. "Alter yourself to look like me."

I was stunned by his impudence. He gave me an order? A reprimand was on my tongue, but I realized that unfortunately, he had a point. I didn't want to be caged each time we encountered a new tribe. I reformed my clothes, my robe swirling and collecting extra matter to form hides and a fur cape like Valthgar's. I kept my likeness my own, since I already vaguely looked like I was born in that region, but I extended my hair to my chest. Valthgar applauded my new appearance. He was especially glad I lengthened my hair because now we truly looked like twins. It bothered me to hear him say this. Would this transformation negate all I had been trying to teach him?

When we reached the familiar woods outside the village, I could tell immediately that something wasn't right. "Do you smell that?"

His smile grew wide. "They have lit the pyre in celebration of our return! The scouts must have seen us coming."

But the scent in the air wasn't just wood. There was something else, something acrid.

"Valthgar, wait," I said, but he clapped my shoulder and sprinted through the trees. I followed him, the smell growing stronger. The closer we got, the more unpleasant it became.

I pushed through the brush, low branches bending back and snapping, sticks and leaves crunching underfoot. Dry twigs and thorns raked my face and drew blood. I called matter to heal the cuts as I ran, frustrated that Valthgar seemed to have no trouble running the same path.

I finally stepped out from the trees onto the hill overlooking the village. Valthgar stood at the edge of the incline, and when I walked beside him, I saw what held his mortified gaze.

The village was destroyed. The entire valley had been scorched, only the skeletal remains of Valthgar's hut poking up from the charred debris. Persistent flames still burned in places. The ground was black and even from the hill I could see the ash covering it. Memories of the destruction of my hall filled my mind.

Valthgar stared down at the scoured land as though he couldn't process what he saw.

"Valthgar," I said, placing my hand on his shoulder. As soon as I touched him he jerked around and slapped my hand away. A mixture of fury and shock colored his eyes. He scowled and took off running down the hill.

I gathered matter to my wings and soared down, landing near the place our prison cart once stood. Valthgar called out the names of the Chatti as he ran. It was unlikely anyone would answer. The stench of the ruin was as stifling as the heat. I knew what the pungent tinge in the smoke was even before I saw a charred hand protruding from the rubble of a nearby hut. Before Valthgar reached me, I threw mud over it to hide the remains. I thought of Theokritus.

"Bulwyn! Heindl!" Every step he took left impressions in the layer of soot. His face was flushed with despair. "Answer me!"

"They are gone. No one is left in this place."

He grabbed my cloak, enraged. "How do you know? Have you checked every home? Have you given enough time for anyone to answer our calls?" His voice cracked in despair.

"There are no souls left in this valley besides yours."

He fell to his knees and sobbed, his face to the ground and his shoulders shaking. Something glinted in the blackened ash. I stepped to the object and pulled it from the soot, dusted it off. A Roman shield, the imperial eagle embossed on the front. Turel had been thorough. I handed the shield to Valthgar. "Looks like a Roman strike."

He turned it over, inspecting the back. Valthgar's face cringed and his head lolled back onto his shoulders, weeping.

"What is it?" I asked him.

"It was not the enemy," he murmured. "It was the Hermunduri."

"I don't think so. That's a Roman shield. My fallen brother clearly led them here looking for me."

Valthgar shook his head. He turned the shield over in his hands, pointed to a pattern of wavy lines etched into the metal. "They mark all the weapons they steal." Apparently Theokritus and I had only delayed the raiders. "I should not have left them. I should have remained here to protect them."

"You could not have stopped an army," I said.

"No, but you could have!" he spat at me. "We should have waited!"

The anger was immediate. "We are not mercenaries! The power we possess is to be used in the fight to protect this world and the kingdom of Heaven, the true Heaven, the *only* true Heaven! We were not sent here by some earth goddess to protect your tribe. I serve the Almighty, and now that you have joined our war, so will you!"

Valthgar threw the shield down and stood to face me. "I serve Wodan and the rest of the gods, and because you have shown me the power of your Almighty, I will serve him as well. But do not think you can make me stop serving those powers I have witnessed all my life just because you are the newest. You think you are special? There were others before with wings like yours—only black like a raven's. The magics they showed us were far more powerful. They brought rain, returned life to the dead and foretold the future. You want me to abandon the black-winged gods to follow yours when you have done nothing but make a sword from the air and tried to tell me my own gods are false?"

"Others like me? With black wings?"

"Yours are white, so I know you must be special, as the white wolf is special, and I will help you. But I refuse to forget all I have been taught."

"How long before me did the black-winged ones pass through this land?"

"You missed them by a few days."

The vice gripping my chest closed tighter. It had to have been Turel and whatever others were traveling with him. Valthgar had lied to us all along. Theokritus and I might have caught them if Valthgar hadn't slowed us down. *Theokritus, I'm so sorry.*

Valthgar looked around at what was left of his village. "I must leave a message for the king that this area is no longer safe."

"The king?" I asked. I felt like I was losing my mind.

"The Chatti king. When others come here, they will want to know who did this."

"You are the Chatti king!" I protested. Was everything around me a lie?

Valthgar laughed. "I could never be king. I was not even born Chatti." He paused as though he'd just admitted some important secret. Covering, he explained, "The king is with the main tribe farther south. He has been waging war with the enemy's army for many years, but the enemy still presses into our land. He fears what will happen when they reach the Chatti home. So he sent me to make a new home. The king must know this place is too close to the Hermunduri before we go."

"We?" I asked. "Where are we going?"

Valthgar's eyes filled with determined fury. "To avenge the deaths of my people. Those who survived the attack were likely sacrificed to Wodan or Tiwaz, and favor will not be with the Chatti again until we sacrifice their warriors and make it right."

I said, "Do you know how ridiculous that sounds? What kind of god lets his worshippers slaughter each other back and forth to keep his favor?"

"Wodan is a warrior god. He demands our rivalry."

I rose to my feet. "We are not going to retaliate! The wars will only end when the killing ends. There are more important things we must do, and even if you were to try to earn Wodan's favor, you are not even a true Chatti."

"The king himself made me Chatti. I was not born Chatti, but this is my tribe!"

His unique features now made sense. "What tribe were you born into?"

"I was Angle. But in a battle with another tribe, I did not fight, and I was banished," Valthgar said. "Heading for the enemy's land so I could regain my honor, I was captured by the Chatti. I prayed to Wodan for strength, to help me get free. Then the king told me I would be set free if I defeated one of his warriors in battle. So I did, and the king allowed me to take the warrior's place at his side."

I knew from that strange knowledge I had of the Earth's people that the Angle tribe resided near the sea to the north. "Where did the black-winged ones go when they left here?"

Valthgar pointed north. "Toward the sea." He paused, seeing my train of thought. "We will follow them only after we win back the favor of Wodan!"

I needed to follow my fallen brothers. Now. If they had stopped at the Chatti village to spread their lies, they would stop with any other tribes as well, including the Angles. Valthgar, although he'd been banished, knew exactly where to find them. Making him a warrior of light might have been a good idea after all.

"Valthgar, you are not Chatti anymore. You are a warrior of light, my warrior, whether you understand this fully or not. Your allegiance to the tribes is over. You are a warrior of the host. That is your tribe now. Let the Chatti king believe you died defending this village. It is a warrior's death; they will honor you."

"I will not abandon my tribe!" Valthgar said. "The power you have given me can restore honor to the Chatti. I will not walk away. You are my brother in this gift. You will help me."

Valthgar headed south toward the trees where the Hermunduri had appeared during the raid. I looked north where my fallen kin had gone. Turel was still within my reach. I could finally take his black heart, but I had to follow the trail while it was hot. If I could just show Valthgar what we were truly fighting, perhaps he would accept the responsibility of being a warrior of light. I could not let him walk around empowered without understanding.

I spread my wings and lifted into the air. Calling my sword, I sped toward Valthgar and struck him with the pommel in the back of his head. Scooping my unconscious warrior into my arms, I flew for the land of the Angles.

CHAPTER TWENTY-EIGHT

"I told you not to come here," Valthgar said. He sat cradling his head, the swelling already going down thanks to his new healing abilities. The waves of the Visurgis lapped the rocky shore, feeding into the dark waters of the North Sea.

"You do not tell me what to do. You are my warrior; you go where I need you."

"Do you not understand the Angles will kill me if they find me?" He rose on shaky legs. "I must avenge the honor of the Chatti."

"You can hardly stand up yet. Sit down."

Valthgar remained standing. "You hit me."

"You forced my hand." The sound of a splash drew my attention, but I saw only ripples. "You must realize your old life is behind you now. What will Wodan's favor matter if the world is destroyed and the demons we seek claim the throne of Heaven?" His expression was unchanged. "You and I have the power to stop them. It's time you begin fighting *our* war."

"You leave me no other choice," he said through gritted teeth.

"There is no other choice! The blessing gave you abilities not meant for this world. You cannot just use them however you wish. Your allegiance is to the host now; you swore it."

Valthgar's sword burst out to point at my throat. "I swore nothing! How dare you take me from my people? Let me go to them, or I will swear an oath—to take your head."

I looked up at him along the length of the blade. My own warrior, challenging me! It was unbelievable. Disobedient, rebellious; how could I get through to him? He was a warrior, following only the faith of his weapon, the code of honor in battle. Perhaps the only way he would truly understand would be through conflict. If I showed him that the power I served could suppress those he stubbornly clung to, he might learn his place.

I rose, shoving his blade away from my face. "You want a fight, I will give you one. If you can defeat me here, I will allow you to go free. But if I defeat you, you will follow me without question." My sword slid into my hand. "Agreed?"

Valthgar laughed and raised his sword. "Then let me say good-bye now," he said. I wondered whether I was the first of my brothers to do battle with his own warrior. I couldn't imagine Gabriel or Raphael having this problem.

He struck with the force of lightning. The impact of our swords sent me staggering a step. My hand ached. He charged again and our blades crashed together, the metal screeching. The pressure on my forearms was unyielding. I sidestepped and his sword plunged into the wet earth. Yanking it free, he spun to face me again, clearly getting angry. I modified my body, allowing for quicker than human movement. This time after I deflected his attack, I answered with my own. His eyes went wide as my sword flew at an impossible speed. I recalled my fight with Lucifer beneath the streets of Jerusalem. As I had then, Valthgar managed to block each strike of the speeding sword but couldn't form an attack of his own.

I relented and stepped back to let him recover. He shook out his hands. His smirk told me he thought I paused because I was tired. So I attacked again. The sound of our swords reverberated across the waves. Again and again I pummeled him, finally nicking his arm.

"Finished?" I asked.

He looked up from his wound and with bloodied hands grasped his sword again. "I will be finished when you can no longer stand."

Changing his grip, he brought his blade down in great arcs. Deep whooshes of air preceded the crash of our weapons. When metal struck metal, Valthgar brought his fist around and smashed it into my face. The taste of blood accompanied the sodden crunch of my nose breaking. My vision swam and, when it focused again, I was on the ground.

Bits of damp earth clung to my face and hands. I spat blood. Before I could gather myself, his sword came again. I rolled as he tried to impale me, then rose and slashed at his neck. But he drove his fist into my stomach with an incredible power. It hit like a battering ram. I sailed through the air to smash into a tree fifteen feet up. I hit the ground hard and had to repair my damaged stomach, kidneys and nose. So, Valthgar had inherited Theokritus's strength.

To be honest, I was impressed. I was holding back, allowing him to block all the potentially fatal strikes, but he was an extremely strong swordsman, and I couldn't forget that. Against another human, he would have won already.

I decided to really test him.

Sword raised, I sprinted at him ready to strike, but just as I reached him, I released my physical body. Discarded matter pelted him as a shower of dust. I rematerialized behind him and struck his head with the flat of my blade. He toppled in a groaning heap.

He turned over, enraged. "You are cheating!"

I laughed. "So are you. That punch was a little stronger than you expected, was it not?" He growled and leapt into an attack.

I met his every strike and beat him back, taunting him, fueling his rage until he finally struck so hard I was driven to my knees. I wanted to push him, force him to discover more of his abilities. But he was getting tired. He struck a few more times before I decided to end it. I conjured a wall of flame between us and as he flinched, flew behind him and pulled his head back, my blade at his throat.

"Now it is finished," I said. "If I were one of the fallen, you would be dead."

Valthgar swallowed and held out his hands. Defeat thick in his voice, he said, "I will guide you to the Angles. But I warn you, they will not give us welcome."

"That is not your concern. I will deal with that when we find them."

Valthgar asked, "And when they try to kill me? Will that be my concern?"

I took my sword from his throat and smiled. "Hit their biggest warrior like you just hit me. I assure you, the rest will leave you alone."

The rain started within hours, and it was still pouring when I touched us down outside the Angle village Valthgar once called home. The layout was strikingly similar to the village Valthgar had established. We sloshed through muddy water heading up the main road, with freezing rain dripping from our hair and clothes. Valthgar's pale skin had turned almost transparent. Only a few of the Angles were outside when we approached. The majority shared Valthgar's features, but they stared at him like he was an abomination.

A broad man stepped to block our path, his beard slick with rain beneath a hooded cloak. His hand gripped the handle of the sword strapped across his back. "So, the coward returns," he said.

"I should strike you down where you stand before anyone else here beats me to it."

"I have been forced back by this one." Valthgar threw a finger back toward me. "He claims you may have been stupid enough to shelter a group of demons that passed through here recently, Hrondel. Hearing your voice again, I am inclined to agree."

Hrondel bristled. "You have not heard me, exile. Leave now or find yourself on the wrong end of my blade."

"We came to speak with Konr. Anyone else is a waste of our time."

Hrondel frowned, eyes darkening beneath thick eyebrows. He drew his sword, ready for a fight, but before things could escalate, I stepped up to him and he froze.

Staring him in the eye with empty sockets, I said, "Inform Konr he has guests." Hrondel turned and ran into the village. I let matter come back to my eyes and turned to Valthgar. "Do not use my name. If the fallen were here, they may have warned the tribe about me."

"What, then, should I call you? Liar? Betrayer?"

I searched my memory for a name they would respect. "Ulfarr."

Valthgar scoffed. "The wolf? Lofty choice. You'd better live up to it."

I nodded. "Do not forget."

The hut of the Angle king looked a lot like Valthgar's, only bigger and made of stretched hide. Armed guards at the door monitored our approach. The one on the left stepped forward and asked for our weapons, rain glistening like dew in his hair. I assured him we had none, but he searched us anyway. When he searched Valthgar, I saw recognition in his eyes. Unlike Hrondel, however, this warrior said nothing. Hrondel pushed aside a flap of hide and held it open for us to enter.

"I told you never to return," Konr said to Valthgar as soon as we stepped inside.

Valthgar shook the rain off his cape and slicked back his hair. "The next person to remind me of that will taste my blade."

Hrondel looked more than ready to meet the challenge, but Konr waved him off.

"Who are you?" Konr asked me. "I would know the name of the one who spooked our mighty Hrondel." A thin braid of hair ran along the tattooed markings on his face down to his chest. He was shorter than Valthgar but even more muscled. To think, I had once considered Theokritus large.

"I am Ulfarr," I said.

Konr looked me up and down. "You must be skilled … or another coward hiding behind a warrior's name. What do you want here?"

"We need your help in tracking a group of men through your lands."

Konr's eyes flashed at Valthgar. "You dare ask my help? After your cowardice, you think I would spare even a woman to help you?"

"Not me. Him," Valthgar sneered.

Konr returned to his chair. "You waste your time. Be gone from my lands by nightfall."

"Please," I said, stepping toward him. Hrondel drew his sword on me. The clash of egos happening here was grating on me. "The consequences of our failure are too great to let your anger with Valthgar drive your decision."

"You challenge my decision in my own home? You tread a dangerous path, 'Ulfarr'."

"Only dangerous for you," I replied. "My patience for wasted time has run out."

Konr chuckled. "Provocation will do you no good. You can't force me into aiding you. What makes you think you have any power here? You're not even armed."

I leveled my hand at him, my sword jolting out to prick his throat. "What makes you think that?"

I'd never threatened a human with force before. It was so much easier than reasoning with them. No wonder Lucifer and the others did it so often.

Konr's eyes remained locked on mine. "You found good company, Valthgar. I understand now how you mustered the courage to return."

Valthgar's sword came alongside mine. "You imply I do not have such courage on my own. Things have changed since you sent me away, Konr."

"Making powerful friends does not change someone. I see the same fear and insecurity in your eyes. The only change is your arrogance has grown."

"Enough," I said. I retracted my sword, the trick more easily observed this time.

Konr grabbed my arm, inspected my sleeve. "Where is it?"

I pulled my arm back. "Within reach. Now, you will provide us with what we require."

"I have no supplies to give. We are at war with both the Langobardi and the Chauci. All supplies must be kept for my people."

Valthgar withdrew his sword. "We require warriors, not supplies."

"You had a better chance with supplies. I need our men here; these are dark times." He stared at Valthgar. "Not all Angles run from battle."

Valthgar's fists clenched. I could almost feel his anger in the air. The rain beating on the stretched hides grew louder and I had to shout. "If you cannot help us by sending men, then you can tell us where to go."

"If it gets you out of my lands, I'll point you wherever you want."

"A group of men passed through your land not long ago. They may have had black wings on their backs." Konr said nothing but I saw it in his eyes. He knew. "They search for something, and if they find it here, they will destroy you to claim it. We have to stop them."

"Stop them?" he asked.

"Kill them."

Konr stared at me for a long moment. Then he nodded. "They tried to stop here. We lost a lot of men forcing them out. If you seek to slay those creatures, you will need *real* warriors." Valthgar seethed but said nothing. "I would enjoy the chance for some revenge. We will bring five men with us, but no more. If we leave now, we might still catch them."

⟞⟝⟞⟝

By the time the rain finally stopped, it left the forest blanketed in muck and debris. Our group cut a path through the brush heading west toward the sea. We followed Konr's lead for a full day, and when night came, we found a small cave in the side of a hill. Konr told us it would be the best place to sleep for the night, and in the morning we could continue. Valthgar asked how they knew the cave was not inhabited by some beast. Konr told him to stop being a coward; it was a common Angle waypoint. The words quelled Valthgar's protest, but I had other concerns. My angel sense poked at my mind, faint but unmistakable. If I could feel them, whoever it was could likely sense me as well.

Lying in the dark later, the sounds of slumber filling the cave, I was unnerved that my angel sense continued to buzz, as if the angel causing it was sitting out in the woods, waiting. Perhaps Turel was tired of being hunted and had come to me instead. The shadows disappeared as I shifted my vision to the spiritual. Beside me, Valthgar's breathing was slow and rhythmic. Careful not to wake him, I sat up and turned to leave the cave.

Konr's man Alrekr froze, eyes wide, only a foot away. His dagger unsheathed.

"Konr!" I yelled, but it was the Angles that jumped to their feet. They were wide awake and armed, positioned between us and the cave mouth. "What is this?"

"The black-winged gods warned us of your mission to open the portal between Hell and this world. They told us you are trying to prevent them from closing it forever. We should have known the one trying to stop them would be a banished coward."

"You fool!" Valthgar yelled, his sword exploding into his hand as he rose. The air seemed to quiver. "They want to use the portal to conquer Ensigart!"

"You are the only fool here. Believing you could summon demons to return vengeance on us. Now you have become one of them!"

Valthgar yelled, "This is madness! You knew my parents! I am no demon, and I do not care about vengeance!"

Konr shook his head. "You have been possessed. Everything you say is a lie."

"You want to see me possessed? Vengeful?" The air was definitely trembling. His shoulders were tense, his knuckles white on the sword. "So be it! I will kill you all!"

I needed to control this situation. I called matter to my wings and ignited the embers of our fire. The Angles backed away in fear, now able to see my outstretched wings and vacant sockets. "Listen to me, all of you—"

It was all I managed to get out. The warriors cried for demon blood and rushed us. But just as the first sword swiped for Valthgar's head, he bellowed in rage ... and the trembling air answered.

A wave of energy blasted out of his body. Those closest to Valthgar were killed instantly, flattened from front to back in chunky bursts of gore. I was thrown back and held pinned to the wall. The crushing power of the wave was excruciating. I felt bones crack and cried out. When the wave finally dissipated, I slid to the floor, barely able to move.

Valthgar surveyed the chaos with wide eyes. The surviving Angles lay strewn about, their pulverized comrades nothing but heaps of bloody pulp. Amazed, thrilled, Valthgar looked down at me and his laughter filled the space. Then the cave gave a great moan, and collapsed.

The wave of energy had weakened the ceiling and walls. They crumbled in an avalanche of stone and debris. Valthgar's laughter turned to a shriek as a massive boulder fell directly onto his up-turned face and his body buckled under the weight with a sickening crunch. Then I was suddenly transferred to the spiritual plane, my physical body crushed instantly.

I didn't move at first, dumbstruck by what just occurred. But my awe quickly turned to fear as I realized that if the cave-in had left no spaces to pass through, I was trapped. Rock still settling around me, I frantically weaved through the maze of cracks and holes searching for a path out to open air. How had this happened? The extent of Valthgar's audacity … I couldn't believe it. I tried to teach him, tried to make him understand the responsibility he'd taken on. He killed himself with the very power I gave him! I thought of Helena and Theokritus, how each of them even at the height of their training had been so easily slain. Now Valthgar, a casualty of the gifts meant to help him survive. It was clear what message I was meant to take from their deaths.

After what seemed like hours, I found a path through the debris and escaped the earthen tomb. Reforming my body, I took a moment to get my bearings. Wolves howled in the distance. Moonlight cascaded around me through the leaves overhead. My angel sense had gone quiet. Whoever caused it had moved on. The cave was utterly destroyed. A pile of rubble stood as a marker to the place where there had once been an opening. I placed my hand on the stone.

"Now you will find out all you would not learn from me," I whispered.

I wheeled around at the sound of a loud scraping behind me to see Konr, still alive, at the base of a nearby tree. The trunk was splintered a few feet off the ground as if struck by lightning. He must have been pitched through the cave opening before the collapse. One of Konr's legs was mangled, wet bone glistening in the moonlight. It was this shattered appendage that made the scraping as he dragged himself across the debris. Dark blood spilled from his mouth over his chin. He retrieved his sword and grimaced as he used the broken tree to help him stand on his good leg. His gaze came back toward the cave and found me.

"Konr," I said, holding out my hands and stepping toward him. His eyes went wide and he raised his sword. "You have to stop moving."

"Keep back, demon!" His eyes were wild in shock; the sword wavered in his hand.

I didn't understand why my fallen brothers were always seen as gods, but I was consistently labeled a demon. "Let me help you."

"Back!" he yelled.

My patience ran out. "Put down the sword. I do not wish to fight you, nor do I want your help. Too much has gone wrong; too many have died. I am just going to leave and you can return to your village."

"You will not," he said, forcing himself a step closer. His defiance of the pain was astounding. "In the name of Wodan you must be slain!"

I sighed, tired of that name. "Valthgar was a fool. He did not understand the importance of my task. Do not be a fool as he was."

"You will not leave this forest, I swear it! I will not let you attack the gods."

"Konr, you are not listening."

Konr yelled, "I'll send you back where you came from, demon!"

Even with all his injuries, he sought to fight me. I was so sick of men's misconceptions, arguing about my identity and mission. When Konr lunged at me, I sidestepped his strike and calling my sword, swiped it over his arms. My blade retracted again before Konr's head hit the ground. His body fell beside it.

I closed my eyes and sank to my knees. The sounds of the forest surrounded me. Wolves cried. I listened to their howls, sorrowful, lonely, comforting. The wolves understood my pain, it seemed, though I was ignorant of theirs.

I looked down at Konr's body: The fate of all humans who encounter our war. I knew now why the Son needed to come to Earth—it was because mankind wouldn't listen. Their minds and hearts were closed. I could not stand the heartache of teaching and training them, only to watch them fall. This was our war, and humans—no matter how willingly they would join it—were not welcome. Their involvement always ended in tragedy. For them, and for me.

I was exhausted. I'd never felt such despair in all my life. In trying to avenge Helena, I had lost Theokritus, seen an entire village razed and created a new warrior only to watch him kill himself and five others, including me. Now, after all that, I had literally severed my final human connection on Earth. Turel needed to pay for all the pain he caused. But the night whispered the truth; in trying to catch him, I'd succeeded only in losing everything I cared for in the world. I had no idea where Turel and the others were, where they were going. My last hope of finding them lay decapitated on the ground behind me.

Damn Michael for this! It was all his fault. First he didn't let me mourn Helena, then he sends me on an impossible errand with Theokritus. Leaves me to wander Europe in the hope I'll come across the gateway by chance. Alone, abandoned, I understood why he really sent me here—punishment. He sent me away as a lesson, hoping I would return sufficiently castigated. Now because of my presence, my adherence to the war, hundreds of people were dead. I never even wanted to fight this war! I didn't want to leave the kingdom, hated that I was forced into this. Michael, Lucifer; damn them all.

Michael wanted me to chastise me? To give me a time out? Fine. I would show him just how much time away I needed.

In the woods of Germania, I had reached my end. I had enough of it. The war. The lies. Me. I looked down at Konr's body and had the strangest idea. He had no family, no personal connections. And for the first time, neither did I. The wolves howled again. This time, I understood.

As I headed back to the Angle village, assuming Konr's form, I wondered how difficult becoming someone else would prove to be.

CHAPTER TWENTY-NINE

For the next twenty-two years, I posed as Konr, king of the Angle tribe. When I returned to the village, the Angles didn't question me about what became of Valthgar and his strange companion. They only asked about their own warriors. I lied, claimed they were slain by the demon-bringers. And the Angles accepted it. It was obvious Konr's betrayal had been planned. They actually praised Wodan for protecting me from the same fate.

As Konr, I once again had to keep my true nature secret. This time, it didn't bother me. For more than two decades, I played king and no one was the wiser. I led the Angles in defense of our land from the Langobardi, the Chauci and later, the Cherusci. At first, it was difficult accepting that I had to kill humans, not for the war against the fallen, not to protect myself, but over something as trivial as land disputes, tribal honor. As time wore on, though, my conscience fell silent even as my hands grew more bloodied. Every limb I severed, every life I extinguished, became another tie cut between Michael and me. A tribute to his decision to keep us from home.

I grew to love it.

I gave myself over entirely to being human. After only a short time, I completely relinquished all responsibility of the war. I thought about it from time to time, but the duty which for so long had kept me from actually living on Earth was no longer a real concern. If Michael wanted us stuck here, I would not waste another minute. The tribe worshipped me as a great warrior, and when they called me blessed by Wodan or Tiwaz, I didn't correct them. I participated in their rituals and greeted the procession of Nerthus. I told stories of the gods and mighty warriors to children, sometimes making them up and other times simply changing the names of my brothers to those of the Germanic pantheon. It was odd how easily the truth fit into their beliefs. I was the most powerful king in all the time the elders could remember. They believed I'd been rewarded with uncanny skill for slaying the demons who once visited the village. Idolized by the men, lusted after by the women, I basked in the attentions of both.

I was also quite mad.

I enjoyed the battles among the tribes. Immensely. Perversely. Every opposing tribesman I encountered became Michael, or Lucifer, or any one of the others who forced me from my home. I reveled in bloodletting, the adrenaline of battle and the bonds of my tribe fueling my every strike. With my angelic abilities, I was unstoppable. A juggernaut of death and destruction. The very sight of me sent our enemies running. My tribe was soon feared by all those surrounding us. We put down any attempts to destroy us. We ravaged the villages of our enemies. We defended our land and conquered new territory. My blade and hands felt the blood of hundreds as I actively forgot who I really was. Why remember? My life before was spent watching friends die, struggling to accomplish impossible tasks that only led to greater challenges. Life as a brutal human was so much simpler.

I never directly encountered another angel when I was Konr, but I did sense them occasionally, which led me to believe the ability was getting stronger as time passed. When it first stirred in Jerusalem, I could only detect angels a few feet away, but as Konr I sensed them for many hundreds. These alerts always reminded me of whom I was, but nothing more. I had no desire to find the ones causing it. I was no longer part of that war. Michael hadn't come to bring me back, so I must not have been wanted or needed.

I was to find that the biggest problem in playing human is that humans get older, and the signs of age progress rather quickly. After only a few years, those closest to me had changed immensely: hair thinning, faces wrinkling, health failing. I needed to keep up, or even after all I'd done for the tribe, they would suspect I wasn't what I appeared and try to banish or even kill me. I took to observing one of my guards closely, for his hair was roughly the color of Konr's and he was about the same age. When the lines deepened around his mouth or in the corners of his eyes, or when streaks of white appeared in his hair, I mimicked the changes. When he was finally replaced by a younger guard, I decided my time as Konr was at an end.

I went into my tent one night and spent the entire night calling matter together to form an exact duplicate of myself. I could not, of course, build a human body with all its intricacies intact. I was not the Almighty. I was, however, a master at creating likeness. I formed the skin and hair to look like mine, all the exact bone structures. Then I filled the body with gelatinous matter. Like a puppet full of stuffing. When it was finished, the false Konr looked and felt so real, no one would know the difference. My friends found my "corpse" in the morning and there was a day-long funeral. I watched from the spiritual plane as they prepared Konr for the afterlife with gifts of weaponry and precious items, then floated him out on a raft into the sea.

Released of my false mortality for the first time in years, I took a break from everything. I swam out to sea, wandered the woodlands and studied the natural world and its many wonders. For weeks I kept my own company in the wild, but loneliness caught up to me eventually, and I knew it was time to return to the Angles. But I couldn't just waltz in and rejoin the tribe; I was dead, after all. It would take a cleverer tactic to integrate myself again.

Taking the form of a four-year-old boy wearing tattered rags, I returned to the woods just outside the village and cried loudly until I was found. The men sent out a search party for any invading tribes that I, only a small child, might have wandered from. They found nothing and, as I hoped, a few of the women pleaded with Ofeigr, the new king, to allow me to stay. He relented, as I knew he would; he was a good man when he'd been on my war council. I was given to a young couple without children to be raised in the tribe. It was much more difficult than I expected having to play the role of a child, never allowing my mature thoughts to slip in conversation. Still, it was a wonderful experience growing up, forming friendships that followed me through all the different stages of life. When I was finally big enough, my adopted father trained me to fight. From the start, he was fascinated by how quickly I mastered any weapon put in my hands. He often said I must have the spirit of a great warrior. If only he knew.

Over and over I played out my charade: found as a child, raised into adulthood, killed in battle, and then repeated again. I excelled at playing any age, at faking my own death, and also at flirting. In my years as Konr, I'd mastered the ability to court women without moving beyond a certain point. I learned early on the danger of showing no interest at all. Physical intimacy is part of being human, after all, but after the pain of Helena's death, I could not bring myself to form any lasting connections. I never wanted to experience that kind of loss again.

I stayed in the forests of Germania with the Angles for nearly four hundred years. Eleven full lives, and I loved each one. I could have remained there forever, the perennial phoenix, living and dying only to live again. I hardly even considered my time in Jerusalem to be part of my life anymore. It was like a failed practice run. I felt truly free in those forests, and I had no desire to ever leave. It all came to an end however, with the name "Vortigern."

Vortigern was the ruler of a place no Angle had ever been, an island far to the west. His men arrived on our shores seeking our aid, and our current king, Ottarr, agreed to an alliance against a tribe called the Picts. In exchange, Vortigern granted us the right to settle on his island. At the time I was a young, talented warrior, and I was selected for the war party.

We set sail and followed the king's ships across the sea, a shorter voyage than the trip from Jaffa to Athens, though the conditions of the North Sea were much worse. The air was frigid and the waves relentless as we headed west along the mainland, then south toward the island kingdom, our ships finally scraping rock on its southeast shores. We weren't the only hired warriors; Saxons and Jutes had been called to the island as well. Our benign relationship with our neighbors from the mainland became the bond of military alliance as two Saxon brothers, Hengist and Horsa, rose to take command of our combined forces.

The Picts were easily defeated. We conquered them almost without resistance. It was as though these island people had never seen real warfare before. We routed them from Vortigern's land and kept pushing, taking full control of the island before we'd even been there two full years. The weakness we observed on the battlefield wasn't just on the Pict side, however, and after the Pict war was ended, we sent a pointed message back to Ottarr. What returned to us was the majority of our tribe, along with large groups of Saxons and Jutes. We didn't all stay in the same camp, but we were all allied against our new common foe—Vortigern's army. The war began immediately, and the king's soldiers and towns fell as easily as the Picts' had. We slaughtered his heir, razed his kingdom and forced him into exile. When it was all over, the three tribes split up the island and made it our own.

For three hundred years, I stayed on the island as the new kingdoms squabbled for territory, bloodying my hands in every battle, taking so many lives I can't today even hope to count them all. I only went into the spiritual plane when I chose to be reborn. I stopped using my angelic abilities. I never thought of my brothers or Heaven. All traces of my former existence were erased. In every respect, the angel Sabrael was gone.

Near the end of my time with the Angles, a new breed of conquerors arrived on our island—people calling themselves "missionaries." When I learned their purpose in coming, I avoided them at all cost. Monasteries, convents and churches sprang up around the island over the course of many years, but I remained at the head of the armies, conquering, slaughtering. I never set foot in these so-called "holy" places. I had neither the time nor the desire. It was a long time before I would even allow myself to stand outside them and gaze up at icons of Jesus and Mary, of the men I had seen walking with Jesus that last day in Judea. The memories these images stirred were not welcome. I couldn't ignore that over and over, the Roman torture device called a "rood" was employed both in the art and structural design of these places. I refused to venture into the churches to find out why. That life had been only pain.

Still, after seven centuries of continuous war, it was all beginning to wear thin. My tribe held firm control of a good amount of the island, but there were seven different kingdoms vying for power at that point, and three of these had sprung from my once unified Angles alone. There was no longer any sense of community. Mercenaries moved from place to place; allies when they went to bed and enemies by morning. People no longer knew everyone in their own villages, let alone those serving the same king. The way of life that I embraced and that had kept me distracted from my past for so long vanished a little more each year.

My angel sense, however, flared more and more frequently, sometimes so strong my head pounded with it. In my last years on the island, it was a rare day I did not feel angelic presences and, with this constant prodding, I started to rouse from the fever dream I had slept so long.

CHAPTER THIRTY

"Hello? Aldhelm?" My friend Iuwine lay beside the fire in the flickering light. Most of the village was asleep, but Iuwine always stayed awake with me late into the night, as he had ever since we were children. "Your soul wanders again."

A shooting star blazed a trail across the sky. Its luminescent tail vaguely reminded me of a robe. "I was just thinking."

"That does not sound like you," he said with a smirk.

"I was thinking about those people we heard about at Lindisfarne. The men from the sea."

"Ah. That does sound like you, then." He chuckled and bit off another hunk of venison from the loaded skewer in his hand. "Hoping for a chance to test your blade against them, that it?"

I gazed at him through my long hair. "Do you ever wonder when the fighting will end?"

"End? You love the battlefield. Every tribe fears the vicious and cunning Aldhelm! They say you are the legendary king Konr reborn!" he yelled, arms held high. A few hoots of approval came from nearby. Iuwine chuckled. "Why would you want the fighting to stop?"

"Our people once fought as one to claim this island, sea to sea. After we took it, instead of peace, we just started fighting each other. Our greatest enemies now were once our brothers. Are all kin fated to such an end?"

"Our kin are right here where they have always been, and always will be once we put down the Mercians for good. Where is this coming from?"

I shook my head. "Nevermind."

Iuwine looked at me squarely. "Perhaps you should visit the monastery. Sounds to me like you are having a crisis of spirit."

"What does that even mean? Besides, the missionaries remind me of … harder times."

"When? I have known you your whole life. You have never been to a church."

"Does it not bother you that they come to change everything you believe?"

"Not when the message they bring is one of hope," he said. "In these dark days, we could use as much of that as we can get."

"If they speak of hope, why adorn themselves with a symbol of torture? Do they threaten crucifixion if we do not listen?"

Iuwine laughed. Seeing my confusion, his smile faded and he cleared his throat. "You should hear what they have to say. Even if you believe none of the stories about this Jesus person, the words He preached hold wisdom. When I listen to the monks, I cannot deny the calm I feel. I bring it with me to battle and somehow, amidst the chaos, I am able to find peace."

"Jesus was against bloodshed," I said, then quickly added, "I heard."

"He was. Yet even He recognized that sometimes it is unavoidable, even necessary, when the cause is righteous."

"How do you know when that is?"

Iuwine rose and patted my shoulder. "Visit the monastery. You will not regret it."

Converted from an old pagan temple to support the church in Canterbury, the monastery near our village housed only a handful of monks. I had done my best to avoid them since their arrival more than a century earlier. Standing in the building now, I wasn't sure what I felt. All along the walls, murals and iconography stared back at me, images of a half-remembered life from long ago. Dozens of eyes looked at me, and I found it difficult to hold their gaze. I could feel their judgment, their condemnation. I wanted to scream at them.

Hardest of all was looking at Jesus. Not surprisingly, the painted images didn't truly look like Him, but this did not steal from the artistry. The comforting gaze and open arms of this idealized Jesus were inviting, forgiving, as the presence of the true Son had been. I felt naked before Him, stripped to my very core where all my doubt and shame was laid bare. This was a stupid idea. I shouldn't have come. Yet, despite the overwhelming urge to leave, my feet wouldn't move.

"You have the look of one who seeks answers."

I nearly jumped. A gaunt figure stood among the prayer benches. He wore a simple brown habit with a hood, said to demonstrate humility but always seemed to invoke reverence and condescension instead. His hair was cropped close, his face shaven. It was clear his had been a life of study, safe from the elements and physical toil. What could he know of the world?

"Do I?" I replied. "How exactly does that look?"

"Amazingly similar to that of one who believes he already knows them."

Riddles and mind games, as I always expected. Circular arguments to give the layman pause. The fallen used to use the same tactics. I wasn't impressed.

The monk continued, "I am Brother Gottfried. Welcome. I have not seen you here before. What brings you to the house of God?"

"I am not sure," I said, the truth of that becoming more evident with each moment.

"Oft times that is the best reason of all." Gottfried moved to stand beside me. His eyes remained fixed on the large rood standing over the altar. "Have you heard the message of peace we offer here?"

"I knew it well once."

This seemed to surprise him, though he masked it well. "Not well enough, apparently."

"The message and the promise no longer seemed meant for me."

Gottfried nodded. "You are a warrior. I can see it in your calloused hands and hard gaze. You have probably experienced horrors most of us can only imagine. That can make it difficult to see the light."

"I am not looking for the light."

"Yet you came here. I see no soldiers or escorts; you came of your own volition. There must be something here you seek."

"A few moments of quiet," I said. "Apparently that was too much to ask."

Gottfried gave me a knowing smile. "There are only two reasons anyone comes here. To find the courage to do something they do not know they can, or to find forgiveness for something they have already done. If you would like, I can guess which one drove you here."

I stared at him, the light of the altar candles flickering on his face. He wasn't going to back down.

"Some of my friends say you changed their perspective. Gave them a new path. My perspective has changed lately as well, though no path has been revealed to me. Only wrong turns in the road now passed."

"Decisions always become clearer when viewed after the fact. Fortunately, all forks in the road can be revisited."

"Not all forks," I said.

"Have you ever tried?" he asked.

"You speak as though you have experience facing your past."

Gottfried's eyes were warm, trusting. Fulfilled even. There was nothing hidden in them as he replied, "We all have pieces of our pasts that trouble us. We are creatures of sin; it is in our nature to make mistakes, whether in ignorance or anger. I am no different, but through God's Word I have made my peace with my mistakes, and understand fully they were the very means by which I was led to be here, now."

"Is this truly where you want to be?" I asked.

"If it were not, I would do everything in my power to get to the place I did."

It was not the answer I wanted to hear. My gaze lifted to a portrait of Jesus. Again, I felt His eyes on me.

"Where is it you want to be, friend?" Gottfried asked.

"Somewhere I cannot return to," I said, unsure why I was telling him this. Yet it was invigorating to talk about this with a man who seemed to understand better than anyone I'd known in ages.

"Why not?"

"I was bound to a most important task, but I walked away from that duty."

"Regret is a heavy burden, but one you can always choose to put down."

"Not mine. My brothers would not let me return if they knew what I have done."

"All regrets. That is the power of the salvation we received through Christ's sacrifice."

"He did not die for me," I said.

Gottfried put a hand on my shoulder. "He did. I assure you, the pain and suffering He endured, the humiliation, was for all men across the entire world."

His words shocked me. "Pain and humiliation? Jesus had followers, disciples who walked with Him and crowds that would gather to hear Him speak. He died a king."

He cocked his head. "I am afraid you are mistaken, friend. Our Lord Jesus was crucified."

CHAPTER THIRTY-ONE

Crucified.

Nailed to a cross.

Suspended on display to die before a crowd.

The Son came to Earth, gave up His throne to save mankind, and they executed Him on one of the most sadistic devices ever made. I couldn't fathom it. It was inconceivable.

And I wasn't there.

Sitting near a fire away from my friends in the village, I stared into the flames, despondent. Wringing my hands. Terrified as the veil of denial was torn from my mind. What had I done? We came to protect the Son and stand at His side until the end. When He breathed His last, undoubtedly excruciating breath, where was I? Somewhere in the forests of Germania, pitching a fit like some petulant youth over the actions of my brothers. I knew, obviously, that I had missed His death; I'd been reveling in my own world for centuries. But crucified? If I had only known…

How could Michael have let this happen? We were angry with each other, yes, but this was the death of the Son! All he had to do was call, or send someone to find me, and I would have returned. He could have done something, anything, to retrieve me, but he did nothing. My blood boiled, old rage stirred again, and I wanted to drive my sword into something that would scream. But no. I took a breath and unclenched my fists. It was just as much my fault as Michael's. All of it. I could not let anger drive me any longer. Anger led me here, drained from me all that I was, and kept me far too long. I had spent lifetimes wallowing in its iron grip. I would not slip again.

I was standing over the body of Konr again, the future just as unclear as it was then. Seven hundred years and nothing had changed. Nothing except everything. Gottfried's words had eradicated the last vestiges of the illusion of my humanity. I could not ignore that Jesus was dead anymore. Crucified! I wondered if He even completed His mission. Even as I thought it though, I recalled that day in the Chatti village. The sun going black, the souls of the dead disappearing. It suddenly made sense. He did it. He won. Our mission, our original mission, ended in victory. It must have. The mission Michael imposed on us, though…

The gateway. It had been so long since I'd even thought about it. Impossible that it hadn't been found in all this time. It was obvious what must have happened. Jesus was crucified and opened Heaven to mankind, while Michael and my brothers sought out the gateway and sealed it shut. My brothers then returned to the kingdom, victorious, and left me behind, punishment for my disobedience. That was why Michael never came for me; he was already gone. They abandoned me. The thought terrified me, but did I deserve any less? Anxiety swept through me. With no gateway and no knowledge of how to return home, I was truly exiled. Did my brothers consider me fallen? Was my name erased from the archway over the first hall? My mind swam in horror, but there was nowhere I could go for answers. I was alone, and for the first time in seven hundred years, the idea drove me to despair.

Unable to sit still, I ran into the safety of darkness in the surrounding woods. I tried to outrun my nerves, the terror creeping into every thought, but there was no escape for me. Not this time. When my legs finally tired and I could go no farther, I fell to my knees and wept. I had doomed myself. I had not listened to Jesus's last words to me; I let anger consume me exactly as He warned. Whatever "great things" He alluded to in my future, I was sure I'd missed them long ago. I was exiled, and worse still, without purpose.

Then, I felt it.

The back of my head tingled and I jumped to my feet. My angel sense. I closed my eyes and for the first time in centuries, I focused on it. Hope rose that it was Michael or Raphael, searching for me, following my screaming, flailing thoughts. I waited, expectant, but no one came. Opening my eyes to the spiritual plane, I saw no one either. But I felt them. Whoever it was, I felt them. I waited for a time, still hoping for my brothers to appear, but the more I paid attention to the sense, the stranger it felt. Something was different. I could feel where it was coming from. It was subtle, but unmistakable. The angel sense was drawing me to the west. Tracking the feeling like a dog locating a scent, I turned in different directions. The sense remained fixed. Whoever caused the flare was straight ahead of me.

I burst into the spiritual plane and took flight, soaring after the phantom signal. I flew for miles, yet the sense did not grow any stronger, and my certainty of its direction came and went. Sometimes I was sure it was ahead, other times it felt far off to one direction or the other. Finally I lighted on the ground again. If it was Michael or one of my brothers, I was sure they would have found me by now. That meant it was the fallen I felt. Despair crept up again as I accepted my exile was real, but I forced it back down. I had missed the death of Jesus, missed the destruction of the gateway and been abandoned by my brothers. If I was truly stuck on

Earth with no one but the fallen around me, I wasn't going to pout and do nothing as I had for so long.

I would hunt down the fallen, alone, and kill every one of them. Not for revenge, not out of bloodlust, but to stop their continued infection of mankind and to help as many of the humans find their way into Heaven as possible.

Though I remained with Iuwine and my tribe for some time yet, my attentions wholly turned toward honing my ability to track the fallen. The reach of my angel sense had obviously grown exponentially in the years I spent as a human, but if I was going to use it effectively, I had to be able to follow it like a moth to a flame.

Luckily, flare-ups were a daily occurrence. Every time I felt the sense buzzing, wherever I was, I would sneak off and try to follow it. It was difficult at first, like trying to make out a whisper in the wind. But as the weeks and months passed, the whispers grew to shouts, then became the wind itself.

It was perhaps another six months before I finally felt ready to follow the sense to its source. During that time, the battles with my tribe continued and new foes even appeared, attacking our shores and ravaging the monasteries and convents along the coast in fast ships bearing dragon heads on their bows. Each warrior I cut down only strengthened my determination to get away from it all, as did Iuwine's savage death at the hand of these men from the sea. It was time to leave. Every day the flare-ups grew more frequent, stronger, though I couldn't know if my burgeoning proficiency only made it seem so. If my fallen brothers were truly moving closer, I could ignore it no longer.

On an overcast evening in the spring, the familiar tingle started, and this time, I was ready. Taking one last look at my village, at the warriors I fought beside for decades, the only family and friends

I had left in this world, I burst from the physical plane and took to the sky. I closed my eyes and let the sense draw me. Hovering, I waited, making absolutely sure I truly felt its pull and not simply overexcitement giving me false confidence. The sense grew weaker; whoever it was, they were moving away. But they were definitely to the west. This was it.

I beat the air as quickly as I could, flying for the hills in the distance. The sense grew stronger with each flap, the intensity guiding me like the needle of a compass. I whisked over the land, concentrating, trying to discern how far away I was.

Then it was gone. As quickly as it had come, I lost it. Setting down in the dark countryside, I waited, expecting it to flare up again at any moment. It didn't. My quarry had eluded me. Unsure of how far the sense could reach now, it was impossible for me to know if I'd even gotten close. Somehow I had not been fast enough to catch the angel causing it, or they'd suddenly veered off in a new direction, and I hadn't been sensitive enough to notice. Either way, I had left behind my human life. There was no turning back now.

Wandering in the general direction I last felt it, I patiently awaited the sense's next flare up. When it happened a few hours later, I darted back into the chase. I lost this one too, but in this manner, I crossed the whole of England in sprints, dashing after the sense until it faded, then waiting for the next occurrence. It was over a day before I hit the coast, and when the sense again flared, it was leading me away from England altogether. I followed.

Across the open water I soared until the next coastline sped to meet me. I was familiar with this neighboring island, Ireland. For years it had been a favorite plundering spot for the dragon ship raiders. Though the Irish had called to us for help in defending their shores, we'd always been too embroiled in our own battles to care. It was no surprise to me, then, when passing over the Irish coast, I spotted a village under siege by these Viking warriors. I felt bloodlust rising again, the sight of open warfare drawing out the darkness that had held me for so long, but I continued on. I had to follow my angel sense while it was fresh.

Only a short way inland, I suddenly found what triggered it! But my excitement was immediately quashed. Not just one of the fallen stood on the hillside ahead, but six of them: Rimmon, Turel, Balam, Armaros, Mammon and Dagon. So I still couldn't ascertain how many demons caused the sense. Good to know. As soon as I spotted them, I dropped, flying so close to the ground the grass tickled my chin, then folded my wings and collapsed onto my stomach. Scooting along the ground, I found a clear vantage and laid low.

The fallen stood in a circle, their mouths moving, though I could hear no words. They were all in the physical plane. I gathered matter to my ears, but not my eyes; I might lose sight of them in the dark of the night. They were chanting. I couldn't make it all out, their voices too quiet and too far. I understood a little though, and when I heard the word "gate" my heart leapt. When I heard "open," I was immediately in the air again ... heading the other way. Gate. As in gateway. It could not be. That gateway, the gateway from my Jerusalem days, had been destroyed ages ago; it must have been! Yet what other gateway would possibly inspire chanting?

Hope and confusion clashed in my mind. Had my brothers left it here all this time? Had Michael decided to go home with the Son after all? If that were true, then this was my chance to earn their notice again. To find my grace again, so to speak. Surely they wouldn't just leave me here if I single-handedly finished the last part of our mission. I had to stop the fallen, but I needed help. Six against one were not good odds.

As fortune would have it, I had two entire fighting forces ready to back me up.

Flying back to the edge of the Viking attack, I found the raiders and Irishmen embroiled in bitter battle. Half the village was already a raging inferno. If I could just divert the fighting somehow, I would have all the help I required.

Forming into the physical likeness of an Irish farmer, I ran to confront the nearest raider. He saw me coming, and as I called my sword into hand, I allowed him to call for help so the rest could watch as I stabbed my blade clean through him. Withdrawing my sword, I flicked the blade toward the raiders and spattered them with their dead friend's blood. Cursing and provoking them, I took off across the plain, the sufficiently riled mob not far behind.

A few raiders soon broke off the chase to return to easier game, but nine kept up the hunt. Plenty for what I needed. As we ran, the skies opened up in a heavy downpour, turning the ground to mud. Their pace slowed, the wet ground churning beneath their boots, and I feared they would give up. Thankfully, the hillside was just ahead. As soon as they caught sight of the six figures chanting in what looked like a religious ceremony, these raiders, who pillaged dozens of monasteries along the English coasts as though sent by Lucifer himself, quickened with zeal.

Scaling the hill, I sprinted past my fallen kin and noticed they stood inside a ring of limestone boulders jutting skyward. The demons stopped their chants when they saw me. They looked tired, drained. Probably the reason they didn't attack me outright.

Turel glared at me. "Sabrael? What are you still doing here?"

"Finishing what I should have long ago," I said, shifting my appearance back to my own. I tried to hide the fact that being so near them, my angel sense blared painfully in my head. The raiders finally reached us and encircled my brothers, battle cries announcing the song of skirmish as it broke the night air. I swung my sword in a wide arc, putting all my strength behind it, and the Heavenly metal sliced through the nearest boulder. The top half thumped to the ground. I destroyed a second stone, then moved to join the fight.

Four raiders were already dead. The fallen were in no danger despite their exhaustion and the experienced technique of the humans. Without the special abilities of the blessing, the raiders stood no chance. I dashed up behind Rimmon and thrust my sword straight through his back. His raider opponent stumbled back, fear and questioning in his eyes. I twisted my blade then plunged my hand into the hole to grasp Rimmon's heart.

"Two of the stones are gone, Rimmon," I growled in his ear. He gurgled, his head leaning back on my shoulder. "I will destroy this gateway. You failed."

He spat blood onto his chin, shaking in my grasp. "You are a fool, Sabrael. You have always been a fool."

"That may be," I said. "But at least my eyes are finally open."

I ripped his heart out through his back and incinerated it before his body even struck the ground. The raider ran screaming.

I next tried to divert Armaros's attention from the two men facing him, but this time, the raiders did not stand idly by; they moved in to kill us both.

"I am a friend," I yelled, blocking the first raider's attack. "Do not fear me!"

My words had no effect. The man slashed at me again and his sword caught the edge of mine, momentum driving him into the mud. My angel sense flared, and I spun just in time to deflect Armaros's cudgel swinging at my head. The second raider who had attacked Armaros lay motionless in the muck.

Armaros laughed, "What is all this, brother? Cannot handle your own battles without calling for help?"

He swung for my side, and I dove into the spiritual plane, rolling behind him and rematerializing. My sword punched into him just below his right shoulder blade. He shrieked when I withdrew the blade, dark blood washing away in the rain.

Chest heaving, Armaros said. "Not bad for a throne drone. Last I recall, you were all pushovers."

"I have had centuries to practice," I replied.

He chuckled, his wound closing immediately. "When you hit a few millennia, maybe we can do this again."

He pushed me toward the first raider, standing again and covered in mud. The man grunted and shoved me back, following with his sword. I was trapped between them. When Armaros swiped the cudgel at me, I vaulted past him to snatch the sword from the dead raider behind him. A blade in each hand, I rose to face the demon and the remaining raider. They circled me, the movements of their weapons skirting through my periphery.

Armaros suddenly lunged, and I ducked under his slash to shove the dead man's sword up into his gut as I rolled out to the side. My own sword swung up to meet the raider's attack on the other side, but he froze as he looked past me.

Armaros had dropped his cudgel in the mud to grasp the blade impaling his stomach. With pained grunts through gritted teeth, he struggled to pull it out. The raider stared in disbelief. Armaros threw his head back and with an agonized cry, snapped the blade in two. The hilt fell to the mud. He shoved the remaining metal through, forcing it out his back. The raider fled, terrified, but Armaros howled in rage and threw the bloody, splintered blade, burying the iron between the retreating human's shoulders and sending the man sprawling.

Before he had a chance to recover, I pounced on Armaros and drove my sword into his chest. I had his heart in hand in but a moment and just as quickly burnt it.

Slicing another stone in half, I became aware of growing silence around me, and when I turned back to the circle I found only demons remained standing. Turel stood behind Dagon, Balam and Mammon. His smile dispelled the thought it was due to fear.

"Sabrael, brother," Mammon said. "Lucifer will not be pleased. We all know he has a soft spot for you, but after this…"

I let none of my surprise at his words show. "Where is he, Mammon? I would've thought he'd want to be present at the opening of the gateway."

Mammon smiled and slicked his hair behind his ears. "I am in charge of this search."

"You mean you were too afraid to tell him," I said. The demons glanced at each other nervously. "Can't imagine he'll be happy to find your secret quest caused the gateway's destruction." I focused on the stone just behind them and released some of its matter. Its top half crumbled with a definitive thud.

"You have no idea what you're doing," he said.

"Getting you into a great deal of trouble, I would imagine." Another rock crumbled.

Mammon's lip twitched. "Maybe. But you will not be around to enjoy it."

I tightened my grip on my sword as all four of them sprouted black wings. Mammon and Balam hunched down and sprang toward me, wings beating the air. I raised my blade, but they just swooped past me to snatch Armaros and Rimmon from the mud before retreating. I turned and found Turel and Dagon gone as well. Shifting my eyes to the spiritual plane, I saw them soaring into the sky the opposite direction.

I looked between them, my wings quivering in anticipation. The gateway was destroyed! By my hand! Surely the Almighty would forgive me for the past lifetimes after destroying the thing we sought for so long. I smiled looking at the pulverized stones, the circle more of an arc now. I was positive Michael would appear right there, come back to take me home for good. I had fulfilled the Almighty's prophecy that my journey home would be different than the others, as well as the Son's words that the future held great things for me. Any second, Michael was going to appear. Any second.

But he didn't, and my mind kept returning to the same thoughts. Why only six of them? Was it true; did Lucifer really not know they had found the gateway? Mammon must have been planning something big to risk the scorn of Lucifer. I couldn't imagine what that would be, but if it meant such a drastic shift in the chain of power, Heaven needed to know. Following Mammon, I could root out the meaning of this apparent mutiny. Then again, I could still see the receding forms of Turel and Dagon. Turel. After all these hundreds of years, he and I still had unfinished business. This might be my last chance at him.

I made up my mind and soared into the spiritual plane.

CHAPTER THIRTY-TWO

The land sped by as I raced after Dagon and Turel. It had taken more than eight hundred years to find Turel. Though my hesitation gave them a head start, he would not escape me again.

Countryside gave way to ocean and still the chase drove on. Across horizons of open water, the demons led me west to parts of the world we host angels had not yet gone. Turel somehow maintained the distance between us, no matter how hard I flew. I knew he couldn't fly forever though. Whenever he chose to land, wherever, I would be there, blade ready.

A snow-covered coastline appeared on the horizon, and Dagon and Turel veered south.

Down the long coast of this unknown continent, ice gave way to forests and grassland. I'd never flown so far before; even in the spiritual plane, I was exhausted. Unlike the coasts of Europe, there were no signs of settlement here, no ships riding the waves. My quarry turned as the coast bent, and I followed them southwest over the sea again. They showed no signs of slowing.

A peninsula soon crept over the water, unlike any stretch of land I'd ever seen. Beaches of white sand bordered lush jungles, devoid of the boulders and sharp rocks which marred the northern shores. A flock of vibrant birds scattered from the trees, and I swooped under them, skimming the canopy. I made sure to stay just high enough to avoid contact. Just as with all physical objects, the plants were impenetrable barriers to my immaterial form.

Then, at last, as the sun rose behind us, Turel and Dagon plunged into the trees.

Swooping down into the canopy, I spotted Dagon far below, maneuvering through the trees along the ground. Flitting through the dense forest, it was difficult to keep him in sight. I couldn't see Turel anywhere. Vines and branches whipped past, a grasping, tangled web. I couldn't flap my wings fully, forced to glide with them tight to my back. Just before a clearing ahead, Dagon risked a burst of speed and snagged his right wing on a vine. His spiritual essence burst around it and he whipped out of control in a meteoric fall to smash into the clearing. I shot through the remaining trees after him.

A domed structure rising from the trees ahead caught my eye, but I kept my focus on Dagon. I landed as he rose to his feet.

"Sabrael," he said, dusting off his robe. "You're like a horse fly, persistent and annoying. But look where it's gotten you. All alone. Far from the protection of the host."

"I've been without their protection for centuries. Where is Turel?"

My angel sense blared as Turel hurtled from the trees in ambush. Dagon swung his mace at the same time. I called matter to myself, keeping only my eyes and ears spiritual. The mace struck impotently against the armor of my new physical form.

Turel, however, became physical to clash swords with me. He attacked with superhuman speed, seeming to slash at my feet and head at once. I adjusted my own matter to match, but something was wrong. Turel now moved as though through water. His sword swung lethargically, as though he fought just to drive it forward. It wasn't just his arm though; his whole body slowed! What was this?

Behind me, Dagon had also slowed in mid-swing, having taken physical form to rejoin the fight. His mace crept up as though he were trying to tap me gently, and I redirected it into Turel's languishing sword. The two of them toppled over each other as I watched their slow tumble in awe. I realized they hadn't slowed; I was moving at an incredible speed. How had this happened? Dagon rose and leapt at me, inching through the air. I grabbed his robe and spun, using his own momentum to throw him. This time he floated up and away from me, flailing as he struck a tree twenty yards away and shattered it to splinters. I felt like I had lost my mind. I hadn't strained at all, nor increased the strength of my physical body. Like a tornado, the sheer speed of my movement had sent him soaring.

I turned to find Turel smiling. "Impressive," he said. "Maybe you are worth all the attention Lucifer reserves for you."

"What attention? I haven't seen him in hundreds of years," I asked.

"Doesn't mean his plans for you have changed." Before I could question what that meant, he tried to strike my legs. The movement was so slow I just stepped over the blade as it passed. "Are you planning to fight fairly, or continue this ridiculous game?"

I replied, "Since when have you respected a fair fight?"

"Why are you even still here?" he asked, anger besting the frustration in his tone. "What could you possibly want so badly that you would follow us across the world?"

"To keep a promise to an old friend. You should remember him. You manipulated a squad of Roman soldiers to help murder him after you killed his wife."

Turel's eyes narrowed before realization came over his face. He laughed. "You are still hung up on that? They were only humans, Sabrael! You can just get more."

Heat rose into my face, and my teeth clenched painfully as I ignited the grass beneath him. He jumped back from the flames, but I was already waiting there for him.

Turel's eyes went wide as my blade sank in. I retracted my sword and pushed my hand into his chest, forcing him to the ground with my hand gripped tight around his heart. He spit blood in my face. I squeezed.

After he stopped screaming, I said, "You stole from me all that was important in this world! The friends you killed meant more to me than anything on Earth, including you. You have no idea what you put me through."

His skin was deathly pale in the growing light of dawn. His lips quivered as he whispered, "It was almost nine hundred years ago. Let it go."

I turned my hand slightly. He screamed that wretched cry of our kind on the brink of physical death. I leaned down to whisper. "Never. Not even tomorrow, when you are dead and stowed where no one will ever find you." He tried to struggle, the motion only bringing more pain. Looking him in the eye, I said, "This is for Theokritus and Helena," and ripped his heart out. I forced him to watch as it burned in my hand.

A stifled cry came from the trees nearby. I looked up to see two humans, their souls aglow in the spiritual plane. A young man and a young woman. I was so startled, I only noticed my angel sense too late. I spun just in time to see the handle of Dagon's mace as it smashed down into my head.

CHAPTER THIRTY-THREE

Sounds came first. Murky. Dozens of voices all at once. The laughter of children rising above the din. Then I felt the heat, and sweat. A woman shouted, "Get away from there!" I murmured Helena's name, realized I must have been asleep. How did I lose consciousness? How long had I been out to have such a terrible nightmare? The heat and the familiar noises of Jerusalem brought me back, and I waited for my mind to clear and my warriors to find me. I could feel I was lying down. Humidity drenched the air around me, my skin sticking to what must be a bed. My head was screaming, and a sigh of pain escaped my lips. The light came then, and my vision returned. I recognized the shadowless spiritual plane and blinked, gathering matter to my eyes.

I was indeed lying on a bed of crushed plants covered by a strange, soft material. Sunlight illuminated everything; it seemed strange somehow, its hue different. Clay pottery lined a set of shelves beside a doorway I didn't recognize. Then a child ran past outside. Tan skin and black hair. He was shirtless, with a number of beaded necklaces around his neck and a skirt at his legs. I'd never seen such fashion before. Then I realized I'd never seen anything around me before.

My heart hammered as everything came flooding back. My warriors were dead, Jerusalem was just a memory, and I had no idea where I was. Worse, I had been unconscious … for the first time ever. I sat up and almost cried out, pain in my head blaring. I touched the swollen knot where Dagon hit me and repaired the matter. Another child ran past, laughing; this one wore necklaces like the first, but carried a dozen more in his hands. The woman pursuing him stopped just outside.

"Bring those back and pay for them or I am going straight to your mother!" she yelled.

I'd never seen a woman like her. Her long, black hair floated on the wind. She reached up to tuck it behind her ear, bracelets shining in the sun. Her skin was bronze, her eyes a rich brown. My heart skipped to see I was still in my own pale likeness, wearing my angelic robe. How many people had seen me?

The young woman turned and her eyes met mine. She covered her mouth in surprise, then came into the room. The peach hue of her dress was adorned with exotic feathers and beads, its warm color reflected on her neck and arms. "You're awake!"

"Where am I?" I asked, though knowledge about this place and her people had already sparked in my mind and was filling in as we spoke. "How did I get here?"

She sat next to me on the bed. "Let me see." She touched my forehead where the bump had been. Her eyes were large and her face round. Each ear was adorned with a few piercings, and three beaded necklaces hung above her sloping collar. She caught me looking. "Your bruises are gone," she said, shocked. "You could not have healed so fast."

Memories of Valthgar popped up. Explaining anything to her was dangerous.

"Perhaps it was not as bad as it looked," I said.

She gave me a look. "I know what I saw. You are lucky to be alive."

"That I cannot argue."

"Does it hurt?" She prodded my head. "What about here?"

"No," I said, pulling away. "Are you not afraid of me, even after what you saw?"

She smiled. "If I was afraid, you would not be in my home."

"Someone else was with you. Does he have no common sense either?"

"My brother fears nothing," she said. "Hun Balum helped me carry you here after the others had gone. You spoke in your sleep. You called for 'My Kul.' Who is that?"

After the others had gone. Her words echoed in my mind and I almost missed her question. "My brother, who also fears nothing. But he is a long way from here."

She rose from the bed and moved to the door. "Are you thirsty? I can bring—"

"What is your name?" I interrupted her. My mind reeled as information about the Maya continued to pour in. I was so much farther from Europe than I thought.

"Ix Nuk," she said, looking back at me. "But most people call me Malietta."

"What happened to the men I fought in the field, Malietta?"

"When you were struck down, Balum ran to confront them. The one who hit you picked up the other and..." I waited for her to finish. She blinked away whatever she was remembering. "Fled into the jungle."

It was obvious she was hiding something. "Why help me when you were so eager to drive the others off?"

She shrugged. "You were the one they left behind."

Malietta forced me to relax for a day, despite my assurances I was fine. I could have left if I really wanted, of course, but where would I go? Michael hadn't come to my aid, hadn't appeared in Ireland at the destroyed gateway. Convinced he and the others had gone home, and finally having avenged my friends, I felt a moment's peace was well deserved.

Since Malietta had discovered me with my own appearance, I was reluctant to change it now, but I also didn't want to show my face to anyone new. A strange, pale visitor might not be so welcome with the rest of the Maya. Thank the Almighty I had not formed my wings while fighting Turel and Dagon.

Malietta spent the day with me, and I gleaned a great deal about her from our conversation. Her parents were both dead, her mother in childbirth and her father in a war with another city. Balum had raised her, which was why she didn't have the angled head shape common to the Maya; he hadn't known to place her in the device that pressed the developing infant's skull between two wood boards. This apparently made her something of an outcast. Balum was training to become a priest, with the hopes of being appointed to serve directly under their new high priest.

"What about you?" she finally asked. "Where do you come from, with your hair like the sun and your eyes like the sky?"

"That is a very long story."

Malietta's gaze softened. "You seem troubled even thinking about it." She put her hand on my arm. "What happened to bring you here that could be so sad?"

I met her gaze after a few moments. "I lost my way."

We fell silent for a short time, just listening to the sounds of those outside. The day was growing old, the light waning and the town slowly falling silent. Malietta's skin reflected the changing sunlight, the deep tan turning golden, and her hair took on a new shimmer as well. I found I could not tear my eyes away.

Finally Malietta said, "You were sent here from Heaven."

I was so shocked, I answered truthfully. "Yes, I was."

She smiled. "I knew it. I knew when your wounds healed so quickly, when you made fire from nothing fighting in the field."

"What about when you saw what I did to the one I was fighting? What did you think then?" We had managed to avoid talking about my killing Turel all day.

Malietta looked away for a moment. "I am sure you had no choice." Her eyes suddenly widened. "Oh! I forgot. Your sword ... you must have dropped it in the field, but Balum and I could not find it. The warriors must have found it by now. Or the children!"

I took her hand, squeezing it. "It's all right." I held up my arm and my sword exploded from my sleeve. Malietta stifled her cry, then laughed at herself. I smiled and let her take it from me, fascinated as Theokritus had been all those centuries before.

"How did we not find it when we carried you?"

"When do you think Balum will be back?" I asked, dodging her question.

Malietta put the sword on the bed. "If he is training, he will probably be gone all night."

I knew I couldn't remain there too long. The fallen knew where I was; I had no doubt they would return. Malietta and Balum had rescued me from death, but in doing so put their people at risk. They were ignorant of the demons and the war. They would accept the fallen just as Malietta had accepted me into her home though she'd seen the things I had done. I wanted the chance to thank Balum, but not if it meant risking the destruction of their city. The longer I stayed, the more dangerous it was.

Then another thought occurred to me. What if the fallen came looking for me and learned I was gone? They might seek to punish those who helped me to recover. Even if I left, someone had to protect these people—someone with the abilities to fight the fallen and drive them off. The candidate was obvious. But no! I dismissed the thought even as it came to me. I would not bless her into the war; I couldn't. I was done making warriors of light. I couldn't bear to be the cause of her death; I had too much blood on my hands. But I had to do something.

What seemed an obvious compromise then occurred to me. I could simply inform her about the war without blessing her into it. She was obviously interested to know about my past; she shared her own with me. What could it hurt if one human outside the war knew? Maybe if we had started that way, *telling* humans instead of *involving* them, Theokritus and Helena wouldn't have been killed. If I taught Malietta about the fallen, what they were and how to recognize them, she could rally the city's defense. I had no misconceptions that they could kill the fallen, of course, but if they proved a big enough annoyance, the fallen might leave them alone.

Besides that, looking into Malietta's eyes, I felt … something. I knew I could trust her.

"You invited me into your home and cared for me, Malietta. For that I am in your debt," I said. "I have not been entirely honest with you, though. I think that time has come."

I picked up the sword and slowly so she could see, retracted it. Malietta's jaw dropped. "What … what have you not been honest about?"

"Close the door. I will tell you everything."

Once I started, I couldn't stop. I had not shared my life story with anyone before, not all of it anyway. I told her about Lucifer and the fall, about Jesus and our coming to the Earth. I explained the planes to her and the reason the hearts of angels had to be stripped to ensnare them. I showed her the way I could control matter, how I could change my appearance. I told her about Theokritus and Helena, Valthgar and my lifetimes in the tribes. Finally I told her about Turel and the gateway, and my longing to go home. She listened intently, and the longer I talked, the closer she moved to me. By the time my story was finished, her head was on my shoulder.

"Sabrael," she said, taking my hand. "Let me take you out tomorrow, show you the city."

"I don't think we should risk that. I will not really fit in with your people."

She laughed and tightened her hands around mine. "No, definitely not. We will find Balum. With a priest at your side, no one will question you."

"Priest? I thought he's still in training."

"Everyone thinks of him as a priest already."

"All right then," I said. Malietta kissed my cheek and squeezed my hand, then rose from the bed. She glanced back at me from the doorway, then headed to her room.

I sat back, feeling at peace for the first time in centuries. It felt wonderful to share so much, to talk freely with no fear of repercussion. I felt ... whole.

I barely noticed the soft patter of footsteps retreating from the window.

CHAPTER THIRTY-FOUR

The Maya city was the most beautiful place I'd seen since Athens. The architecture was completely different than any I had ever gazed upon. Buildings weren't just buildings; they were testaments to science and religion. It was the first city I'd ever seen centered not on economy and commerce, but on the worship of gods and knowledge of the natural world.

Malietta led me by the hand past dozens of buildings where the faces of gods and ancient kings watched over their people from richly colored mosaics and bas-reliefs. The path wound us from her home past the market to a step pyramid Malietta called the Temple of Warriors. Flanking the structure on three sides, thousands of columns with carvings of soldiers formed a forest of stone under ornate roofs. Dozens of warriors sparred amidst the pillars under the scrutiny of others in ornate headdresses gazing down from the peak of the pyramid. I watched, reminded of the Romans in the Antonia Fortress of Jerusalem, until Malietta pulled me along.

It wasn't until we reached the center of the city that I saw the most incredible sight. A marvelous pyramid, at least one hundred feet tall and still under construction, rose above all other buildings. Men wearing brilliantly colored skirts worked to haul huge stones to the top.

"They build the temple for Kukulcan, the feathered serpent," Malietta told me. "Does your Almighty demand shrines made in His honor?"

Again my thoughts turned to Jerusalem and the Temple, the shining gold and the decoration. It was still clear in my memory, yet how many hundreds of lives had I cut down since I stood within its courts?

"He appreciates it, but it is not required," I replied. "In a desert far across the sea, there is a monument to Him that shines like the sun and can be seen from all directions."

Malietta said, "El Castillo will reach high enough that every city will see it and know Kukulcan favors us best." I couldn't help shuddering at how like Herod's mentality that sounded. Or Valthgar's. "Our king consulted the star watchers from El Caracol in planning its construction. He says that once it is built, Kukulcan will descend the great stairs into the city each day when the sun sits on the land."

The domed, cylindrical observatory called El Caracol was a building like I had never seen before. Together with the Temple of Warriors and this gargantuan pyramid, I was again amazed how like Jerusalem with its Temple, fortress and palace this city was. I realized after a few moments that Malietta was staring at me. As our eyes met, she smiled and pulled my hand to lead me back toward the market.

The Maya men and women who saw the two of us together seemed curious. Malietta emphatically introduced me to everyone. I could see the uneasiness in their eyes, but they were surprisingly welcoming. Some even offered gifts of jewelry and clothes. A few asked about my origin, but before I could answer, Malietta would reply that I'd come from another land and had lost my way. I was happy to meet them all, but longed to be out of sight again where it was safe. And to be alone with my alluring host again.

When Malietta and I returned to her home, we sat at her door and ate tortillas, melon and papaya. I'd never tasted such things. Malietta laughed as juice dribbled down my chin, reaching over to wipe it away with her hand. She whispered gossip as people passed by, clearly knowing everyone. I was in awe of these people, this civilization. Everyone worked to enrich the city, from those tending the fields to those building the pyramid. In England there had been so many wandering the roads with no purpose, and even more whose purpose was questionable at best. Mercenaries and thieves creating trouble. There was none of that here. I felt I could trust everyone, except perhaps the two boys I'd seen the day before. It truly felt like paradise.

Malietta's brother Balum returned home as we finished our lunch. He shared her dark eyes, but his head was angled in the traditional shape. They believed it was attractive, though I personally didn't understand why. In my opinion, Malietta was far more beautiful than anyone else I had seen. Balum wasn't much older, but there was an intensity to him that she did not share. His expression was serious and his shoulders rigid as he approached. Two flat, obsidian discs stretched his earlobes, and a plume of turquoise feathers sprouted from a headdress with symbols for the gods Chac and Kukulcan across his brow.

"Balum! Where have you been? Come meet the man we saved," Malietta said. "This is Sabrael. I have been showing him the city and introducing him—"

She yelped as he grabbed her wrist and pulled her away from me. Keeping himself between us, he spoke low to her. "I told you to stay away from him! You parade him around for people to see? Have you lost your senses?"

Malietta wrenched her arm free. "There's no need to fear him like he's some animal!"

"Tell that to the king when he hears of the man with dead flesh walking in our city. Word is spreading, Ix Nuk! If the king finds out I had any part in bringing him here—"

"Let them talk!" Malietta countered. "I do not care what people think! I have lived with their whispers my whole life!"

"This is not the same!" Balum yelled.

"Why? Because this time they might be talking about you, too?"

Balum raised his hand to strike her. I grabbed his arm. "Balum, stop, please. I do not want to cause trouble."

He yanked his arm away, whirling to jab a finger at me. "Do not touch me!"

I held up my hands. "Your sister has done nothing wrong. She is a talented healer. She stayed with me through most of the night and has shown me nothing but kindness today."

He glared back at her. "Through the night?" Balum drove his fist into my face. I felt the warmth of blood on my lip.

"Balum!" Malietta gasped. "What is wrong with you?"

"We know nothing about him!" he snapped. "Or the other white ones that fled from me. They cast fire from the very air! Whatever they are, I do not want them returning to finish what they started."

"How can you—"

"No," I interrupted her. "He is right to fear them."

Balum took a step toward me, growling. "I do not fear them! I only seek to keep our people safe. That is the only reason I listened to my sister and brought you here instead of letting you die in that field. I wanted to know where you came from, what you are, but I will not have you consorting with her."

I held his gaze. "If you are so worried about her being alone with me, why was I not bound or guarded?"

Balum's jaw tightened. "You were." Malietta shrank under his gaze. "I meant to be there to question you when you woke. No man heals from such a wound in one night. Your very presence puts us in danger."

369

"I do not want to put you, or her, in danger."

"Then go. Leave our city and tell all those like you to stay away."

Malietta stepped between us. "He is my guest, Balum. If you do not like it, then stay at the temple. He's not going anywhere until he wants to go."

Balum eyed her like she was some creature he didn't recognize, then marched off down the road. Malietta glared after him.

"Perhaps he is right," I said. "I do not want to cause conflict between you."

"He is a fool. Everyone is happy to have you here; forget what he said. He is just…"

"Protective?"

She met my eyes. "Overly. If you were a woman that would have gone differently."

Warmth rushed to my cheeks at the implication.

"I could use a break from all this," she said. "Come. I know a perfect place."

Malietta took me away from the city and led me down a winding path through the jungle. Bright flowers lined the path in arranged patterns, and I realized the colors were a guide to various locations. I wanted to follow each to see where they all led, but Malietta skipped along, and I didn't want to let go of her hand. We finally reached a place where the trees grew strikingly close together. The trail ended at a hole on the opposite side of the copse. A stairway descended into the earth, sunlight trickling through the canopy to light the top steps.

"Come on," Malietta said. "Follow me."

"Where does it go?"

She smirked. "Not afraid, are you?"

She removed her sandals before starting down. I understood why when I followed. The incline was incredibly steep, the steps carved from the existing rock face. She stepped gingerly down, gripping my hand for balance. There was no handrail, just an open fall to the floor some twenty feet below.

At the bottom, I was astonished at the sight before me—a lake, completely underground. Reflected light illuminated the entire cavern, spread evenly through the water, giving the pool an ethereal glow.

"Beautiful, isn't it?" Malietta asked. She laced her fingers in mine.

"I have never seen anything like it," I said.

"There is more." She pulled me after her, her green dress dancing with refracted light.

I ducked under a grouping of stalactites, passing into an area hidden from the stairs. The pool spread before us like an underground sea, and despite its clarity and the light, I couldn't see its bottom. A dense tangle of impossibly long roots cascaded from the ceiling, twisting down dozens of feet to dip into the surface.

Malietta crouched to scoop water in her hands. "It is always cool. You should drink."

She was right; the water passed through my lips and soothed my entire throat.

"This cenoté is a gathering place for the spirits. It's usually forbidden," Malietta said.

"There are no guards?"

"With all the building in the city, the men are kept from many of their usual duties. Guards are only here in the days before the king comes to purify himself or appoint new priests. Balum will be anointed here if he completes his training."

I looked down at my reflection. I thought it looked much older than the last time I'd seen it, though this was impossible since my appearance never aged without my consent. Malietta slid beside me, her reflection staring up from the crystal clear surface.

"Are there people who look like me in the land across the sea?"

Side by side, her features starkly contrasted my light skin and golden hair. "Not exactly," I replied. "There are some with hair and skin even darker than yours, but no one is like you."

"Does your appearance make you uncomfortable here?"

"It has been a long time since I felt so … at peace. Even after meeting Balum." I smiled at her and she laughed. "Besides, I could look like you if I wanted, you know that." I altered my appearance to match her black hair, tan skin and brown eyes. It was the first time I had watched such a transformation on myself. Shocking how unsettling it was.

"Change it back," Malietta whispered. The color bled away, leaving me pale and blond.

I looked at her—the real her—and wrapped my arm around her shoulders. Teasing, I mimicked her voice and said, "Not afraid, are you?"

Keeping her eyes on the water, she smirked and with a finger, tilted my face back down. "No," she said as she wrapped her arms around my waist, putting her head on my shoulder. "I just like you the way you are."

We sat together for a short time without saying anything. Then she turned to face me.

"How long will you stay?"

"With the gateway destroyed, I assumed my brothers would come for me. Since they haven't, I'm not sure what to do or where to go."

I could see she struggled with the words before saying, "Then stay here with me."

"Malietta," I began, but she took my cheeks in her hands.

"If your Almighty brought you here and gives you no reason to return, then perhaps you are meant to stay." Her hand moved to rest on my chest. "I prayed to the gods for so long for someone like you. I am not beautiful. I know this."

"You have no idea how—" I interrupted, but she put her fingers over my lips.

"I had no parents to meet with the atanzahab matchmaker. No one will take me the way I look. I prayed not to be left alone. Now you have come, sent to this world by the Almighty and all the way to the field where Balum and I went walking one night. You have met my friends, seen the city, and still you are here. You are my gift, Sabrael, I know it. I feel it when I look at you, and I think you feel it when you look at me."

Thoughts of Nephilim and the flood filled my mind. For hundreds of years I had avoided romantic relationships for fear of such consequences. I tried to answer her, to tell her it couldn't be, but I couldn't find my voice.

She said, "You will be happy here with me, I promise you. I know what you are; you do not have to worry about keeping your secrets. And I know you have loved before. It was in your eyes and your voice when you spoke of Helena." My throat closed up. "You could not show her your love, and I know you suffered for it. It does not have to be so with us. You have in your eyes the beginnings of love when you look at me. I see it. Stay with me. Be with me here."

I may not have been able to find my voice, but my thoughts would not be silenced. I knew the coupling of angels and women in the past had always ended in tragedy. I did. But every relationship between angel and human had involved one of the fallen. Would a host angel's love bring about consequences as good as the fallen's had been bad?

Just looking at her there in the light of the cenoté, I felt so at home. It was the feeling I had before I told her the truth about me. It was so easy to open up to her, so thrilling to hold her hand. Her hands were so warm. She was intoxicating as Helena had been, but in her own unique ways. And I had reached her in such a strange set of circumstances. Was this the great future Jesus once spoke of? The religion of the Maya had striking similarities to the following of the Almighty; could it be that the Almighty was one of the Maya gods, and Malietta's prayer was answered through me?

My answer, as I decided it was, came as Malietta brought her lips to mine. She held me tight, kissing me as only humans kiss. I was at first shocked it was happening, but the scent of her was so alluring, her lips so soft, I relented and pulled her closer. Of all my human experiences to that point, this was the one that felt most natural. When our lips parted, I felt like a connection to something unknown and exciting was broken.

I struggled to find logic amidst passion. "I have spent so many lifetimes at war," I said. "I'm not sure I remember how to love."

She simply whispered, "I will help you."

CHAPTER THIRTY-FIVE

After the chaos of the last few centuries, life with Malietta was truly a release from the darkness that had haunted me for so long. I imagine I felt what soldiers feel after returning home. We rarely ventured apart during the day, and when we were forced, our reunions would make up for the time lost. She slept in my arms every night, and I counted the minutes by the beats of her heart, the slow breaths of her slumber. With Malietta, everything felt like home.

We kept our relationship quiet for the most part to ensure it wouldn't get her into trouble. While the Maya accepted me as a visitor to the city, we both knew such a drastic move might still carry repercussions from those who harbored any mistrust. Balum never came back to the house after our first meeting. I felt terrible about this, but Malietta assured me it was just part of his training. We carried on in that fashion, showing our affections in the night and masquerading behind the façade of innocent attraction during the day. We could take as long as we wanted developing our relationship in the public eye. As long as we had our time together under the cover of darkness, we were happy. It was exciting, our secret romance. I'd never dreamed I could have such a thing. We stole away to our cenoté whenever we could manage it, talking for hours in the place where we shared our first kiss. It became our special retreat when we needed a release from our daytime charade. Everything felt like a lucid dream after the nightmare of tribal Europe. I was happy with Malietta, absolutely so, and I didn't think anything could ever shake that feeling as long as she was by my side.

It wasn't all perfect though. My mind was plagued. After only a few days, jarring memories started flooding back of their own accord, consuming the present and thrusting me into times long since past. I would see blood on my hands when there was none, spot familiar dead faces among the crowd, even relive battles in all their intensity. Sweating and panting, I was forced to experience the most nightmarish parts of my many lives again, crying out at the bite of a phantom blade or the adrenaline of crushing the life out of one of my many victims. When it happened in private was one thing, but sometimes it would happen when we were in the city square. Malietta was always there to hold me, cajole me back to the present and quell the fires within, but every time I awoke from these fits to find people staring at me, I was equally terrified and embarrassed.

One night, I was startled by the sounds of someone outside our window. My angel sense was silent, but I was sure it was someone and not something I heard. I held my breath, listening. The noises came again. I slipped my arm out from under Malietta, careful not to wake her, and tiptoed to the window, transitioning my sight to the spiritual plane. The shadows disappeared and the nearby houses came into view. A few glowing warriors strode past, but too far away to be what I heard. I leaned out the window, scanned the ground. No one. Behind me, Malietta murmured in her sleep.

Then a sharp sting suddenly pierced my back. I swatted at it, thinking it was a bug. My fingers found a tiny fluff of feather embedded in my skin. I turned to find Balum standing in the doorway, wearing a priest's headdress. He lowered a short tube from his lips. I plucked the feather and held it up. A small barb protruded from the projectile. The area where it hit stung like fire.

"Balum, what..." I saw the bed was empty. "Malietta?"

"Stop," Balum said, drawing a knife. "She is gone."

"Where is she? What is this?" The sting was getting worse. And spreading. I tried to reform the matter there but my thoughts were scattered. Balum watched me like he was studying a wounded animal. The room began to tilt. "You poisoned me?" I asked, though forming the words was surprisingly difficult.

"Keep talking, keep wasting your energy. It will be faster that way."

I took a step toward him and suddenly found myself on the floor. I could not push myself up. Balum pulled my hair to raise my head and pressed the knife to my throat. "We both made a mistake. You should never have come here, and I should never have left you alone with her." His features swam on his face. The feathers on his head coiled around each other like serpents. "Kukulcan has told me what I must do. You're going to Hell for what you have done to my sister." I wanted to tell him he didn't understand; it was love, not lust, which held me to Malietta. I wanted to tell him she was innocent. But I could barely keep my eyes from rolling back, let alone speak. The poison on the dart had been an excellent choice. I was completely at his mercy. Three more priests entered behind him, and Balum helped hoist me onto their shoulders.

I struggled to focus as they carried me through the city. We went up the road toward the pyramid of Kukulcan, and I could just make out two figures ahead. They also carried a body—one I recognized even from a distance. She didn't struggle. Warriors stood around a bright fire burning at the pyramid's base. Silhouettes of headdresses and spears danced in the dark. I hoped they would stop us, ask what was going on, but they said nothing as we passed.

Into the jungle my bearers continued onto a path lined with flowers. It was similar but much wider than the path to our cenoté. Our cenoté. Somewhere in my mind, I knew where they were taking us and feared it, but I couldn't remember why. Something Malietta once said.

Fire lapped at the darkness high up on a ridge as we emerged from the trees. A giant well, at least forty yards across, formed a pit in the earth, and I remembered then why I was afraid. The Great Cenoté. We turned and started the ascent up the rim, climbing higher and higher. Finally, I saw an altar at the peak, the blaze now only yards away. A man with an enormous headdress and glyphs covering his clothes was seated on a throne carved to resemble a jaguar. More priests stood around the altar, all costumed as animals. The altar itself was streaked with chunky blue paint.

My bearers threw me onto the ground beside Malietta. It was obvious she'd also been drugged. Her eyes wandered, half closed. I tried to say her name, but managed only a mumble. Her eyes found me and opened a bit wider. Looking down, the movement of her head slow and shaky, she slid her bound hands over the dirt to mine as though driving them by her gaze alone. When our hands intertwined, a gentle smile formed on her lips.

The first time I noticed the loud incantations of the head priest was just before a lizard-man lifted Malietta off the ground, forcing our hands apart. Balum yanked me up into a sitting position and held my head up. "You will watch what you have caused," he growled, tears in his eyes. "You will watch!"

The priest in a monkey costume scooped a handful of the chunky blue paint from a bowl and ran a trail down Malietta's body after the lizard tore off her clothes. Her binds were cut and a ceremonial headdress thrust on her head. She moaned, helpless, and Balum sobbed into my ear. I was screaming for them to stop, for her to run, but my voice didn't work. The flickering orange light stained everything except that blue paint. I tried to speak into

Malietta's mind directly, praying my abilities had reached that level. I received no answer. She was beginning to shake off the stupor though, and she weakly thrashed in the grip of the lizard. Her fist found the monkey's face, but the other costumed priests moved to restrain her. The head priest touched her forehead and said a few words, then the four of them dragged her to the altar. Tears on her cheeks glistened in the firelight. They forced her onto the block, her breasts pointing up as she arched over the stone. Her screams were frantic as she kicked and flailed, but the four animals held her pinned and the head priest continued.

I desperately fought the numbing poison in my veins. Balum's grip on my face tightened, his fingers digging into my cheeks as he whimpered, "Look what you have done. You made her the consort of evil!"

Malietta screamed for me to help her. All the bloodlust and rage of my centuries as an Angle boiled up, turning the world red. Had I not been drugged, the priests would have been dead already. The head priest pulled a long, curved knife from his belt. He stepped to the altar, blocking my view of Malietta from hips to head, then spoke words of ritual and raised the knife above his head. I growled and thrashed against Balum's grip, my skin tearing as I wrenched my arm free. I shoved him back and tried to throw myself at the priest. My legs were still too weak. I fell hard and couldn't get up. I tried to go into the spiritual plane, to scream. All I managed was to crane my neck to meet Malietta's gaze. Through her tears, she said, "I love you."

The priest's blade plunged down. My scream finally found its way out.

Malietta grunted, and I heard the unmistakable scrape of bone. The priest drove his hand down, and when he turned from her, he held her heart. The sight of it was more paralyzing than any poison. Balum grabbed me, flipped me over and beat me, viciously, unleashing his rage on me. The priest smeared the nearby idols with blood from the heart. The monkey priest caught the blood draining from my love in a bowl, and when no more came, he poured it over the flames. The head priest tossed her heart in after the blood, the morbid grins of the stone faces all around us glistening with crimson. I still couldn't focus enough to let my physical body dissipate, but at that moment all I wanted was to let my eyes go into the spiritual plane so I could see her soul depart. I hoped she could at least see how I suffered for her. My tears would not stop. Had I been in full control of myself, I doubt I could have stopped them any better. Between Balum's crushing blows to my head, I called out my confessions of love. It only made him beat me harder. I knew what was coming next, and I prayed I would go blind before I had to watch it. I couldn't bear it. Thank the Almighty, Balum couldn't bear it either.

"Please, my lord!" he cried. "She has given her blood to the gods and paid for her crime. She has been cleansed. I beg you, let that be enough."

The king on the jaguar throne waved his hand, and Malietta's body was peeled off the altar. The four animal priests heaved her over the edge of the cenoté like rotten garbage.

When the priests turned toward me, for the first time, I thought of myself. I started screaming for my brothers. Without even knowing it, the Maya priests were going to kill me the only possible way they could. I cried out over and over, praying some brother of mine was still on Earth. But I could sense no one. Was this what Barachiel felt when the fallen took him? Did he know he had no hope of being heard, and did he also scream anyway?

The lizard dragged me to the monkey, who smeared me with blue paint. The head priest touched my forehead and they sprawled me over the altar.

Michael! Raphael! Anyone! Hear me! Please!

The knife was raised above my chest.

Please Father! Guide them here! Let my brothers save me!

The entire assemblage grabbed their ears at my shriek when the priest tore out my heart. I felt that terrible cold sweep over me, death flooding my body, overpowering the poison. The world closed in and I slipped down into myself, released of one paralysis to be cast into another. I cried. I screamed. I watched the priest burn my heart. I tried to swim back from the abyss, to kick free of the weight pulling me down. Nothing.

The most horrifying, painful, nightmarish thing ever to happen to me happened then. It was the final part of the ritual, the part from which Malietta had been spared: The priests came back and slowly, methodically, flensed the skin from my body.

She would not have felt it. But I could.

The stone knife slit groin to sternum and the priests worked their fingers in to separate skin from muscle. Inch by inch was peeled from my body. The wet muscle beneath was cold in the night air. All my sins from Europe were being paid back on me. It was also my punishment for wanting to marry Malietta. I knew that. Balum had been right; I had caused it all. Even as Balum spit on me, even as the head priest danced around the fire wearing my skin, even as they tossed me over the rim and I felt the rushing air as I plummeted all that way into the cenoté, I knew I had brought this on myself, and there was nothing I could do.

I plunged into the black water, bobbing to the surface again, the whole of my right side stinging from the impact. My face was submerged as I floated on my stomach. Chunks of gore detached to sink into the inky depths. I wondered what creatures might dwell in the blackness below to be roused by the scent of blood. At least I would see them rising to feed.

I started drifting along a weak current, though which direction I couldn't know. Slowly, limestone entered my view, and I passed into an underground chamber just below the water line. Through the dark I floated, bumping gently against the walls and ceiling of the passage. Where the line would end, I had no idea. When I finally came to rest, my face was turned to the right and I could feel the pressure of something bobbing very near. I could see nothing in the absolute dark though, and the spiritual plane was closed to me.

Floating there, trapped, blind and paralyzed, I finally let out all of my pain and fear, screaming without tears or sound into the darkness that had claimed me.

CHAPTER THIRTY-SIX

Morning came. Light filtered into the cavern. I couldn't turn my head or even move my eyes to find out how, but somehow day was different from night. There is no describing the relief that brought me. The changing light provided my imprisoned mind a way of tracking time. It also brought something else, something so terribly felicitous it felt planned.

Floating mere inches from my face, a body bobbed on the water. Malietta. Her face formed out of the dark like some apparition as sunlight trickled down, her soulless eyes twinkling before it even reached her face. After the initial shock passed, her presence was a comfort. I was not alone. Her head had come to rest on the same outcropping as mine. Long, black tendrils of hair clung to her cheek and reached out for me as the water lapped against us. She was ghostly pale, blue in some places. Thankfully, the way my head was positioned, I couldn't see the hole in her chest. I wondered what I must look like. I was ashamed that while I had her beautiful face to look upon, I was merely a hideous monster of muscle and tendon staring back at her. Then I remembered she was gone.

The water chilled my exposed tissue. I wondered if I would ever acclimate to it, or if I would have to float there freezing forever. *Forever.* The word carried a new weight. How can I express the despair I felt in that cavern? I spent that whole first day trying to distract my thoughts from the fact that I might never move again. The few times I thought about it sent me into fits of screaming for my brothers, for the Almighty, for anyone who could possibly hear the anguish of my terrified mind. I couldn't sleep. I couldn't dream. There would not be any respite from this nightmare. I was utterly, horribly trapped in the experience of every moment.

As daylight traveled across the cavern and darkness returned, I continued to call for help from anyone who might be able to hear me. When the sun rose again with no answer, I wondered how many days would pass before I lost count.

After about a week, Malietta was bloated beyond recognition. Her face had stretched into a rainbow of pallid hues. I was thankful I could not breathe; the stench of decomposition, both hers and mine, must be heavy in the air. With its expansion, Malietta's body had shifted against the rock and actually slid closer. Our hands were now touching, her skin taut and clammy. The first time she brushed against me had been in the night, and I might have had a heart attack if I still had a heart. In the morning when I realized it was her, I wept uncontrollably. The woman who had been so warm and lovely was now the fetid corpse floating beside me. Perhaps the worst of it, her bloated cheeks obscured half of her eyes. With the gentle rocking of the water, Malietta now maniacally peeked over the mounds of flesh like she couldn't stand the sight of me, or avoided eye contact as she plotted revenge. As the days wore on, I went back and forth seeing it one way then the other.

Memories of England, as well as memories of my life before it, continued to haunt me, even worse than when I was alive. Battles replayed in vivid detail against the darkness. Hundreds of warriors challenged me only to be eviscerated, generations rising and falling by my hand. Whole armies had not the number of soldiers that I alone was responsible for slaying. I stood again in the midst of slaughtered hordes, blood soaking every inch of my body and the rush of combat pounding in my chest. Why had I ever let myself enter that world? Why had I followed the glint of the blade rather than the light of Heaven? Flashes of Michael's face appeared in the shadows. I thought back to that night nearly a millennium ago, on the hill under the olive trees with all my brothers. We were expressly told not to go out and change the course of man's history by involving ourselves in it. Our sole reason for being here was Jesus. I hadn't even stayed in Judea long enough to see Him reach the end of His ministry! The moment He reached adulthood and the knowledge of who He was, I embarked on my quest of defiance and vengeance. He was my only responsibility, and I left Him without looking back.

But if I was so wrong, why had I been permitted to carry on? At any time, Michael could have come to retrieve me. The Almighty could have given me some sign. If I was wrong, they should have corrected me. Not to mention the fact that we should have returned home to Heaven the moment Jesus learned His role. I never agreed to spend millennia on the Earth! A distant memory surfaced of telling Raphael that leaving the kingdom was a mistake. Almost one thousand years later we were scattered, Barachiel was lost, and I was a victim of ritual sacrifice.

The gateway seemed the most ridiculous part of the whole thing. The fate of Heaven and Earth rested on whether we found it before the fallen, and we were left to duke it out on our own? Ridiculous! Seven angels, six without Barachiel, were supposed to scour the entire planet—which was crawling with the fallen—to find some relic that had apparently never been recorded in all the annals of history. Yet somehow it was my fault I'd come to the end I had?

The longer I floated there, the hotter the embers of my old anger burned. Had I not single-handedly found and destroyed the gateway? Had I not been the only one of the seven to risk everything?

I should not have been punished; I should be praised! I admitted that all the killing I'd done was wrong. I should have found better uses for my abilities, but did I deserve an eternity in the ground staring at my dead and decaying lover for it?

⊫⊧

The cavern eventually crumbled. I have no idea how long this took. Days, weeks, years; did it even matter? All I know is it happened in the daytime. It started with just a trickle of dust, then in a deafening avalanche, the ceiling came down and thrust me down into the water. Everything went dark. Mud filled my mouth and coated my unprotected eyes. I could still feel Malietta's hand, and I knew she too had been pushed down into the muck. How deep under the surface were we? If sunlight had been able to penetrate the cavern, it couldn't have been far. Even if it was only a few feet though, there was little chance of being found by anyone now. My tomb had been sealed.

With the loss of the only way to know day from night, I lay interred in the sodden earth with only my thoughts to keep me company. How far would I decompose now that the creatures of the underground could reach me? Was Barachiel still in some far away land, nothing left but a physical skeleton? Scavengers found me soon enough. The sliding of worms, the frantic touch of antenna, claws and noses. I felt them come, pausing to sniff or prod. I lay there waiting for the inevitable biting, sucking, burrowing, all the terrors I knew were in store. If they were indeed eating away at me though, I couldn't feel it. At least I was helping something to survive. Better that than being buried for nothing. This reminded me that Malietta was still only inches away however, and I tried not to think about what was happening to her.

In the unrelenting dark, my visions beyond the grave intensified. Most of the time, I saw the faces of dead friends. They never spoke, but hovered in the abyss staring at me. Always staring. Theokritus and Helena appeared to me. Glowing in the black, silent as I asked them about Heaven, about my hall and who was in charge of it. Only when I finally gave up the notion they were really there and started thinking of them as nothing more than projected memories did they find their voices.

"You should not have continued to run, Sabrael," Helena said, her expression grim beneath dark eyes. "Look at you now; look what has happened to you."

Helena, Theokritus, please help me.

"Help you?" Theokritus asked. "How?"

"Would you have us talk to the Almighty to have you released from death? He hears your pleas, Sabrael. What could we say that you have not already?"

If He hears, why does He let this go on? Why should I be trapped here when I could be back home in Heaven? The gateway is destroyed. What else must be done?

Helena's expression did not change as she repeated, "What could we say that you have not?"

"Why did you go on living in that horrible place after I was gone?" Theokritus said. "I failed to avenge Helena. Why did you continue on?"

How can you say this? Was it not a worthy cause that took us together into the forests of Germania? It was the path you wanted to follow!

"I was wrong. We were wrong."

We were avenging the murder of your wife, the woman we both loved! How can you question this now? I yelled. Turel deserved our retribution!

Helena asked, "Did I ask you to avenge me? Were you still avenging me all those lifetimes later?"

Away from me, phantoms! Which of my fallen brothers stands above and plagues my mind with these horrible images? I wasn't wrong! Turel had to be punished for stealing you away from me, and none of my brothers would have helped! Get out of my mind and leave me in peace!

The two of them faded, but it was only the first time I would be visited. They continued to appear and declare their disappointment in what had become of me, asking questions like the one Helena had repeated. Over time, I calmed down and appreciated when they came. It was much better than sitting in the dark by myself, or having to talk to Valthgar.

Yes, he came as well, but only to blame me for his death. His phantom came with an air of sorrow sometimes, anger at others. Over and over he reminded me that he died fighting my war, not his. He hated me for not teaching him to properly use his "divine" abilities, despite my arguments that he never gave me the chance. He gazed at me with piercing, sunken eyes, yelling at me for my foolishness, my haste, my selfishness. I yelled back about his irresponsibility, his stubbornness, but it was no use. In yelling at him, I only understood my own failures. We'd been instructed to keep our presence on Earth a secret. How many humans had watched me hurling conjured flame and cutting down dozens on the battlefield, miraculously healing before their eyes? How many heard me speak of Judea and my time there, giving away my age to be hundreds of years at least if any of them had been educated enough in history to catch it?

Only after a long period of these malicious, depressing haunts was I finally visited by the one I wanted to see. Her scent would precede her appearance, jungle flowers and mango surrounding me before I would feel her hand close around mine. My Malietta. She would lie close and reassure me that I wouldn't be alone in the earth forever. With her forehead against mine, she would calm my crazed anxiety. She never analyzed my past or blamed me for what happened to her. When she left, I would still be able to catch traces of her scent. Since I wasn't breathing, I assume it was more her essence, but it was all the same. I often wondered what life with her would have been like. Theokritus and Helena never spoke about that at all. They came bearing visions of me in battle, madness in my eyes as I ran my blade through countless bodies. They never showed me images of Malietta and me in our cenoté together, the two of us holding each other in the night while she slept and my mind healed from centuries of pain.

The sounds of the world above sometimes seeped down. The beating of rain, the howl of storms, even animals treading over me. The sounds of people were much rarer. I wished I'd been buried closer to the city so I might have listened to the Maya complete the pyramid, maybe even perhaps have been able to know how much time was passing from the conversations of men. Away from the city, I had none of this. I was simply left to wonder how long the darkness held me in its cold embrace.

Had my brothers ever found Barachiel? Was he in a place where he could listen to the world of men, or was he like me, hearing only the voices of those that visited him in the dark? Being buried, I found a new respect for my brother. I prayed the others had found Barachiel, or would at least find him before me, if they hadn't already. Death was too horrible a thing to let someone suffer for long, and Barachiel had suffered far longer than I thought I would be able to last. If my brothers ever did find me, I worried they would discover I'd gone insane.

Time passed. Theokritus and Helena stopped tormenting me and instead now came to reminisce about when the three of us had been together. I enjoyed their visits, and Valthgar came less often to ruin it. They convinced me that I really should have gone back to Judea after Theokritus's death, even if only to check in and ask Michael's help in finding Turel. I did not agree that the journey for vengeance was wrong. My brother deserved death for what he did. But I agreed I had taken the wrong path to do it. My exploits in England were undeniable proof.

The sounds of men finally began to trickle down to me. Voices, though I couldn't make out what was being said. The city must have expanded. The world above seemed to rumble now, much more violently and frequently than during the worst of storms. What kind of beast could make the earth tremble so? I had not seen a great deal of the jungle before I was sacrificed. My imagination created numerous possibilities of beasts wandering the surface, their growls and footfalls shaking the earth and sifting more dirt into my mouth and nose. The creatures' movements were strange, going from deafening to totally silent before repeating again, each stage lasting only moments. When did they ever sleep or eat?

With the coming of the voices above, and with my departed friends opening my eyes to the fool I'd been for so long, I finally felt ready to do what I'd been avoiding for centuries—I prayed. Not in anger, not to plead for help. I had accepted my well-deserved fate. I had no way of knowing how long I'd been there, but it didn't matter. I'd given up the hope that I would be found. I accepted that I was to be buried for rest of the Earth's existence. Fitting punishment for one who so vehemently abused his freedom.

No, I prayed to apologize. I prayed because I had not yet told Him I was sorry for my disobedience. Theokritus and Helena helped me to control my own anger, truly control it this time, and not just force it to the back of my mind. Even when I left the tribes behind, I hadn't let my anger go; I only denied it. I had abandoned duty for vengeance rather than using common sense and realizing that the Almighty would avenge Helena's death in the end. I prayed that Barachiel had been found before my brothers had returned to Heaven. That mankind could finally recognize the demons for what they were. I prayed that the Almighty would forgive me for all the murdering I'd done and might someday accept me back into the kingdom. I prayed that eventually He would free me from my underground prison. But I knew it was His decision. I had sacrificed my right to expect anything.

The next time Malietta came, she held me and kissed me, and as she faded with a smile, told me to be good this time. Then, a loud scraping broke the soil above my head. I cried out in joy as sunlight touched my face. I thanked the Almighty with tearful cheers and laughter, and as a bit more soil was lifted away, a finger touched my head.

A voice from above cried, "Professor! I think I've found something!"

CHAPTER THIRTY-SEVEN

Into the darkness from the world above I'd been thrown, and when the light found me again, everything I knew was gone.

Inch by inch, my soil tomb was cleared away by people dressed in bizarre fashions and using strange tools. Though I watched them, heard them speak, my knowledge of their culture would not come. Even more troubling, I couldn't understand their language, though it seemed composed of familiar sounds. And the way they moved! Frenzied, abrupt, and faster than any humans I'd ever seen. These men and women were as alien as the creatures in the deepest sea.

I called for Michael and my brothers, though I knew they were gone. They might at least hear me from Heaven. The sunlight soon waned and the humans draped a sheet of material over me. It was unlike anything I ever felt. Cold and waxy, flexible yet unyielding; much less comfortable than my earthen womb.

In just moments, the sheet ripped away and the humans were back. The sun was rising before my very eyes, and it slid across the sky in minutes. Had the Earth's rotation somehow accelerated while I was in the dirt? Was this why the humans moved so quickly now?

Beads of sweat covered their foreheads and necks as they worked to clear away the dirt. There was a look on the faces that passed before me, a look they all shared. Like Adam and Eve discovering the forbidden fruit.

When they had fully exhumed me, the group stood back, whispering in awe. A man with a curly gray beard crouched to stare at my face. Dabbing the crown of his bald head with a cloth, he motioned to the others and someone handed him a few small items that looked like pyramids. They were adorned with numbers written by some hand so controlled there were no stray marks. He arranged the pyramids around me, then a younger woman stepped up with a small, black box, a circle of glass protruding from its front. The man leaned toward me but turned his face to her. Suddenly, a flash of lightning erupted from the box! I cringed for her, but when the light faded, she wasn't harmed!

What miracles had I missed? None of the humans seemed afraid of this box, and in fact, most of them even smiled before the woman fired it again. I was astounded that mankind had somehow learned to harness such terrible energies.

Over and over the woman circled me, flashing her lightning. The older man walked away as a number of the others assaulted him with questions, if I was reading their bodies and expressions correctly. He must be the leader then, though I doubted he could defend his throne for long in a fight. I saw no weapon, and his arms and legs were frail. Thin circles of glass rested before his eyes in a metal frame which connected to his ears, much like the glass on the lightning box. Could he shoot lightning from his eyes then? Was that how he kept the throne?

A few days passed. The digging continued. But when a pretty, raven-haired woman with blue eyes eventually uncovered something directly in front of me and shouted excitedly to the others, I knew what she'd found.

She'd discovered my Malietta.

I wished she would hurry and move so I could see my love in the daylight again. It should have been long enough for the bloating of her body to have dissipated. Remembering the animals that crawled over me under the soil, I knew she would be a little worse for wear. I wanted to see her anyway. Hers was the only familiar face left me. The older man knelt to help, tools scraping away earth. My face was then closer to the rear of another person than it had ever been. They stayed there, meticulously removing dirt until the sky turned bronze, then rose to prepare the sheet. But when they walked away, it wasn't Malietta I saw. They had unearthed an age-worn skeleton.

The sheet came down over me and beneath it I was left to stare into hollow sockets once filled by gorgeous, brown eyes. Malietta's skeleton lay in the same position as when the cavern crashed on top of us. How had she decomposed so far! A wave of fear swept through me. How long had I been buried? My right hand, stretched out before me where I could see it, still looked freshly flensed. Why had Malietta decomposed and I had not?

It rained through the night, and beneath the crinkled sheet, I remained dry. I understood then its purpose. I spent the next day trying to decipher the language of these people, needing to hear some explanation, even just shared wonder, at the condition of my body in contrast to Malietta's. It was futile. They spoke so quickly I couldn't even separate words.

Just before sundown, the older man returned with a few others. He directed them into a circle and they gently lifted me from the ground. As soon as I realized what was happening, I strained and screamed to stop; they were taking me from Malietta! I knew she was no longer in the skeleton. It didn't matter. It was still her. They couldn't separate us now! But I couldn't move, couldn't escape the paralysis, even for a moment. In death, just as in life, I was powerless to stop others from tearing us apart.

As the humans carried me away, however, I discovered something that had not been apparent before. Something had grown on me in my time underground. I could feel through it like skin, but it was hard, like a shell. It kept me completely rigid even as I was passed around. The sun gleamed off it, giving my hand and forearm a frosted, crystalline appearance. Where did this casing come from? I hadn't called this matter to me. What, or who, had?

The hands of my bearers were so calloused I felt it even through their gloves, yet they carried me with the utmost care. So unlike Balum's warriors, who had all but dragged me. The men hefted me up an incline and at the peak, the entire excavation site lay before me.

The site was huge, at least two dozen men and women digging in four separate locations demarcated by grids of string. Unearthed skeletons peeked out of each location. The grids formed a curved line, my burial site the farthest down. As the men carried me along, I realized it was the course of the underground tunnel leading away from the Great Cenoté. Perhaps the collapse that had buried me had only been the first of many, and each excavation was a step in the progression. Were there more sites even farther down than mine?

My bearers stopped and lowered me onto another rain sheet. This one was bright orange, and when they wrapped the sides around me, I was sealed in perpetual sunset. The material crinkled loudly as hands lifted me up again and laid me on some surface too high to have been the ground. The loud bang of feet on metal near my head was followed by more hands pressing down on me. Then, to my horror, whatever was beneath me grumbled and began to shake. They had placed me on the back of one of the earthquake creatures! Someone yelled over the rumbling, and the beast suddenly heaved forward.

The journey lasted the remainder of the day, and when darkness came, the beast stopped and rumbled no more. I couldn't even feel it breathing. Men stomped past and again it sounded like metal under their feet, though the space beneath me felt soft. Their voices faded, and soon only distant thunder broke the silence of night.

I wondered what they would do with Malietta's remains. Why were they removing the deceased from the ground anyway? I was grateful they pulled me out, even excited to see where they were taking me, but I'd never heard of a people who did such things, save grave robbers. Where were the Maya that they allowed these people to tear into their land? Had the pale raiders of the north finally conquered all of England and come across the sea in search of new kingdoms to subjugate? To think that the Earth had come under the rule of a people who joyously butchered so many was horrifying. But even if this were true, the raiders I knew never unearthed the dead.

It was still dark when voices approached and I was lifted up again. With the days and nights passing so quickly, I had no idea how long I'd been there. As they carried me, we passed into sunlight, the orange around me suddenly blazing. They kept the earthquake beast inside? The ground felt flat, reminding me of the paved roads in Athens and Jerusalem. We climbed what felt like stairs and the sunlight again disappeared. Here I was gently put down and when the men clomped away, I thought I was alone again. Then the sheet suddenly pulled away.

The room where they left me wasn't completely dark; dull red light cast a pall over everything. It was freezing. Quiet beeps and humming filled the air. And in the reflection of a smooth, metal panel only inches away, I saw myself for the first time.

Wide eyes glared insanely from a face of exposed teeth and tendon. Perfectly preserved muscle, sinew and veins. All blood red in the scarlet glow.

I raged against the paralysis, desperate to look away, close my eyes, anything! Unable to look away from my own grotesque face, I was nauseous at the sight. The horror before me reached out, trying to ensnare me with bony fingers like white spikes from a club of meat.

Finally, someone stepped behind me, their legs reflected in the panel. The person bent down, but what kind of person I could not tell. It was clothed in bright red, but this could have been due to the light. The material was uniform over its entire body, including its head where hair should have been. Eyes behind glass, mouth and nose covered, its impossibly smooth hands prodded me. A second person appeared, identical to the first. What odd breed of twins was this? The two of them attempted to pull my legs straight but the shell held me fast as stone. They hoisted me onto a metal table.

The ceiling burned red above me with a dozen tiny suns, but then one of the humans pulled down a large dome, and blinding, white light suddenly cascaded over me. Not only could man harness lightning but they'd learned to create light! I felt like I'd never seen this version of mankind before, but had only been witness to a first trial in the Almighty's creation process. The terrifying thought occurred to me that I might have missed a second flood or some other catastrophe that started humanity over.

The two alien humans sped around me, writing notes. They tried to push thin metal sticks into my shell, but these snapped each time. They tried to cut away the shell and found equal frustration. Their tools all broke against me. Through it all I couldn't help becoming increasingly terrified. If none of their implements could break through the shell, how would I ever be released of it? In the end, one of the genderless humans attached a paper tag to one of my toes, then wrapped my entire body in a soft, stretchy material. I was in darkness again once my eyes were covered, but I could feel the humans wrapping me in other, heavier linens. When they were finished, I could only faintly tell when I was lifted again. I couldn't feel their hands at all.

Long periods passed of being carried, put down, lifted and carried again. At some point, I heard thunder rumbling as though I was riding storm clouds, and it felt as though I were being lifted into the air. The movement leveled off, and then I wasn't sure if I was moving or not.

I started calling for Michael again. I didn't scream as I used to; I simply called out his name. I actually began to sing a little song for all my brothers who had once been on the Earth. I wasn't afraid of what was happening. The humans couldn't crack my mysterious shell; what did I have to fear? I just sang, and in doing so, realized how very long it had been since I last sang anything.

When I finally felt a downward movement, weightlessness gripped my stomach. I felt like I'd been flying. Humans could not fly now, could they? At that point, I was open to any possibility. If they'd gathered lightning into boxes and harnessed the sun, flight seemed like the least of their achievements.

For many weeks, the humans kept me in a room illuminated by false suns. I knew this from the cycling of the real sun past the mercifully close window. During that time they poked and prodded me with all manner of tools and devices. None broke through the shell. Though it appeared thin as ice, it was hard as diamond. Dozens of men with the lightning boxes came and went, shaking their heads with broad smiles and whistles. A few who saw me vomited. I didn't take it personally. I understood all too well. They came and went, these people of all colors wearing strange clothes. Only those in the long, white coats remained, though they always took these off before leaving at night. I slowly learned some of their words, even came to know the names of a few regulars. I figured out that those called "professor" held power over the other, usually younger ones. While at first I thought these professors to be the masters and the younger ones their servants, their title was similar to the Latin for teacher, praeceptor, and in that light, things made more sense—I was being studied. I recalled hearing the same title being used for the bearded man in charge of the excavation site. Although these professors made their students perform most of the work, they also seemed to genuinely enjoy their company. There was a sense of camaraderie that I would not have expected.

I especially enjoyed when the students were left alone with me. They would stand next to me and gesture at the lightning boxes, or bend down to eye-level and make absurd faces like they were challenging me to change my expression. They kept me laughing, and for that, I was grateful to them. But in the night, when all was dark and silent, I couldn't help but think of Malietta. Her remains never followed me.

Though I didn't mind being mulled over by the people there, I was sure the humans would eventually tire of their cocooned prize, and what then would they do with me? I sang for my brothers often, and prayed to the Almighty. I hoped one of my brothers would be sent soon to free me so I could join them in Heaven again.

Then one night, sixty-eight days after the first one, my prayers were answered.

The room was dim, most of the false suns extinguished for the night. Occupying myself by trying to form a sentence in the students' language, I became aware of a strange sensation creeping into the room. A trembling, or vibration in the air, as though the entire room was nervous. I could hear it as well: a low drone, barely audible but steadily growing. Then, suddenly, particles of matter drew together before me. As they formed into a figure, terrible fear gripped me. But as the physical being took shape, it was not Lucifer.

It was Michael, wings outstretched and arms open!

I screamed in joy the moment I recognized him. Relief washed over me, and for the first time since my death, exhaustion overwhelmed me. His ebony hair with the silver bangs, his perfect face—it was a sight I will never forget. I cried, apologizing for running away, pleading with him to forgive me. I told him he'd always been right, and it had been stupid of me not to listen. I begged him to release me so I could make it up to him. I was so afraid that he was going to tell me how angry he was and leave me there.

Michael bent to lay his hands on my bald, skinned head. Tears welled in his eyes as he kissed my cheek.

"Sabrael. After a thousand years, thank God, you are found."

CHAPTER THIRTY-EIGHT

Michael didn't reform my heart there. If I screamed at the terrible burning sure to overwhelm me as it had beneath Jerusalem, my life throes would attract unwanted attention. Instead, he scooped me into his arms, his silky robe and warm arms comforting after months of cold metal tables. He moved to the door, the handle turning without him touching it.

Can you hear me, Michael?

He looked down at me and smiled. "Of course I can."

Where are the others? Have you come alone?

He cradled me like an infant, my right arm still rigid over his shoulder. Passing into the hallway, he freed the matter from his wings and scanned for guards, then ran. The smooth ceiling passed before my dead stare. What kind of stone was that?

"You will see them again soon." Michael moved swiftly through the deserted corridors, slowing to check each direction at the intersections. His flawless beauty was so much more striking than my memory of it. My own hideousness was like a reflection of the disparity between his perfect obedience and my falling away from it.

How did you find me? After all this time, I thought you were gone.

"Quiet now, Sabrael. All will be explained."

I had so many questions, but I struggled to silence them. The dual effect of Michael's presence on humans—calming to the most tortured of spirits yet terrifying to those of evil ways—worked even on me then. As the maze of passages that made up the professors' home flew past, I knew that for the first time in more than a millennium, I was truly safe.

We rushed out of the building into the night outside. The night sky seemed to glow a dull red, the stars above far fewer than I remembered. Had even the sky changed so much? The drone of civilization coursed through the night as I'd never heard it before. Strange horns in the distance resounded over what sounded like waves or gusting wind, yet I felt none. False suns on tall posts blazed against the darkness. The air seemed to buzz. Where was I?

Michael ran, jostling me in his grasp. His footsteps soon changed from the hard slap of stone to the cushioned patter of grass. Yelling came from behind us, but Michael continued on as though deaf to it. Commands in the new human language were shouted after us, insistent footsteps giving chase. I understood the words "you" and "stop," as I'd heard the professors yell this at their students quite often.

Michael, they are yelling at you.

He smiled and said, "Yes, I believe they are."

Running away from the light of the buildings into a field, he suddenly spun to face our pursuers. Their breaths came in quick gasps as they caught up.

"Put it down and back away," a man said. I might have understood what he was saying through the gestures he made, but I could only see Michael's face and the sky beyond.

My brother smiled and gathered matter to his wings. His eyes ignited to that wonderful gray glow. "You will let me take him. He is to be studied no longer." Then Michael flapped his great wings and the weightlessness of flight gripped my stomach.

I longed to see the world below, how different it looked. The energy in the air was palpable, like the night itself pumped adrenaline. I wanted more than anything to see what caused this feeling.

"Not yet," Michael said. "It's not time." He covered my face with his robe and flew faster. The wind on my body sang of my lost freedom. I could not wait to be revived.

Michael didn't uncover my face until we landed in a small room. He laid me down facing the wall on a bed so soft I couldn't imagine what it was made from. Exquisitely smooth sheets reminded me of the cotton used in Athens. I heard him pull curtains, casting the room into darkness, then light a false sun beside the bed. The wall before me was made of the same smooth stone as the professors' building. A painting hung in its center, displayed behind glass. Surely this was a king's city with the number of scholars and luxuries. I had never seen so much glass. Had it replaced gold as currency in my time away?

Michael knelt at the side of the bed. "Before I free you, you must realize that you have been dead for so long the transition back will be harder than you can imagine."

I understand, I thought, the anticipation of moving again almost more than I could bear.

Michael shook his head. "No, listen to me. The longer you have been dead, the worse it is. Do you recall that night in Jerusalem when I brought you back after only a few minutes?"

I remembered all too well the horrible quickening, the burning pain of dead flesh resurrected. I also remembered the comfort I found in Jesus's young arms.

"This time, Jesus is not here. You are going to burn like you're in Hell, and there is nothing I can do to ease the pain for you. You've been in the ground so long I can't even guess what it will be like."

Have the others been slain and brought back?

He nodded. "Most of us. A few times."

I was shocked. *Then, you have not returned to Heaven?* Michael's eyes narrowed and he shook his head. Scared to dwell on what that meant, I asked, *Are you saying none of the others have ever been dead as long as I have?*

"So far, you hold the record," he said with a smile.

Have you ever been slain?

"Not exactly. Not yet."

Not exactly? What does that mean? You speak as though you have experienced the quickening for yourself.

Michael's gaze grew distant. "The ability to share another's thoughts is not always a blessing."

I was terrified. The memory of the pain beneath Jerusalem, conjured for just a moment, would not subside back into the past. It had been so unbearable, and I'd only just been killed. The knowledge that there was no way around this was the worst. How does anyone willingly walk into the arms of suffering?

What's funny? I asked, seeing Michael's expression change.

"You sound like someone else. From a long time ago."

Who?

He shook his head. "Believe me, now is not the time."

My fear was rising. I needed a distraction. *Then tell me about this shell. How did it form?*

Michael ran his fingers along the shell on my arm. "To be honest, I don't know what it is. Uriel and Gabriel each had one once. It seems to form when we're buried in the earth for prolonged periods. Did it keep the animals from feeding on you?"

Yes, I replied, remembering the scavengers beneath the soil. *They just passed over me for...* I thought of Malietta and felt ill.

Michael nodded. "Placing a heart into the empty ribcage of a skeleton would be difficult. I think the shell is a gift from the Father to ensure the possibility of revival."

This discussion was only making my fear worse. With each moment the anticipation of pain brought more doubt about my ability to bear it. Reluctantly, I finally said, *I'm ready.*

"Are you sure?"

The sooner it's done, the better. Michael nodded and exhaled, rising up on his knees beside me. *Just promise me one thing.*

"Of course."

If I should not be able to take the pain, release me and give me a moment before trying again. I could see he had a difficult time with the idea. *Knowing what the pain is like will make it easier to brace myself than going into this blind. Please, Michael.*

Michael took a moment and then nodded. "Ready?"

No, I said. *But do it anyway.*

"When it's done, free yourself into the spiritual plane and rest there. Do not try to reform a new physical body right away."

I remember, I said.

He took a deep breath and raised his hands. His eyes narrowed, his gaze focusing on my chest. I felt the shell recede beneath his hands like wax from a flame. I was shocked. How many times had the humans tried to crack it and failed? Cool air rushed into the exposed hole where my heart should be. His hands balled into fists, and as matter gathered in the hole where my heart once was, a terrifying scream tore out of me into the air. The bed became a blazing grill, and the entire world seared white.

CHAPTER THIRTY-NINE

I screamed until I was mute and still I cried on. My entire body constricted, violently contorting as atrophied muscles strained against the influx of blood. As tissues reformed to connect the new heart, I felt each and every vein and artery welding back together. Three times Michael formed a beating heart in my chest, three times I was lost to voracious pain, and three times he dissipated the new hearts back to nothing. With each try, my conscious mind disconnected from my body and only the immeasurable sting of new life branded the silhouette of my body into the white void of madness. But the fourth time I desperately held on, and though my screams and the quaking of my body were no less than before, this time I clung to their presence amidst the flames. I tried to keep still as Michael instructed, though it was probably just the constriction of my muscles that held me grounded.

Finally, after an eternity of only a few minutes, the flames cooled and the screaming of my mind slowly subsided. My legs crept back from my chest, my clawed hands relaxed. Silence swept through my mind as I sank into the mattress, exhausted. I couldn't close my lidless eyes, but it didn't matter. I only wanted to lie still, freed of that horrible pain.

"Sabrael," a voice said. I remembered where I was then, and I smiled to think that Michael had not been a dream from somewhere in that burning place. The sensation of my expression changing was exquisite. I relaxed my mouth so I could feel it again, not caring that it wrung fresh blood over my chin and teeth. "Sabrael, let your body go. You remember how to return to the spiritual plane?"

The spiritual plane. Visions of a shadowless place came to me, where there was no suffering like that which clamped my limbs and mind to that bed. I formed the word "Yes," but had no voice to utter it. My vocal cords were literally shredded from screaming.

"Do not linger in that ravaged form. Free yourself from death completely."

I understood, but the idea of doing anything at all was inconceivably daunting. Just let me rest awhile. The sheets were so comforting, so cool against me—

"Those are the thoughts of a human. You are an angel; you require no rest! That is not your true form, brother; wake up and release yourself of it!"

"I can't," I exhaled, even that effort draining me.

He put his hands on my chest, which was still open, and then a terrible pressure forced a squeaking scream from me. My arms mindlessly thrashed. The pressure released.

"Only you can stop this suffering! Focus!" The pressure came again and my body arched in pain. I thrashed again, slapping Michael's hand away from my chest.

"What are you doing to me!" I pleaded, my voice weak.

"You cannot heal in that body," Michael said. "If you refuse to leave it, I will drive you from it!" He squeezed my exposed heart again.

"Michael, please!"

"Free yourself, Sabrael! Do it now!"

A choked cry escaped me. I held my breath and focused, growling with effort, and the matter exploded from my body for the first time in … I still didn't know how long.

My screaming filled the spiritual plane, a proclamation of my escape from pain, exhaustion, and from that flayed and tortured body I'd worn so long. My mind started to clear from the murkiness of revival. My voice gave out as the sobs came and the last vestiges of death released their hold. I sat up and drew my knees to my chest, crying into my robe.

Free. Finally. Mercifully. Free.

A hand touched my shoulder. I looked up into Michael's eyes, their gray glow full of pride. "I knew you had it in you."

I fell into his embrace, crying onto his shoulder. He held me and said nothing, letting me work through the transition at my own pace. When I finally lifted my head and sat back, I saw tears in his eyes as well. "I have not the words to tell you how relieved I am," he said. "For years, we scoured this world for you. I dared not imagine what horrors you suffered." Michael put a hand on the back of my neck. "I missed you, brother."

All the years I spent furious with him, all that time fearing his anger, running away, and Michael missed me. I cried my apologies into his robe, confessing all the terrible deeds I'd committed. Michael just held me, forgiving without hesitation. All was laid bare to be washed clean in a rain of tears, and finally, after centuries of life and death, I found my way again.

Michael made me learn to control matter again before anything else. My questions about the world and the past were answered with commands and instruction. He wouldn't even permit me to look out the window. He sat in front of it with the curtains drawn to keep me from sneaking a peek.

The path back to my former control was a long one, and like any great journey, it began with one step. Literally. I had to re-learn how to walk in the physical plane. I spent the first day of my new life just traipsing around the room, toying with the matter of my body. I stood before the mirrored closet and formed my body again and again into the likeness of myself, of my brothers, of Theokritus, Valthgar and Konr. I remembered how to do it, but I was sorely out of practice. The effort required was exhausting in ways I'd never known. By the time my ability was up to par again, the sun had set.

"Why did the days and nights pass so quickly when I was first unearthed, but now move at a regular pace again?" I asked him.

"Your perception of time sped up so you saw the days and nights going by faster. Perhaps so death does not feel as long as it truly is. It happened to Uriel as well."

"So Uriel is still here? On Earth?"

"Where else would he be?"

I felt the anxiety in the hollow of my stomach grow a small amount.

It was another three days before my skill with a sword was back to normal. With the bed standing against the wall and the suite's furniture pushed to the sides, I trained as I had in Heaven, first against nothing, then against foes which I gave substance and finally against the opponents of Michael's controlling. When I had overcome them all, I wanted to fight Michael. He would not, however, raise his sword against mine.

"I do not ever wish to take up my sword against you in battle, real or imagined," he said. "Besides … it is time to expand your horizons." He pushed his chair back and, for the first time since I'd been revived, he pulled open the curtains.

Immediately the room filled with the glow of a huge, domed structure, shining white against the night sky. I stepped to the window without realizing my feet were moving. A golden statue of a woman stood atop the high peak of the dome, pointing toward the distant horizon. Looking at the building, my hidden knowledge stirred from its long slumber. The building was a monument for politicians, and I was shocked when I received an image of these men. Words came to me such as "suit" and "tie." I put my hands on the glass and looked down. People below moved like figurines through a giant model. "Figurines," "model," words I'd never heard before popped into my vocabulary as, everywhere I looked, new sights met my gaze.

I stepped back from the window, nauseous. Information poured into my mind so quickly I couldn't process it. The city, the culture— it was all so different from the world I knew. Not even Athens had been as this city was, this place called Madison, Wisconsin.

I sank to the floor, trying to remain calm as it all came flooding into my head. I tried not to think, lest I cause another torrent of information. I had not known how different the world was, could not have known. In the suite, I only had access to lamps, mirrors, bathrooms; things that weren't so different from what I already knew.

Michael sat back in his chair. "Now you understand why I kept you from it all."

"Yes," I said, pressing my fingers into my eyes. Images of the new world kaleidoscoped across the darkness. Thank God Michael hadn't turned on the television.

"You will never walk out of this room without feeling this. Every new sight will trigger updates to teach you about the world today, and believe me, there is no end to the changes that have been wrought since you were killed."

"But why must I go outside?" Careful to avoid looking at the window when I opened my eyes again, I replayed the memories of my battle on the hill in Ireland for Michael to see. "I told you; I destroyed the gateway. Our task here is done; can we not just go home?"

He silence spoke volumes. My stomach knotted with the confirmation of what I feared. I looked away to hide the rising heat behind my eyes.

"The gateway," Michael said clearing his throat, "is not destroyed."

"I destroyed it with my own hands! If I didn't destroy enough of the stones, let's fly back there now and finish it! I know exactly where it is!"

"Mammon may once have believed it was, but what you found was not the gateway," he said. "The fallen still search for it as we do. I am sorry."

I absentmindedly looked out the window. Information assaulted my mind, and I spun away, slamming my fist on the table as I saw construction crews, cranes, cables and power tools. In an instant I knew how buildings were constructed in the new world. No wonder such tall structures were now commonplace.

"Sabrael," Michael said from the bed. I looked at his reflection in the mirror on the wall. "That will keep happening until we resolve the problem."

"My lack of knowledge is not the problem. It's that we're still here. How have you stayed so long? Don't you miss home?"

"Of course I do." A flash of intensity burned in his eyes for a moment. "But our missing it is irrelevant. Would you let the fallen find the gateway so they can destroy our halls simply because you miss being there? The gateway still exists, so we stay. We remain now so we will have a home to return to when the time comes."

"What of Barachiel? Have you found him at least? You told me I've been dead the longest."

"It would be best if you let me just show you what you've missed. All your questions will be answered."

Seeing there was no way out of it, I relented. "Fine. Show me."

Michael rose and moved toward me. "You will be disoriented as the knowledge sinks in. Do not fear; it will pass."

"Why would I be afraid? Is it going to hurt?"

"Maybe. You will experience a thousand years in mere seconds. Absorb it, don't fight."

"How should I do that?"

Michael sat me on the bed. He placed a hand on each side of my head, using his thumbs to cover my eyes and his fingers my ears as Raphael once had in Heaven. He even repeated Raphael's line. "Try not to think."

The passing of knowledge was instantaneous. The moment my eyes and ears were covered, an explosion of images and sounds destroyed the room, and I was thrust out of time.

I saw Judea, Jesus riding a donkey over palm leaves strewn about the ground. A crowd shouted the name Barabbas as thirty silver pieces fell from a hanging man's hand. I saw Jesus spit on and whipped, his hands nailed to the cross. A boulder rolled away, and then He was resurrected and visiting the apostles, the same men Theokritus and I had seen on the road to Jaffa. I watched as Jesus lifted into the sky, then heard the screaming of thousands as Roman armies conquered Jerusalem and destroyed the Temple, slaying those who did not escape and banishing the Jews from the land. The apostles each met horrific deaths as they spread Jesus's teachings in various lands. Peter was crucified upside-down in Rome. I witnessed the fall of the Roman Empire and the division of its lands. Europe's forests thinned as new nations rose, the clatter of hooves and the clang of armor filling the wilderness. Monumental castles sprang up in the lands I had once known so well. Strange smells came to me, and I watched the spread of gunpowder. Naval fleets journeyed out and found no monsters lurking in the unknown. I saw with horror the fall of the Maya empire and the conquests of explorers and conquistadors in the western world. Ships ran from continent to continent, spreading goods, people, and animals to new places. Colonies were built across oceans only to sever ties with their parent nations. I saw dark-skinned people being captured and sold, wars fought over their freedom. Continents were explored and wild lands tamed, ravaged by the spread of cities. The last cries of the last members of millions of species rang out as the human population multiplied exponentially. Rulers rose and fell in revolutions across the world. Crusades were fought, dynasties broken. Lands were conquered, inhabited, civilized, bled dry, and abandoned. Blood soaked the earth in every kingdom as two great wars engulfed the world. Man overcame gravity, learned to talk over wires, harnessed electricity and even set foot on the moon.

I saw everything Michael had witnessed, heard every sound he heard in the centuries I had missed. I didn't exist as a corporeal being while the thousand-year history worked its way into my memory. I was a leaf on the winds of time. It was at once fascinating and horrifying. Men had cured all manner of diseases, and men had made weapons capable of killing entire cities. The world was opened to anyone with a computer and a phone line, and deadly epidemics spread through the mail. Food and supplies were brought to the starving, and millions were carried by train to camps where they would be experimented on and murdered. My brother had been among the best and worst places throughout history. The fallen were there as well. I knew everything, as though I'd experienced it as it happened. Finally, the link trickled down and the room came back into focus.

I was lying on the bed, my arms at my sides as my eyes fluttered open. My head ached like never before. I sat up as I realized the room was bright. I had missed the night. The sun was in the sky, giving the white capitol building a statuesque gleam. I received no jarring knowledge at the sight of it. I knew what it was, and I knew of those who worked inside.

Michael sat in a chair looking out the window, hands steepled before his face. I knew his thoughts were miles away. My own were on only one thing.

"Jesus," I whispered. "He knew it would happen, and still He allowed it."

Michael blinked a few times as his thoughts returned. "Not without tremendous fear and doubt. The night of His arrest, He begged

413

the Father for a different path. I begged too, but it was meant to be. He came to take the place of mankind in their deserved punishment; they deserve unending pain and damnation. His mission was never going to end in anything but unimaginable agony. Yet He faced it and destroyed death's power. Through His resurrection, mankind's sins were forgiven and Heaven was opened to their souls."

"But to willingly face that kind of pain… If I had known, I would have returned."

"By the time you found out, you would have been hundreds of years late. None of us were long in Judea after His ascension. The search for the gateway took over."

"I should not have left," I said. Michael didn't protest. I changed the topic. "You have never taken on a human companion…"

Michael took a moment before replying, "The others have all had numerous 'warriors of light,' as you called them. I have seen many great men and women enter this war beside us, and I have seen many mistakes made as well." The memory of Valthgar's death came to me. Michael nodded. "Exactly. Too many have been blessed for the wrong reasons. Finally I decided there had been enough deaths. Only those of great faith should be allowed into the war. It has been that way for more than two centuries now; the warriors of light chosen for their devotion and knowledge of the various true religions. There have been no exceptions."

"Various true religions?" I asked.

Michael raised an eyebrow. "Did you think there is only one? I know you noticed similarities between the religions you encountered. Why would God make Himself known to only one group of people when He loves them all and has opened the gates of Heaven to their kind? Jesus was the form in which God made Himself known to the Roman world. His sacrifice there was necessary to free the souls of mankind, and His teachings continue to spread throughout the world. But do you really think the Maya, or even the

Angles, would have believed that a man from Judea was their savior? The Son once said no man can be saved but through Him. He never said that meant knowing Jesus and His teachings specifically. God has revealed Himself to man in many forms, in many lands, at many different times in history."

My mind was exhausted. I couldn't argue with him. He must be right. Michael rose from his chair. "Take as much time as you need to recover. This room is one of our havens, a safe place looked after by our network of warriors. You won't be bothered. Take a walk when you feel able. Knowing how the world has changed is different than experiencing it yourself."

"Where are you going?" I asked.

"I am being called away. It's something easily handled while you recover."

He turned to the window and waved his hand. The glass dissipated. A brisk wind blew through the opening despite the bright sunshine.

"Michael?" I asked as his wings appeared on his back. "How did you find me?"

A broad smile parted his lips. He pointed to the nightstand beside the bed. "See for yourself." Then he flew out the window, and as the matter of his physical body dissolved, the particles shot back to reform the glass.

Pulling out the drawer in the nightstand, I found a stack of magazines. Science mags, pop culture rags and a variety of others. One detail linked them all. Each featured articles and pictures of me, my hideous, flayed body lying on the cold table with the professors posing next to me. The headlines ranged from "Maya Miracle Man" to "Look What The Badger Dragged In." I opened the first of them and read some of the article. It featured the anthropology department of the University of Wisconsin-Madison and its project in and around the ancient city of Chichén Itzá. There was some information on what was unearthed, but most of the article was dedicated to the experiments run on me and the puzzlement over the preservation of my body. Theories abounded about my being buried recently, or underground minerals halting the natural decomposition; there was nothing conclusive. I smiled thinking about how the professors' faces must have looked when they found their prize had disappeared.

So much had changed in the time I was kept from the world. I couldn't even comprehend it all. World wars, crusades, conquests, holocausts, all had transpired while I lay motionless in the earth. How had I missed so much?

I stepped to the window overlooking the city. Dozens of people scurried through the urban labyrinth below, all of them saved from eternal death if they chose to be. I had faltered and missed the finish of our mission. I let down my brothers and let down the Almighty. Again. There would not be a third time. I would see the destruction of the true gateway with my own eyes, not through the memories of another. I would lend my sword to the battle that ended this war. The new life given me would not go wasted. But before I could fight again, I needed to see and feel the new world for myself.

Manipulating the matter of the window to part for me, I jumped through the hole and re-sealed the glass with my shed body as Michael had, soaring down to form a new physical body and joining the loud, quickly moving world that had formed out of the darkness.

CHAPTER FORTY

I t was night when I returned to the hotel. The air was cool, the dark sky masking my form from those who might look up to see an angel, wings spread, passing overhead. Most of the people in the city were young. At least, young in the new world. Humans lived so much longer now than what I was used to. During the day I had seen men and women in their eighties, nineties even, moving slow and steady among the frantic youth. Before I was buried, people were lucky to see fifty. No wonder the Earth had become so crowded.

The window parted as I entered Michael's room at the Concourse Hotel again. I reformed the glass with my back to it, then looked to see I had done it correctly. The room had been cleaned, the furniture put back in its right place. How nice that my brothers had established these havens where human allies allowed my brothers to come and go freely.

Dissipating my wings, I sat on the bed and turned on the television. The image on the glowing screen was that of a man and a woman arguing, yet laughter erupted at each pause in the fight. I watched for a few minutes, then changed the channel. Again, and again. I listened to the way people spoke, studied their movements and expressions, the subtleties of gesticulation that had evolved in my time away. My long hair was apparently out of fashion. Everything seemed designed for aesthetic rather than function. The designer clothes, the unnatural hues, the sleek shapes; the days of utilitarian huts and heavy furs were gone. It seemed somewhat absurd to me; how long did these women think they could brave the elements in clothes that barely covered even their most intimate parts?

My angel sense suddenly flared. I bolted up and backed against the wall, controlling the sensation before it debilitated me, as it had that night in Ireland. Had it really been so long ago? The sense intensified. Someone was coming. I should draw my sword. But the thought paralyzed me. My hands shook and adrenaline surged as memories of war flooded back. My heart leapt as the window dissolved and two winged forms appeared outside against the massive, gleaming capitol. I retreated into the safety of the spiritual plane where death wasn't possible, but as they flew into the room, I relaxed and took physical form again.

Uriel ran to embrace me even as his wings were still dissolving. He laughed and lifted me from the floor in a bear hug. "Look at this guy! A thousand years sleeping on the job and you still look exhausted." His hair was still long, almost white in the light from the capitol. "When I called for Michael's help today, I never dreamed to hear your name."

He clapped a hand on my back. I shrugged off the sting. "Where were you? I had no idea you were so close."

"Tracking a demon out over Lake Michigan before we lost him. But who cares? Where on Earth have you been! How could you let the fallen get the drop on you?"

I laughed. "They fled from me, all right? I only fell after a human slipped me poison."

Uriel's eyes widened with intrigue. "The plot thickens."

Another flare of my angel sense and the window dissolved again. Raphael rushed in, frantic. His emerald gaze found me, staring like he didn't believe I was really there. Then he stepped past the others to pull me into his embrace.

"Praise God you are found," he said. He held me tight, like he was worried I would disappear. "When we saw the articles, I could not let myself hope it was you."

"I missed you too," I said.

Even as he backed away to look at me, he didn't take his hand from my shoulder, his fingers curled around my robe. "Do not ever, ever run away like that again."

He looked to the door as my angel sense flared and there was a knock. Uriel waved his hand and the door opened to reveal Gabriel and a woman.

"I thought you were in Paris," Uriel said, moving to greet them. "How did you get here so quickly? Michael only sent out the call this afternoon."

Gabriel stepped past Uriel into the room. "Caim's not going anywhere. Paris can wait. You honestly thought I would miss this?"

Gabriel grinned at me then and swept me into his arms. "And look at our brother who was too good for us all these years. Took his own death to bring him back."

I was embarrassed beyond words, but laughed with them, relieved that after so long, no one held any grudges. Perhaps they felt I had already been through enough. It was like coming home. Michael sat in his chair by the window, watching us all with a smile. Gabriel went to him and spoke privately while Raphael and Uriel prodded me for details about my time away. The shame of it was still strong, but I relented. As I charted my journey from Jerusalem to Chichén Itzá, my gaze kept wandering to the woman who stood alone near the door. Long curls of deep brown fell around her face. She had brilliant blue eyes. These stayed on me as I told my story, their intensity almost tangible.

"Who is she?" I finally whispered to Raphael.

Uriel held out his hand to her. "Join the party, girl. What's with the shy act?"

She stepped to his side and smiled as Uriel draped his arm around her shoulders. "I was just letting you all have your moment."

"This little doll is Adrienne," Uriel said, "one of Gabriel's war-riors. Don't let her looks fool you though; she wields a sword as well as any *real* warrior."

Adrienne mocked offense and elbowed him in the ribs. He chuckled and held up his hands. Her eyes returned to me. "Gabriel said you have been gone a long time. I did not want to interrupt."

"Not at all. Forgive me for not inviting you in. After a thousand years, my manners are a little rusty. You are from Paris?"

"I am. Gabriel found me when I was sixteen, living on the streets. I have been with him ever since."

Raphael said, "She cut her teeth in some of the most vicious battles of this century. Have her tell you about Versailles some time. My warriors would not have made it if not for her."

"You all still have human warriors?" I asked, afraid the answer would be yes.

"All but Michael," Raphael said, looking at our ebon-haired brother still deep in conversation with Gabriel. "The warriors of light patrol the entire world now, looking for the gateway and try-ing to keep the movements of the fallen in check."

Had even one human survived an attack of the fallen in all the time I'd been gone? "How many are there?" I asked.

Uriel said, "Not as many as we need. Nowhere near the number that follows the fallen."

Raphael added pointedly, "Only a few still join the battles."

He must have caught what I was thinking. I was not comfortable with the idea of humans continuing to get caught up in our war, whether they actively fought or not.

Adrienne's eyes were still locked on mine. Their color was electric, hypnotic even. I felt as though I were being studied again, though for different purposes than the scientists had once looked at me. Almost like she was afraid of me.

"I saw you. In the magazines," she said. "You look more put together in person."

"I wish I felt more put together, but thank you," I said. My next thought was interrupted as my angel sense flared painfully. Uriel and Raphael simultaneously stepped in front of me.

The window suddenly exploded inward. Gabriel shielded his head and Michael jolted out of the chair, reaching into the cascade of glittering shards to catch a large form crashing through. He toppled backward with the force of the impact. I instantly recognized Haniel in his arms, the two of them covered in glass and blood. Wind whipped my robe as Adonael swept into the room.

The sight of him stunned me more than Haniel's body coming through the window. The engraving on the archway of my hall read, *First Hall of Heaven, Protected In This Time By Adonael In The Absence Of The Guardian Sabrael.* What was he doing here!

"Forgive us, Michael," he said. "It was an ambush!"

Before he could explain, a swarm of black wings descended from the night. Adonael shouted a battle-cry as he swung his halberd out and caught flesh, leaping back through the shattered window and yanking the ensnared demon out of sight. A few of the fallen pursued them, but the rest poured into the room. Uriel and Raphael drew their weapons and stood ready as Michael and Gabriel faced the first wave of attackers. My heart sank when short swords appeared in Adrienne's hands.

Four of the fallen made it past Michael and Gabriel. Uriel's sword cleaved two of them while Raphael's swords barred the others from reaching Adrienne and me. The suite filled with the deafening sounds of battle, the window hemorrhaging new opponents. Adrienne yelled and jumped in, short swords gleaming as they twirled and slashed, and saved Raphael from being impaled from behind. Her hair flew about her face, blue eyes burning with furious focus as she skirted the mad swipes of Gadreel's scythe. But how long could she keep it up?

I couldn't move. Breath caught in my throat, I was like a child seeing war for the first time. I hadn't seen so many fallen gathered together for a single strike since the last assault on Heaven. "No," I whispered, paralyzed by the fear of being killed again. But I couldn't ignore the quickening of my pulse, the stirring of old bloodlust deep within. Watching my brothers amidst the swarm, I felt my sword scratching at the spiritual plane, desperate to join the fight. I started to see red—

The door behind me suddenly blew open, the sizzling crackle of the electronic lock firing sparks onto the floor. More of the fallen rushed in, and the only free hands left were mine.

Michael's voice boomed in my head, *Flee! Wait for my call to regroup.*

Glass knocked free of the window as a group of the fallen chased Michael and Gabriel into the night. Haniel was gone, and I prayed that Michael had grabbed him before flying away. Glowing green eyes seething, Moloch led the demons in the doorway toward me. His sword flew at me and my own appeared in my hand to defend the strike. I was knocked back like a novice and stumbled into Adrienne, her shoulders bracing me and keeping me on my feet. Helena's beauty. Theokritus's strength. Her wild eyes turned to me as Gadreel's scythe blade swiped at her neck. She didn't see it...

The door to the next room burst back on its hinges, buckling under my reinforced shoulder. The room was thankfully empty, the fallen right at my back. Adrienne writhed in my arms, screaming at me to let her fight. I ran for the window, retracting my sword and wrapping my arms tight around her waist as she squirmed. The scents of lavender and chamomile filled my senses as her body pressed against mine. I dissolved the glass ahead, but her swords managed to make contact with someone behind us and I lost my balance, tumbling into the still-dissipating pane. I pulled her down into my arms and shielded her head with my forearms.

The night was freezing as we burst through the window. Glass particles glimmered around us as we plummeted fast. Only then did I remember my wings weren't in the physical plane. Adrienne grabbed onto me, realizing it as well. My robe fluttered loudly as the ground sprinted up to meet us. One hundred feet…Fifty…Forty…

"Sabrael!" Adrienne screamed, but I was already forming my wings. I spread them and we swooped back up, missing the ground by only ten feet or so. Praise the Almighty there was no one standing on the sidewalk to see us hurtling down.

There was someone waiting above us, though. Gadreel had not given up. I could feel him flying just behind us, my angel sense tracking him like radar.

"Are you hurt?" I yelled, the wind whipping past so I didn't know if she could hear me. I wiped blood from her cheek and showed her.

"Put me down!" Adrienne replied. "How dare you!"

Her hair flew in my face, and I shook my head to clear my eyes. I wasn't sure where we could go; I barely knew the city, and I couldn't just disappear into the spiritual plane with her in tow. Flying along the lake, I headed back toward the university campus, though I knew this would take us straight over a crowded avenue called State Street. With the massive, glowing backdrop of the capitol building behind us, it would be impossible not to be seen by anyone on the ground. I veered to skim the rooftops of the stores and restaurants along the street, hoping the thick ducts and other protrusions would hit Gadreel. Adrienne continued squirming, stretching her feet down in an attempt to catch ground. I wrapped one of my legs around both of hers and flew a bit higher.

"No!" she yelled, defeated. "We can finish him! He cannot stand against us together!"

"I cannot let you fight him!"

423

"Why not? I have fought the fallen before!"

How could I explain to her the horrible, inevitable deaths that awaited humans who challenged the fallen? I would not allow her to come to that end. The memories of my friends demanded it. I swore I would never be responsible for another human death in this war; I wouldn't make an exception for her, even if she was technically Gabriel's responsibility. When Gabriel fled that hotel room, Adrienne came under my care.

Ahead, the steep incline of Bascom Hill rose up toward a quieter area of the campus where taller buildings would shield us from view. I could already make out the twin walking paths leading up and over the hill where during the day hundreds of students walked to class. Now, in the night, they were thankfully empty.

Adrienne looked back over my shoulder. "He's still there! We have to face him; he's not just going to give up now!"

Trying to ignore her, I beat the air with my wings, and the last of State Street sped past. If I could just get some distance between us, I might lose Gadreel yet. Just as we started rising up the hill though, something slammed into the back of my head. Everything went black.

Blind, dazed, I heard Adrienne scream as she slipped from my grasp. The fall was a good distance, her scream lasting a few seconds. Then I slammed into something at full speed, my arms and legs tangling around the limbs of what had to be a tree. Bones shattered. Blood flowed. I concentrated and broke free of my physical body, the world reappearing in spiritual light, and found I was indeed tangled in a tree nearly at the top of the hill. Working to free myself, I dropped the last few feet to the ground.

What had knocked me from the air? I scanned for Adrienne and finally found her. She was lying in the grass, having rolled nearly all the way back down to the bottom of the hill. Digging her heels into the ground, back arched, she was clearly in agonizing pain.

Gadreel landed at her feet, the matter loosing from his wings. Scythe gleaming in one hand, he hefted what looked like a cannon-ball in the other. Mystery solved. He dissolved it as he smiled down at Adrienne. She cradled her arm, defenseless. There was no way I could reach her in time. I sprinted for her anyway.

But even before I had fully formed a new physical body, a young man came running from the nearby pedestrian bridge. I dropped the matter away from all but my ears, running invisible. The distraction might give me the opportunity to surprise Gadreel before he could harm anyone.

"Hey lady, you all right?" the young man called out, but slowed as Gadreel turned. The backpack dropped from his shoulders as his eyes fell on the scythe.

"Run! Get away!" Adrienne yelled to him, but it was in French.

"Better keep moving and forget what you saw here, boy," Gadreel said.

"I'm right here, demon! You want to kill me, then kill me!"

The young man stood his ground, though it was obvious he was regretting playing hero. Hands held out defensively, he said, "I—I think you should leave her alone. Let's not make this into some-thing, all right?"

Gadreel lunged at him. Adrienne screamed. I pumped my wings, soaring for them.

The metal blade of the scythe glinted in the light of the near-est lamppost as Gadreel slashed with enough force to cleave the student in two. His wings blocked my view of the attack, but the jolt of impact in his shoulders was unmistakable. Crying out in rage, I flew harder. Even when I tried to save humans from fighting, they ended up dying!

As I reached Gadreel, I entered the physical plane, ready to drive my sword through his damned back and tear his heart through the hole. Before I could though, he crumpled to the ground like a marionette with clipped strings.

Standing there, the young student was shaking. Face pale, covered in blood, he stared down at Gadreel. I quickly retracted my sword, hoping he hadn't seen it.

My eyes met Gadreel's gaze. I knew that gaze. Vacant, frozen in surprise. I looked at the young man again, thinking, *It's impossible.* Then I saw what he was holding.

Clutched in his hands, Gadreel's scythe looked monstrous. And hanging off the end of the blade in a tangle of gore, the demon's heart beat its last.

CHAPTER FORTY-ONE

"Where have you been?" Raphael asked. His voice echoed off the bare concrete walls of our construction site rendezvous point.

With Adrienne downstairs, arm broken, unable to talk to the student who hadn't spoken a single word since Bascom, and me, dragging our burden up to the fourth floor, Raphael couldn't possibly have known the complexity of what he asked.

I dragged Gadreel into the room, leaving a thick smear of blood across the gray dust on the floor. It looked almost black. As did the blotches on my robe; the stairs had been especially fun. Unable to reveal what I was to the student, he and I had carried Gadreel in tense silence from shadow to shadow all the way across town. It was a miracle we made it undetected. When we finally reached the unfinished building where Michael and the rest were gathered, the boy was still as pale as Gadreel's emptied corpse.

The scrape of wood on concrete filled the room as my brothers pushed their seats back from an elegant table that stood in stark contrast to the drab, gray walls. It was the only object in the room not covered in construction debris.

"What the hell happened?" Raphael said, jumping up to help me drag the limp, but not entirely lifeless, body to the table.

Uriel laughed and said, "Back on his feet not two days and already a kill!"

I didn't smile. Neither did Michael. I was replaying the memory for him.

"Where is Adrienne?" Gabriel asked, worry in the glow of his eyes.

I dropped into an empty chair, exhausted and relieved to be done sneaking around. "Downstairs. She's hurt."

Looking like his fears had been realized, he rushed toward the door.

"Wait," Michael's voice echoed. He gazed out at the lights of the city. The capitol dome was farther than it had been from the Concourse, but still dominated the view. I looked at Haniel, whose heart had been replaced since the attack. He nodded, seeing me for the first time since my resurrection.

Adonael stood next to him. The newcomer. What happened while I was gone to bring another of the host here? Was he the only one?

"Sabrael," Michael interrupted my thoughts. "Go with Gabriel. Bring our guest to the back room on the first floor. I will meet you there."

The others looked confused. I almost asked Michael why he wanted to meet the student, but I had defied and questioned him for hundreds of years. I knew where that road led.

My soiled robe peeled from my skin as I stood. I couldn't wait to change the matter of my clothing and cleanse myself of the blood, but if I was to continue the ruse for the student, it wouldn't do to look differently than I had just moments before. I followed Gabriel back to the stairs, forced to keep on a bit longer.

"Our guest?" Gabriel asked as we descended.

"Just a boy. He saw everything that happened. Why would Michael want to meet him? He's gone through more than enough tonight without our making it worse."

We took the stairs two at a time. At the bottom, Adrienne sat waiting with the student.

"I thought you meant a child," Gabriel said when we turned around the final landing to see them. "He must be nearly twenty."

"He's too young for all this."

Gabriel looked at me as though I were the child. "Adrienne's not much older."

"Had I been around for her blessing, I would have said the same for her."

Adrienne rose when she saw us, wincing as she supported her arm but still managing to look relieved. I doubted the two humans even tried to talk. They most likely sat in silence and exchanged hopeful glances that the other would somehow turn bilingual through force of will.

"Gabriel," she said, her accent rolling the name from her tongue. "I'm sorry we were late. It was my fault completely."

"No," I said before Gabriel could reply. Adrienne's gaze snapped to me. "We discussed it upstairs. It was my fault and there will be no arguing the matter."

Gabriel gently tested her forearm with his thumb. "We should get a splint on this before you start healing."

"What of the young man who saved me?" she protested, though I could tell she was in terrible pain. A sheen of cold sweat covered her forehead.

Gabriel gave me a puzzled look at the word "saved."

"Come on," Gabriel said, wrapping his arm around her shoulders. I waited until they were past the second floor before turning to the student.

He sat on a stack of drywall planks, feet dangling. From the waist up, he was caked in blood, but he didn't seem to notice. His eyes were fixed on the floor.

I sat beside him and waited. Eventually he blinked and looked at me, as though only then realizing there had been movement around him. Parted in the middle and nearly chin-length, his hair was dusty blond except for two streaks along his face that were almost white. He had an intelligent, hazel gaze, but right now he looked lost.

"You must have questions," I said.

"Who are you?" he asked quietly after clearing his throat.

"Someone you should not have met."

A police siren suddenly wailed from the street. The light played along the edges of his hair as he straightened, then relaxed with the passing of the squad.

"I killed that man."

"He would have killed you if you had not." I thought to myself, *He still might,* but I didn't share this. Instead I asked, "How exactly did it happen?"

The student's eyes narrowed. "It was like he was twenty feet away and then right next to me, swinging that … thing. A scythe, right? Like the Grim Reaper. I just reached out and caught it. I don't know what happened." Tears welled in his eyes. "I swear I didn't mean to kill him. Am I going to jail?"

I held back a smirk. "I would not worry about it," I said. Amazing. This child had accidentally done what not a single trained warrior had accomplished in two millennia. I wouldn't have believed it if I hadn't seen it.

He stared at me, suddenly terrified. "What are you going to do to me?"

"Nothing. My brother just wants to meet you, and then you can go. Promise." I motioned toward an empty room where the light was brighter.

"Are you guys like the mafia or something?"

I gave him a smile. "More like Homeland Security."

Michael nodded throughout the boy's account. The student heard a woman scream as he passed over the walking bridge to the hill, and when he saw Adrienne and Gadreel, he thought she was being mugged.

"I didn't even see you until after," he said to me, the shock of the experience fading. "If I knew you were there, I probably wouldn't have done anything."

"Believe me, Gavin, it was a very good thing you did," Michael said. My eyes darted to him, realizing he read the boy's mind to learn his name. The student hadn't yet said it.

Gavin didn't notice. "What will you do with the body?"

"We will take care of it. Do not worry. No one else will learn what happened tonight."

Gavin smirked, the light from outside shining on his face. "So you are like the mafia." His smile faded instantly as he realized the situation he was in if we were. Then his eyes went wide. "We left my backpack! If someone finds it in all that blood..."

Michael's eyes were locked on the boy with the same intensity he'd maintained through the entire meeting. Amazing the way his eyes held so much power even when made to appear human. He seemed fascinated by the boy, the unlikely and until then impossible slayer of a demon. I was just anxious to get the boy away from us. "I will send one of our brothers to retrieve it and escort you home safely."

One of our brothers? Not me then?

Gavin looked relieved. Raphael appeared at the doorway as though he'd been waiting all along and beckoned Gavin to him.

The boy looked back at me. "Don't worry; I won't tell anyone you guys are here."

I nodded though I wanted to laugh, and then they were gone.

I waited for Michael to say something. He was listening to the echo of their receding footsteps. Finally out of Gavin's view, I reformed the matter of my robe, Gadreel's blood disappearing. I wondered if Gabriel had revived Gadreel upstairs to interrogate him yet.

"You will bless him," Michael said, snapping my thoughts back to the room.

"You're joking, I hope." His eyes returned to their natural, glowing appearance. His expression dead serious. I held my tongue earlier, but I couldn't let this happen. "Absolutely not. He's far too young."

"Were Theokritus and Helena any older when you met them?"

"Yes!" I blurted out, though I realized immediately this wasn't true. "Those were different times. Theokritus and Helena were mature adults at that age."

"He killed Gadreel. With nothing but the quickness of his human hands. Think what he will be capable of with the abilities we can give him."

I struggled to keep from yelling. "Did you not see what killing Gadreel did to him? He was in shock until he started talking to you. He won't last."

"He was overwhelmed. It is only natural. Ending a life isn't easy to deal with, especially the first time, but he will overcome this. It will be easier when he finds out it was a demon."

"How?" I yelled, unable to suppress it any longer. "They bleed like humans, they scream worse than humans, and removing their hearts feels just like removing a human's. It's still killing. I will not teach one so young to be comfortable with that."

Michael sighed. I was getting nowhere. "This cannot be overlooked. He's done something miraculous. Never before has a human been so fit to help us."

"You told me that for more than two centuries, no human has been brought into the war without first showing extreme devotion and knowledge of the Word!"

"That is true," he said. "The rule was made to protect the humans who might be blessed for the wrong reasons. Without strong faith, they will not be committed to our cause."

"Exactly. Thank you. We know nothing about him, least of all his beliefs."

"He believes."

"How can you possibly know that?"

"The whole time he was here, he was praying we wouldn't kill him." Michael tapped his temple. "Talk to him. Convince him if need be."

"No," I snapped. His persistence was appalling. "This is absurd. He's a kid with almost his entire life ahead. I will not strip that from him as I did from…"

Michael cocked his head. "From whom?" he asked, clearly already knowing the answer.

I sighed and shook my head, moving to look out the empty window. I thought of them, their tears and pain. Their blood.

"You do not know what it is like. To give them power and then watch them run headlong into death. Theokritus and Helena were great warriors. They had strength I didn't know humans could possess. Turel killed them both, and his smile never even faltered. Valthgar stood against entire armies, and that was before the blessing. He moved among deadly weapons as though they were flowers in the breeze, and he died collapsing a cave on top of himself using a power I gave him. Malietta wasn't even in the war, yet simply knowing me was enough to get her killed. Tonight, Adrienne would've been next but for Gavin's timely arrival. She will die just like my warriors did, just like Malietta did, because this war is not theirs. They don't belong in or anywhere near it. I told you, I am finished bringing death to mankind."

Michael sat staring at me for a moment, contemplating, then nodded.

"We've had this conversation before," he said. "Long ago, in Jerusalem. I admit that back then, I longed to have human companions as you did. I wanted to have the relationship you shared with Theokritus, Helena. I envied you that. Until Helena died and I saw how you suffered. I began to understand then why you thought it better to be without that bond.

"Then Jesus was crucified.

"You watched Helena killed and could do nothing to save her. Imagine what it was like watching the Son hanging there and knowing I *could* save Him. Think how I felt, standing there on Golgotha, the man I had watched being born now dying before a crowd, slowly, in agony, but knowing that if I saved Him, I would destroy the very thing He had been sent to do.

"I know what it is to face the horrible knowledge that yes, humans will eventually die. Jesus's death is the reason I never took another human into my care. They are not as we are, no matter what abilities we awaken in them. When one of us falls, we have the ability to rise again. The men and women who fall do not, not here at least. And you're right; it didn't start as their war. But when Jesus walked out of that tomb, He made the kingdom their home. If Lucifer and the fallen wrest the throne from the Father, human souls will suffer for eternity alongside us, and that makes this their war too. All of us, angels and humans alike, depend on the outcome of this hunt for the gateway to keep our home safe.

"That's why we need them. Despite the fact that it takes us mere hours to fly around the world, it is still a big place with many secrets. We are but seven. We cannot beat Hell's legions in this race to find the gateway. It's inevitable they'll discover it first. We need the humans' help, even though they are not as strong, not as fast, and even though they can die, because they have strength where we do not—in number and knowledge of this world. They think differently than we do, and they may point us to the gateway when we otherwise would've overlooked it."

Michael stood, moving to the window, his voice lowering almost to a whisper. "Gavin killed one of the fallen tonight. For more than two thousand years, countless men and women have stood against the fallen with weapons they have mastered and amazing abilities that give them the power to contend with the demons. Not one has ever, with all those advantages, managed to kill a single member of

Lucifer's army. That 'boy,' as you insist on calling him, did it with his bare hands. In all the time we have been blessing humans, never has there been one with such potential to stand against the fallen."

"Michael, please," I begged. "I cannot do this."

Anxiety washed over me. There was no arguing anything he said, but I wasn't ready to take on another warrior of light. I could not be a mentor in this new world where I was still learning so much. I could not be a mentor in any other world. The thought of caring for another warrior and watching him die was unbearable. How did we know the slaying of Gadreel hadn't been a horrible, misfortunate accident? Perhaps Gavin had exaggerated his role in the demon's death. How could we know for sure that he would be able to do it again? I would be taking him from everything he knew to bring him before death and tell him it was all right to spit in its face.

"I cannot be the one. Let Raphael or Gabriel do it. He met them both. He will trust them, and I can be nearby in the beginning to put him at ease. Or let Uriel take him. Uriel would love to take such a potentially powerful warrior under his wing."

Michael put his hand on my shoulder. "You found him. It has to be you. It has been the tradition since the beginning. That is why I am *ordering* you to do this." I moaned in anguish at the word. "Make sure his devotion is clear, then invite him to join us. If his soul is not in the right place, spend time with him and teach him before bringing him into his new role, but you will bless him and be his guide."

I lost. He ordered the blessing; I would not disobey him. At least that promise I could keep. I wholeheartedly disagreed and wanted to fight him on it further. Gavin, despite what he'd done, wasn't ready. He would never survive. I knew this, but what could I do? No amount of objection would change Michael's mind.

Michael left me to gaze out at the sky, hoping to see the moon but instead finding only a black expanse of clouds. Were my brothers still up there watching us, pointing and screaming, "Look, the gateway is there!" It didn't matter. Even if they were, we couldn't hear them.

Thinking about the host, I ran to the stairwell. "Michael!" I called up.

He looked down at me from the second floor landing. "I will not argue any further."

"Why is Adonael here? When did he come to Earth?"

"About fifty years after you were killed. He told me he was sent to act in your place until you were resurrected, just as he was your replacement in the kingdom."

"Who guards my hall now?" I asked.

"Suria was appointed," Michael said, starting his ascent again.

"But I am resurrected. Why is Adonael still here?"

"I would imagine the answer to that question," he said, "is linked to why no one was sent in Barachiel's place."

His words hit like a fist. He was right; there should have been a replacement for Barachiel ages before. I realized why Michael hadn't answered my question in the hotel room.

Barachiel was still missing.

This revelation was too much. Old anxiety rose up, but I checked it. I had been ordered to a task that would take all my strength. Barachiel, sadly, would have to wait a bit longer.

I wasn't prepared to take on a new warrior. Michael didn't understand. How could I train Gavin when I had not even been able to raise my own sword against the fallen? I had been frozen, not by awe or indecision, but fear. How was I to guide anyone when I couldn't even bring myself to fight? I prayed to the Almighty to help me be the guide Michael believed I could be. I prayed for His help in befriending Gavin and for the safety of the boy who was much too young for the responsibility Michael was placing on him. I let my physical form dissolve into the wind and tried to gather my will. Then, spreading my wings, I soared out to do the one thing I had vowed never to do again.

CHAPTER FORTY-TWO

"I don't understand why you're so opposed to this," Raphael said. A cool breeze swept over the roof as I looked down at the bustle of State Street. Despite the brisk air, it had been crowded since sunrise, first by delivery trucks, then by university students and shoppers. Even the sidewalk cafés were packed in the shining spring sun.

"He has a good heart. Confidence in the abilities will come with training," he added.

I met his glowing gaze. "That's the problem. The confidence. They all come to it eventually, running blindly toward death, led by the belief they might just be able to handle the fallen on their own."

"Lighten up, Sabrael," he said. "The warriors of light have grown more mature and more responsible in your absence. The mistakes of times past have all but disappeared."

"Only because warriors today are selected more carefully. Gavin was chosen as hastily as Theokritus and Helena, as recklessly as Valthgar." I leaned forward to rest my arms on the roof's ledge. "What happened to them will happen to him. It is inevitable."

"It's really not. Many of my warriors have died from natural causes. Takes longer than it does for normal humans—some pass their hundredth birthday and still live a decade or more—but it does happen. Gavin may see those years as well. No one can know."

"I can," I said. After a few moments I could still feel Raphael's gaze on me. "What?"

He was smiling. "Everything's always so black or white. After all that happened to you, you're the same hard-headed fool. I have missed you."

He came at me with open arms. "Get away," I said as I pushed him back, but a reluctant chuckle ruined my delivery. I couldn't help it. He looked ridiculous with that grin. I laughed and let him embrace me. "I missed you too," I said. "Idiot."

Raphael motioned to the street. "There he goes. Better get to it."

Gavin emerged from a store in a black long-sleeved tee with a skull print. He scanned the street as he walked, looking for someone … or perhaps ensuring no one was looking for him.

Raphael patted my shoulder. "It will be fine."

I couldn't hide my skepticism as I leapt from the roof into the spiritual plane. Spreading my wings, I swooped low over the pavement, landing just behind him. I followed him a few steps, but he slowed as his gaze fell on a bar window.

His eyes narrowed, and he spun to look right at me. I froze. Could he see me? He took another glance at the reflection before shifting the straps on his shoulders and continuing on more quickly than before.

I looked back down the street just as a young couple walked through me. I dispersed for a moment, the woman shuddering and pulling her collar up. What had Gavin been looking at? I gathered myself together and ran to catch up.

It was another two blocks before he stepped into a corner restaurant. I wound through the crowded tables inside to follow him to the second floor.

There, at a table overlooking the street, a young woman sat reading in the sunlight. Gavin moved behind her chair, then leaned down to wrap his arms around her. The girl jumped, then elbowed him before kissing his cheek.

Oh no, I thought. A girlfriend. His family we could have slowly introduced to the idea, told them about the blessing after it was already done. But a girlfriend changed everything. How could he possibly hide the transition from someone who lived on the campus?

Gavin disappeared downstairs again and the girl returned to her novel, the light gleaming off a silver ring strung on a chain around her neck. What would she say if she knew an angel was watching her, come to steal her boyfriend away into a war he couldn't hope to survive? She was as young as Gavin, though sitting there absorbed by a book in the middle of the busy restaurant, she had a more mature air about her.

I remembered thinking the same of Helena and Theokritus.

Walking to the window, I stood at the head of the table beside her. She looked up at me, but I knew she saw only the window and the street beyond. Her eyes were a delectable chocolate brown, almost the exact same hue as her hair.

As Gavin returned with two sodas, she put the book down and I saw the cover. *Pride and Prejudice*. He scoffed. "I want to know who decides what gets to be a classic."

"Right, like you read enough to be an authority," she teased.

"I read plenty," he argued.

"Uh-huh. How'd the studying go last night?"

Gavin's jaw tightened. "Fine," he said, his voice trailing off as he drowned the lie with a drink.

Her eyes narrowed. "You didn't study, did you?"

"Why don't you ever just trust me? I was at the library late, I told you."

"Then something else is going on."

"Nothing's going on," he said, averting his eyes. At least I would never have to wonder when he was lying. He was terrible at it.

"I know that look."

Figuring it was a good time to interrupt before he ended up admitting anything, I rushed to the bathroom door and passed under it to form a physical body in private. I kept my own likeness so he would recognize me, but gave myself appropriate clothes.

I returned to the table just as the interrogation was getting ugly. The color drained from Gavin's face as he saw me.

"Morning, Gavin," I said, as casually as possible. "Have a moment?"

He nervously held out his hand to the chair across from him. The girl's eyes moved between him and me, and after a moment she nudged him.

With all the emotion of a machine he said, "Sabrael, this is my girlfriend, Lena."

She said, "Sabrael. That's a beautiful name."

"Pleasure to meet you. Gavin speaks very highly of you." That should earn me points with her.

I saw the flash of surprise in her eyes. "He's never mentioned you."

Gavin said, "We just met last night." He was still staring at me.

"Really?" She gave him a raised eyebrow. "At the library?"

"How'd you know?" I asked. And that should earn some with him. "He helped me out of a certain … predicament."

"Which I thought was all taken care of," he prodded.

Lena's gaze moved between us. "Are you in trouble?"

I reached out and laid my hand over hers. Gavin's eyes narrowed. "No one's in trouble. There's no need to worry." The concern evaporated from her eyes, and she nodded.

"However," I said to Gavin, letting him watch me take my hand from Lena's, "you and I need to speak. Privately."

A waitress arrived with their order. I waited until she was gone to continue.

"Will you have time to talk today?" I asked him.

Gavin ran his fork through rigatoni and marinara. "I guess."

I nodded. "I'll find you later then."

"Why don't I just give you my number?"

"I prefer to talk face to face. It is not hard to track you down," I said, inwardly laughing at his attempt to conceal his terror at the thought. I stood and gave Lena a smile. "Wonderful to meet you."

"You too," she said, smiling up at me with her chin resting on her hand.

As I headed downstairs, I heard Gavin whisper, "He's in the mob, I swear to God," and Lena reply, "Long hair is so totally hot."

⊷ ⊶

"You're a what?" Gavin asked.

We were walking along the shore of Lake Mendota, the bigger of the two lakes bookending the campus. The trees lining the path were already full with spring leaves.

"An angel."

"Yeah. Look, it was great meeting you and all, but..."

"I swear, it is the truth. I've been on the Earth since the days before Jesus Christ." I fell quiet as two students walked past, heading the opposite direction. "The one you killed last night, he is an angel too. One of the fallen."

Gavin laughed. "I would think an angel could put up more of a fight."

"You have no idea."

"If I killed an angel, what happened to him? Did he go back to Hell or something?"

441

"He is trapped inside his body now." His eyes narrowed and I waved my hands. "You will learn all of this later. There is too much to explain here."

"Listen, I'm really glad you were there to cover up … whatever happened, but I don't want any part of this. Okay? I told you, I'm not going to say a word to anyone about your operation here. So you can just forget about me, and tell Michael your secret's safe."

I shook my head, frustrated. A group of five men walked by, looking at me with wide eyes. I checked the spiritual plane to make sure they were human. "For the last time, we are not the mafia. What can I say to convince you?"

"How about, 'Kid, we're the mafia'?"

I would have traded a wing for the ability to transmit thoughts as my brothers could. "Today you stopped in front of a bar on State Street, looked around, and then continued the way you were first going. How would I know this?"

"Wow. That's some impressive intel. Next you're going to tell me I went to class, fell asleep during the lecture, twice, then went to Noodles."

"Lena was reading *Pride and Prejudice* when you snuck up behind her. She elbowed your stomach and kissed your cheek."

He shrugged, the skull on his chest bobbing. "So you were sitting at one of the tables. Not like I was looking for you."

I looked toward the sky, the sun peeking though the branches overhead. What did I have to do here? I had an idea and made sure no one was close enough to see me clearly.

"Look at my eyes." I shifted the matter to reveal their blue glow for a moment before transforming them back to human appearance. "Explain that."

He stared open-mouthed for a moment, then said, "You can get all kinds of weird theatrical contacts online. Doesn't prove anything."

I was appalled. "There must be a way to prove to you what I am."

"Where are your wings? I've seen plenty of movies and angels always hide their wings under a coat or something. You're in a hoodie and…" he patted my back, "I'm pretty sure there's nothing under there."

Why is it my wings are always the first thing humans ask to see? "They are there, but not in a form you can see or feel."

"That's incredible! Mine too," he said, mocking me.

"All right," I said, taking his hand and holding it open. I concentrated and gathered matter to form a leather pouch. Turning it over, I poured gold coins from inside onto his palm.

He stepped back from me, eyes wide. "Jesus!" he whispered. "That's…"

"Keep walking," I said, trying to avoid a scene.

He followed me, but his eyes were transfixed on the pouch. I made sure no one else had seen what had happened.

"I am telling the truth. I am an angel, and last night, you cut out the heart of a demon."

His hazel eyes in the sunlight reflected a kaleidoscope of every possible human eye color. "Why are you here? I mean, why aren't you up there singing and playing a harp or something?"

"Is that really what you think Heaven is like?"

"What is it like then?"

I set myself up for that. "I am not sure I am supposed to tell you that. Perhaps someday Michael will."

"Michael? The guy with the silver dye job, he was…?" His disbelief melted into laughter. "My mom is going to flip."

"Your mom?" I asked.

"Angel freak. Big time. Church nut and all that."

"What about you?" I asked, glad this had come up without my having to pry.

"I get there when I can," he said, averting his eyes. Then they went wide and he said, "Oh God! That guy was a fallen angel? And I killed him! The rest of them are going to hunt me down, aren't they? That's why you're here."

"No one knows about last night except those you met. Understand?"

He nodded, but his expression didn't change.

"In time though, other demons will find out and come looking for Gadreel, the demon you killed." I paused as a young woman passed, giving me a coy smirk. "Gadreel is perfectly conscious in that dead body. He knows your face, believe me, and he will not forget. If the fallen find him and he is released, danger might find its way to you then."

His eyes filled with fear. The conversation thus far wasn't convincing me that he should be allowed into the war. Had it been my decision, I would have left him right then, telling him that he should be careful, and we would do our best to make sure he was safe.

"There is something you need to know though, something so incredible it has caused quite a stir."

"Something besides all that?" he said.

"You are the first human in all of history to do what you did. What happened last night was impossible until now. We have always had humans working with us, warriors who fight with weapons and abilities that should give them the necessary skill to kill the fallen in battle. In two thousand years, it has never happened. The greatest human warriors to ever walk the Earth have been unable to kill even one demon. Now you, without a weapon or any training, killed the first demon you came across."

"But I didn't even mean to!" he said, clearly afraid he was in trouble. "I told you; it just happened! Can't you tell Gadpeel or whatever that it was an accident? It wasn't my fault!"

"You misunderstand. My brothers are intrigued by you. They want to meet you again."

The fear remained in his eyes, but curiosity now colored it. "Why? They want me to submit a report or something?"

"No. We have something much greater to ask of you."

"Which is?"

Everything in me screamed not to continue. I forced the words out. "Michael believes last night was a sign that you are meant to become a warrior of light."

Gavin stopped, shocked. "You want me to go toe-to-toe with the devil?"

"Not me. Michael. And no, you would not fight Lucifer. You may face demons like Gadreel from time to time, but there is no way you could fight Lucifer himself. Trust me."

"But we're talking about angels fighting demons? Like real Bible stuff?"

"The Bible doesn't really talk much about all this, but yes, essentially." At least he knew about the Almighty and Lucifer. Made things a bit easier. "Many have died in this war just like any other. Those we fight can control the matter of the universe as I did when I formed that pouch, and they will always be around even when you cannot see them. They can pluck the greatest fears from your mind and make them reality."

"What about my family? Lena? My friends?"

"You must be prepared to leave it all. Depends on what Michael has in mind. There are those who never take up a weapon against the fallen. Many lead normal lives and simply serve as researchers or scouts." I was a bit surprised at all the details contained in my mind from when Michael had bestowed on me the knowledge of the modern world. "My guess however, is that Michael intends a more active role for you, given the way you caught his interest."

"You want me to say yes without finding out what happens to my life first?" he asked.

Good. He was being cautious. "Michael wants to meet you again, tonight. I'm just here to offer the invitation. Do you remember how to get to the building? The one from last night?"

"Yes," he said. I was surprised and impressed how serious he'd become when only moments earlier he had been practically giddy at the concept of fighting in the war.

"Go there tonight. We will talk to Michael together."

He nodded, and I placed a reassuring hand on his shoulder before turning to leave him.

"Sabrael," he said. I looked back at him. "I'm sorry I didn't believe you."

"This may surprise you, but no one ever does."

CHAPTER FORTY-THREE

I t was an hour past sunset when we spotted his approach. Only Michael, Raphael and I were present, the others busy interrogating Gadreel or guarding our position. After the hotel attack, many of the fallen had scattered, but we could still sense them nearby. Police were investigating what happened at the Concourse. The hotel manager insisted the rooms in question were under renovation and had no known occupants. Some of our warriors fight the good fight with words.

We were on the roof discussing where we should go next when we saw Gavin coming down the street. Only he wasn't alone.

Lena walked beside him, their hands clasped in the sodium orange glow of street lights.

Raphael asked, "Is that Lena with him?"

I was surprised. "How do you know about her?"

"She was all he thought about on the way home last night. You invited her too?"

"No," I said, glaring down at them. Had he heard nothing I said? Just bringing her here endangered her life.

"That's not true, Sabrael," Michael said. "Calm down."

"The fallen don't even know who he is yet," Raphael added.

I looked at each of them in turn. "Is it really that difficult to stay out of my thoughts?"

"When you think so loud, yes," Raphael said smiling.

Gavin and Lena reached the building and, as they entered, Gavin did something no other passerby had done all evening—he looked up. Seeing us, he waved.

"He's not afraid," Michael said. "That's good."

"Or very bad," I replied. I caught his look as we walked to the stairs.

We met the pair on the second floor. Raphael went ahead of us into a room to form a table and chairs, as it was still uncertain how much of our power we would allow them to see.

After Gavin introduced Lena to the three of us, this time introducing me for what I truly was, we sat around the table. Lena was shaking with excitement, had even dressed up for the occasion. Gavin had not.

"Let me begin by saying that you do not have to receive the blessing. You are free to leave here and nothing will come of any of this," Michael said. "It's entirely your choice."

Gavin said, "Would you just erase our memories or something?"

"No," Michael said. "There is no need for such a thing. You're in no danger."

"What about the fallen?" Lena asked, revealing that Gavin had told her everything. "Won't they come looking for him?"

"Only if you start telling people about what you saw here," Michael said.

Raphael added, "Even if they did, from what we have seen already, he can defend himself better than any other human in history."

Gavin smiled, but Lena didn't.

"Your decision shouldn't be based solely on whether Gadreel can find you," I said. "If you agree, you will be with us for the rest of your life, and this might simply be the first in a long line of dangerous encounters."

"You said there are different kinds of warriors. What kind would I be?"

"There are not really different kinds," Michael said. "They are all given the same training. The difference is only in what tasks we assign them. You'll be whatever kind of warrior Sabrael needs you to be."

"What about my family?" Gavin asked, pushing his hair from his eyes.

Michael smiled. "No family has ever disapproved of someone becoming a warrior of light."

Lena laughed, covering her mouth with a hand. "Sorry. It just sounds so stupid, 'warrior of light.' Does the blessing come with twenty-sided dice too?"

I frowned at her. I happened to like the title I gave them.

"There's no way to leave the war once I've entered it?" Gavin asked.

Raphael replied, "Would you ever really want to once you stood against the fallen?"

"That is not to say you will be actively fighting until your death," Michael added. "When our warriors grow too old to fight, they find other ways to help."

Lena took Gavin's hand and held it between her own. "What about Lena?" he asked. "Could she become a warrior as well?"

Michael said, "My recommendation is no. It is a dangerous thing and requires great sacrifice. But I leave it to Sabrael to decide. You would be his warrior, and so would she."

All eyes turned to me. I should have known that was the reason she came along. I was only ordered to bring Gavin into the war, though. No one said I had to bless Lena.

"Lena, do not misunderstand me, but I do not think you should be part of this. I am not even sure Gavin should, but after last night, the choice is not really mine. You are young and this war has taken the lives of so many. I would rather you did not subject yourself to this."

"But I already have! How am I supposed to go on like everything's normal when I know Gavin's out there fighting a war you just said has killed so many people? I know as much as he does about all this, and besides killing a fallen angel, we're even."

"That's a big 'besides,' " I said.

"Whatever the risks, I'd rather be by his side than sitting at home wondering if this is the day an angel will come to tell me he's been killed."

"Hon—" Gavin said.

"No!" Lena interrupted. "I'm not going to let them whisk you away and I never see you again. If you go, I'm following you." She turned back to me. "I'm going to be helping you whether you like it or not. Why not just make it official?"

"Because the fallen can tell the difference," I said, remembering the unique glow of a warrior's soul. "If I bless you into the war, it would be like putting a target on your back."

"Won't they figure out that I'm always with him? It's going to happen anyway."

"It is not the same." How could I tell her that I wasn't ready to have a couple as companions again? How could I tell her that being blessed had killed the last pair of lovers I took under my wing?

"If you are serious about helping, why not just do that until Sabrael feels you are ready?" Raphael said. "You can aid them with all but the fighting. We could use the help, believe me."

He gave her a wink. Gavin implored me with hopeful eyes. I looked at Michael for help.

I see no problem with it, his voice said in my mind. *It may even make the transition easier for him.*

"Fine," I said, defeated by the four of them. I would have to smack Raphael later. "You can help, but when I tell you to stay behind, you will not argue."

"Deal," Lena said, beaming. Gavin looked relieved. I flashed a glance at Raphael, who wore the broadest smile of all.

Michael asked, "Has it been decided then?"

Gavin said, "I'm being asked by angels to serve God and fight demons. Who would say no to that?"

Michael smiled, and Raphael reached over to pat Gavin on the back. Lena laughed and kissed Gavin excitedly. I realized Gavin's mind was made before he even came here. This whole show had been to negotiate Lena's involvement.

I closed my eyes. *God, give me the strength for this.*

Gavin was blessed that night. I asked him to take his time, to spend a night or two as a normal nineteen-year-old. I told him to go out with friends, or take Lena somewhere for one last date night. I wanted him to enjoy life before I stripped it from him. But he would hear none of it. After some arguing, I reluctantly proceeded.

In that same room on the second floor, Gavin knelt before me on the bare concrete. Lena stood nearby with Raphael. My emerald-eyed traitor. Michael sat in the chair behind me flanked by Gabriel and Haniel, his fingers steepled. Gavin was awash in the artificial light from the street lights outside the window. My child warrior. Had he any idea what he agreed to?

"Gavin, today you become a warrior in the service of the Almighty God. You have been called by Him to rise above the flock and become a shepherd of your brothers and sisters. To protect them from the influence of those who would see them ruined, and to guide the light of Heaven onto them all."

Again I came to the place where the old words didn't apply. I remembered the blessing of Valthgar, how different his had been from that of Theokritus and Helena. Had the ritual ever sounded the same in all the instances when the words had been uttered through history? Or was I the only one whose every blessing was unique?

"The life of the Messiah was the most important life ever to come to the Earth. You have been asked to guard the memory of that life and the gifts it bestowed. You have been asked to spend your days serving the Lord and preparing the way for His return. Your God and His angels on Earth are calling you to join our war, to fight and ensure the salvation of all people through the faith in the kingdom of Heaven and the power of the resurrection over death."

Lena covered her mouth, but her eyes gave away her smile. The ring on her necklace sparkled as she turned to Raphael, an excited giggle hunching her shoulders. Too young for this.

"In the name of the one true God, will you, Gavin, give your life in the service of Heaven, fighting alongside the angels of the Heavenly host, to preserve the promise of peace for all mankind, and to defend the world from the touch of the fallen?"

Gavin nodded, his hazel eyes so resolute it was shocking. "I will."

"Called to God's service you have willingly taken upon yourself the responsibility of being a leader among mankind in the ways of the Almighty. Let us pray."

All of us lowered our heads, but before I could speak, Michael placed his hand on my shoulder. *Let me.* I was confused why Michael would interrupt the blessing, but I stepped back to let him have the honor.

Michael bowed his head. "Almighty God, You have brought this young man to us through a most miraculous act. Never before has there been a blessing so important, never before a warrior so graced. With his induction into the war, let his strength only grow, and make him an example for the warriors of today and in the days still to come. Guide him through the darkest moments of his service, and never let him lose sight of You or Your teachings. Protect and lead him closer to You always, and help him to become a powerful companion to Your servant, Sabrael. We know there is a reason You have led this young one to us. Grant him the confidence and courage to become that which You have planned. Amen."

The room echoed with the repeated "Amens." Gavin looked up at me, the weight of Michael's words heavy on his shoulders. I raised my arm and called my sword. When it burst into my hand, his eyes gleamed. I touched the blade to his shoulder.

"I, Sabrael, guardian of the first hall of Heaven and minister to God the Son on Earth, bless you a warrior of light, to fight the fallen and defend the throne until death parts you of this world, in the name of God the Father, Son and Holy Spirit."

I retracted my sword and leaned to kiss his forehead. "Rise now, Gavin, a soldier of the faith, and a warrior of light." He smiled, and I reluctantly returned it. "Amen."

Gavin stood, and I backed away from him, coming beside Michael in his chair. Lena laughed and jumped into Gavin's arms. They kissed, laughing and smiling.

"Clear your mind of those thoughts," Michael scolded quietly. "This is meant to be."

"We shall see," I replied.

Gavin embraced Raphael, who came forward with Gabriel and Haniel to welcome the boy into the war. They all embraced Lena as well, as in a way, she enlisted that night as well.

As Michael rose to join them, I sat in the empty chair and watched my brothers, the baby warrior and his beautiful girl. They acted as though they won some sort of prize. I wanted to share their optimism, their hope that everything would work out fine. But I couldn't. Gavin had done something extraordinary, true, but there was no reason to believe that he would adapt to a war. Could he be counted on to kill again? Could he cope with the unique horror of killing another human? Would he still be at my side when the gateway was finally found, or would he fall before then, proving my brothers wrong? He would have to show me much more before I accepted his place among us, and trusted him to guard my back when the time came to do so.

CHAPTER FORTY-FOUR

Gavin was no more prepared for the training than any other had been. He brought no special knowledge or experience that made him stand out from my past warriors, though he was an incredibly fast learner. Like the others, he often impressed me with his abilities once he learned them, but I held fast to my belief that this was all wrong.

His weapon turned out to be a metal rod about a foot long, which extended to a six-foot staff with a quick flick of his wrist. Another simple twist sharpened the ends into points that cut through concrete as easily as my sword. I wondered what the construction crew would have thought each morning if I didn't call matter to repair the damage our training caused. Lena watched every night, working on homework in the window well and encouraging Gavin to keep up with the opponents I created for him, and later against my own sword. She was a boon for him, helping to focus his determination, and I'll admit that at times, I was glad she was there. Adrienne came to watch us during those nights as well, and though she didn't speak English, she laughed along with Lena when Gavin or I would take a fall or when Gavin would occasionally smack his own head with the staff.

During breaks, Adrienne and I would walk the Madison streets together. I knew Gabriel planned to take her back to Paris soon, and I found myself dreading the day. I secretly hated when the two of them went out on short missions. My mood soured when she was away; I knew it, but I couldn't help it. There was just something about when she was around, and when we took our private walks, I led her on ever-longer routes. If she noticed, she never complained.

One night as we walked, she looped her arm in mine playfully, and when I didn't pull away, she kept it there.

"What do you think about Gavin and Lena?" I asked her, searching for some reason to keep us out longer.

Adrienne said, "I am surprised you allow them to attend classes during the day. When I was training, Gabriel kept me at it for months without reprieve."

"The only reason we do not meet during the day is that we would be seen. I do not want the fallen to find them before they are ready."

Adrienne raised an eyebrow and smiled. Her blue eyes were striking in the false glow of the night. "Is that it? Or are you trying to shield him from joining the fight?"

I couldn't look away from her, but I had no answer.

She said, "You cannot shelter him forever. He will be fine, just as we all are. He cannot learn to survive until you allow him to experience real danger."

"What if he doesn't learn? What if he falls like so many before him?"

She pulled me a bit closer. Touched my cheek. "You are sweet to try to protect him. But his fate is not up to you. Do not let him know you have been prolonging all this or he may resent you for it."

I took this in and nodded. A moment passed, neither of us pulling away, then Adrienne said, "You can't always get away with stretching out your time with those you care about."

My cheeks grew warm and she smirked, playfully nudging me and then continuing on.

⸎

When we reached our building again a bit later, Lena was already back to her homework while Gavin stretched sore muscles. They looked up at us and Gavin stood straight.

"Ready when you are, boss," he said.

Adrienne squeezed my hand and gave me a look, then joined Lena. "How about we pick things up a little?" I suggested, and Gavin's eyes lit up.

"That," said a voice from the doorway, "is just what I was going to suggest."

When my eyes connected with that particular cobalt glow I hadn't seen in millennia, it paralyzed me. How could he be standing there, in our hideout, that horrible, beautiful child's face looking at us? It was impossible.

I stood for a long moment, and then dove at Lucifer screaming. The sound seemed to shake the very foundations of the fetal structure around us. It exploded without my desire, without my effort. I didn't care it might draw attention to the building and force us to relocate again. I didn't care that my new warrior and his girlfriend saw me lose control. I didn't even care that the last time I'd seen my demon brother he'd easily killed me and swore to do it again. In that moment, thousands of tortured voices stretching back across millennia cried out in unison, hurtling me toward him.

His golden sword appeared in his hand instantly. He deflected my blade as easily as he had beneath Jerusalem. I'd gained nothing on him in two thousand years. How had he broken in unchallenged? Or had he? Were my brothers all dead and I the last one standing? It couldn't be! I heard no screams, no calls for help. Surely he wasn't so stealthy that even Michael didn't detect him. I'd grown so accustomed to the constant tingle of my brothers' presence that I hadn't even noticed the peculiar flare when Lucifer had drawn close.

The vibration of our weapons rippled through my bones. I didn't even see Lucifer, only the screaming dead, those felled by my hand cheering and taunting as I beat my sword against his, striving to see his heart on the ground and that expression of death sweep over his features. Vengeance for wreaking so much havoc on the human world through me.

I don't even recall when Gavin and Adrienne joined the attack. My attention was so completely focused on Lucifer, I didn't notice them until Gavin's staff whistled past, just missing the end of my nose. He had promise, but had not even begun to master the weapon yet. I dodged the razor-sharp point, giving Lucifer the moment of respite he needed.

Adrienne was hurled back first, my brother simply waving his arm to send her soaring. She slammed into the wall and crumpled to the floor as Lucifer turned to Gavin. Flashbacks of Valthgar colored my vision as my young warrior was lifted off his feet and thrown as Adrienne had been. He struck the wall and managed to plant his feet on it, shoving off like a missile right back into battle. But the wall literally reached out to ensnare him! Like a living creature, the concrete stretched to wrap around him, encasing him in a cocoon with only his head free.

I continued the attack but it was too late. Lucifer caught my wrist and drove his blade through my forearm. Bolts of pain spread from the wound and my sword slipped from my powerless grasp. Lucifer tripped me with a sweeping kick, and immediately when my back hit the ground, the floor rose up to envelop me as the wall had Gavin. When I tried to free myself into the spiritual plane, a lancing pain shot through my side. Something was inside the concrete with me! I thrashed against the stone and called for help. I took no solace in the fact that my chest was shielded and my heart unreachable. Lucifer promised to kill me again, my weapon was out of reach, and I had no idea if my brothers were dead. Lena was screaming, clawing at the wall that held Gavin immobile. I had no idea how Lucifer manipulated the building itself to grab us. How had he done all this so quickly?

"Sabrael!" Lucifer yelled, his voice booming over my own. "Be quiet, little brother!"

"What are you doing here? How did you get in here?"

"Please. I escaped Hell without anyone noticing; I think I can slip past your pitiful sentries on the roof."

"You may have gotten in, but you will never get out. The others will sense you. They are probably already coming." I tried to struggle free, but it was hopeless. I couldn't move.

"We both know you're full of it." He picked up my sword, only a few feet from where Lena slouched on her knees at the base of Gavin's stone straightjacket. Tears coursed over her cheeks. Lucifer's tone softened. "Lena, darling, you do not have to fear me."

"Leave her alone!" Gavin yelled. "Or I swear to God I'll hunt you down!"

My brother's laughter filled the room. I glanced at Adrienne. She wasn't moving.

"Tell me this is not your new warrior, Sabrael," Lucifer said. "All this attitude. Like a Chihuahua that has no idea how easily it can be broken." He trailed off, looking from Lena to Gavin and then back again. "What is this? Trying to fool us now by not fully initiating all your warriors? Or is she really only here for him?"

"Did you come simply to bore us with talk?" I asked, still struggling.

"I see." Lucifer nodded, turned back to Lena. "One so pure and beautiful has no place in war. But do not worry. I promise I will not hurt you."

Gavin raged in his restraint. "I said leave her alone!"

Lena, amazingly, wiped the tears from her cheek. She seemed calm now. Or in a trance.

Lucifer said, "Better, *mellita*. You have nothing to fear from me."

"Is that how you gain trust, with Latin pet names and lies?"

Lucifer crouched next to me. He held my own blade to my exposed neck. "I never lie to them. I simply tell them the uncensored truth, and they love me for it."

"What do you want?" I asked.

He considered my sword, then laid it down. "I have not come to fight. We danced that dance long ago, and I have felt nothing but remorse since. Do you remember the way we were in the kingdom? Who would have guessed we would ever have come to that battle with the…" His jaw tightened for a moment. "With the *child* under that city."

"Who would have guessed you would ever lead an army against us?" I said.

Lucifer's eyes glazed over. He chuckled. "We were all so ignorant. But, even the seeds that sprouted then have withered, and the wheel turns again."

I narrowed my eyes. "What are you rambling about?"

"So many things have changed. So much more than could have been expected."

"Lucifer," I yelled. "What…do…you…want!"

Anger flared in his eyes for a moment, but faded. "Little brother," he began, "I have come to beg for your help."

CHAPTER FORTY-FIVE

Glistening pools of wax collected beneath candles illuminating our gathering. Tension hung in the air like humidity. Looking around, I couldn't decide with whom I should be more infuriated.

To my right, Raphael's knuckles were white on the table's edge, his burning eyes locked on Lucifer. Then Gabriel, listening to the devil spout his tale, as though ready to pounce. Where had they been when Lucifer had me pinned to the floor, powerless to defend myself? Could he have killed me, again, and walked out unchallenged by those keeping watch? Gavin and Lena were next, hands linked and chairs pushed close. Gavin, whose destiny the others extolled, and Lena, who stowed her way into the war. What good had either of them been? The one overpowered so easily, and the other still in a daze. Adrienne sat on my other side, her head swollen where it had slammed against the wall. She'd been even less effective than Gavin. It wasn't her fault though; she was still recovering from the hotel assault, after all. Beyond her were Haniel and Uriel, who were supposed to have been guarding us from detection just as Adonael was supposedly doing right then. Fantastic job they'd done. Finally Michael, brow low, fist at his chin. Why had he even allowed this meeting to happen? Why was Lucifer's heart still in his chest? Why were we allowing him to tell us how he had come to be in our hideout, alone and unarmed until I "forced his hand"? Most importantly, why had Michael commanded me to stay at the far end of the table, and why had he insisted I turn over my sword before the meeting began?

"Do you understand now why I have come?" Lucifer asked. "Why I need your help?"

Lucifer. How many times had I sworn vengeance on him? How often had I felt the ghostly sting where his sword had carved into my chest all those centuries ago? To think of all the souls he helped pull into Hell was maddening. To think that Hell itself was created because of him was worse. His beautiful, little mouth formed each word with such aplomb, the thin sliver of his teeth flashing in the candlelight. So alluring, so striking. Even in pleading for help, he maintained the illusion of such innocence that to listen to him unguarded would be to succumb. I focused on the memory of his burnt flesh, the tiny horns, the black wings; these would keep me from empathizing with him as I had in times past. They allowed me to keep the flames of my anger from cooling to embers.

"You want *us* to help you find *your* followers?" Raphael asked.

"Yes. Because I believe they have found the location of the portal into Heaven."

All of us took a moment to process what he said. "Come again?" Raphael asked.

"The gateway. That marvel of creation forgotten by all for eons and now the prize that brings us together again—they believe they have found it."

Uriel said, "Can't have that, can you? Allowing your peons to succeed where you have failed for so long."

The spark of rage in Lucifer's eyes was gone quick as it came. Had anyone else seen it?

"Perhaps you fail to understand how they intend to use the gateway. Should I explain it again more slowly?"

"Sounds to me like a ploy to get us to help quell a rebellion," Raphael said.

Gabriel added, "After all this time and all the suffering he has caused, who's to say he isn't lying through his teeth to send us into an ambush?"

Uriel growled, "We cannot trust him!"

Michael raised a hand. "We have to hear him out. If he is, for the first time since before his condemnation, telling the truth, we cannot risk the fallout."

The room fell silent, each of my brothers wrestling with the reality of the situation, and the humans watching all, afraid to make a sound.

"We could kill him," I said. "Leave him here while we investigate."

The corner of Lucifer's mouth turned up in a smirk. He winked at me.

"I think we should help him," Lena said. All eyes were directed toward her. She stared at Lucifer, swaying slightly in her chair. "I think we need to help him."

"I think you need to wait outside," I said. Gavin frowned at me, unaware what was happening. Lucifer had ensorcelled her like so many women before. I wondered how often he actually resorted to tempting anyone. It seemed all he needed to persuade humans into following him was to simply let them look at him.

Michael asked, "Where do they think the gateway is?"

Lucifer replied, "If I knew that, I wouldn't be here. I know only where they were last. Something there must have directed them on. We might still find clues they left."

Nothing was said for a moment. Then he smiled, raised a finger to his temple. "Are you trying to get in here, Michael? Trying to see what game your older brother is playing? You think you have the power to do such a thing?"

Michael's lips pursed in irritation. Gabriel asked, "Where do you want us to go?"

Lucifer turned to Gabriel, the candlelight dancing in his cobalt eyes. "They paid a visit to a priest in the Vatican. I believe you know him. Father Maurizio."

Haniel sat straight at the name.

"I know he's one of your pets. I also know he has access to records and ancient texts that no one outside the Holy See has ever seen." He smirked and waited for a laugh, but none came. "The venerable father was calling out for you. Said he 'found something of great import,' I believe, and wanted you in Italy at once."

"We heard him," Michael said. "Shortly after, he followed with a warning to stay away and await his next call. You think I was not aware of this?"

"I think you have no idea what what happened after that second call." Michael blinked and cleared his throat. Lucifer nodded. "Adramelec and Mammon. They heard him and went to find out what he'd uncovered."

Haniel's chair toppled loudly as he jabbed a finger toward Lucifer. "You sent them there! If anything happened to Maurizio—"

"Haniel," Michael said calmly, motioning for him to sit again.

Lucifer was enjoying the show. "Of course I sent them. Do not be a fool. Maurizio sent out the call for anyone to hear. The important matter here is that Adramelec and Mammon have not returned, nor have they sent word of what is happening, and now..." He paused for a moment. "Now I cannot find the rest of them."

"Funny," I said. "About a hundred of them attacked us here a few nights ago."

"Not that it went so well for them," Uriel added with a smirk.

"I'm sure you had no part in that, right?" I said.

"Why would I send an attack just before coming to ask for your help?"

For the first time, Gavin spoke. "To flush us out. Make sure we were here. Maybe even test us. Then you could claim you knew nothing of it so we'd still trust you."

Lucifer looked at him, impressed. "Oh my, little warrior. You are a surprise! Where did you find him, Sabrael?" He leaned toward Gavin. "Sure you still want to work for them? I'm always looking for promising young—"

"Stop," Michael commanded. Lucifer rolled his eyes at Gavin and Lena. Lena's expression warmed as she basked in Lucifer's attention. I should have sat nearer to her.

Michael said, "Are you telling us you have lost control of even your closest followers?"

"No one has lost control of anything," Lucifer snapped. "Adramelec and Mammon are carrion, always watching and waiting for the opportunity to scavenge power. I want to know why they suddenly disappeared and how they managed to take so many with them."

"I remember similar events long ago in the kingdom," I said. "No one lost control then either?"

Lucifer said nothing. Uriel barked, "Find them yourself. Or better yet, go back to your cell and lock yourself up tight; let us return them to you one by bloody one."

Raphael asked, "How do you know they found anything? They could just be busy deceiving new people for you. It is what your kind does best."

"They are your kind as well."

"They have not been our kind for eons," Uriel argued.

Gabriel said, "The fact is they turned from us willingly to follow you. If you have now lost them, it is no concern of ours."

"No. Lucifer's right." Michael shook his head, defeat heavy in his tone. "It makes no difference who stands at their head. If there is even a chance the gateway has been found, we must make sure it is not opened."

"You cannot be agreeing to help him?" I asked.

"No," Michael said. "I am agreeing to investigate what the fallen found, nothing more."

"Fine," Uriel said. "Then let us stash the devil away while we are at it. If we find he was lying, we leave him to rot."

Lucifer's eyes flashed again. He must have been at war with himself to remain calm.

"We take him with us," Michael said. "I don't want him out of our sight for a moment."

"I will not be shackled like a dog," Lucifer said, his voice low.

Lena added, "Of course you won't. We would never treat you like that."

Gavin returned my gaze, finally starting to catch on. He squeezed Lena's hand, whispered to her and tried to break the spell.

Michael rose from his chair. "You will do as you are told. Be grateful we have not struck you down already. There are those here that would do it in a moment."

Uriel cleared his throat pointedly, but Lucifer looked at me. I was shocked by Michael's words. Was he actually trying to provoke Lucifer? Lucifer was bristling, his jaw tight, eyes burning. My heart thundered, my hand open beneath the table in anticipation of calling my weapon from where it lay at Michael's feet. But Lucifer remained silent.

Michael nodded. "Everyone get ready. We leave right away."

"Please let me go with you!" Lena pleaded. "I'm better now, I swear!"

I finished piecing together matter to form a harness for the flight. Much the same as the harness which once carried Theokritus, this would allow me to carry Gavin all the way to Italy.

Lena kept at me, her color having returned and her mind cleared. "Lena, I do not know what dangers await us there. You might be left behind in the middle of the Vatican with no money and nowhere to go. I do not want to risk that happening."

"But I'm resourceful!" she said. "If something happens, I can just call home. My parents would have to believe I was kidnapped. How else could I get to Italy on my own?"

"What can it hurt?" Gavin asked. "She hasn't stopped us from training."

"That is different. You have seen what can happen when only one of the fallen attacks. Imagine if Lucifer had come with an entire force."

"But it's Rome! Please! I swear I'll stay away from any fights," Lena said.

"I will not change my mind."

Lena turned away and covered her face. I was sorry it hurt her, but I wouldn't allow her anywhere near Italy if that is where the battle was to happen. I couldn't be focused on her safety with the end so incredibly near.

I placed my hands on her shoulders and said, "I have seen the battles that can erupt in what seem like perfectly safe places. If we are surprised by the fallen, if we step into a trap, I know we can fight our way out of it. I do not know if we can fight someone else out of it as well. Do you understand?"

"I understand. This was your plan all along. I'll always be left behind to wait with no word, wondering if you're all dead. I'm no more part of this than my roommate in the dorm."

When I said nothing, she moved to embrace Gavin, her shoulders shaking as she cried into him. Gavin led her outside to walk her home.

What could I do? I hadn't wanted her to be a part of this from the beginning. She wasn't blessed into it; she was helpless against the fallen. She would be safe in Madison, and I would rather she be angry with me here than dead in Rome.

When Gavin eventually returned, he said, "She'll be fine. She just needs to cry it out."

"I am truly sorry. There is no other way, you know that?"

"Oh, I know." He looked down at his hands. I noticed he was now wearing all black. He'd stopped to change his clothes. "Don't tell her I said this, but I'm actually kind of glad. For my first mission, I don't want to have to worry about her."

Perhaps he was more mature than I thought.

"She made me promise to buy her something nice though," he said with a smirk.

"Sabrael," Raphael said from behind me. "It is time."

I pulled the straps of the harness over my arms and around my legs. "Ready to fly?"

"Can't be much different than a rollercoaster," he replied.

I laughed. "Oh, trust me, it is far less exciting."

"Well then," he said, "let the good times roll."

CHAPTER FORTY-SIX

The flight over the Atlantic went quickly. The others flew in the spiritual plane, invisible, but with Adrienne and Gavin in tow, Gabriel and I had to remain physical. Two angels would be difficult for anyone looking up to make out in the clouds; eight would not be so easily dismissed. Michael kept a close eye on Lucifer; Uriel and Raphael flanking him with weapons in hand. For his part, though, Lucifer led us straight to Italy without complaint.

Despite our past, I had to admit—it felt right having him on our side again.

Dangling below me, Gavin lay at the edge of the harness. He knew perfectly well what might await us ahead, yet he kept a steely silence as he watched the coast speed by below. His acceptance of my decision to leave Lena behind was commendable. I knew he was probably thinking about her just as much as anything else, but he understood the responsibility upon him. He seemed ready. As ready as any human can be, that is.

Thunder rumbled over Vatican City as we descended from the night, the ground still wet from what looked to have been a vicious storm. We had to be especially careful to avoid human detection here. If the Catholic order and those visiting the holy city saw us descending from the night, it might trigger a wave of religious fervor that would engulf the world in a matter of hours. Other cultures would only see men with wings, maybe even try to drive us away; the clergy would see an affirmation of faith.

The moment our feet touched the ground, our wings dissolved and our clothes altered to modern fashions. I chose a pair of khaki pants and a short-sleeved silk shirt.

The air was mild, the wind carrying none of the chill in the Madison breeze. The moon fought through the scattering storm clouds to illuminate the alley around us. Gavin rolled out of the harness and its matter dissipated.

Haniel pointed across a brick walkway to an immensely ornate building. My special knowledge was hard at work filling in with information about everything with all the new sights. "Beyond the Basilica there is a library. He spends his nights there researching."

"Researching what?" Gavin asked.

The others started walking toward the massive Basilica of St. Peter. "Old records, books from ages past. Across the world our warriors scour libraries for any mention of the gateway. None are as vast or specific to our purpose as the collection here, however."

Worry flooded Haniel's green eyes, and he hurried toward the Basilica.

Lucifer called out, "I do not think—"

Uriel shoved him as he walked past. "No one cares what you think."

Gavin and I followed the group. My eyes traveled over the buildings around us, names and other information coming to me with the sight of each.

My attention was wholly diverted, however, as we neared the Basilica. Every inch of the structure's façade was decorated with ornate masonry, all serving as the mere foundation for the dome reaching to the heavens above. The sheer scale of the building inspired awe. In the night, with no crowds in the square outside its front doors, the Basilica was a monolith of human ingenuity and a testament to art in design. Across the roof's edge, statues looked down upon us, saints and popes mostly, but I smiled when I realized some were angels. I tried to memorize every detail as we circled the building. To think such a monument stood in a land once ruled so passionately by Jupiter and the pantheon of adopted Greek deities was beyond incredible. I thought back to Jerusalem, the oppression the Romans exacted on the Jews there. How amazing the shift of mankind's beliefs can be.

Around the back of the Basilica Haniel led our group of seven angels, two warriors of light and the devil himself. Only days ago, the idea would have been absurd. He directed us to a door northeast of the piazza. It was locked, but he disappeared into the spiritual plane, and a moment later the door swung open. We passed quickly through a series of darkened hallways and winding corridors filled with priceless treasures and relics of the past. It was breathtaking to see such a trove of history preserved in one place. I found myself thinking about all the people who'd walked these halls before us, all the generations who had seen them since their creation. The passageways were well lit and immaculately clean now, but I wished I could have seen them in times past, dusty and illuminated by torches. I missed those days.

Haniel's rushed tour finally ended at a private library. Priests sat with leather-bound volumes, others at computer stations scrolling through digital archives. Obviously a restricted area, there was a palpable sense of reverence here. A doorway across the room opened, and a priest came into the reading room already carrying a book. I knew the majority of the huge Vatican collections were kept in underground vaults, rooms that could only be entered past the eyes of the librarians at the desk against the wall.

"I do not see him," Michael said.

"Nor I," said Haniel, his neck craned. "Perhaps he's in the stacks."

"Perhaps the others found him and research is the last thing on his mind," Lucifer said.

Haniel wheeled on Lucifer with murder in his eyes. Michael put a hand on his chest and pointed a finger at Lucifer. "Stop. You are only here because I allow it. Do not make me rethink the decision."

Lucifer smiled and held up his hands. Enraged, Haniel said, "I will look for him. Wait here." He made sure no humans were watching and his body dissolved.

Michael's gaze still burned on Lucifer. "Why would you say such a thing? Are you so indifferent to human life that it has become a joke?"

"I care more for life on this planet than anyone. You fight to keep things the way they are; I fight to provide mankind with what they truly want."

"Which is?" Gabriel asked.

Lucifer looked at him. "Freedom. To live without restriction. To walk through that door over there without question; to allow themselves the pleasures their bodies scream for but His Dryness forbids."

"Their restrictions are earned. They were put in place only after you provided them a taste of the 'freedom' of which you speak."

Lucifer shook his head. "Lighten up, Michael. Besides, what I told Haniel may be true."

"You'd better hope Father Maurizio is alive and untouched when we find him. I will hold you responsible for anything that has happened."

"Please, the man is on his last legs. If he was any older—"

Michael's eyes widened, and he grasped Lucifer's shirt, pushing the devil against the wall. "No one said he was old!" he grunted. "How do you know what he looks like?"

A priest with gold-rimmed glasses scurried over. He didn't look happy. In Italian, he said, "Excuse me. What do you all think you are doing in here?"

Michael and Lucifer looked at him, and the man was visibly struck by their perfect beauty. "Ah. Padre Gianni," Lucifer smiled. "One of my favorite people."

"I am sorry; have we met?"

"More than once."

The priest looked confused. Raphael draped an arm around Gianni's shoulders. "Speak with me for a moment, Padre." He led the priest back toward a desk near the wall.

Michael's grip hadn't loosened.

Uriel said, "Well? How you know what Maurizio looks like?"

Lucifer looked between them, then scoffed loudly and said, "I sent someone to find him, remember? They saw him, and I saw him through their eyes." Michael's head dropped, his jaw tightening. Lucifer said, "If you had let me say as much when we landed, I was trying to point out they confronted him at his home. If something happened, it happened there."

My brothers rushed for the door. Raphael saw the frenzy and hurried out a few last words to Gianni before running after them.

"What about Haniel?" Gavin asked, falling in step with Raphael.

"I called him."

Michael and Lucifer remained. The corneas of Michael's human-looking eyes faintly smoldered as he leaned toward our devil brother. "Pray he is not harmed." He shoved Lucifer away and headed outside.

Lucifer rubbed his throat and muttered, "Pray to whom?" He looked at me, and I could see the anger in his eyes before he followed Michael.

I was sad to leave the beauty of the city so quickly, but the others had already taken flight. I took hold of Gavin's arms and lifted us into the sky.

Gavin's legs whipped up into my shins with the speed of our ascent. Away from the museums and Basilica we flew, west into the residences of the clergy. Old lampposts stained the night a hazy yellow. Ahead, Haniel's legs extended beneath him as he headed for the ground, his feet touching down, and his wings fluttering before folding to his back. His weapon was in his hand almost instantly. I spotted what startled him.

The dark road glittered in the moonlight, covered in glass. The house ahead had been ransacked. Furniture and personal effects littered the front lawn. I helped Gavin find his footing before I landed. His staff dropped into his hand and extended to full length as he trotted after the others. Only Lucifer and I kept our weapons retracted. I felt no flare in my angel sense.

Haniel and Uriel rushed to the shattered bay window, glass still lining the frame like a spiked collar. Adonael lifted his hand to the window and the shards blew harmlessly away. Uriel and Haniel jumped through, Raphael and Adonael following.

"We are too late," Lucifer said, rubbing his forehead. Michael shot him a glance that made me wince.

Adrienne came up beside me and asked, "Where will we go if Maurizio is missing?"

Her lips sparkled in the moonlight. I said, "No one thought that far ahead."

Michael stood behind Lucifer, his sword poised to strike if the devil made any quick movements. Voices called out as lights inside the house came on. Michael retracted his sword and ran to leap through the window.

"This is a waste of time," Lucifer said, the tension lifting from his shoulders. "If they are not here, they already have what they came for."

"The location of the gateway," Gavin said, defeated.

"We do not know what is in the house," Gabriel said. "Let us wait to see what they find."

As though on cue, Michael's voice echoed in my mind, *Come inside. All of you.*

Lucifer said, "Is that how he beckons you—like dogs? Why do you put up with that? You could be free of such treatment. Amongst us, you would give the orders."

Gavin stepped to the window. "Yeah, cuz that's working out so well for you right now."

I smiled, but Lucifer was not amused.

Inside, the house was ravaged. Shelves broken, furniture overturned, books and belongings scattered everywhere. The cracked lamp in the corner cast odd shadows on the walls. Amidst the mess, my brothers tossed aside the clutter, looking for clues. Near the front door, a pair of shoes sat neatly together, the sole bastion of order in the chaos.

"They were definitely here," Uriel said from the doorway leading to the next room.

Adonael said, "The question is whether they found what they came for."

"Not right away at least," said Raphael as he stepped over the thick carpet of books.

Gavin retracted his staff, looking around wide-eyed. When he stepped toward the door to the next room, Uriel turned him away.

"Don't look back here," Uriel told him.

"What is it?"

Haniel sat crumpled against the wall. "Father Maurizio. He did not even get the chance to draw his weapon."

Adrienne grabbed my hand and squeezed it tight.

"He was holding this," Uriel said, tossing a book to Gavin. "Had to pry it from his fingers."

The boy caught the volume, sinking with its weight. He opened it and looked confused.

"What language is this?" he asked.

"Aramaic," Uriel said, looking over Gavin's shoulder. He smirked, "Why, know it?"

Gavin scoffed, "Yeah, right. I can't even remember last semester's Spanish."

"Why was the priest holding it?" I asked.

"He has a name!" Haniel shouted.

I lowered my head. "I am sorry, Haniel."

Gavin turned a page. "I don't know, but…" He glanced at Haniel. "…there's a lot of blood on it. Especially this page."

Uriel snatched the book back. "Look," Gavin said, reaching over Uriel's arm to lay his hand on the page. "It's a handprint, see?"

Michael flipped an overturned table back onto its legs. "Bring it here. And a lamp."

All of us crowded around. Ornate handwriting and drawings filled the page. A dark handprint covered a faded sketch. A ring of small circles surrounded by larger ones spread farther apart. A third ring, this of rectangles, circled the first two, and then led down the page in parallel rows. The whole thing looked like a key.

"What is it?" Adrienne asked.

"The gateway," Raphael said as his emerald eyes traced the text. "It's a description of its layout."

Gavin asked, "Does it say where it is?"

"No. Only that it is in the north, on an island of stones."

Gavin flipped the page, but Raphael smirked and turned it back, flipping one more to the left. "Aramaic reads the opposite way," he said.

I couldn't help but smile as my young warrior laughed and shrugged. "Well how was I supposed to know? How old is this thing anyway?"

Raphael said, "This was written by a descendent of Noah's grandson, Tiras. Possibly during Christ's lifetime." Gavin's eyes went wide and returned to the book.

I was enthralled by the image on the new page—a woodcut, obviously a view from just outside the eye of the key. Massive stone slabs stood in the background, the farthest like doorways with two upright stones supporting a third, horizontal one. These must be the rectangles on the previous page. In the foreground, a group of men stood with arms raised, each standing against a stone in the innermost circle. Strewn around them on the ground were bodies, dead eyes staring Heavenward. Directly in the center of the ring, a white ellipse like a cat's pupil hovered over the ground, a sliver that seemed to emit lightning. Though faded and hard to make out, there was what looked to be a figure inside it, arms outstretched and face to the sky as though caught in rapture.

"Is that...?" Gavin asked before stopping himself.

Michael's studied the drawing, eyes wide. Uriel said, "God in Heaven."

"Think they saw this?" Gabriel asked.

"Obviously," Lucifer said. Leaning on the wall, he tossed aside another book he was casually flipping through. "If they had not, they would still be here."

"A page is missing!" Uriel said. He held up the book. A jagged tear was all that remained of the page at the start of the gateway description. "It must have listed the location!"

"How long ago did you send them here?" Raphael asked.

Lucifer looked up from another volume to meet his gaze. "Yesterday."

Questions and suggestions flew as my brothers argued over each other, the urgency of the situation driving everyone into a frenzy. Haniel escaped into the room where Father Maurizio lay. Only Michael and Gavin still read the book, though Gavin simply looked at the pictures.

"Anyone have any idea where there are circles like that in the north?" Gabriel asked.

Raphael shrugged. "Where's north? It would have been north from wherever that book was written."

Adonael said, "Aramaic limits its writing to the region near Judea."

Uriel added, "That drawing could be thousands of places. Without more, we are lost."

"Stonehenge!" All eyes turned to Gavin. "Look at it. A stone circle with doorways like that, built so long ago no one can remember why it's there. It's even on an island in the north."

Gabriel said, "It is too famous, and not old enough. Stonehenge was not there when the flood occurred."

"If it were that obvious, we would have figured it out long ago," Uriel added.

"But look at it! It looks just like it!" Gavin protested. "People have been drawn to that spot for thousands of years. Wouldn't it make sense that God put it in our minds to go there?"

My brothers started to argue again, but the sight of Haniel silenced everyone. He stood in the doorway to the next room holding Maurizio's ravaged body. Staring at us all, his expression cold, he walked to the table and laid Maurizio on it. Lacerations and cruel, unholy carvings in the flesh of his forehead and chest made Gavin retch. "He spent most of his life looking for the gateway. He knew what it meant if his findings were discovered, so he only kept one record."

Grabbing hold of Maurizio's bloodied pants, Haniel ripped off the left leg. There, tattooed upside down along the inside of Maurizio's thigh, lines of numbers were revealed.

"What are they?" Raphael asked.

"Coordinates. Of all the possible locations backed by research. We checked some in the beginning, but after many disappointments, we decided to wait until hard evidence showed us the correct one. He just kept adding to the list, carrying it with him so those bastards would never find it. If he found the gateway, its location will be in this list."

Everyone scanned the list, even Lucifer, who was now perusing a third book. "There must be more than twenty here," Uriel said. "How are we supposed to know which one it is?"

Michael stared at the numbers, pondering. "We check them all."

"That's madness, Michael," Uriel said. "These coordinates are spread across northern Europe and into Asia. We don't have time to fly all over the globe."

"We do if we split up. Sabrael and Gavin can take all the sites between here and Stonehenge while the rest of you head in other directions. Whoever finds it can alert the group."

My heart skipped at Michael's words. England. How could I return to that place? Before I could argue though, Lucifer did it for me.

"Do you know how ridiculous that sounds? Maurizio must have kept notes, even if no specific locations were listed. Why would you search a whole continent when you could search around a single house to find more direction first?"

"I intend to, but there's no guarantee we will find anything. Wherever the gateway may be, your followers are headed there already. We have very little time. It does not take ten of us to look through a house this small."

"I am not going to waste my time on some wild chase," Lucifer said.

"You are staying right here and helping me. Where I can watch you."

"Unless you want to fly with me, devil. I will gladly be your watchdog." Uriel reached for Lucifer's shoulder.

A brilliant flash of light blinded me for a moment, and I felt a body fly past me through the air. When my sight returned, Uriel was on the floor, Lucifer's hand still outstretched.

"Keep your hands off me or next time I take them!"

"Enough!" Michael yelled. "Sabrael, take Gavin. The rest of you choose some coordinates and go."

CHAPTER FORTY-SEVEN

Time was growing short; at least Lucifer was right about that. Despite how bizarre it sounded, we had to get him back at the head of the fallen. With Lucifer powerless among Hell's legion, I feared who might take his place. At least we understood Lucifer. When it came down to it, he just wanted to be like the Almighty. He wanted to rule the kingdom, not destroy it. But the others ... I could only imagine the burning debris of Heaven falling onto the Earth if Adramelec or Mammon led the damned through the gateway. They had to be stopped.

The flight was more torturous than any I'd ever made before. We stopped at eight possible sites where the gateway might be, and at each one, nothing. No fallen, no angel sense. With each failure, my anxiety grew until finally, there was nowhere left but the one place on Earth I never wanted to see again.

England. So many memories. So much pain. The bitter cold over the sea stung my face and hands, the wind pushing against my wings as though trying to force me back. Gavin lay shivering below me, so I formed a shield on the harness to curb the wind. I was glad for his company; I didn't know if I could handle returning to my old home on my own.

The phantoms of those I had slain rose again to confront me as I neared the island. It seemed they would haunt me forever. Are human murderers as terrorized by the souls of their victims as I have been by mine? Out of the night they materialized, their disconsolate, hollow stares finding me from beyond the grave. Had any of them moved on to Heaven or Hell? Were they in Sheol? Or had they stayed to follow me and remind me of the atrocities I committed? In the pitch abyss of night, I was nauseous with the illusion of being buried again.

The specters did not, this time, opt to haunt me with tales of the hopes and earthly ties I severed with my blade. They simply formed an aisle that continued to the horizon, their black stares and silence worse than any words. Some appeared as they had in life; others bore the fatal marks of my blade. I couldn't help myself from meeting their mournful gazes. I wondered if this avenue of shame continued around the entire Earth? Had I killed so many to make such a thing possible? I feared I knew the answer.

By the time we reached the Salisbury Plain west of London, the air had grown mild. My hands, however, continued to quiver. The moment the sun peeked over the horizon, the spirits mercifully faded, leaving me alone to face the land where the haunting began.

I pulled in my wings and dove, swooping low to land near the famous stone monument. Stonehenge stood as it had for centuries, silently vigilant over the morning, stoic and ancient. Gavin stepped into the early morning haze. No sign of human or angel anywhere. My angel sense twitched, but nothing more. Whoever caused it wasn't close enough for alarm.

"Maybe they didn't get here yet," Gavin said, his voice muted in the fog.

I scanned the haze, desperate. "If the gateway is here, they would have come right away. Where the hell are they?"

"Are you okay?"

"How many sites do we have to check before we find them?" I yelled. "When is this search going to end? We may be too late already! They should be here by now!"

"Maybe they're waiting until the moon's right or the stars line up or something."

"The Almighty would not have based the gateway's operation on superstition!" I snapped. I didn't mean to, but this entire situation was infuriating. Dark memories clawed at the back of my mind. I had to get away from England.

"The Lord works in *mysterious* ways," he said, trying to lighten the mood.

Michael, I called in the spiritual plane. *There is no one at Stonehenge either. This entire trip was a waste of time. We are coming back.*

His reply echoed in my mind. *No, stay there. We may have found something important.*

Then let me return, I said. *I do not want to be here any—*

Just stay there and keep watch until I call you again, he said.

Michael. Michael? He didn't answer. I kicked one of the upright sarsens.

We spent the morning at a café in Amesbury. I had not been so uncomfortable since waking from death. The very air stirred memories of chaotic nights in the wilderness tracking down the Picts or some other group. Vortigern's last stand hadn't been far from here, and when the Heptarchy divided the island, this area of Wessex was bathed in the blood of war all too often. I could not remember a time when there had been no wars among the tribes here. Flashes of running into a line of screaming men came to me, my sword dicing flesh and setting countless souls free from their physical bodies. I could smell the sweat around me, feel the warmth of blood on my hands and face. Screams pierced my ears as deafening as they had been all those centuries before. I leaned forward and cupped my mug with both hands, waiting for the visions to pass. Sweat beaded on my forehead, but gradually, the sounds of the café returned. I wouldn't be able to stay here for long. Whatever Michael was making me wait for better be good.

Stonehenge. In the days of the feuding kingdoms, we never paid any mind to the site. I could recall times when we trekked past it, wondered about its construction, but never with such awe as the modern world. We never believed beings from another world created it, or that it was a miracle. It was just a landmark to guide our travels. I never felt any special compulsion to it. But I hadn't really been looking for the gateway then, had I?

Gavin returned to the table with a chocolate mousse. "She says 'Hi' back. She also said to make sure you're not mad at her for being a jerk before we left. I know you're not, so I just told her."

"I appreciate it," I said. I watched two men walk past the café, releasing my eyes of their matter for a moment. Only humans. "What else did she say?"

"Well, she laughed when I told her that Stonehenge might be the gateway. She said it figures it would be something so obvious after all this time and that if you let the women do the searching, you would have been home a long time ago."

I couldn't help but smile as matter gathered back to my eyes.

"She looked up a bunch of stuff for us, but nothing we probably couldn't find for ourselves. The public is only allowed there until four, and tour groups have access until about seven. After that, no one's supposed to be there, so…"

"If they are coming here, it will be then." I didn't put it past the fallen to simply kill any humans there during the day if they arrived earlier, but I doubted even they wanted to attract the attention of the authorities if they could help it.

"So what do we do until then?"

It was only just past noon according to the clock behind the counter, but I was restless. "You should rest. I am going to have a look around."

"No, I'm cool. I want to see the sights."

"You haven't slept in over a day. If the battle happens tonight, will you have the strength to fight it?" He thought about it a moment too long. "We will find a hotel for you."

"Why do I have to sleep while you get to explore?"

"I am not going sightseeing. I said I was going to have a look around. If the fallen are planning to use the gateway tonight, they can't be far."

"Can you sense them right now?"

"Not yet. Doesn't mean I won't soon, though."

We rose from the table, and I put my hand down, forming a large tip for the waitress. Gavin asked, "You angels ever hear about a thing called inflation?" I flashed him a look.

We found a small inn down the road, privately owned and out of the public eye. Gavin hit the pillows already asleep. So much for being "cool." I headed back outside to a bench where the inn was in plain view and took up my vigil. Hood raised, I kept my vision in the spiritual plane, keenly monitoring my angel sense. Hoping for something, anything to make it flare. Everything seemed so tranquil. Was this the calm before the storm, I wondered, or was it proof we picked the wrong target?

With the dawning of the night came a chill wind and downpour. Running through the storm, I returned to the inn. My shoes tracked water into the foyer, the footprints quickly evaporating under my focused gaze. A fire burned in the hearth, safe from the rain drumming the roof. I stepped quickly past William, the innkeeper, asleep in a chair and snoring loudly.

Gavin answered my knock, and I handed him a hooded poncho, knowing he would be cold in the sodden air of the Salisbury Plain. The beige color would ruin the effect I'm sure he planned in dressing all in black, but it was the best I could do. He held out his arms, the material bunching at the shoulders.

"Great. This should make maneuvering fun."

"Hold your arms up," I said. I called my sword and with two quick slashes, I cut down his sides to free his arms, then called matter together to seal the material around his torso. The poncho now had flaps for sleeves.

"Thanks," he said, then took a defensive pose. "Does it look like samurai armor?"

"Sorry, I missed that era. At least you will be dry."

"Guessing that means we're not waiting for the rain to stop."

"Think the fallen will wait?" He nodded, understanding. "Are you ready?"

Gavin laughed. "Do I have a choice?"

I smiled. I was glad he was with me. In having to lead him, I could ignore my own fear.

My hair and clothes were plastered to me in moments after leaving the inn. The torrential rain had cleared the streets, and Gavin and I ran through the downpour past lighted windows filled with silhouettes. The edge of town wasn't far, and when we reached it, I formed my wings and lifted us into the black sky.

"Wait! I thought feathers don't work in the rain!" Gavin shouted.

"I am not a bird!"

My angel sense began to tingle more strongly the farther from town we flew. I couldn't believe it. I freed the matter from my eyes, but could see no one in the rain ahead.

When I yelled as much to Gavin, he said, "Maybe it's Michael coming to check on us."

"More than one of my brothers waits ahead." The sense was too strong.

"Whose side are they on?"

"I can't tell without seeing them. But there's been no word from the others."

Gavin said nothing for a few moments, then shouted, "From now on, don't tell me your sense is flaring until you know who's causing it."

The unmistakable shape of Stonehenge came into view. A single, winged figure stood in the center of the monument. Looking right at us.

"Someone's down there," I shouted to Gavin over the wind. Lightning flashed for a moment, and the air shook with the following boom.

"Fallen?" Gavin called to me.

I smiled. "Fallen."

It was Balam, one of the last demons I'd seen before my flight to the Yucatan. His wings weren't even hidden, their glow encased by matter. Something was wrong, though.

"I thought you said there's more than one," Gavin yelled.

"There must be!" I replied, "Damn it, where are they? Do you see any more?"

"I can't see anything in this rain!"

Balam drew his sword, his long coat fluttering.

"Be ready," I shouted to Gavin. "He is holding—"

"*That* I can see," Gavin said.

I pulled in my wings, and we sped toward the monument. The wind whipped at our faces as the stones rose to meet us. Balam grasped his sword with both hands, bracing himself. My angel sense screamed in warning. But I couldn't see anyone else!

Gavin yelled, "Let go! Let go of me now!"

Before I could reply, he twisted free of my grasp. "No, wait!"

He plummeted straight toward Balam and brought his legs up to his chest, his body rolling into a somersault. He came out of the flip and in one arcing motion called his staff and turned his momentum into a devastating strike.

He crashed onto Balam like a bolt of lightning from the heavens. Balam managed to block the strike though, the clash of their weapons resounding like thunder. Gavin ricocheted into the mud and sprang to his feet, staff whirling. I swooped down to double the attack, but Balum spun, deflecting Gavin and meeting my sword in the same motion. Our weapons rang as I struck for his chest, Gavin's staff twirling, my demon kin moving deftly between us. A flash streaked the sky, and thunder melded into the sounds of our skirmish. With the next whirl of Gavin's staff, Balam leapt up following the arc and kicked me in the chest. He pushed off me and flew over Gavin.

I stumbled back, planting a foot in the mud to steady myself. My ears blared at the sight of Gavin rushing to challenge Balam alone. I pumped my wings to help pull my feet from the muck, rocketing to join the fight again after only two parried strikes between them.

Gavin's loose sleeves whipped around him as he spun through a series of attacks. Each end of his staff jabbed and swung, seeking a break in Balam's defense. Nothing landed. Balam kept up with us, still in control, but I could see the strain on his face. I might have overpowered him already had Gavin not been in the way.

As if hearing my critique, Gavin unleashed a flurry of strikes. Dull metallic thuds rang out as his staff whacked Balam's arms and legs. Gavin growled as he continued trying for a solid blow. I was impressed.

Finally, Gavin swung his staff at Balam's feet and, as the demon blocked, whipped the other end at Balam's head and made contact. My brother cried out, falling into the mud, but Gavin didn't stop there. He flicked his wrist to sharpen the staff's end, and thrust the point at the demon's chest. I'd never seen a warrior of light fight so fluidly. Valthgar had been fierce, and Theokritus had heart, but Gavin seemed born for this. Balam barely rolled out of the way and pushed off the ground to his feet. He held his head, blood running between his fingers, and cried out in rage.

"Where are the others, Balam?" I yelled above the storm.

He spat on the ground. "I am going to take that brat's head, Sabrael! You should have taught him to respect and fear us."

Gavin shouted, "Answer the question!"

"You do not speak here, boy!"

My angel sense was still blaring. Where the hell were the others?

"Have you come here as a scout?" I yelled. If the sense was being stirred by a group of the fallen on their way, they couldn't be far off. I did what I should have done long before—I called for Michael.

"A scout? I come as a herald!" Balam yelled, his head repairing itself. "Tonight the kingdom will be ours!"

"Not while we still stand," I replied.

Balam ran toward us and stuck out his arm. An invisible wave of matter threw me from my feet. So he was going to use his angelic abilities after all. I recovered quickly, but not quickly enough. Balam took only three strikes to fling the staff from my warrior's hands. Undeterred, Gavin jumped to kick the demon, but Balam slammed his fist into the boy's face. I cried out as Gavin fell limp into my fallen brother's arms.

Desperation surged through me. I hurled fire at Balam's feet to keep him from running, but I couldn't harm him with the unconscious boy in his arms. My mind seethed and my jaw clenched so tight it was painful. "Let him go! Face me, you coward!"

Balam retracted his weapon and hefted Gavin over his shoulder. "You were never the one I wanted," he yelled and, to my absolute horror, he beat the air with black wings and soared away with Gavin in his grasp.

I snatched Gavin's staff from the mud and flew into the storm after them. So desperate was I to catch him, I didn't even notice right away that my angel sense had forked. Rain beat against my face as I looked back. Lightning illuminated the sky, revealing three of the fallen following us with weapons drawn. It dawned on me why Balam had not simply killed Gavin. The boy was being used to lure me away from the gateway.

I cried out for Michael and the others, called for them to get to Stonehenge right away. Gavin had been right; the simple answer was correct. My God, we had scattered around the globe; could they even get back in time? I could still turn back, fight to stop the fallen from opening the portal, or at least delay them until my brothers reached it. I knew it was the smarter move, but if I turned back, Balam would kill the boy immediately. I had no doubt of that. Abandon the gateway or allow another of my warriors to die. It wasn't fair!

I gritted my teeth and made my decision.

I couldn't tell Lena I let Gavin die. I couldn't face her tears, let alone adding another phantom to my past. Even if I turned back now, how was I to hold off the entire legion of the fallen by myself? I retracted my sword and clutched Gavin's staff tight. It had been so obvious; how had I not seen this coming? I yelled and beat my chest. My fault, all of it. I cried out for Michael and the others again and again, praying they would make it in time. If they didn't, all would be lost.

Across the rest of that damned island we flew, the place where hundreds had been slain by my hand and would now serve as the portal through which Heaven was destroyed. I returned my eyes to the physical plane, sick of the sight of England. Darkness filled in and the ground below disappeared. I implored Michael to answer me, to tell me they were at least on their way. No answer came. The war rested on my shoulders now, and I was powerless to do anything.

City lights below gave way to the black waters of the Irish Sea, the chase continuing northwest across Ireland to the coast of Galway. We flew free of the rainstorm and the stars shined bright from between the last wispy fingers of dark cloud. Off the coast ahead, Balam swooped low, and I saw a small island approaching. The tiny landmass was almost completely dark, only two areas lit in the night. I pushed with all my strength. If I could catch Balam before he landed, I might grab Gavin and make it back to the gateway in time to stop the fallen. Balam soared down toward an area isolated from the towns. I drew my wings in, speeding as fast as I could in the physical plane. Wind screamed in my ears, and my face ached as it pulled from my skull, but I continued pushing faster. Then, my prayers were answered.

Out of the darkness ahead, two forms rippled into the physical plane. Raphael and Michael. Balam tried to pull up, but it was too late. Raphael drove his fist into the demon's hurtling face, the crack of bone reaching me more than forty yards behind. Gavin's body dropped to freefall toward the Earth, limbs tossing. Michael dove and caught the boy. I turned to face those tailing us, calling my sword into hand, but Uriel, Haniel and Adonael appeared behind the trio. At once, Uriel reached around Armaros to cover the demon's mouth as he plunged his sword through Armaros's back, Haniel clubbed Raum over the head with his mace, and Adonael drove his halberd into the ribs of Sealiah. All three of my brothers removed the hearts of the wounded demons, letting the lifeless bodies plummet to the ground. Raphael cradled Balam, whose skull was crushed but his heart removed before his body had broken apart.

I could not find the words. Michael's smile forced tears to my eyes, though they were just as much tears of exhaustion.

"We heard your call, but could not risk them hearing our answer," Michael said.

I couldn't believe what had just happened. I realized everyone was there and what that meant. "The gateway," I yelled. "It is Stonehenge! We must return to it at once!"

Raphael covered my mouth. "The ritual is about to begin. But not where you think."

CHAPTER FORTY-EIGHT

Flying low over the small Irish island below us, I soon saw them. Glowing forms lay strewn across a field crisscrossed by short, stone walls, all of them hunkered in hiding and staring toward some structure in the distance across a rocky plain. All bearing the mark of the blessed, weapons in hand. Each of my brothers must have blessed two dozen warriors, I realized, as I counted them. 144. The army of light.

Michael told me everything. He and Lucifer discovered a journal in Maurizio's home, and in it, the names of three books. The third was the one we'd all seen. The other two took some searching, but both were found; one in the priest's bedroom and the other in the Vatican library. When viewed together with the notes left by Maurizio, everything pointed to the island of Inishmor. Matching coordinates were also on his leg. It had taken some time to decipher the message even with the guidance of the priest's notes. That Maurizio had even found the three texts, written centuries apart, and thought to put them together was miraculous. But then, our side is used to miracles.

We landed at the head of the gathering where Gabriel and Lucifer were waiting. Lucifer smiled as he saw us coming in. Gavin stirred as I set him down, mumbling and gripping his head. He was awake, but still rattled.

"The fallen have all gathered," Gabriel reported to Michael. "Adramelec has begun."

I slid up to peer over the nearest rock wall. Across the field ahead, scattered ruins broke the earth like a twisted cemetery, some tall, others flat against the ground. The vast, rocky plain led to high cliffs overlooking the North Atlantic. Gathered there was a sight I hoped I would never see again.

The fallen stood united in a monstrous front, every demon who fell from grace except those my brothers had just dispatched. Black wings jutted up from the crowd as the stones did from the ground, filling the spiritual plane with their glow. Thousands of weapons pumped the air in time to what looked to be a chant. It was a terrible spectacle. I didn't know how the warriors behind us could possibly have kept their courage at seeing such a force.

The fallen weren't the only ones there. Around them, I saw for the first time the humans blessed into the war on the other side—the warriors of darkness. I expected them to look evil, twisted or marred in some macabre way. Most looked no different than our warriors, and in a way, this was far more disturbing. All that separated them was their glow, similar to that of our warriors but unmistakably different. Thank God for that; I was seeing so many of our own warriors here for the first time that keeping track of them all would be impossible.

It wasn't the sight of the damned that struck fear into me, however. The fallen and their warriors could be killed. It was what stood in the center of them that terrified me.

Hell's legion stood crowded inside an ancient ruin butted up against the cliffs. Four concentric arcs of stone formed a horseshoe, which opened to a three-hundred-foot drop to the sea.

The outermost wall must have encircled at least a dozen acres. Thousands of upright, jagged stones turned the field between this and the third wall into a death trap, a cheval de frise guarding the fortress from attack. Amidst this medieval defense, nine stones twice the height of a man stood arranged in a circle.

It was the gateway. Not a myth. Not a bedtime story. Real and ready.

Nine limestone spires to open the portal between Heaven and Earth; nine reminders of a time when the Almighty would have allowed mankind free access to the kingdom. The architects of this ancient fortress, Dún Aonghasa, had incorporated the stones into its design, never knowing what it was they were building around. It was the perfect camouflage. It stood as sturdy as when the Almighty created it, capable of destroying the whole of creation if activated. After so long hearing about the gateway and the terror it would unleash, I found in that moment, looking at the army waiting to invade the kingdom, I couldn't believe it was actually there.

In its center, I recognized Adramelec with his arms raised and face lifted toward the night sky. The traitor of the ultimate traitor. Faintly, I could hear him shouting an incantation, one I refuse to write in these pages lest it ever be repeated.

I felt a hand on my back and turned to find Adrienne crawling up beside me. I embraced her, enraptured again by the scent of her skin, the softness of her hair. Her arm had finished mending in the day since I'd seen her. Just in time. I gathered matter to my eyes again before she looked into them.

"I did not think you were going to make it," she said.

"We ran into some ... problems," I replied. "How long have you all been here?"

"Since sundown. Michael sent out the message that every warrior capable of fighting was needed here this night. Those close enough to get here by boat or plane did so; the rest were gathered by your brothers."

"How have they not seen you?" I asked, motioning to the crowd in the field ahead.

"They were already here when we arrived. Probably too caught up in all this to notice."

A pained groan came from behind her, and Gavin slowly sat up, his hand pressed firmly against his forehead.

"Oh God. I'm gonna puke," he muttered.

"The concussion," I said. "Sit still, it will pass."

He blinked a few times and rolled his head around his neck. "Can't you just fix it?"

"It may kill you if I try." I reached into my sleeve and gave him back his retracted staff.

"Big, bad warrior angel falls short against everyday aspirin. Mankind has been duped." He looked around. "Where are we?"

I tried to think of what exactly I should say. I didn't think it would be all that pleasant to wake from unconsciousness to find oneself on the brink of war with the whole of Hell's army. Sometimes the truth hurts though.

"We are on the island of Inishmor, off the coast of Ireland. The fallen have come to open the gateway, and you are sitting at the head of an army waiting for the command to stop them."

Gavin held his temples and turned to face the thousands of damned warriors below. "Yeah right!" he said. "Just knock me back out and wake me when it's over."

Adrienne said, "Why do we wait? We should just fight our way to the center. They cannot open the gateway if we keep them distracted."

"How many do you think could possibly make it all the way alive?"

"It only takes one to destroy the gateway," she said.

The conviction in her eyes was unnerving. "Michael would never have us rush into battle that way."

I could hear the stirrings of the warriors around us, sense their anxiousness. They wanted to attack. When the fallen began singing some ancient song, I thought I should find out what the plan might be. I crept to where Michael, Gabriel, Raphael and Lucifer were talking.

"Michael, what are we waiting for? You do not want them to actually open the gateway before we attack?"

"We will wait no longer." Raphael and Gabriel crept away, whispering to warriors as they went. "The humans will charge the fallen from here. With the focus on the outskirts, we will fly over the battle in the spiritual plane and surprise those performing the ritual."

I was mortified. "Our warriors will be slaughtered before they reach the first wall."

"Once we reach the center, we will be the threat. The fallen will leave our warriors to theirs."

"Michael, this cannot be your plan!"

"We have no time to argue, Sabrael. We must stop the ritual now before the gateway begins to open. Nothing else matters."

"There has to be another way," I said. "You cannot send so many to their deaths!"

"We have only one chance to stop this. If we do not attack the center directly, the gateway may be open before we reach it. "

I looked to see Adramelec stepping away from the center of the circle, the entire field of the damned now singing in unison. Michael's hand touched my shoulder.

"You know I despise sending even one of them to their death, but distraction is necessary to get us where we need to be. They would all willingly give their lives to save the world."

I looked at the field again and scoured my mind for some brilliant alternative. None came. Instead, I met Michael's eyes once more, then conceded. He squeezed my shoulder, and I crawled away from him.

Sabrael, his voice echoed in my mind. I looked back at him. *Fight well, Brother. I will see you when it is over.*

And you, Michael, I thought. I made my way back to the warriors.

Gavin was in bad shape. "Your head?" I asked him.

"Oh, fine. It's the fear that's got me now," he replied.

Adrienne crawled close. I said, "Get ready. You are going to make a frontal attack while we strike at the portal itself."

"See?" Adrienne smiled.

"You won't be with us?" Gavin asked.

"No. We will fly directly to the gateway while you handle their warriors."

"You're kidding me." He looked at the legion below. "This will be a blast."

"Spread the word. Every warrior needs to know the plan."

The three of us split up to deliver the news. Reactions ranged from excitement to near fainting. Most of the warriors were in their thirties or forties, only a few younger, though none as young as Gavin. There was also a good deal of older warriors, many of whom had probably never lifted a weapon against the fallen. I prayed for the safety of them all.

Perhaps taking a cue from me, Michael's voice suddenly filled my mind and from the attentive silence that swept over the gathering, I knew he was projecting to us all.

Father in Heaven, we are gathered here together for the first time in the history of this terrible war. Never before has a peril so grave threatened the whole of Your creation. Never before has there been need for every angel and warrior alike to come together and take up arms.

The warriors near me bowed their heads. One man with gray hair thumbed a pair of rusted military tags. He met my gaze and gave a stoic nod.

Guide us in this darkest hour, Father. Lead Your children safely down the path with death to every side and deliver us from this terrible evil.

A young woman pressed her forehead against the handle of her sword, her knuckles white. The woman beside her made the sign of the cross.

May You embrace those who fall this day, and reassure them they are being called home to the kingdom. Wipe their tears and grant them peace after a life of service and the great act they have performed here.

A couple held each other tight. Matching gold bands on their fingers glimmered.

May those of us left standing have the strength to carry on, to ensure that a battle such as this will never occur again, and that any deaths that occur will not have been in vain.

Adrienne and Gavin rejoined me. Adrienne took my hand.

All this we ask, Father. In Your grace, we know You are with us as we head into battle. You are our strength and in You, victory will be found this day. Amen.

The crowd raised their heads. Weapons were taken up, final tidings of luck shared. Warriors embraced one another and shared last smiles before the battle would strip them away.

Adrienne kissed my cheek. "I will be waiting for you in the middle of that field. Do not leave me there alone for long."

"As soon as the gateway is destroyed, I will find you," I said.

Gavin grasped my forearm and smiled. I looked into his hazel eyes in surprise. I was so shocked I couldn't find my voice. "They do this in the movies before big sword fights. Always wanted to do it."

"This was the way my first warrior greeted me on my first night on Earth."

"Then there's no better way to welcome the end." I saw the fear he was trying to mask. "If I don't make it, tell Lena—"

"You'll make it," I said, saving him from having to go further.

He nodded, and his hand grew tight on my forearm. "Strength and honor." I frowned, and a smirk turned up the corners of his mouth. "Nevermind. See you on the other side."

Looking up at the night sky as the two of them went to join the other warriors of light, I spoke into the air, "So my friends, you are with me still."

The fallen were still singing. I could now feel an electric energy around me, surging in time to their voices. The air on Inishmor quivered. Our time was almost up.

Michael's voice again echoed in our minds. *Take care, warriors. Do not let them hear you until the last moment before you strike. May the Father protect you all.*

With that, the army of men and women ran over the lip of the ridge to charge the army of Hell. Adrienne looked back at me, our eyes meeting one last time, then she was gone.

"Stay together," Michael said to the eight of us that remained. "Follow my lead. We must destroy the stones; let nothing else draw your attack." I nodded as his eyes passed over me, and when he had a response from us all, the matter of his body sifted apart on the wind. My brothers disappeared into the spiritual plane after him. All except one.

"Ready for this, little brother?" Lucifer asked.

"Yes," I lied. "Are you?"

Lucifer smiled. "I will be at your side until the end. As it should have been ages ago. Stay with me, and everything will go as planned."

"How can we trust you to destroy it? You are the one who started this madness."

"I do not need the gateway. The throne will not be won by secrecy and ambush. It will be taken in glorious battle."

"You are really willing to fight your own followers then? Kill them?"

"They betrayed me. They will learn on the edge of my blade what a mistake that was."

"When this is over, what happens to us? We just go back to fighting and forget all this?"

He just raised an eyebrow, then the matter of his body flew free.

His speech did little to assure me of his allegiances, but there was no time to dispute it. I joined him in the spiritual plane, and we flew together to catch up with the others.

The final battle had begun.

CHAPTER FORTY-NINE

The warriors of light reached the gathering of the damned just as we overtook them. I scanned for Gavin and Adrienne but could not see them. At the back of the fallen legion, the warriors of darkness stood with fists raised, oblivious as they sang that mystifying song. We could hear it even in the spiritual plane, the incantation welding the planes.

I skimmed low over the crowd and, as I neared the front line, our warriors met the first of theirs. Throats were slit and heads sheared off by Heavenly metal as the spearhead of the assault drove silently forward. Some noticed the onslaught in time to raise weapons in defense, but even they were overpowered by the wave of opposition crashing into them. Our warriors stabbed through the crowd, a trail of bodies left in their wake. The battle escalated quickly, and stealth was abandoned for full-scale warfare.

The slaughter spread like pestilence. I was glad I could not hear the screams. All across the field, confusion and panic rippled through the fallen army as they caught on. Pockets of resistance clawed into the ranks of our warriors, mounting a defense that finally broke the momentum of the attack. Above the chaos, we streaked through the air toward Adramalec and the gateway. Then the inevitable moment came when the first demons noticed what was happening hundreds of yards behind them and dropped their matter to guard the spiritual plane.

They spotted us instantly.

Dozens of black-winged angels took flight to intercept us. "Brace yourselves!" Uriel yelled as we soared toward the wall of wings and Hell-forged steel. I pointed my blade and ducked my head, accelerating as the distance closed.

I slammed into the fallen like a cannonball. Pained howls and the crack of bodies filled my ears, my head ringing from the impact. Cries of resistance surrounded me as robes brushed my arms and face. Strong hands raked my skin, yanked my hair, trying to rip me from the air.

"Push forward!" Michael cried out from somewhere ahead.

I pulled in my wings and shoved against the demon blocking my path, using his body as a battering ram through the crowd. Gabriel fought against Meresin and Rosier just ahead. Aiming for Meresin's blond mane, I sped forward and cleaved off part of his skull, blood mushrooming into the air. Bodies whistled past as I dodged and twisted. More and more demons scrambled to join the fight. The gateway was no longer even in sight, but as long as I could still glimpse my brothers, I had a direction. My wings spread just long enough to beat the air before I pulled them in, gaining as much speed as I could to catch Michael and Raphael.

"Yes, Sabrael!" Lucifer yelled as he flew up beside me. "Give them Hell, little brother!" Blood spattered the air as he struck a demon in the face and gave a satisfied shout.

Someone came up directly from below, grasping my leg just long enough for Jetrel and Verrine to ensnare my robe and yank me from the air. I heard Lucifer yell my name just before I smashed into the stone spikes of the cheval de frise. Shards of jagged rock snapped off under my weight, embedding deep in my arms, legs and back as I careened through the formation. I rose to my feet, healing the wounds, but could no longer see my brothers amidst the swirl of battle.

A serrated machete blade whizzed past my head. I ducked just in time, spinning to face Jetrel. "Make this easy on yourself, Sabrael. Give up now and I will not make it hurt … much."

He swung again, and I caught his arms. Straining against him, I had to dive away as Verrine thrust his spear at me for a cheap shot. Before I could even get to my feet, Nelchael swooped down from the raging cloud above and crashed into me. I stumbled back into a physical body, sturdy as a wall. Balberith, who of course, felt nothing. Nelchael drove his fist into my stomach. I threw a punch but missed, rewarded with a painful kick to my face. Slamming against Balberith again, my sword fumbled from my grasp. Verrine's spear jabbed down, barely missing me as I dropped to the right. The point glanced off Balberith, and Verrine spun to attack again. Snatching up my sword, I stabbed up and sank it deep into his stomach. He stared in disbelief as he slumped to the ground.

"If you know what is good for you, stay down," I said.

I pulled my blade free just in time to deflect Nelchael's mace, but beneath my raised arm, a heavy war hammer slammed into my side. Ribs buckled, and blood filled my mouth.

The earth rose to catch me. Nelchael laughed with my other assailant as I clawed the ground and pulled myself away. A hand yanked me back, scraping my chest across the hard ground. When I flipped over, it was to face Azaradel winding up the hammer again. I slashed up and glowing blood rained onto my legs as his severed arms fell, still clutching the hammer.

Searing pain spread from my shattered side as I drove my shoulder into Azaradel, toppling us both, then plunged my sword into his chest. I had to lean on the blade to help me from the ground as he screamed beneath me. Immediately, Nelchael was upon me again, and I parried his mace, using the friction of the metal to draw him closer. I spun the weapons in a low circle and brought my elbow up into his nose with a sickening crunch.

My ribs throbbed. I couldn't lift my left arm past my chest. Had I been physical, I could have repaired the damage. I ran in the direction I'd last seen Michael and Raphael. Burning eyes found me and demons gave chase. Crowded bodies slammed into me, the fallen clambering over each other to strike me down. I sprinted past the physical fallen still performing the ritual, unaware of the insanity happening all around them. I'd lost all sense of where the gateway was. The madness of battle overloaded my senses, threatened to overwhelm me. All I could see were bodies and wings, taunting faces, fists and feet and flashing weapons. I couldn't even think. A shoulder down here, a sword slash up there; I cleared a bloody path as I ran screaming through the army of the damned, that terrible song underscoring it all.

Where were the others? I had to find them. Alone in the rolling sea of Hell's legions, I was losing my mind. The hair on my neck stood and fingers grabbed my shoulder. I cried out and spun, the blade of my sword slicing through Nelchael's throat. His eyes went wide to each side of his shattered nose and, when he tried to speak, a spray of hot blood washed over my face. I spat the alkaline taste, standing over him as he gurgled on the ground. The screams, the bloodletting, the utter savagery of battle—it was Germania again. England. All those years spent warring in the human kingdoms came flooding back again, and in that moment, I realized those experiences were all that were keeping alive now. I saw red as the taste of blood unleashed the fury within, and suddenly I was no longer tired, scared. I was ravenous for more.

Ribs aching, wounds bleeding, I turned to face my pursuers. Four of them, black hair all. Black like their wings. Their hearts.

"Is this where you try to stem the tide?" Asbeel leered. A curl of hair clung to his forehead. "You think you can stand against us?"

"In a minute, I will be standing *over* you," I said.

He laughed. "Bring it on, traitor."

Weapons gleamed as Asbeel and the others rushed as one. Good. I welcomed it. I swung my sword into the pack and smiled at the tearing of flesh. The agonized screams. I laughed and swung again.

They all fell to my blade, my instincts from the ancient killing fields driving my every move. More demons rushed to replace those I struck down. Luminous blood soaked the earth, covered my hands and chest. They landed a few strikes, but I barely felt them. Until a chain lashed me from behind. Barbs punctured my shoulders, raked down my back. Even in the heat of bloodlust, I felt that. My entire being shook with my cry, and I flew to escape. The demons took up the chase. My robe clung between my wings where the flesh had been stripped away.

Voices taunted from behind me. "Sabrael, you cannot escape!"

"The kingdom will be ours this night."

"All of you will die before you leave this field!"

I pulled in my wings and arched down toward the earth again. Upside down I caught sight of the gateway. I felt a strange compulsion toward it as a light grew in the center circle. I caught sight of Michael fighting his way through the broken crags. A crowd of demons tugged at his robe, pulled at his hair, and still he cut them down by twos and threes. A short distance behind him, Haniel struggled less successfully against the horde. Hands grasped at him as though reaching up from a drowning sea. Lips peeled back in determination, he swung his mace into the crowd one last time before the demons pulled him to the ground.

I caught a quick glimpse of our warriors, still fighting to reach us. Then the ground was near, and I righted myself, slashing up into the air. Blood rained down from my closest pursuer. I couldn't even tell them apart anymore. I braced myself as they formed a circle around me.

They came at me as one this time. I blocked three blades at once, driven almost to my knees. Wet muscle slid beneath my robe. Rising to strike, I barely had the chance before they attacked again. The clash of swords echoed on the air. My angel sense flared, and I whipped around to stab a demon sneaking up behind me. I tore my blade free and faced the others again.

Chest heaving, a sheen of blood covering me head to toe, I felt like the air crackled around me. It was a moment before I realized it wasn't just adrenaline. The demons slowed as they felt it as well, and I used the opportunity to run Flauros through, then flew into the air again.

For one moment I had the chance to take in the sight of how many demons had not even joined the fight yet. There were still thousands. For one moment, despair sapped my strength and made my raw wounds flash with fiery pain again. For one moment, I lost hope.

Then, I felt something coursing through my body. A tingle, like a jolt of electricity. Not unlike calling matter to form a physical body. My hair stood on end. Then, from somewhere inside the fortress, a tremendous flash of light preceded a thunderous boom that drowned out all other sound. The air itself exploded. Purplish-white energy rippled out over the plain like a tidal wave, and as it crashed into me, my vision seared as I felt myself being swept off the ground.

CHAPTER FIFTY

My mind reeled. I was sure I had blacked out. My first sensation was the feeling of falling. As my sight finally returned, I discovered I was indeed plummeting—through water. Bodies rained down like macabre hailstones above me, violently penetrating the surface to float limp, the light of their souls extinguished.

Farther and farther I fell, shell-shocked, until I struck the bottom. The water above was littered with bodies. Clouds of bubbles surrounded the few survivors flailing against the tide. Dazed demons landed around me, just as confused as I was. Before they took notice, I flew for the surface high above.

What was that blast? I'd never felt or seen anything like it. I was vaguely reminded of Valthgar's death, but it was like comparing a brisk autumn breeze to a hurricane. That both planes had been affected sent chills down my torn and bleeding back. Whatever caused it, it wasn't good.

I threaded through the floating dead, taking a closer look. None of the bodies were marred by burns or shrapnel. The impact on the water must have killed them. The sea was a graveyard, so many dead I wondered how many could possibly still remain on Inishmor.

It was impossible to tell our warriors from theirs after their souls departed, but passing through the nearly indistinguishable surface, I found a small number of men and women still lived, frantically treading in the waves. The vast majority bore the mark of the fallen. I scanned them quickly, hoping and yet fearing to find Adrienne or Gavin among them. But they weren't.

Searching the horizon, I spotted the island. The explosion had thrown us nearly a mile out to sea. Its dark contour jutted up from the rolling waves, and on the cliff where the gateway sat, I could barely make out the spiritual forms still at war.

Far below in the deep, a number of demons had recovered, and now sped toward the surface. Some took physical form in the water, but not their own. Gargantuan beasts of horror rose to pluck the helpless warriors from the surface and rend them apart beneath the waves. They didn't discriminate. Light, dark, it didn't matter; they took out their rage on all.

My ears filled with the roar of the physical plane as I dove down to stop what was happening. Humans cried out from every direction, the waves drowning them out with every crash. Blowhole sprays and the hisses of unnatural beasts punctuated piercing screams. A woman's shriek just a short way to my left was abruptly silenced by vicious thrashing. Salt burned my face and lips as I skimmed the surface. Hands were raised to me and random cries of hopelessness became pointed, desperate screams for salvation. I formed matter together into a large, flat raft and dropped it into the water.

"Pull yourselves up!" I called down. Soaking warriors of light swam to the platform, coughing salt water as they helped each other up. Warriors of darkness quickly closed in, and as soon as the last of our warriors was up, I wrapped the long tethers connected to the raft around my arms and pulled it along as I sped for the island.

Racing against the nightmare hunters in the water, I tried to scoop up as many warriors of light as I could. The warriors of darkness did their best to grab on, but the men and women of the blessing beat them back in a new, smaller battle for survival. Many had lost their weapons in the fall, but they beat their fists and feet against the converging damned. When a warrior of darkness managed to gain a foothold, I hurled a fireball at her chest, sending her back into the black water.

Everything was under control until one young woman was pulled up, and as her body left the water, the waves violently parted beneath her. A horrible perversion of a whale, jaws brimming with teeth, burst through the surface and narrowly missed biting her in two . Huge, bulbous eyes caught sight of me and narrowed. This was no creature made by God; it was a vision borne of the fears of men. The beast bellowed as the woman was plucked from its maw and flicked its angry tail into the bottom of the platform. Three warriors catapulted into the air as the platform bucked. The creature growled in satisfaction, but before it could claim its prey, I swooped low and ripped my sword down the monster's side. A long gash peeled apart the leathery flesh, and the air filled with a shriek as inky gore poured into the waves. Then I stabbed one of its huge eyes. Blood and ocular fluid gushed in a torrent, and the beast thrashed wildly, roaring before diving beneath the surface again.

When I'd gathered all those the platform could carry, I soared for the island. The warriors clung to each other to keep from falling. So many were still out there, but I had to get back to the gateway. I created planks of wood and dropped them as we passed, hoping this would give them a fighting chance … or at least a floating one.

The island drew near and for the first time I shifted my sight to the physical plane.

Dún Aonghasa was a maelstrom of violence, bodies of angels and humans alike strewn everywhere. Weapons clashed amidst the cries of the wounded. Smaller skirmishes spread throughout the fortress, and I picked out a number of humans still fighting. They hadn't all perished! Gabriel and Adonael broke through the line of fallen together to join Michael as he pushed Adramelec, Tumael and the other leaders of the damned away from the gateway. None of the fallen remained at their positions against the spires.

I could see all this despite the dark. I could see, because in the center of the fortress, a beam of light so thin it was almost imperceptible now reached toward the sky. The gateway had opened a crack, and the light of Heaven trickled through onto the Earth.

The awed reactions of the warriors I carried suddenly became screams. I looked down to find a few of them collapsed, ecstatic smiles on their lips and the blank stare of death in their eyes. The others yelled as they tried to revive them. I realized what was happening.

"Do not look into the gateway!" I called down. "Shut your eyes!"

As quickly as I could manage it, we were over land again. I set the platform at the edge of the cliff and dropped the tethers, yelling to the disembarking warriors, "Take weapons off the dead if you lost yours. Avert your eyes from the gateway and help whoever you can!"

I didn't wait to lead them. I flew straight for Michael at the front line.

My sword shot into my hand as I neared the gateway. My ribs and back still ached from my injuries in the spiritual plane, but I could not slow down. It wouldn't be long before the field filled with the fallen again; some were already returning with warriors gathered from the sea as I had. I prayed that somewhere, Adrienne and Gavin were safe.

Still more than fifty yards away, I was spotted by the fallen. We collided in the air, and the battle dropped to the ground. I swept my sword through the demons' ranks, sparks flying as metal met metal, but I was one against a dozen. The barrage came from all sides, razor-sharp weapons nipping pieces off my robe, my flesh.

I enhanced my body to that inhuman speed, and the attack slowed to a crawl. For the first time, I was not unnerved by it; I was empowered. I dodged the fists and blades like they were choreographed and turned the attack back on them. They sped up their own bodies. I was still faster. Ducking under the thrust of a spear, I caught it with my left hand and with my right, drove my sword up through Shamsiel's jaw and out the top of his head. He tried to curse, blood seeping between his lips, but his mouth was held shut. His body disintegrated, and I brought my sword around to bury it in Agares as I punched Shamsiel's spear into Gressil.

But a spiked club smashed into my side, piercing my skin and crushing my already wounded ribs. I dropped, crying out in agony. The demons converged and, even with all my speed, I couldn't get free. There were too many of them. Vicious kicks pummeled my sides. Blades hacked into me. Curled up on the ground, I tried to slash at them, but someone caught my hand and a sword cleaved flesh and bone, severing my arm at the elbow. A spear punched through my stomach. Pinned like some research specimen, I choked on blood as warmth poured down my sides to pool beneath me.

I did the only thing I could—I started the grass beneath me on fire.

My robe and hair became a blaze. The stench of burning flesh filled my nose. All my effort went into grabbing my sword and retracting it before I died. Two demons shrieked as their robes went up. The pain was far worse than I imagined it would be, but I died quickly. My body dissipated to free matter. The field grew light again, and the pain left me.

I ran from them in the spiritual plane, but a pack of the fallen's warriors returning from the sea stood in my path. Their escort, Yomyael, caught sight of me. His spiritual gaze locked on and he drew in his wings to speed toward me.

I called matter to my body again. Yomyael strained to strike in time, but he faded as the world turned dark again. Sandwiched between fifteen humans and six demons though, my situation had not improved. There was only one direction to go.

My sword danced into the flesh of the fallen's warriors as they swarmed. They were far easier to take down than the demons would be. I didn't want to kill them, but I had no choice. With the path cleared, I lifted into the air.

Of course, the demons were ready for this, and I was tackled from the air almost instantly. In that moment though, I saw something that shocked me to the core.

I saw Barachiel, alive, and it was he who led the song to open the gateway.

CHAPTER FIFTY-ONE

My mind disconnected from my body as I was beaten mercilessly. All the pain meant nothing. Just a reminder that what I'd seen was real. The demons heaved me into the air, and I crashed back down deep inside the cheval de frise. They landed around me to continue the assault. Their taunts were lost on me, their jeers an incoherent babble. The image of my brother leading the fallen was branded onto my mind. How long had Barachiel been alive? How long had he been working to bring down the kingdom he called home? Or did Michael know this whole time? Had Barachiel gone undercover all these centuries and Michael kept it from us?

I called for my ebon-haired brother. *Michael! I saw—*

My cry was silenced by a fist crushing my nose. Cartilage snapped and blood filled my throat. I dropped to my knees, and the six demons swarmed me. My cheekbone shattered; my eye socket caved; something metal boxed my ear. When another strike splintered my right radius, a piece of it punched through the skin. How long could my body hold out?

When my skull cracked, they finally let up. It was a short-lived reprieve. A blade punched through my chest, shoving me to the ground. I knew what was coming next. The identity of my slayer was blurred through the mask of blood and swelling. I saw only a pale face with dark hair above the shoulders wrenching the weapon in a yawning circle.

"How's it feel, Sabrael?" I heard him say from beyond the blanket of pain. "Get used to it. I claim you. You're going into the kingdom with me to serve as entertainment for eternity."

I don't know if he actually thought I was capable of responding, but I definitely wasn't. He ripped the blade from me, then plunged his hand into the hole. Fingers wrapped around my heart, plucking veins like harp strings. My entire body constricted, but I craned my neck toward the gateway so I might at least watch the finish of the battle from death.

A shrieking death cry erupted nearby just before blood spattered my attacker and a wet clump struck his face. A heart. He recoiled and looked up as a gleaming sword swooped over me and buried deep in his chest. He pleaded for mercy as someone caught the handle and tore the sword out of him sideways. His hand did not leave my heart, but his fingers went limp as he slumped over me. I didn't need to see the features of my golden-haired savior to know who it was. Lucifer severed the demon's hand and shoved him off me, plunging his blade down. When he stood again, Lucifer tossed a bloody heart to the ground, teeth bared and eyes blazing.

He crouched at my side, carefully plucking the hand from my chest. "Still alive, little brother?" Dark blotches clung to his face and robe, his hair doused in blood and sweat. I knew the others standing around had been dealt with as swiftly as my would-be killer. "Don't die yet, Sabrael. I need you now."

He held his hands over me. I felt my chest closing and my face mending.

"The ritual is almost finished. It is nearly open. Dozens lie dead at the sight of it."

"Have our warriors reached the fortress?" I muttered through chipped teeth and shattered bone, blood still caked in my throat.

"Finally," he scoffed. "Though a good number of them continue to look at the gateway, and you will soon run out." He grinned. "Temptation. I love it."

Another moment, and I felt nearly whole again. "Finish it yourself," he said. "Hurry." Immediately, a pair of the fallen attacked, and he rose to dispatch them. When my body was fully repaired, we ran for the glimmering sliver of Heaven's light.

He saved me. The same fallen angel that once tore out my heart and threatened to one day do it again had slain his own followers to keep me alive. Had I been wrong about his coming to us? Could he really be fighting to shut the gateway for good?

The sight when Lucifer and I passed the inner walls of Dún Aonghasa and came close to the gateway was the most beautiful and the most horrible I've ever beheld in this world. The field was a wasteland of corpses, the bodies of thousands blanketing the earth. The dead stretched across the entire cliffside, the ravaged cheval de frise like bloody, skeletal fingers reaching for Heaven. Humans still clashed in groups farther down the cliffside, and fallen angels sped over the battlefield to join the skirmish. Only Michael and Raphael still stood at the gateway, backed against each other, defending against a crowd of the damned. I couldn't see if any more of my brothers fought beyond the gateway. The light was too bright.

My God, I thought as the glow filled my vision. The rift was still too small to admit a body, but wide enough to allow a glimpse into Heaven. Remarkably, that glimpse was the one thing I longed for more than anything else—my hall. The tall trees, the vast fields, a single bend in one of the many rivers; I froze at the sight, and my entire being yearned to shed the matter of my physical form and fly home.

"Do you see?" I whispered to myself. "Do you see it?"

I didn't realize I was running, but my legs carried me closer and closer to the kingdom. I felt the light of the Almighty on me, and I ran faster. He was calling me. After two thousand years, He was calling me home! Somewhere far away I heard Lucifer crying out for me to stop, but how could I? The songs of the host were on the wind. My hall was there, the warm, comforting light of the kingdom beckoning. The warriors of darkness pushed in on the circle, and my brothers struggled to keep them at bay, but I didn't care. *Oh, Michael, Raphael, Lucifer, do you see? Can you see what we have been waiting for?*

Without thought, I cut down any warriors of darkness standing between me and the gateway, and when the last of them fell, I sprinted for it. The world suddenly spun out of control as Michael came hurling through the air to tackle me.

"Michael, no! Let me go! My hall is there; I can go home!"

"Stop, Sabrael! You must stop!"

I screamed and thrashed in his grasp, desperation surging through me. The light. I needed it; I would do anything to have it! He heaved me from the ground and spun me to face the angry mob cascading toward us.

"Sabrael!" Michael screamed at me. "Ignore it, brother; it is a mirage! You see only what you want to see! Force it from your mind and help us! All the others are lost!"

My visual link to the gateway broken, the shouts of battle suddenly filled my ears again, and the songs of Heaven disappeared. Raphael fought desperately to keep the damned back from the gateway. Michael let me go and ran to help him. I forced my back to the gateway despite the light caressing my wings, promising such peace. It took all my determination to ignore it. The wall of Hell's legions charged. I swung into them again.

The piled corpses were soon as much a hindrance as the living. With each slain warrior, three more clawed over them to continue the attack. We couldn't kill them fast enough. Blood ran in rivers. My hands were covered in it, my lips tasted of it. My sword swept through the unending line, chests splitting and limbs severing in its wake. The screams of those stricken were drowned by the shouts of those rushing to take their place even before they hit the ground.

Struggling to find room, I backed into one of the nine spires. The gateway tugged at my robe, beckoning me to return to the light. As the fallen's warriors drew near, they looked past me and their eyes widened, smiles forming before they dropped dead, one after the next. Not a single one could resist. Behind them though, Astoreth and Procell marched steadily on.

The demons moved in quickly, Astoreth striking at my head while Procell's sword swung low. I had no choice; I dropped my physical matter so their weapons would pass through me. That moment I was in the spiritual plane, I was paralyzed by the sight of it.

In the presence of the gateway, the spiritual plane was in turmoil. The entire field teemed with souls being sucked into the gateway as though it were a black hole! From every direction, they flew past me, ripped from the bodies of those who looked upon the gateway. Amazingly, not a single one tried to escape Heaven's pull. It didn't matter which side the warriors had fought on; in the moments after death, they all desired to call Heaven their home. They screamed and laughed at the sight of the kingdom, half running and half drawn by the inescapable force. Then I was physical again, and the fight resumed.

I brought up my sword to turn away Astoreth's mace as I kicked Procell in the chest. Astoreth gasped as I jammed my blade into his chest, but I couldn't grab his heart before Procell's sword hacked into my left leg. I cried out, my blade tearing from Astoreth and his body exploding. I desperately needed a moment to mend my wounds. Procell didn't relent though, forcing me back toward the gateway. Astoreth rejoined the fight, the light so bright on his face I knew the gateway couldn't be more than a few steps behind me.

Then, I suddenly felt it siphoning the matter from me! Pieces of my wings and back detached and turned to dust. Horrified, I strained against the gateway's power, trying to hold myself together as it shredded my physical matter. My left leg buckled as my sword blocked a simultaneous strike from both demons, the weight of the twin blows too much for my damaged limb. I sank onto my right knee, bone protruding from my left thigh, flesh gathering like a sock at my calf. Throwing up my arms, I shoved their weapons away and then, using Valthgar's technique from centuries before, swiped straight across their unguarded stomachs. Entrails spattered the ground and the demons disappeared from the physical plane. More demons moved to replace them, even as Astoreth and Procell reappeared almost instantly. Stopping them was like trying to cut sand. They swung their weapons, and I braced for the killing blow.

Then, as before, a golden sword came to my rescue, guiding the attack safely away. Lucifer stood between the demons and me, and I used the moment to mend my leg.

I rose, ready to fight alongside him, but then, Lucifer calmly lowered his weapon. The demons smiled as one, but not one moved against him. He turned to face me.

"What is this?" I asked.

"This, little brother, is the end," he said with a strange smile. The demons laughed.

"I don't understand."

"I told you long ago that I would return for you, and the pain you would know then would be worse than you can imagine. I always keep my word."

"No. You were..."

"What?" His tone spoke volumes. "I offered you a seat at my side. A chair beside the throne of creation where all would bow and worship you." His smile transformed into a scowl. "You spit it back in my face!"

I was so shocked, I could only stutter gibberish.

"I would have given you everything! From the very beginning I wanted you at my side, the highest in our ranks and ruler of all eternity second only to me! Even when you insulted me by refusing the first time, I offered again because of my love for you. Did I not raise you up when I might have left you to wallow alone in the forests of the kingdom forever? Did I not lead you by the hand among our brothers and make you great in their eyes?"

He stepped toward me, and I raised my sword.

"I gave you the keys to Heaven, and I would have given you the keys to the Earth as well. All I wanted in return was loyalty, trust, friendship!"

He was only a breath away. I could see the fire in his eyes.

"Why follow Michael and the old ways still? What binds you to them that you would dishonor me so? I offer you the vestment of a king, but you choose the robe of a slave."

"I choose the truth. We are His children. He provides everything we want and more."

"When you wanted nothing more than to stay with Malietta, did He give you that?"

My teeth ached as my jaw tightened at the mention of her name. "That was different. I was ignoring my responsibility and disobeying both Him and Michael."

"By wanting something for yourself? Seeking just a moment's privacy, an instant of relaxation, one human lifetime of peace? You only sought to make Malietta happy, and He snatched her away!"

"He did not kill her!" I yelled. "Her brother's fear of me caused her death."

"He could have stopped it, could He not?"

The cries of battle echoed across the field, and I looked to find Michael and Raphael had been overwhelmed. I could see no sign of our human warriors and fear gripped my heart as I wondered about Adrienne and Gavin.

"This entire battle has always been in my control," Lucifer said, turning my attention back to him. "Did you really think seven angels and a handful of humans could stop me from opening the gateway?"

His confession sapped the strength from me. "Lucifer, you came back to us. Do not do this again, brother, please!"

"Haniel and Uriel are dead," Lucifer said. He smiled. "Both by my hand actually. I wish you could have seen the look in Uriel's eyes when I tore out his arrogant heart.

"Gabriel I gave to Adramelec for his work in locating the gateway, and Adonael fell to our warriors—after we softened him up, of course. They're only human, after all. Your warriors, well, you know better than anyone how easily humans, even armies of them, fall to our swords. For you though, who disrespected me above all others, I saved something special."

"I am not afraid of you."

"Oh, but you are. Horrified. I smell it, taste it. I am even tempted to act on some of those exquisitely painful ideas passing through your mind, but not even those would be enough for one whose betrayal was so great."

"Killing me will not matter. You failed. The gateway isn't wide enough for your army, and no one knows the last part of the ritual to fully open it. It was missing from Maurizio's research."

Victory cries spread across the battlefield from the fallen and what remained of their human followers, though I thought I could still hear the clashing of weapons somewhere far off.

"It was there, just hidden in Maurizio's notes. In his excitement to tear the entrails from the venerable father, Adramelec forgot to force him to give up that crucial piece." He held up a torn page from what looked like a handwritten journal. "Why do you think I led you all to Italy? Argued to keep searching there instead of scattering? While Michael fumbled around looking for the gateway, I found the key to open it."

He waited for me to respond in some way, to acknowledge his cleverness somehow. I didn't give him the pleasure.

"Once I had what I needed, it was just a matter of leading you here to a battle you could never win, thus ensuring no surprises. Now I'm free to take the throne that is rightfully mine, and all will recognize me for exactly what I am."

"The biggest disappointment in creation?" I said.

He just smirked. "Like all the best rituals, this one demands sacrifice. A being with ties to both the physical and spiritual planes. The blood of one will allow an army to pass through and make right what was been wrong for so long."

The gateway sheared off more matter from my wings and I realized I was retreating from Lucifer. I stepped forward again, out of its reach, and repaired the damage. Lucifer drew near, looking into my eyes.

"What better punishment for the one who refused me? What worse fate could I give you than making you the linchpin of my coup? Ensuring your final thought will be that it was you who put the crown on my head. That you won this war for me after fighting so long to stop—"

I thrust my sword at him with all my speed and force. Somehow, he still blocked it. I struck again and again. Lucifer's blade flashed against mine, gold and silver shining in the ethereal glow. The rest of Hell's army kept back, no one daring to come between us. I swung my blade around toward his neck. He blocked it, driving my sword up and slashing my chest. Blood flowed, the air stinging, but I didn't let it slow me. I stabbed at his chest then swung for his head, but he darted to the side.

"How pathetic that the last one standing between Heaven and Hell would be the one angel here who cannot defeat me. You can't stop this, Sabrael. What is meant to be will be."

I answered by slicing his arm. He staggered from the unexpected blow, staring at his blood. I felt a swell of pride. "If you believe that, why the sudden doubt in your eyes?"

In the next moment, he redoubled his attack. His movements were so fast, so fluid, I barely saw them. Instinctually, I altered my form to allow that superhuman speed, and amazingly, found it was a perfect match. Was this why I had gained this ability? I deflected his strike at my ribs, spun to parry a slash aimed for my thigh. Then I did what I'd never been able to do before; I broke his attack and fought back. My sword danced around Lucifer, cutting his arm here, slashing his robe there, and the look of surprise in his eyes gave me such satisfaction that I drove harder still. My blade hacked into his leg and sliced his shoulder. I moved more quickly than ever before, emboldened by Heaven itself. I pounded on his sword until his wrist gave and then, with all my strength, buried my sword in his heart.

Lucifer looked down at my blade, eyes wide. My chest heaved with exhausted breaths. It was over. I had won!

But when his gaze rose again to meet mine, I didn't see defeat. Only fury.

Growling, he jerked his body to the side and ripped the sword from my grasp, then drove his blade straight through my leg, severing it mid-thigh. I fell to my remaining knee, holding the wound. In horror, I watched as my leg on the ground dissolved, absorbed into the gateway.

Blood dripping down the handle of my blade protruding from his chest, Lucifer stared down at me defiantly. "As I was saying, inside the gateway, where the planes converge, you will be consumed, ripped apart, body and soul, in order to open the portal. You will cease to exist."

My strength was literally being sapped through my wounds. The gateway was trying to suck the soul from my body as it had the human warriors before. Since I had no soul, however, it was instead drinking up my very essence from the physical plane.

"You put up a good fight, little brother," he said. "I am impressed, but I have a bigger battle to prepare for now."

"You will never win," I said through clenched teeth. "You'll be back in your basement before you know what He's done to you."

The fallen laughed. Lucifer smiled. "We shall see." He added, "Actually, *I* will see. You will just be a faded memory."

I called matter to mend my wounds, but couldn't keep up with the drain of the gateway. The fallen cheered as Lucifer rallied them, proudly exhibiting the sword in his chest. An army of demons and loyal humans ready to march into the kingdom. *I'm sorry, Lord,* I thought. *I've failed You again.*

The cry was raised to begin the siege, and Lucifer crouched near me. Looking to see that none of the others were listening, he said, "As you face death, little brother, know that you brought this on yourself."

I looked into his cobalt eyes and saw nothing left of the one I'd known in the kingdom before the war. He was utterly gone. "I would rather not exist than watch you rule Heaven."

"Then let my final kindness to you be the granting of your wish," he said. He lifted his golden sword before his face, a warrior's salute, then swung it hard at me.

For a long moment, I felt no pain. Even thought he somehow missed me. When I looked up at him though, I saw the horror in his eyes. Revulsion at his own handiwork. Then, the first of the blood and feathers rained over my shoulders, and I knew.

He had severed my wings.

Pain so excruciating I couldn't bear it suddenly ignited across my back as the initial shock subsided. I crumpled to the ground, agony racking my body. The acidic laughter of the fallen erupted across the battlefield. The pull of the gateway intensified tenfold, siphoning matter and spiritual essence from the fresh wounds like a ravenous beast. It burned worse than even waking from death.

Blood slathered the ground from my stumps, staining the grass and stones beneath me. Lucifer pulled me from the ground, lifting me up to display me above his head for his army. The eyes of the vast crowd burned with anticipation, eager for the end. Our efforts to stop them had accomplished nothing. Every single demon that lost his heart had been resurrected. After the long search for the gateway seeking to close Heaven's doors to the fallen for good, in the end we made no difference. Had the Almighty known it would be so, or was even He surprised?

Lucifer turned toward the gateway, the glow of Heaven pouring over us as the rift whipped our robes and hair. He said, "Goodbye, little brother," and without another word, heaved my body into the opening.

I was engulfed by the light. Floating without weight. I lost all sense of direction. The light penetrated and emanated from me all at once. I wasn't in the light; I was the light. The sapping of my essence flared for a few moments of utter agony, and then I felt nothing. Blind, deaf and mute, I hovered for an eternity.

Then, I saw everything.

The brilliant glow cleared before me and as my sight returned, I saw Heaven. The Hall of Song stood in all its majesty before me. The walls gleamed, the twinkling colors inside them so beautiful. More marvelous than any memory could capture. Yet it paled in comparison to my own hall. The trees stood proud just a short distance away, exactly as I left them, my city expanded far beyond what I remembered but still recognizable after all this time. I saw the multitudes of flowers in every color imaginable, my murals and work still intact. The gateway's pull was nothing compared to the relief that washed over me at the sight, cleansing the anger, guilt, exhaustion and shame that had built up over centuries, over millennia.

Then, to my amazement, I saw something new. In that moment, all our pain and bloodshed and sacrifice finally felt worth it. Throughout every hall, I saw the souls of humans. Laughing and conversing, aiding my brothers in the ongoing beautification of Heaven. They shimmered in the light, their appearances wavering between various ages, never settling. They were everywhere, but I quickly noticed the vast majority crowded around a new hall. Enclosed like the Hall of Song but many times bigger, it seemed it had been prepared solely for them. I was desperate to know what was inside those walls!

That beautiful incantation began again all around me as the fallen resumed the ritual. The gateway pulsed around me and then, it was like a fog lifted from before me. Heaven grew even brighter, the colors more vivid, and I felt a warm breeze on my face. Nearby souls suddenly turned and looked at me, curious. Horror settled over me as I realized what was happening. The gateway was opening the rest of the way! Then it began to devour its sacrifice.

Sparks of white-hot pain shot through my back where wings had once been. Blood siphoned out into the air in a crimson whirlwind. I screamed as my bones condensed, crunching under tremendous pressure, my limbs snapping at odd angles. Through the fire erupting inside, I saw the souls watching, terrified. Some ran to get help. What help could there be? Agonized cries welled up from within me. Every particle of my physical body burned, a thousand times worse than being revived from death. Bits of matter chipped away, breaking free to fly off and cling to the sides of the gateway. A thin layer of physical material gathered like a frame around the portal. I cried out to the Almighty, *Please Lord! Save me from this! I do not want to die!*

Then I saw some of the souls return from Raphael's hall, pointing and lamenting the sight of me as they led Iophiel and Behemiel to see. My brothers slowed, unable to comprehend what was happening. "Sabrael?" Iophiel called out. I couldn't answer him. Instead, the gateway ripped a screeching cry from my lips as one of the stumps of my wings tore free, its matter bursting to slam into the rim and form a piece of frame. "Hold on! We will get you down!"

Iophiel and Behemiel started toward me, but I forced every ounce of willpower to yell, "No!" They stared at me in horror, confused and suffering to see me so. Shaking, sweating, barely able to speak, I growled, "The fallen are coming! You must ... prepare! Warn the host!"

They stood uncomprehending. Surely to them what I was saying was madness. My remaining leg burst in a sickening crunch, my scream shaking them from their stupor. They fled into the Hall of Song, and I heard a great trumpet call issue forth through the kingdom.

My arms buckled, matter sloughing off to sprinkle showers of loose particles onto the gateway frame. The crowd of souls grew with each second as my cries drew in more and more of them. Two souls in particular finally shoved through the pack. Theokritus! Helena! They ran to embrace me but my touch scalded them and they recoiled.

"Sabrael? What is this?" Theokritus said. His face was that of a teenager, then of a middle-aged man, then a boy, as if I were looking at him through a kaleidoscope of time.

"Theokritus. Help. The gateway is opening." My other wing stump shattered into billions of particles that swirled around me like dust. As they clung to the sides of the gateway, the portal expanded out a bit. I grabbed the frame, struggling to pull it closed.

Helena looked past me, and I knew she could see Dún Aonghasa. The rift was setting. As if awakening to a forgotten nightmare, her eyes slowly grew wide and she said, "The gateway. Oh God! Theokritus, the gateway! Remember? What can we do?"

"Help me hold it closed!" I screamed, but pain lanced through my sides, tearing off chunks of flesh to bolster the gateway's frame.

Theokritus and Helena wasted no time. They dove to grab the bottom of the frame beneath the dangling tatters of what used to be my legs.

Behind me, the song of the fallen swelled, metal weapons clanking in anticipation of battle. *Please God! Do not let it end like this!* I pleaded. The gateway swelled, and Helena lost her grasp as the portal sheared off the back of my head sending brain and skull into the air.

The crowd of souls cowered at the sight. More and more emerged from the new hall to watch. Soon another stepped forward from the crowd. My heart cried out to see her. Malietta. Michael was right; the Almighty must have revealed himself to her people in a different way. In fact, as I looked around the crowd, I realized there were multitudes of cultures and peoples there, from every part of the world.

Malietta flew to me, placed a hand on my cheek. She winced as smoke rose from her hand at my touch, but didn't let go. "They are coming. Your brothers are coming."

I could hardly find my voice. "Malietta, my love. Please, it hurts."

"You were right about everything. The Almighty, the kingdom. Hold on just a little longer."

"I can't," I cried, arching as it felt like a sledgehammer pounded my lower spine. The gateway yawned a bit wider.

"You can. You have to," she said, then kissed my cheek and took hold of the frame beside Helena. "You are not alone."

My three companions, together. I never dreamed it would be possible. It was a miracle.

The Hall of Song's trumpets blared twice, insistently. A group of angels flew from their halls toward the central structure, then more, all unaware of the army standing poised to destroy our home. "Brothers, please! Arm yourselves! The fallen are here!" I pleaded. They did not hear my voice, too weak under the gateway's strain. The scalding power of the rift gnawed at the flesh I had left, and siphoned the spirit where flesh failed.

"Malietta, Helena; I cannot do this," I said through gritted teeth. "It is too much. Theokritus … please."

Malietta turned back toward the crowd of souls hovering there in shock and yelled, "Do not just stand there! Help us! He fights for us all!"

The crowd surged, and everyone grabbed the frame. One by one, souls piled on, wrestled to keep it from expanding further. My body still shook despite the help, but the expansion slowed. Incredibly, I realized I recognized many of the faces around me. Friends from all my many human lives, Angle warriors who followed me into battle, children I trained and taught, women I flirted with, Malietta's friends. Even many of the phantoms that had haunted me for so long, their stares no longer dead and black as I knew them so well. All the people I had known on Earth joined the effort, and together we strained to keep the gateway closed.

The song of the fallen behind me escalated, the gateway throbbing in our grasp. I could feel the last of my strength ebbing away. The frame suddenly lurched, throwing off many of the souls helping me. My torso splintered and my right arm disintegrated. I cried out as the gateway consumed more of me. Souls were dragged into the rift as they struggled to hold on, and others dove to save them. Theokritus groaned in effort, and the gateway snapped free of his grasp, sending him tumbling. The remaining souls stood back, terrified as the insatiable portal shaved the last of the matter from me. It was now big enough for ten angels to fit through. I fought as it consumed my spiritual essence. My friends and allies wailed, helpless, watching my spirit die.

Then, at that moment, the great wooden doors of the Hall of Song burst open and Iophiel strode through, Behemiel at his side. They held banners bearing angelic script … and they were not alone. Behind them, two more of my brothers strode from the hall, then two more. Weapons in hand, they sang a glorious and beautiful song. The sight of my brothers after millennia enthralled me, even as I felt myself dying. Souls from every hall flew out to form an aisle as the host marched forth, joining in the angels' song.

They threw flowers and glimmering light into the air around my brothers, transporting me back to the last time I'd gazed into the kingdom. Only then did I listen to the words. It was a war hymn, a summons to battle that soon every being in the kingdom sang together, voices mingling into one great sound.

The winged warriors marched up to me and stopped, fanning out to form a line so vast I lost sight of the ends of it, the procession extending all the way back into the Hall of Song.

Struggling to hold myself together, agony in every movement, I turned back to the fortress on Inishmor. It was only a step behind me, just as the kingdom was only a step ahead. I could see the entire battlefield, every detail visible as though I was everywhere at once. Michael and Raphael were still alive, but under constant assault. They fought demon after demon, but when they tore the heart from one, another would take his place while others resurrected those slain. I saw Haniel, Uriel, Adonael and Gabriel lying amidst the hundreds of dead warriors from each side. So Lucifer had not been lying then.

Lucifer carefully drew my sword from his chest, taking a relieved breath and healing the wound. He dropped my blade and raised his own, rallying the fallen for the invasion of Heaven. But confusion soon swept over their faces. The war hymn! They could hear it!

Pulling with all my strength, I yelled through gritted teeth as the dueling incantations threatened to tear the frame from my hands. The souls around me could hold on no longer. I felt the last of my light fading. Then the gateway surged, and I screamed as my spirit ripped apart.

The space inside the gateway exploded as the kingdom and the Earth fused. Every fiber of my being fueled the effect. A supernova of spiritual energy burst from me, and the gateway solidified, brilliant light flooding Inishmor. Lucifer and the fallen covered their eyes and stumbled back. Michael and Raphael flew free of their blinded assailants and soared for the gateway. Heaven's light bathed my four slain brothers and healed their wounds, life returning to their eyes as they rose to join Michael and Raphael. The two armies on each side ran for the portal, and as the first weapons clashed, it all faded away.

⊱⊰

I was dead. I had to be. There was only darkness, and yet, I was conscious. Or was I? Disoriented, confused, I wasn't even sure I had a body. The pain was gone, at least. Then, as though I opened my eyes, the darkness was replaced by the purple-white light of the gateway all around. "What is this?" I asked.

"Sabrael," a voice said. Beautiful, awesome, unmistakable even after so long.

I turned, and He was there. "My Lord?" I said, unable to believe it was true. Somehow I ran to embrace Him, though I had no form. I had become pure consciousness.

He caught me and held me. The warmth and light of His presence enveloped me, His love soothing the confusion racing through my mind. "Do not worry. I am here, my child; you have nothing fear. You did so well."

"But I failed," I said, despairing. "The gateway is open."

He smiled. "No, Sabrael. You triumphed. You held it long enough for the host to prepare. You and those who loved you, who admired you, those whose lives you touched. Did I not say you are special among your brothers?" He motioned behind me. "Look for yourself."

I could suddenly see it all again. My brothers fought inside the rift, the host pushing through the gateway onto the battlefield. "How am I seeing this? Am I dead?"

"The gateway consumed you, but you are not dead."

"You saved me."

"There was no need," He said. "Lucifer misunderstood the portal's effect. I only wanted to hold you here a moment, to tell you how proud I am of you."

"How did Lucifer misunderstand?" I asked.

"He was right about one thing. What is meant to be shall be," He said. I felt His love wash over me one more time, and then I felt myself flying through the air.

⇒⊱ ⊰⇐

I crashed down hard and, though I felt no pain, I was powerless to move.

"Stop them!" Lucifer screamed from nearby. "Get inside the gateway! Push them back!"

I was back on Inishmor! Brilliant light flickered on the faces of the fallen, their angry cries filling the air. The song of the host swelled over the sounds of brutal fighting. The fallen charged past me toward the fight, and though I couldn't move to watch them, they quickly returned, pushed back by Heaven's army. The procession of my brothers did not let up. The demons stood their ground at first, but it wasn't long before they were forced to retreat. Blessed weapons flashed across the field, Michael and the rest of our team leading the surge.

No one could have imagined such a rout. No one, that is, but for the Almighty. The bodies of the damned littered the ground as the Heavenly force drove the fallen from Dún Aonghasa. The host poured forth without pause, covering hundreds of yards and still coming.

The battle lasted for a short time after that, and then, it was over. The fallen had failed.

CHAPTER FIFTY-TWO

In the light of the gateway, among a sea of the dead, I lay with a body that didn't obey my commands. In the distance, I could still hear shouts and the clash of weapons, the pursuit of the fleeing fallen. The march of the host was over, though. With the fallen denied any hope of gaining Dún Aonghasa again, my brothers began filing back through the gateway. A few sentries remained, disappearing into the spiritual plane to guard the host as they returned to the kingdom. Flickering light danced on the ground and the bodies nearby, the gateway itself behind me. The warmth of its glow caressed me, and slowly, I felt my strength returning. Struggling to crawl, I caught sight of my arm. Wisps of white smoke rose from my flesh. I tried to release my physical matter, but couldn't. I wasn't strong enough yet.

I tried to yell to my brothers, but my voice was hoarse. Had I ever been so exhausted? I gritted my teeth against the pain and pulled myself forward. The ground sizzled at my touch, blackened handprints forming as the grass beneath my body burned away.

Only then did I realize I was naked. My long hair was gone as well, the night air cold on my bald scalp.

I continued my tortured crawl toward my brothers, and I finally came near enough to Anafiel and Furiel as they stood guard that I could call to them. With all the voice I could muster, I said, "Brothers, you would not leave me?"

Furiel's eyes went wide as he looked down to see me. "Sabrael?"

"Help me," I pleaded. "Please."

They ran to lift me up, but recoiled at my touch. "What happened to you?" Furiel asked.

Anafiel said, "You are burning up, Sabrael. Why do you remain in that body?"

"I cannot…" I said, my voice giving out. "I cannot release myself from it."

His eyes narrowed, their matter flying free. "Oh my God," he whispered.

I pulled the blanket tight against the cold wind, smoke still twirling from my skin but the heat now cooled. Anafiel and Furiel sat with me as the last of the Heavenly host soared in to return home. My brothers had carried me to the innermost wall of the fortress, away from the gateway. They wouldn't tell me why my appearance surprised them so. Besides the smoke and loss of my hair, everything looked okay to me. Even the stumps of my wings were gone. When I met their eyes though, they smiled as though I caught them staring. I looked out across the field at the bodies blanketing the earth. How the inhabitants of the island, few though they were, had not seen or heard the horrible battle fought on their shore was beyond me. Angels traversed the battlefield and bent to touch the foreheads of all the human warriors who were slain. The corpses burst into flame, incinerated in moments. Ashes to ashes. The host angels that fell in the final surge were revived, and our few surviving warriors carried to a triage point near the gateway. The fallen were also heaped together, the pile of the dead growing by the minute. I had no idea what my brothers planned to do with them all, but we were going home and I honestly didn't care.

I was more physically tired than I ever remembered being. The gateway had drained me so much that I actually felt the strange sensation of needing sleep. Sitting between Anafiel and Furiel, I was only half aware they were talking. Their voices lulled me toward unconsciousness. Images began to form, sounds. I shuddered and opened my eyes, disoriented. What was that?

In the air over the battlefield, silhouettes appeared as Michael and Raphael descended. In their arms, they carried the greatest sight I could behold. Adrienne. Gavin. I lost so many friends in my time on Earth, I had expected the worst. As soon as they were on the ground they ran to my side. I reached out to them, unable to stand, and gathered each of them into my arms. Gavin laughed and rubbed my smooth head.

"What the heck happened to you? Here I thought we had a rough time out there!"

I smiled and shrugged. "Your guess is as good as mine."

"Here," he said as he held out my sword. "Found this on the ground. Shouldn't leave it lying around. Some kid might find it."

"Some kid has," I said, teasing. The sword weighed more than I remembered. This exhaustion was tiresome. I placed the sword at my feet. "I was so worried about you two. How did you make it through?"

"I don't know." He paused and his eyes darkened. "Lots of people died around me in the first push. The fallen's warriors picked us apart, separated us into small groups. I was on my own until Adrienne found me in the crowd. We just stood our ground and fended them off while everyone else kept driving for the gateway."

Adrienne grabbed onto me tightly and kissed my cheek. The flowery scent of her hair mingled with that of sweat, and it was wonderful. She held me a long moment, and when she finally drew back, I saw blood on her forehead and wiped it away.

"It is not mine," she reassured me. "I only received a cut or two."

She showed me her "cut or two"—long slashes down the length of her forearms, as though she blocked a sword with her bare flesh. "Adrienne, my God; we must stop the bleeding."

"It is already done," she said, stroking my cheek with her finger. "I can feel the burn of healing. Do not worry."

"It's a miracle the two of you are still here," I said, and Furiel agreed, introducing himself with warm embraces.

Michael and Anafiel whispered to each other. They, along with Raphael, looked at me with empty sockets, their eyes in the spiritual plane.

"Will someone tell me what's going on?" I demanded.

The wind lifted Michael's hair, the silver streaks glowing in the light of the gateway. He looked both puzzled and horrified. "Gather matter to your wings, Sabrael."

I sighed, my mind swimming with fatigue, and closed my eyes. Nothing happened. "It's not working. I'm too tired."

Michael frowned. The analytical gazes of my brothers were making me uneasy. Adrienne squeezed my shoulder gently and wrapped her arm around my waist.

Michael crouched before me. "Do you feel anything when you try to call matter?"

"No," I said.

"Can you feel your wings at all?"

"No!" I yelled. "Stop asking me questions! Just tell me what is wrong!"

Michael took a moment, then said, "Your wings are not there."

"Of course not. Lucifer cut them off, and the gateway consumed their matter."

"No, you do not understand." His lips parted like he had more to say, but his empty sockets just continued to examine me.

"What? What is it?" I asked.

Raphael looked away. I couldn't help but notice the sadness on his face. Michael's gray eyes flared in his sockets as his sight returned to the physical.

"Your glow. It's changed. It comes from within your body now, like…"

"Like what?" I said.

"Like a human, Sabrael. You look human."

CHAPTER FIFTY-THREE

My only memories of my first dreams are of darkness. Whatever else I dreamt escaped back into the realm of sleep before I could drag it into the light of consciousness. I started awake, feeling as though I were pushed from a great precipice. Shaking, soaked in a cold sweat, I looked around at a room I didn't recognize, in a place I didn't remember.

Cocooned in a down comforter, the heat of sleep was trapped around me, and once my mind cleared and my heart rate slowed, I sank back into the bed. The window was still dark. I must not have slept long, but the journey here from the ruins was a void in my memory.

The door slid open, and I jerked up, trying to call my sword before the memory of what happened returned. I relaxed when a familiar form entered.

"Hey, you're up," Gavin whispered. He gently closed the door. I noticed the sleeping form on the couch beside the bed. "We were wondering how long you'd be out."

A strange urge rose within me, and my mouth opened in a yawn. My arms stretched above my head almost of their own volition.

"Where are we?" I asked, finding my throat dry and my voice raspy.

"Galway. The Connemara Coast Hotel. Michael thought it would be best to get us away from the gateway. Now that you're one of us, he didn't want to risk us looking at it."

"I am not one of you!" I snapped, immediately ashamed.

Gavin stood quiet a moment. "Well, whatever. He didn't want any accidents, so they flew us here and told us to wait."

I stared out the window, a gentle rain collecting on the glass. "For what?"

"Don't know. Michael left yesterday afternoon, promised he'd be back soon."

"Yesterday!" I said, shocked. I'd been asleep a full day!

"Shh!" he scolded, motioning to Adrienne. "After you passed out and we came here, he waited as long as he could."

I looked at Adrienne on the couch, legs drawn to her chest and hair draped over her face. White bandages wrapped around her forearms.

Following my gaze, he said, "She stayed awake at the side of your bed until a couple hours ago. She tried to force me to sleep, but I can't. Not yet. Every time I close my eyes … I told her if she was able to sleep, she should."

"How did she understand you?"

He raised his arms, mimicking a pillow. "Some signs are pretty universal."

"Where did Michael say he was going?"

Gavin looked away, pushed his white bangs back. "He didn't. Not exactly. I know he went to meet with the others…" His voice trailed off.

"They were going back," I said, heat rising to my eyes.

"No, they wouldn't," he said, but his tone told me he knew otherwise.

They left me behind. They were visiting their halls, basking in the light and love of the Almighty, and I was trapped in this room, waiting for Michael to confirm I would never go home again. I clenched my fists around the sheets. It wasn't fair! After all we had been through, all we'd done, how could they leave me here to suffer? *I am not human, Michael! Do you hear me?* The idea was ridiculous. Humans can't become angels; how could the reverse be possible? I had to show them, prove that whatever this was, it was only temporary.

Throwing the covers back, I ignored the cold, the soreness of my body, and rose from the bed. I concentrated on the beating of my heart, the rush of blood in my veins. After sleeping so long, surely the gateway's effects had waned. I focused and flexed my muscles to push the matter away from me. Nothing happened. No change, no release. I tried again. Hissing through gritted teeth, I strained so hard a groan finally escaped my lips. Gavin moved to calm me. I threw his hands from my arms. I could do it; I knew I could! I just had to concentrate harder! Gavin's hands touched my arm again, and I shoved him back. "Leave me be!"

"Sabrael, stop it! Seriously!"

My fingernails dug painfully into my palms as I clenched every muscle in effort. Tears cascaded down my face as I realized I needed to keep breathing. Adrienne startled awake at the commotion and rushed to my side, but I shrugged her off, shaking with the effort. I cried out and tried again. She forcefully restrained me.

For all the strength of her grasp, her voice was soothing. "Hush now, Sabrael. It is all right. You cannot fight this."

I twisted in her embrace and cried out. It couldn't be true! It was impossible! I sank to my knees, sobs racking my body. Adrienne's grasp loosened as the fight drained from me. She pressed her forehead to mine, hands cupping my cheeks.

"We are here for you. We can get through this."

Gavin crouched beside me, and she looked at him, a gentle smile forming on her lips. He rubbed my shoulders and said, "It's cool. We won't tell anyone you cried. Let it out."

I buried my face in Adrienne's neck, tears streaming freely. She kissed my head and crushed me against her.

I couldn't fight them. It wasn't their fault this happened. It wasn't their fault my brothers had abandoned me. I held onto Adrienne as she stroked my neck, like she was the last vestige of reality in this nightmare. Her gentle kisses accompanied comforting whispers. There was no going back. The truth of it sat on my shoulders like a boulder, and it was all I could do to keep from screaming to Heaven.

Gavin gave my shoulder a squeeze. "I'll get you some water."

As he left, I turned my head and for the first time felt it: the scratch of stubble against Adrienne's shoulder and the strap of her tank top. Stubble I didn't command to grow—it was the stubble of a man, a human. Testament to the truth of what I so desperately denied.

I pulled Adrienne tighter and lost myself in tears again.

CHAPTER FIFTY-FOUR

"It is done," Michael said. He appeared in the room, white robe glowing and wings outstretched. It was his preferred way of appearing to humans. He meant it to inspire awe. The fact he now revealed himself to me that way inspired only despair. "The gateway is destroyed, the stones scattered. No one will ever open it again."

I nodded, feeling a pang of regret at the irony that I had worked so hard to shut the one thing that could now deliver me home.

Adrienne sat beside me on the bed, her hand intertwined with mine. In the two days since my breakdown, she hadn't left my side. I owed her my sanity. Gavin had been there as well, of course, and I'm indebted to him, but it was Adrienne who held me afloat when my mind threatened to sink into madness. Her touches, her whispers, her very presence held me grounded. When I woke in the night calling for my brothers, it was she who gathered me into her arms. When I tried to control matter like a child picking at a raw wound, she scolded me to let it go. Now as I needed someone to keep me calm while Michael told me the only way I could return home had been destroyed, she sat close caressing my hand, staying my urge to explode.

"Now you're leaving for good," I said, more a statement than a question.

"Actually, I've decided to remain. The fallen aren't gone, only scattered. We have been fighting them here so long, it doesn't feel right to leave."

I was shocked, but also glad he wouldn't be home while I was exiled. I knew the selfishness in that, but it didn't change the way I felt.

"When will the others come back, if they ever do?"

Michael's wings dissolved and he sat beside Gavin. "If they plan to return, I doubt they will stay away for long."

Gavin asked, "What about us? What do we do now?"

I translated for Adrienne. My knowledge of languages still existed, I was relieved to find, but I now had to consciously speak to my friends in their native tongues rather than how I used to just speak and they heard it differently. It made conversations somewhat taxing.

"Only twenty warriors of light remain, eight of whom are too old to fight. We are back to early Jerusalem numbers—not a very effective force. When I see how many of our brothers return from the kingdom, then we can figure it out."

Michael's eyes turned to me, glowing as mine had only days earlier. Mine were now fully human; brilliantly blue, but human nonetheless. "How do you feel?" he asked.

"Trapped."

He nodded as though he knew what I was talking about. How could he have the faintest idea? Adrienne leaned her head on my shoulder, the lavender scent of her hair calming.

Michael's eyes disappeared for a moment. I knew he was checking to see if I looked any different in the spiritual plane. The gray glow filled his sockets again. "Are you adjusting to it?"

"Adjusting?" I asked. "Look at me. There is no adjusting to this. I have to eat now, sleep now, use a toilet now. I have no control over anything. My legs feel like weights, my hands like shackles. My body does things entirely of its own volition. This is worse than death."

Michael opened his mouth, but said nothing. He stood and crossed his arms. "We must find somewhere where you will be safe. The fallen will undoubtedly search for you if they know you are alive and powerless to…" He bit his lip.

"Say it. I'm powerless to defend myself."

He tilted his head and said, "You know that's not how I meant it."

"It's still true." I exhaled heavily. "Let them find me. What does it matter? Perhaps death will finally send me home."

Annoyance entered his voice as he said, "I will not allow them to find you. Do you really think that after what happened, Lucifer would simply kill you now?"

"Even if he did, how do you know you'd go to Heaven?" Gavin asked. "Do you even have a soul?" Everyone looked at him. His cheeks flushed, and he stared at his feet. "Sorry."

"There are thousands of places you could live until we figure out a way to reverse this, or at least figure out what exactly happened to you. Our havens remain, even if the warriors who ran them are gone," Michael said.

"I call that hiding, not living," I said.

"Why not Madison?" Gavin asked.

"They know you live in Madison. Remaining that close to you will make it too easy to find him. Madison is one of the first places they will look."

"How about Waukesha, then?" Gavin said. "It's where I grew up. It's close to Madison so we can keep watch over you; I'll be around if you need anything; and trust me, the fallen will never think to look for you there."

I looked at Adrienne and, finding her imploring a translation, I gave it to her. She said, "I will stay with you there."

I didn't know what to say. "What about Paris? Your home?"

She sat silent for a moment before saying, "My friends, Remy and Monette ... did not survive the battle. There is nothing left for me there."

Her eyes glistened. I took her hand and kissed it, and she blinked back tears.

Michael said, "Then for the time being, I'll prepare a house there. Take a plane from Dublin back to the United States. You should be safe enough for now. I will contact you once I know where you should go." He placed a hand on my shoulder. "We will find a way to get you home. I promise."

The matter fell from his body as he no doubt left the room through the window facing Galway Bay that Gavin had left slightly ajar. My head ached with the thought that I was truly stuck on Earth, trapped in this human body that looked like my own and yet was nothing like it.

"Did I catch that Adrienne is going to be living with you?" Gavin asked.

I nodded.

"May I suggest then that the first item on our to-do list should be to teach that girl English? I'm really getting tired of this translating."

Upon arriving at Dublin Airport, Gavin heard a call to check his pocket. He was shocked to find a key to a locker. We located it quickly and discovered a trove of passports, boarding passes, clothes and money. Gavin thrilled at the adventure. I was less excited.

The entire flight across the Atlantic into Chicago and then Milwaukee, I was taunted by the fact that I now needed a crude metal tube with wings to reach such heights. Naturally, we found a taxi waiting for us, which then took another thirty minutes down the freeway into Waukesha. I spent the time fighting back my body's new functions and wondering how anyone could bear traveling this way.

When the taxi finally pulled up to an address we hadn't even told the driver, I looked up the driveway at a white, two-story house. Nothing extravagant about it. It even stood at the center of a cul-de-sac. Anguish tightened my throat. Adrienne took my hand.

"It is beautiful," she said. "How can you look so upset?"

I hadn't the words to explain it to her. This house was to be my cage.

"Seriously, I'm making Michael zap English into her," Gavin said as he stepped past.

We followed Gavin as he disappeared into the house. The door wasn't even locked. When we reached the step, I nearly tripped over a mat that read, "Welcome Home." I wanted to focus on its matter and burn it. The knowledge that this was impossible twisted the knife.

Sunlight filled the house, creating a warm ambiance. It was fully furnished, courtesy of Michael. Adrienne laughed and pulled me from room to room. The walls throughout much of the house were painted a forest green, and I wondered if this was Michael's attempt at recreating the look of my hall in the kingdom. The smell of grass and lilacs permeated through the open windows, and the laughter of children next door reached my ears.

"Not bad," Gavin said as we returned to the large living room. "Even has cable—with movie channels!"

Adrienne rubbed my back and leaned against me as I stared out at the backyard. "This is a very nice house, and I will be here with you."

I looked into her eyes. The warmth I found in them was still startling. "I know. It is just not the home I have been waiting for."

She kissed my cheek. "That doesn't mean you can't make it the one you want." She headed off to explore upstairs.

Rubbing my head, I felt bristles of hair scratch my palm, growing unbidden like some disease or mold. "So this is home."

⟞⟝ ⟞⟝

By dusk, I'd seen the entire house, led by my overly supportive companion into room after room, floor after floor. Each room looked new and yet like someone had lived there for years. Two of the rooms on the second floor had beds, the third was set up as an office. I looked at the computer and no knowledge came. I didn't even know how to turn it on. Would I be so lost with every aspect of human life?

A bit later when Adrienne and I were watching a movie with Gavin in the living room, Michael arrived in a brilliant flash of light and feathers.

"What do you think? Did I do well?" Michael asked after the light had dimmed. His wings folded to his back then dissolved so he could sit in the empty chair.

"It's not the kingdom, Michael. It's not my hall."

"You are right. It's not Heaven. It is not your hall and you are not home. Not your real home. But there is nothing we can do about that for now." When he opened his mouth again, it was to finally ask the questions that had been burning since the battle. "What did you see in the gateway? What caused this transformation? Surely there must have been something."

"I have no idea!" I said. I stood and walked to the glass door facing out into the backyard. The yellow phosphor of fireflies winked all across the lawn. The moon was just rising. I forced the calm back into my voice. "I did exactly what the Almighty told me to. He told me He was proud of me. What did I do to deserve this?"

"If I had the answer to that question, I would be doing everything in my power to change it. And, don't forget, you are not the only one," he said. I narrowed my eyes. His face was grim. "Somewhere, Barachiel still waits for us to find him."

I bit my tongue and turned back to the window. I remembered our brother singing that terrible, beautiful song to pry open the doors of the kingdom. Michael truly hadn't seen him. I searched his face for some sign of a test, or a joke, but there was nothing like that. I forced Barachiel from my thoughts lest Michael find him there.

"Why so quiet?" Michael asked.

"Because I don't want to talk about this anymore!" Turning to face him, I hoped to hide behind anger and depression. "I'm tired, more than you can possibly understand. This accursed body wants nothing but sleep. At least in dreams I can forget that I'm trapped here."

Michael's jaw tightened. "It is only a trap if you make it one, Sabrael. You cannot return to the kingdom for a time. You must accept that. This melancholy will not pass until you let it, and as long as you allow it to linger, you will only find despair in everything. I know not what has happened to you, nor how you feel at this moment, but do not forget that you are among friends. We are ready to help with whatever you need. Try not to make enemies of those who want nothing more than to support you."

I caught his gaze for an instant, and then he was gone into the spiritual plane. For a moment no one said anything.

Gavin finally said, "He sounded pretty pissed."

"He'll get over it," I sighed. I sat back on the couch, leaning on Adrienne's shoulder. "He always does."

CHAPTER FIFTY-FIVE

Over the next few weeks, human life tried its hardest to take hold. Adrienne slept in the guest bedroom and was waiting for me in the kitchen each morning. Gavin visited every day that first weekend, and the following one he brought Lena with him. When she learned what had happened, she wanted to visit immediately. The two of them finished out their school year, and then they were at the house each day when vacation came. Adrienne enjoyed having the two of them around, and Lena even started instructing her in English. By the end of summer, she was speaking it fluently.

Most of this I missed. Instead, I isolated myself in depression. Time didn't make it better. The pain of being exiled from the kingdom ate at me, and I could do nothing to escape it. I refused to accept human life. I was sure this was only temporary, that it was only a matter of time before I would find my angelic abilities returned and the curse of the gateway lifted. Each day I prayed to the Almighty, sometimes to beg Him to make me an angel again, other times to ask what I'd done wrong, still others to denounce Him for abandoning me when I needed His voice the most. Sometimes it was all three.

For the first two weeks, I did nothing but sit outside and sulk. Adrienne and Gavin tried to move me; Lena even once set up a sprinkler next to me and turned it on. I knew they only wanted to help me settle into my new life, but I couldn't. I lay awake at night imagining what my brothers were doing in the kingdom. I was still trapped in that gateway; neither in Heaven nor on Earth, one foot touching each. I wondered how long it would take me to die.

What finally shook me from that corrosive state was the return of my brothers. Just before the third week had passed, Michael and Raphael paid me a visit in the night. Sitting in my bedroom with only a single candle burning, I jolted up when Michael's glowing form appeared at the foot of the bed, Raphael materializing beside him. For the first time ever, I was not all that happy to see him.

"Not asleep, are you?" Raphael jested, smiling and moving to embrace me.

"What are you doing here?" I was too depressed to say anything more welcoming.

"We are here to get you out of this bed," he said, shaking the mattress.

Michael said, "You must end this self-mourning. Those that console you are losing hope."

"I never asked them to stay with me."

"They are wearing down. Gavin and Lena agree that they might never shake you from your depression. Adrienne cries in the night and begs the Father to help."

"She came here to be with you, and you have abandoned her," Raphael added. "You have abandoned them all."

"I am in agony in this place! How can you come and tell me to liven up when I am dead in this body and in this house?"

Raphael said, "You are not dead! You are perfectly alive and not only that, you have the chance to live as none of us has since before the Earth was created. Have you once considered that you are free from the burden of the war for the first time in eons?"

I didn't reply. The words on my tongue didn't seem strong enough.

"You sit here in this house each day, without a weapon in your hand, without watching for those that would slay you given the chance. You are hidden from them, with no more obligation to fight than the neighbors you watch across the street every day. You constantly tell yourself this is a curse; have you once considered it might be a blessing?"

"A blessing? I am unnatural! An abomination, neither angel nor man, but some bizarre hybrid. How can anyone expect me to live like this?"

"What has happened to you is shocking; no one questions that. But instead of embracing this new life and discovering what you can make of it, you mope about, bringing nothing but sadness to those around you."

"Sorry I have nothing else to give," I said.

"That is the talk of an angel blinded by self-despair."

I shook my head and leaned back against the pillows and the headboard. "Did you just come to tell me how I'm failing to live this 'blessing,' or was there something else?"

Raphael walked away in frustration. Michael's glowing stare remained unaffected. "Actually, we came to tell you that we are returning."

"What do you mean?" I asked.

"To the Earth. Every one of us decided to stay and try to keep the fallen in control."

"Just the six of you? Good luck."

Michael said, "It will actually be seven again."

"What are you talking about? How am I supposed to help like this?"

"You?" Raphael said. "You're too busy grieving to do anything else."

Michael said, "You know the seventh position cannot be yours, Sabrael." His tone was sympathetic, yet firm. "We must acknowledge you no longer have the abilities you once had. Whether you choose to continue in this state or to wake from it is up to you. But you cannot retake your place with us for now, and you know it as well as I do."

I gripped the sheets and struggled not to scream at them. How could they come to me like this? First they tell me I am wasting my life, then they flaunt in my face the fact that I'm essentially useless.

"So who is it? Who's number seven?"

Michael replied, "The others are deciding that now before they all return."

I was crushed by overwhelming disappointment. This wasn't just some sickness or injury. They weren't waiting for me. They had moved on while I clung to my futile hope for salvation. I blinked and felt tears rising.

"Will I still see you from time to time?" I asked.

Raphael said, "Of course. Just because you refuse to stop pouting does not mean we will let you forget who you are." He smiled, and I was relieved that he wasn't angry with me. "No, not angry. Just concerned, you big dope."

"We'll let you sleep," Michael said. "I am sure the others will be dropping in for your blessing soon though."

"My blessing?"

"Of course," he said. "No one wants to join the fight again without our patron saint."

"Try not to let it go to your head," Raphael smirked. He embraced me and disappeared into the spiritual plane.

Michael remained. "In all seriousness, Sabrael, find your reason to move on and live. Don't stay like this too long, brother. You must learn to see this isn't a curse."

"I can't help it," I said. "All I see is despair."

"Maybe you're not seeing what's right in front of you," he said, then he was gone.

I hated that I had no way to know if they were still in the room. I lay back and stared at the ceiling. Raphael's words repeated in my mind, and I tried in vain to think of a good argument. He didn't know what this was like. None of them did. What did Michael even mean, "right in front of you"? His damned cryptic messages. Restless, I stood and paced. If he wanted to get his point across, why not just tell me what he meant? For once?

Then I heard it. Crying. I held my breath, listened over the accursed beating of my heart. Putting my ear to the wall, I heard Adrienne crying in her room. I grabbed my sword from the hooks on the wall and ran.

The house was dark, the flicker of my candle pushing back the shadows. I rushed down the hall, the carpet rising up between my bare toes, and as I came to Adrienne's door, I heard the unmistakable sound of weapons being drawn. I threw open her door.

Adrienne sat in bed, her brown hair falling over the shoulders of a nightgown in beautiful long curls. She held her short swords poised.

"What is it? What's wrong?" she asked. The candlelight glimmered on her wet cheeks, but she was alone.

I stood there, heart racing, and realized what was happening. When she saw my confusion, her face softened further. "Did you have a bad dream? It's okay, come here."

I sat on the bed beside her, placing the candle on the nightstand. I looked into her eyes, and the tears finally came. *What's right in front of you.* "I think I did have a bad dream." My face cringed, and I crumpled into her open arms.

"It's okay," she whispered. "I am here. I am not going anywhere."

"I am sorry," I cried. "I am so sorry."

She held me tight and I kissed her hair, her cheeks, and then her lips. It was wonderful. It was worth living for. We stayed there together, holding each other until sleep finally took us.

⊨⊨ ⊨⊨

When Gavin and Lena came to the house the following day, Adrienne and I were outside on the wooden porch swing. We watched the neighborhood kids playing their games around the cul-de-sac. I smiled as the pair approached.

"Sabrael?" Gavin asked. "What's wrong with your face?"

"What's that supposed to mean?"

"You're smiling! Shouldn't you be over there in the grass, or collecting dust, maybe?"

Before I could reply, Lena asked, "What happened to finally wake you up?" Her eyes followed my glance at Adrienne before returning to me. Her eyebrow playfully rose.

Adrienne blushed. I said, "I just had my eyes opened. Is that all right?"

She smiled and embraced me tightly. "Yes! It's about time!"

Gavin asked, "So you're totally fine now?"

"No, but I accept it's out of my control. If this is what the Almighty wants of me, I might as well begin living."

The words sounded worse than I meant them. No one commented, though. Instead, Gavin pulled me out of my chair. "Glad to hear it," he said. "And since you're going to be doing all that living, the first thing we should do is teach you how to shave. You're looking pretty shaggy, my friend."

I laughed and followed him inside to take the first step into being a human in this age.

A few days later, I was visited by the last of my brothers to return to the Earth. Gabriel came to our house with Zadkiel, the new seventh, and I welcomed him with open arms. I felt a stinging ache at being officially replaced, but it was inevitable. Zadkiel would do well, and above all else, I was simply happy to see my brother again.

He wasn't the last of my visitors though.

That night, while Adrienne was in the shower, I walked through our garden in the backyard. My fingers traced along the leaves of hostas and low-hanging branches, the fragrance of lilac heavy in the air around me.

"So it is true."

I turned expecting to find a neighbor behind me. The eyes I met were not glowing, nor were there black wings extending from the shirt on his back, but Lucifer's face was unmistakable, even in the waning light of dusk.

"I thought the gateway would kill you, but now I see everything in those old books was even more fascinating than I imagined."

I lunged at him without another thought. He vanished before me, and I stumbled to the ground. I wiped the dirt from my face and spun around.

"Please," he taunted. "You could not even move quickly enough to catch me when you were still one of us."

"I am still one of you!"

"Don't flatter yourself," he said.

"What do you want?" I asked between clenched teeth.

Lucifer laughed. "What could I possibly take from you that I have not already?"

I kept my thoughts clear of Adrienne. "We trusted you. How could you lead us there just to turn on us again? How could you throw me into the gateway?"

Lucifer bent to crouch before me. He was close enough for me to strike, but I knew he would move long before I could touch him.

"I did more than just throw you in." I narrowed my eyes. "Michael sends you away before the battle, so I send Balam to Stonehenge to reel you back. Then the fools partially open the gateway, blast you out into the water, and in their haste for blood, they nearly rip out your heart before the proper time. I had to call in reinforcements to shepherd you toward the gateway for the exact moment I needed you. Do you realize how much I went through to put you where you are now? Credit where credit is due. It was not just a matter of 'throwing you in.' "

"Why tell me this?" I asked. "What does it matter? You want recognition, is that it? Is it not enough that I am human now?"

"No, it's not!" he shouted at me. "It will only be enough when every time you cut yourself and take weeks to heal, you know that I gave you that pain. It will only be enough when you are an elderly man, senile and fouling your pants, and remember that I put you in that body. It is only enough if you know perfectly well that your defiance brought this upon you. I want my revenge to be perfectly clear to you for the rest of your human life."

"I'll keep that in mind, devil, and when I die, I'll return for your heart, and then you will have an eternity of death to think of me in return."

"Big words for one I have killed twice now."

I could hardly control myself. I grasped the earth to keep from lashing out at him. "At least I stopped your precious plan to re-enter Heaven. In all your scheming, did you ever think that you were throwing the one angel who could stop you into the very place I needed to be to do so? Or did I surprise you after all?"

"There are plenty of ways to get what I want. The destruction of the gateway means nothing. I will find my place on the throne."

"Then why haven't you done it yet?"

Lucifer's eyes darkened, but he smiled. "How would your little woman say it? Touché?"

I lunged at him again, growling, but he was already behind me. His laughter drove me on, diving back and forth until I ran out of steam. I lay on the grass, chest heaving, hands and knees covered with dirt and grass stains.

"I know all about her. I have watched the two of you crying together, sleeping in each other's arms, gazing at each other over breakfast with all the disgusting gaiety of lovers. I know what lies in your heart, and the answers to questions you have not the courage to ask yet. I know where your brat warrior and the girl live as well."

"I will die to keep you from them."

"Oh, I know, but where is the fun in that? I want you to live a long and healthy life. I'm going to make sure of it. Wouldn't want you released from that body too soon."

"Are you so blind that you can't see you will never win? You will never be as powerful as the Almighty, Lucifer."

"Sabrael, I already am," he said. "Don't you get it? If even one soul denies His existence, if even one turns away from the path He intended, then creation can never be perfect. It will bear my mark forever. That makes me more powerful than God."

The lights on the outside of the house turned on, and he became a silhouette in the quickly fading last light of the day.

"Enjoy your life, Sabrael," Lucifer said. "Don't worry. I will be around."

A wave of fear and anger flooded me, but before I could say anything, he dissolved into a shower of particles and was gone.

The patio door slid open, and Adrienne stood drying her hair with a towel. "Sabrael? Who are you talking to?"

I quickly ran into the house, slamming the door and locking it. I stared out at the lawn, wondering if he was still there, laughing at me from the spiritual plane I could no longer see. When Adrienne wrapped her arm around my waist, I could not bear to tell her what had happened. She kissed me, pulling me away from the door. "You're a mess! Hurry up and get ready. Gavin and Lena will be here soon, and you know how they tease when you're late."

I walked to the stairs, praying to the Almighty for His protection and wondering if I was truly as free of the war as Raphael claimed. More importantly, I wondered how long it would be before I could sleep without the light on.

EPILOGUE

So I have come to the end. There's nothing more to tell. The gateway is destroyed, and I remain, stripped of divinity, at least for the time being. Yet I'm still alive.

Has it taken me so very long to write what I wished to say? The sun has long since set, the rumbling of the storm outside dwindled to a soft trickle in the night. A thin wisp of smoke dances from the candle before me, its flame giving light to the dark that has fallen around me. The smells of the wet earth, the grass, and the lilacs reach into the kitchen even now to find me. The peace after the storm. Always so comforting.

The war continues as it always has. My brothers are still out there with the few warriors who survived Inishmor, along with some new faces who have been blessed since. With each addition to their ranks, they pay me a visit. I don't feel like a saint, as Michael put it, but perhaps a veteran whose day has passed, though the memory of his actions lives on in the stories of those taking up the call. I don't like to think of it that way, though. I still feel part of the war, though what role is left me now I don't yet know. Gavin and Lena continue to visit when they are able. They've become quite a team, Raphael having blessed Lena officially. Adrienne is still called away from time to time. They all keep me informed. I remain here, sword hanging on the wall instead of in my hand, and to tell the truth, I prefer it this way. I don't envy the others the dangers they face each day.

Still, sometimes, late at night when the world is asleep and the ratchet call of crickets seeps in with the scent of the flowers, I can't help taking up my sword. I can't let myself forget what the blade feels like slicing the air, twirling around me in its fatal dance. I won't let the memories fade completely. For during those times, I can still feel Lucifer nearby, watching and laughing at what he has done. I know he's there, just as I know the fallen are never too far away. Lucifer even lets me see him every now and then, reminding me this isn't some strange dream and that I will never wake from it. In the crowd at a baseball game or out in the garden at night I'll find him, staring back with a smile. One night I even woke to find him standing over me, his face inches from mine, vanishing the instant I recognized him. One day, I'll be released from this human life, and no matter how long that takes, I want to be ready to turn right back around and keep *my* promise to him. I'm not finished with this war. I must only bide my time until the day when I can once again join it properly.

In the meantime, I will patiently wait out this life and enjoy my time off. I'll go to the store to buy food like everyone else. I'll cut the grass until the snow comes, and then I'll shovel the walk and make small talk with the neighbors as we shiver in the cold. I'll watch TV and laugh with the unseen audiences. There's no way to know what I'll see in the time given me here. Nothing is planned or known to me about what's to come. There are no battles that must be fought and no series of events that must occur. There is simply life.

As a last thought for whoever reads this record, I will say this: If you're ever out walking and happen to see something strange flying in the sky, or catch a glimpse of someone behind you in a shop window only to find no one there when you turn, do not be afraid. Rejoice that you have been made privy to the secret. The angels of the Almighty are on the Earth. Not constrained to statues or holy places. We are everywhere you look. We are, have always been, and will always be part of this world.

Take heart in the darkness. We are among you.

—Sabrael, Guardian of the First Hall

ABOUT THE AUTHOR

 Stephen J. Smith is an award-winning screen-writer and author. He grew up in Wisconsin, intrigued by the idea of angels and their ongoing war, as well as being an avid reader of genre fiction, comic books, and spending most of his youth at the movies. While studying animation, he was soon convinced to try writing. His first short story was published, his first collection of short stories won an award, and the writing bug took a firm hold. He moved to Los Angeles and studied screenwriting for both feature films and television, and now writes for both fiction and the screen. He currently lives in Waukesha, Wisconsin with his wife and daughter.